Rings
of Annulment

by

Richard R. Roach, MD, FACP

DORRANCE
PUBLISHING CO
EST. 1920
PITTSBURGH, PENNSYLVANIA 15238

Dorrance Publishing Co
585 Alpha Drive
Pittsburgh, PA 15238
Visit our website at *www.dorrancebookstore.com*

ISBN: 978-1-4809-8768-5
eISBN: 978-1-4809-8791-3

Dedicated to C. Ebenezer Fillmore

He taught me to always leave a generous tip to my waitress.

Prologue

Once I found out that I had cancer, I was certain as to how I would die. The cancer cells would invade my body and set up their kingdom to destroy everything good in my life. Uncontrolled, they would invade my lungs, filling the vital passageways for life-giving oxygen with necrotic debris as they outgrew their blood supply. The exuding progeny would die, but the evil progenitors would live, and I would die gasping for breath.

Or I imagined that the cancer cells would travel through my blood stream and hide in my bone marrow. They would set up islands of non-functioning cells chewing up the nutrients intended to make infection fighters and oxygen-carrying cells. In the process, they would stretch the skin on my bones, producing terrible pain as the nerve fibers yelled and screamed during their destruction.

Or maybe they would cloak themselves to bypass my surveillance system and hide in my brain. They would thrive in their imperialistic colonies, pushing my soft brain tissues through the foramen magnum like toothpaste. Maybe I would be lucky and have a seizure when they invaded my frontal lobe and I would die in the ecstasy of asphyxia and not have to experience unrelenting headaches. But I don't believe in luck. Besides, I felt that I would die without accomplishing anything in my life. Anyway, I was wrong, totally wrong about everything.

Chapter 1
Desperate for a Job

"May I speak to the manager?" I tried not to sound desperate as I handed my check to the dark-complexioned waitress and dropped my backpack beside the counter. Her long black hair flowed over her shoulders. She had high cheek bones, a nice figure for her uniform, and appeared quite attractive despite a lack of lipstick or any apparent makeup. I saw 'Connie' on her name tag, so I added, "Connie, please?"

"What's this about? Was there something wrong with your food?" Her face looked angry and her knuckles turned white as she crumpled my check.

."Sorry, I didn't have any food, only coffee. And it was very good." Her face relaxed. She smoothed out the check on the counter. "Then why do you want to talk to the manager?"

"No complaints," I said with wave of my hand and then stammered, "I'm looking for a job." I hung my head, trying to look submissive. I attempted to keep the panic out of my voice, but I was sure that I had failed.

"Just a moment," she said, "I'll get Mr. Lloyd."

My sweaty fingers searched for change in my empty pockets. There wasn't any, and I knew it. The last of my money had paid for coffee when we stopped at the Hinckley, Minnesota diner, halfway between Minneapolis and Duluth. For distraction, I read the notice on the cash register: "No checks accepted. Management. Lloyd's Café, Cotton, Minnesota." A grin stole across my face. I had yet to have money in any account, much less a checking account. *If only*, I thought.

For three days, I had survived on water and coffee as I hitchhiked north. Much of those three days was spent standing beside the road, wishing someone would stop for me. Several of the truck drivers who picked me up had been generous when we stopped and had paid for my coffee, but no one offered to buy me any food. I survived by drinking half a cup of coffee, then filling the cup with cream and sugar, drinking it halfway down, and repeating the process. Several waitresses gave me curious glances when they noticed the empty cream pitcher and refilled it, to the delight of my aching belly. I tried to count the calories I had managed over the last three days, but my brain refused to calculate. As a result, my jeans hung loose and the skin on my belly prickled.

While waiting, my belly cramped as the coffee, cream, and sugar curdled in my stomach. The latest truck driver I had hitchhiked with, Mack, was hauling a load of equipment to a paper factory in International Falls. I doubted that there would be a chance of finding a job there and certainly not in Fort Francis, Canada on the other side of the border bridge, even if I could get across the border without a passport. Mack had said that he was stopping in the 'Falls' for dinner. So I felt like this was my last chance for a job before the border. Maybe there were other towns, but I didn't know. My calorie-starved brain refused to conceive what to do next. I glanced at Mack while I waited for the manager. He was finishing his hamburger and fries. I turned away at the sight of the delicious food because it intensified the spasms in my gut.

Maybe he would offer to pay for my coffee, I thought.

Wiping his mouth with a napkin and taking one last sip of coffee, he got up from the counter stool and headed to the cash register.

Hurry, manager, I thought. *I can ride with Mack to the next town if there are no jobs here.*

A bald, muscular man in tight jeans appeared. His belly torqued his belt. "I'm Bert Lloyd, miss, the owner and manager. Connie said you were looking for a job?" His voice was deep and musical like a trombone.

"Yes, I'm Rebecca Jean Gottwald. I'm a university student, and I need a summer job. I prefer Becky Jean. Rebecca just seems too formal."

"Do you have any waitress experience, Becky Jean?"

Even though I anticipated this question, I sputtered, "No, sir, but I'm athletic, played soccer, so I'm disciplined and know how to work hard. I've served meals at a nursing home. I have three years of college with a 3.2 GPA, so that proves I can learn. I need a job. I'll do anything." Breathless, I swallowed my saliva.

I could feel his eyes scanning my slight frame. After three days of hitch-hiking with no shower, no change of clothes, I was not the best sight or smell for a job applicant. I ran my fingers through my tousled brown hair, but I doubted that it made any difference. Greasy and stringy, it did not promote my appearance or chance of being hired. Out of the corner of my eye, I saw Mack pick up his check and leave a tip that would have paid for my coffee as he headed to the cash register. He handed it to Connie with a twenty. I glanced his way trying to look needy, but he still didn't offer to pay for my bill which lay wrinkled on the counter. Connie gave him his change.

A sharp pain of anticipation made me blurt out, "Please, Mr. Lloyd, I will work hard, very hard."

"Are you coming with me, Becky Jean, or is this where you get off?" Mack asked, returning his change to his wallet. "I have to be in International Falls by nightfall. I got to go."

My eyes pleaded with Mr. Lloyd. My shoulders sagged, anticipating rejection. I would have to ask Mack to pay for my coffee. Next stop, International Falls.

He pulled a piece of paper out of the drawer under the cash register and handed it to me. "All right, fill out this application," he said.

It was yellowed on the edges and crinkled like parchment as I grasped it. I guessed that no new applications had been printed in a long time. "May I start today?"

"You can start right now if you know how to wash dishes." He grumbled like a bear.

"I do," I said as a pathetic smile crossed my face. I turned to Mack. "You've been so kind. I guess this is where I'm landing. Thanks for the ride."

"No problem. I'll see you, Becky Jean, whenever I pass through. This place always has good grub. Nice chat we had. I'll try what you said."

With a wave, he walked out the door. I was alone. But somehow alone felt good.

I turned to my new employer, "Thanks, Mr. Lloyd. I'll prove to you that you made a good decision." He didn't seem to hear me as he motioned for me to follow him. I picked up my backpack and the job application and proceeded to his office. Out of the corner of my eye, I saw Connie grab my unpaid bill and discard it in the wastebasket under the counter.

"Can I put this backpack somewhere before I start?"

He didn't say a word as we entered his office. He motioned for me to deposit my backpack in his closet. It had no door. The office was small, filled with an old oak desk, checked from constant use. Assorted papers clipped together filled an oak box. I sat at the chair in front of the desk and looked up at the wall. It was covered with faded photos of Mr. Lloyd posed with persons I assumed were local dignitaries. A large picture in the center of the wall showed Mr. Lloyd looking much younger beside an attractive woman in front of the restaurant.

I turned my attention to my application. A mug on the desk held pens of various sorts. I grabbed one and scribbled my name and social security number on the form. I checked the box for Caucasian female and answered a few of the discovery questions such as status: 'No' I was not a felon, nor had I been in jail for any misdemeanors, etc. Mr. Lloyd stood behind his desk watching me as I filled in the questions. Then I was stumped. I wasn't willing to put my parents' address on the form, so I said in my most polite voice, "I don't really have an address or telephone number."

"Leave it blank for now," he said and then added as he focused on what I was writing, "You don't do drugs, do you?"

"No".

"If you lie on your application, I am allowed to immediately dismiss you. You know that?"

"Yes."

I finished by filling in some of my professors' names for references and the nursing home director where I had worked the previous year and handed it to him.

He didn't even look at me. "You're on probation until I check these references," he said, scanning the application. "Minnesota law allows me to fire you without a reason in the first three months."

"I understand." I watched his eyes scan my application.

"You're divorced already? You're so young, only twenty-two years old."

"Yes." I grabbed my chest as my heart and mind raced. *I'm not sure I'm divorced. Maybe I'm only separated. Does that matter?* Yelling and screaming, the sound of the slamming doors, and the smell of polyester burning in the trash barrel as all my clothes turned to cinders flashed through my brain. *Please don't ask about that,* my mind pleaded.

Mr. Lloyd didn't say a word. His finger paused over each reference. "I just fired an employee this morning. She was taking money out of the cash register. I will not tolerate dishonesty." He laid my application upside down on his desk. "You wrote no felony convictions, right?"

"No felonies. Yes, that's what I wrote."

"This is a minimum wage job. You are allowed to keep your tips when you waitress, but ten percent has to be shared with the cook. Connie is in charge of the cash register. You're not allowed to even touch it. After you've worked here a while and I know I can trust you…Well, we'll see."

"What hours do I work?"

"I open at six in the morning. You need to be here at five-thirty. We usually close at six, but we stay until our patrons are done eating. Work out breaks with Connie during the slow time. She's worked for me for many years. She is very reliable, so ask her if you have any questions when I'm not available. Do whatever she tells you." He finished, staring at me. "Do you understand?"

"Yes."

"Do you have any questions?"

"No."

"Good. You may eat one meal during your break. Ron, the cook, will fix it for you. You may not fix your own meals. You are not allowed in the kitchen." He paused, shoved my application in his desk drawer and then stared at me, "Letting employees fix their own meals eats up the profits, shall we say. Coffee, tea, or water is allowed if you're thirsty, no soda, too expensive. Oh, one more thing: no desserts."

He got up and motioned me to follow him into the dishwashing room. Trays with piles of dishes filled a gap through the wall from the main restaurant. We entered through a narrow door on the side. The fluorescent light flickered as he turned on the switch. It was a small room painted with yellow enamel that was peeling from the moisture. It smelled of disinfectant mixed with the sweetness of breakfast scraps. I yearned to eat what people had left on their plates.

Mr. Lloyd explained the controls on the washing machine and the requirements of the Health Department. "Rinse must be at 180 degrees. It is your responsibility to make sure the temperature is correct. I don't want any of my customers ever getting sick because the dishes were not washed properly. And check the silverware for spots. We will not have any customers complaining about dirty utensils." He handed me a pair of gloves and a plastic apron, which I slipped over my filthy clothes. "Wear a hair net." He pointed to a receptacle on the wall. I grabbed a hair net and put it on over my greasy hair.

Judging by the piles of dishes already invading through the opening in the wall, the dry dishwasher that no one had started, and the dish rack standing empty, I concluded that the previous employee must have been fired before starting this morning. Mr. Lloyd left, and I started rinsing breakfast off the plates. When the rack was full, I moved it into the dishwasher, added the soap as Mr. Lloyd had instructed, and closed the stainless steel door and pushed : Start. The gush of water and sound of the sprayer were deafening.

I fantasized and drooled over the good food stuck to dirty plates. My stomach ached, coveting what was going down the garbage disposal. My nose caught the scent of delicious entrees. *Lack of food sure does odd things to one's psyche.* But I resisted the temptation, not wanting to jeopardize my job eating other people's discarded waste. "Focus, Rebecca," I yelled below the din of the washing machine.

It didn't take long to swing into a rhythm, rinsing, stacking and filling the racks. Then, swish, I pushed the dish rack into the washer, added soap, and stacked the next rack. Rinse to 180 degrees. Unload the steaming clean dishes. Next load. I felt like dancing as the beat of the machine swirled through my head.

Within an hour, my blouse was soaked from errant spray that found its way around my rubber apron and trickled down my arms. Sweat dripped across my chest and flowed between my breasts, tickling my belly and flanks. I caught a whiff of my underarms. "I stink," I yelled out at the roaring dishwasher. But there was no one to hear me. I was the queen of the dishwashing world, cloistered with a monstrous machine that magically cleansed the dirty dishes. Stacked when clean, the dishes were put away for the next service, just as Mr. Lloyd had instructed. The utensils were placed in separate racks.

Oblivious to time, I jumped off the rubber pad I was standing on when Connie opened the door to yell that I could take a break. She stood at the door waiting.

A voracious wolf hidden in my belly howled for my promised meal. *How many hours had it been since I had last eaten? How many hours had I worked?*

Starved for energy, my brain refused to calculate. I finished the 180-degree rinse cycle on the last load I had put in the dishwasher. Steam poured out of the stainless steel contraption. I stacked the clean dishes, ready to be put away. *How fortunate you dishes are to have had such a nice hot shower. I need a shower more than you do.*

"Thanks for letting me know, Connie." I followed at her command to the grill like a lost puppy, careful not to cross the threshold of the kitchen. She introduced me to Ron, the cook. I felt like a lottery winner as my eyes feasted on all the delicious food stacked around the kitchen counters.

I swallowed my drool before it dripped out my mouth as Connie shoved a menu into my hands. "You can have any meal on the menu," she said. "Just tell him what you want." The choices overwhelmed me. I couldn't decide. My vision blurred. I couldn't focus. My heart pounded against my ribs. I looked up and mumbled some greeting to Ron. The cook stood waiting for my order.

Ron was a tough-looking guy. Muscles rippled out of his t-shirt. His hairnet compressed his disgruntled, wavy blond hair. Grease stains on his apron reflected all the meals he had made that morning. He looked as delicious as an overstuffed sausage. I could have licked his apron. "What'll you have?" he asked. His sweet tenor voice was surprising, unanticipated from his rugged frame.

I glanced at the clock on the wall behind him. It was almost three in the afternoon. I shouldn't have looked. It just made my angry stomach remind me how long I had neglected its nutrition. "Is a hamburger all right?" I asked, "I just got hired this morning and I'm not sure what's allowed."

"One hamburger coming up, with all the trimmings." He flipped the raw meat on the grill. The sizzling harmonized with the music my stomach was singing. I stood mesmerized. Maybe I should have ordered something healthier, but what's healthy to a three-day-starved, empty stomach?

Ron seemed a genie in a greasy apron offering three wishes when I had chosen only one. His grace with the spatula was hypnotizing. It seemed to me that he danced as he prepared my meal, a ballet with the full orchestra of his spatula hitting the grill and his knives slicing lettuce and tomatoes as he waited for my burger to cook. The finale was the artistry he put into his presentation of my food: majestic and beautiful. Lettuce and pickles graced the open, toasted bun. Crisp French fries lay perfectly parallel. A side salad mixed with cubed tomatoes contrasted with the juicy hamburger. A slice of spiced apple and a sprig of parsley framed the plate. I stared, paralyzed in disbelief that it was really for me.

"Take off your gloves before you eat," he said, laughing in high-pitched musical tones.

I slid off my gloves and folded them into my apron belt. I looked at my hands, swollen like anemic prunes. Flexing my stiff fingers, I took my plate but just stood still staring at my food.

"Go sit in the employees' room in the back, silly," Ron said, laughing at my paralysis.

I shook my head back to reality and retreated to the back room I had seen on my way to Mr. Lloyd's office. I sat on the wooden stool beside the employees' table, unsure where to begin. A child in a fantasy, I was unsure of etiquette.

A set of plastic bottles stood like soldiers at my command. The red catsup bottle in the center beckoned me out of my stupor. After a deep breath, I grabbed it and squirted catsup over the hamburger and all my fries. A second white bottle had creamy Italian dressing, which I dabbled over my salad and finished off with a final large squirt. A third yellow bottle provided a drop of mustard to tantalize my burger. Now it was time to eat: chew and swallow. *Control yourself, Rebecca.*

An upward glance revealed a glass of water full of ice set in front of me. *Where did that come from?* I decided to fold my sweaty hands in my lap and take a drink of water after each bite to pace myself. "Thank you, God, for providing what I don't deserve," I prayed, but I couldn't close my eyes, thinking the whole meal might disappear while I had them closed.

As the flavors of meat, catsup, mustard, and bun swirled around my mouth, my stomach crowed with satisfaction. Hunger is such a great spice. The tang of the pickle and the sweetness of the apple squabbled for priority. The salad dripping with creamy Italian spices soothed my soul. Never had food tasted so good; never had the smell been so intoxicating. Even the water, so clear and cold, rivaled Champagne to my palate. Each mouthful was ecstasy. I was embarrassed as I took the last morsel of bun and wiped up the grease on my plate, but I scanned the room; no one was watching as I popped it into my mouth.

Connie jolted me out of my euphoria. "Back to work, starving girl, the dishes won't wash themselves."

•　　•　　•

I had no watch and there was no clock in the dishwashing room, so as I took the last load out of the dishwasher, Connie bolted through the door, hands on her hips. "It's after six o'clock. We're closing. Are you done? Sign's on the door. Customers have all left."

"Great," I said as I slumped onto the aluminum stool in the corner that I hadn't used all day. Filled with satisfaction of a completed job, I peeled off the yellow plastic gloves, took off the yellow plastic apron and hair net. I folded my hands in my lap, "I'm so thankful."

"Where are you staying, thankful-one?" Connie asked. I sensed sarcasm in her voice.

I scanned the stains and scraps of errant food on my blouse that had slipped inside my apron, but I was too exhausted to be embarrassed. I thought about eating them. Soaked in stinky sweat and dishwasher spray, I replied, "Is there a hotel or…" *But I have no money even if there is a hotel.* "I don't know. I hadn't thought that far ahead."

"No hotels for thirty miles," she braced her right fist against the doorframe, "in either direction."

"Is there a campground nearby? I have a pup tent in my back pack." *Actually it was a laundromat bag, but I presumed that I could make some kind of shelter out of it.* I mumbled, "I sure could use a shower."

She turned and yelled, "Bert, she's got no place to stay. You hired a vagrant." The word stung my ears. *Am I a vagrant, a bag lady, homeless? Well, I guess I am.*

He appeared in the doorway. I felt his eyes scanning my pathetic, hunched-over, sweaty frame, but I was too exhausted to correct my posture. "Do you have fresh clothes for tomorrow?"

I thought about what I had in my backpack. I squirmed on the stool as I squeaked out an unconvincing, "Yes." I could tell they weren't fooled.

"Connie, do you think Joan's uniforms will fit her?"

"A little loose, Bert. She's pretty scrawny, but they'll do if she wears a t-shirt for modesty."

They asked in unison, "Do you have a t-shirt?"

"Yes, and that's the honest truth."

Connie left, "I'll get Joan's uniforms."

Mr. Lloyd stretched his back and gave a sigh. "There is a little coop in the back."

Chicken coop? I wasn't familiar with the colloquialism.

"I used to stay there myself when I first bought this restaurant. Now I use it just for storage. But it has a shower and an old, steel bed frame. Still has a mattress if the mice haven't gotten to it. I haven't turned on the water in years. Maybe it's still good."

"Thanks so much, Mr. Lloyd, for your generosity. I'll pay you whatever you ask." *That was a stupid thing to say. I have nothing and he knows it.* So I added, "As soon as I get my first paycheck."

Connie brought Joan's uniforms and directed us out the back door. I grabbed my backpack from Mr. Lloyd's office and followed him through the door, glancing back at the restaurant. All the lights were off, no car in the lot. It seemed so vacant compared to when I arrived. Mr. Lloyd jangled some keys and took the lead across the back parking lot to a small building.

"It has two rooms, counting the bathroom. A little bigger than a chicken coop," he said and laughed. "Actually, the farmers around here have bigger chicken coops." He unlocked the door.

A blast of stuffy air hit my nose. I sneezed.

"Gesundheit!" he said.

"I'm sorry."

He frowned as we entered. "Oh, it is a bit musty in here. You can see what I use it for." He moved boxes of paper towels and a case of toilet paper aside. Dust flew in the air. I scanned the room as he opened what looked like a closet door. It wasn't. It contained a water pump and a water heater. "I'll turn on the water main." A screech reverberated through the room as he twisted the controls. Then he checked the faucet in the bathroom.

If one could call it a room as it had no door, but why would I need privacy?

Rust-tinged water blasted out with trapped air. Pushing aside a crinkled, stained, plastic curtain, he turned on the water in the shower. More rust and rockets of trapped air shot out the calcified shower head. He waited until the water cleared before he shut it off. A whooshing sound filled the reservoir of the toilet. He watched until it filled and flushed it. "Ah, it works. I switched on the hot water heater. It might take an hour or so, but you should have plenty. It's a thirty-gallon tank. I used to take hot showers after work before I went home to my sweetheart."

He handed me a rusty key from on top of the water heater. I turned it over in my hand. It felt so delicate.

"It looks like everything functions. Enjoy."

"Thanks, Mr. Lloyd. You'll never know how much I appreciate this."

Connie handed me a stack of Joan's uniforms. They both stood and stared at me. I felt like a specimen in a science project. I supposed they were comparing my physique to my mysterious predecessor.

Mr. Lloyd broke the silence. "Remember, we open at six. Be there at five-thirty." He picked up a box of paper towels, and dust flew into the air. He coughed. "I'll just stack these back in the restaurant," he said and left.

Connie held up one of the uniforms. "Will you be all right here?" She blew the dust away from her face.

"I'll be fine."

"Joan's uniforms will be a bit loose on you. She was much better fed than you are. But you'll just have to cinch the belt tight and wear something underneath. Modesty, you know. All right, see you bright and early in the morning." She paused in the doorway as Mr. Lloyd headed for his vehicle. She shook her finger at me. "Don't you dare disappoint Mr. Lloyd. He is a good man and cares about his employees."

"I won't," I said, but I don't think she heard me as she backed out the door and slammed it. The evening wind wafted her long, silky black hair over her high cheek bones as she left.

She must be Native American. If we're going to work together, first priority is to gain her trust.

I clicked the lock in place. *My new home.* The boxes scratched across the floor as I pushed the supplies up against one wall to make more living space. Shades were drawn over the two windows. One faced the restaurant, and the other faced whatever was behind the coop. Despite the urine-yellow walls, the repulsive glow of a low-watt light bulb and a musty smell irritating my nose, a sense of safety melted over me. I dropped my pack down on a corner table and rolled out my sleeping bag on the threadbare mattress over the metal frame along the far wall below the back window. I collapsed on the bed. The squeaky springs sagged like a hammock. I jumped up and lifted the shade to peek behind, then pulled it aside. Out the grime-encrusted window that faced west, I could only see pine trees. The evening sun wouldn't set for a few hours, but an ominous green shadow already crept over the few feet between the coop and the forest. Neglected weeds and wild grass filled the space. *Not much of a view.* I gave the shade a few gentle pulls. It did retract part way. I stopped trying to get it all the way up as it was brittle with age. *If I a tore it, then what would I say to Mr. Lloyd?*

I peeked around the front shade that faced the restaurant. Everyone was gone. The parking lot was empty. Searching what I could see of the sky, I saw heavy clouds dimming the summer sunlight. Soon it would disappear. As I watched, the mercury security lamp started to flicker, unsure whether it should stay lit. Convinced at last to stay on, it cast an eerie glow over the empty lot. Unlocking my door, I walked outside to the other end of the parking lot. Dark green clouds rumbled overhead to the west. It was going to rain and rain hard tonight. There was a sudden burst of lightning. The thunder was only moments behind. I pirouetted around the empty parking lot until large drops of rain struck my face. *I am so thankful for a nest and a roof over my head. I will survive the storm.*

Another bolt of lightning lit the whole sky. Thunder was immediate, and a cloudburst made me scurry for my coop. I was drenched by the time I got to the porch. Slipping inside, I stripped off my filthy, soaked clothes and danced about the room to dry to the music in my mind as the storm mimicked Tchaikovsky's "1812 Overture." I felt liberated, warm, and naked. It felt great. Flinging my arms, I got a whiff of my body odor. Instant revulsion led me to the back "closet" to check the hot water heater.

Turning around, I explored the bathroom. "Rebecca, you don't want to stain your sleeping bag with sweat. It's time to clean up." I yelled at myself just because no one would hear me above the din of the storm. I could think of lots of things that were wrong with me, but I aborted any further train of thought as the stench of my body odor was now top priority.

The water pipe felt hot, and it had been almost an hour since Mr. Lloyd had turned it on. I checked the shower. It spurted, blew a blast of air, then a rust colored burst followed by clear hot water flowed from the rusty fixture. I jumped aside, adjusted the temperature, and crawled in. A cracked, dried-up piece of yellow soap sat in the steel soap dish attached to the wall. I softened it in the stream of water and rubbed it over my breasts and down my belly, laughing as the bubbles collected in my greasy pubic hair. I scrubbed my face and arms finishing with meticulous care of my legs and feet, between my toes. Then the glorious sensation of rinsing followed. Clean, hot water cascaded across my skin in exhilarating waves, especially to the sensitive part of my abdominal scar. Every crack and crevice scrubbed, I felt clean for the first time in a long time. I used the last scrap of soap to wash my hair, thankful that it was short. When the water turned cold, I realized that I had just drained a 30-gallon tank. What would my father have said? I could hear him yelling at me in my mind as I got out of the shower stall. I had no towel, so I took out a t-shirt and a comb from my pack, placed the t-shirt on the one wooden chair and sat down. The comb snagged in my hair, washed with bar soap without conditioner, but with persistence it straightened out. Sitting naked on my dirty t-shirt, air-drying in the stale air, I was the happiest I had been in my whole life.

I better wash my clothes, especially my t-shirts. I need them for tomorrow. Oops, no hot water. I chuckled, and then shivered as hives spread across my chest. "I'll have to wash you in cold water," I explained to my t-shirt. My eye caught a label on one of the stacked boxes: dishwashing soap. *Perfect.*

Then I hesitated. *Would that be stealing?* I held up my right hand. "I promise before God to tell Mr. Lloyd first thing in the morning that I had used his soap." *If he fires me, at least I will have clean clothes.* I emptied my backpack onto the small pine table, pulling out the clothes and laying them on the bed. In the three days since I left, I had worn everything I owned. All of it was dirty and smelly: a couple of t-shirts, one pair of slacks, a pair of shorts, two pairs of underwear, and an extra bra that I probably didn't need. Poorly endowed in the mammary department, most people couldn't tell whether I was wearing one or not.

A check receipt fell on top of the pile. I unfolded it and read, "One cup of coffee $1.75." That coffee had used up my last two dollars, two days ago. I had left the quarter as a tip for the waitress. Folded in a small handkerchief stuck in the hidden pocket of the pack was a small bundle. Wrapped inside were my wedding and engagement rings. The diamond sparkled even in the dim light. "For an emergency," I told myself but couldn't conceive of any emergency that would make me sell them, at least not now. I rewrapped them, folding them into the handkerchief, and hid them back in the small pocket inside the pack. Memories flooded my brain. *Was I still married?* But the horror of the last days before I left made me stop thinking. I stuffed the backpack in the closet behind the water heater. It was heating up again. I could at least wash my clothes in tepid water.

Snitching some dishwashing soap, I filled the sink and dunked all my dirty clothes—panties, t-shirts, jeans, everything—scrubbing and squeezing them out. The water was filthy. After a thorough rinse—I was amazed how fast that hot water heater worked—I hung up my clothes around the room to dry. Everything I owned was now wet, so I slipped naked into my sleeping bag, happy, content, and for the first time in a long time, with a full belly. *What bliss.*

Chapter 2
Contentment

The reflected sunlight off the pine trees peaked through the half-shaded window and woke me.

The t-shirts hanging in the bathroom were almost dry, but my bra felt damp. I put it on, recalling Connie's remark about modesty, and hoped my body heat would dry it. I slipped on one of the t-shirts. I found a dry pair of panties I had overlooked the night before. I had washed them in a bathroom at a truck stop near Minneapolis. It felt comforting to put them on, and they smelled good too, like the soap dispenser at the truck stop.

Joan's uniform was too big. I tried to imagine what she was like to fill the uniform. Obviously she had a bigger bust and wider hips. But my t-shirt covered me, and after cinching the belt tight and gathering the extra fabric to the sides, I thought I looked acceptable in the bathroom mirror. The twisted folds around my waist were irritating, so I loosened the belt a bit and gathered the excess fabric into smaller folds. Another check in the mirror showed a baggy but modest covering. I felt nice despite no make-up or perfume. I was ready for work. I checked my watch: five o'clock. The restaurant didn't open for an hour, but I didn't need to be there until five-thirty. *What to do?*

I slipped out the front door, locked it with the rusty key, and proceeded to explore my adopted town. Cotton, Minnesota isn't much of a town. All the buildings are arranged along the west side of the highway, except a conical building on the east side. Beyond these few buildings, there is nothing but forest. An intersecting road was paved but narrow. I walked south until I could read the sign: Bug Creek Road. I laughed at the name and thought, *There prob-*

ably are a lot of bugs down that road. Searching in the direction of the road to the east, I could see a swamp and waist-high weeds filling the fields, turning the other direction, there was nothing but forest to the west. I saw no crops. Southwest of the intersection was a gas station. I wandered down to check it out. "Wickstrom's" was proudly displayed on a board across the front, but it wasn't open yet. Through the window, I could see that it was more than a gas station. There were snacks and juices stacked in a central aisle. Seeing them made me salivate. I made a mental note of what I might enjoy with my first paycheck. I hoped they stocked toothpaste, soap, and shampoo. I calculated what wonderful things I could buy. Then I thought, *Where could I cash my check? That could be a problem. Where was the nearest bank, and how would I even get there?*

South of Wickstrom's along the highway, there was nothing but jack pine forest, thick, impenetrable, and foreboding. Driving with the trucker, I remembered nothing but wilderness forest north of Duluth for miles. But there seemed to be paths through the brush at intervals. I wondered whether moose or deer had made those trails. There were no houses or mailboxes as far as I could see. I wondered where all the people lived who came to the restaurant every day.

I turned around and walked north. Checking the time, I still had fifteen minutes before Mr. Lloyd required my presence. Besides, his car was not in the parking lot and the key I had opened the coop but not the back door of the restaurant.

Past the restaurant to the north was a school, Cotton School One Hundred. A large sign announced, "Home of the Cotton Cardinals." I concluded that it must have all grades as there was only a single large building. A large plywood cardinal, streaked in red paint, displayed the school mascot. *Why was it school one hundred? Where were the other ninety-nine?*

A windrow of pine trees separated the school from the next building. A dilapidated sign announced the Cotton Covenant Church. It was small, and except for the spire, it could have been a cottage on Cape Cod. Shoulder high weeds grew around the abandoned structure. The locked display case, supposed to announce the sermon, only had fallen letters inside. Even with a key, the lock seemed too rusted to open. But the glass was intact, maybe too holy to be broken by vandals. A small parsonage behind the church was carefully boarded up. Weeds and vines climbed to the window sills.

"I guess they don't have services here very often," I said to the squirrel that hopped on top of the sign. She was chewing seeds out of a pine cone. "Where's the Catholic church? There has to be one, doesn't there?" The squirrel scowled at me as if to say that the question didn't deserve a response.

"Arrogant little beast," I said and snickered as she scooted away with her prize.

North of the church was a highway bridge with a green sign announcing, "Whiteface River." The bridge was wide enough for the two lanes of traffic of Highway 53, the main thoroughfare north of Duluth heading to the Canadian border. What surprised me was a narrow walkway on each side. There was no sidewalk or even a path leading to it, but it provided a safe place to walk across the bridge beside the highway.

Since there was no traffic and I had time, I walked through the brush to the bridge. Part way across, I paused to scan the water below. It was so clean and clear that I could watch fish dart between the rocks. *I'd sure like to go fishing sometime.* I had always dreamed of fishing, but my father was always too busy teaching at Wartburg Theological Seminary. He explained to me that fishing was a waste of time. One time I reminded him that Jesus went fishing and even told his disciples to go fishing. That merited a slap across my face for insolence. I never asked again.

There was nothing but thick forest beyond the curve in the river. Scanning out past the bridge, there was a gravel road that went east and west, but there was no sign naming it. Devoid of buildings and mailboxes, the landscape was wilderness as far as I could see, so I turned back toward the restaurant. A sign caught my eye on the other side of the bridge sign, "Cotton, unincorporated." No population was listed.

Why was this place called Cotton? I wondered. It sure was a long way from any cotton fields I knew about. I would have to ask someone. Walking back, a bait shop next to the large conical building with the initials, MDOT on the other side of the highway caught my eye. "Minnesota Department of Transportation," I read out loud. "M-DOT sounds better." The bait shop seemed abandoned.

There was not a single house except the abandoned parsonage by the church, and maybe one could count the Wickstrom's place if they lived above their store, but maybe not. "Am I the only person living in Cotton, Minnesota?" I yelled at the top of my lungs. There was no one to hear me.

I glanced at my watch and quickened my pace to get back to the restaurant. As I walked across the parking lot, Mr. Lloyd was turning into the driveway. I checked my uniform once more to make sure I was appropriate. *All right, I'm ready.*

"Good morning, Becky Jean," he said as he unlocked the front door and we walked in together. "Connie will be here soon. Do you know how to start the coffee pot?"

It took a brief explanation as it was quite different from the coffee pot we'd had at home or the nursing home where I had worked. I thought about how grouchy my father was until he had his first cup. Mother only drank coffee after he left for the seminary in the morning. The nursing home where I worked required lots of coffee as the residents drank one pot after another.

I added water and figured out where to put the grounds. I had coffee brewing as Connie walked in the door. She smelled it and smiled, "Thanks for having the coffee ready." She poured herself a mug full and took a drink. "Now, I'm ready."

She offered me a cup, but my empty stomach didn't agree with the idea. "Maybe later, thanks."

Mr. Lloyd appeared from his office and applied a plastic name tag to my uniform with "Becky Jean" in black marker on tape over "Joan." "Show her the ropes so she knows what to do when you take your lunch break," he said to Connie as he unlocked the back door and returned to his office. I heard Ron come in the back door like a sleuth. He said nothing to anyone.

Before customers arrived, Connie showed me where plates, cups, saucers, and condiments were and how to write up the orders. "You can help me take orders and serve until the dishes start piling up," she said. "It will give you a few tips. Most people around here are Scandinavian or Finnish and don't tip well, but after they get to know you, they tip better. We're real busy at the start. People want breakfast before they head off to work." She turned to the cash register. "I'm in charge of the register. Keep your hands off when I'm gone, Mr. Lloyd will cashier. You're not bonded yet." She squinted and said with a snarl, "You're still on probation."

The restaurant filled with commotion as soon as the "Open" sign was turned over at six o'clock. Cars started filling the open parking spots in front of the large picture windows minutes before the doors opened. Once open, orders came quickly for eggs over-easy, omelets, oatmeal, pastries, hash browns, pancakes, and lots of coffee. Between my pleas of, "Where's the extra catsup?" and, "How do I refill the salt and pepper shakers?" I managed to help more than hinder Connie for the first couple hours. I bussed dishes when I didn't know what else to do. It gave my gnawing stomach a break from seeing all the delicious food I wasn't entitled to eat yet. I wondered if I should have breakfast for my one meal but decided I would be too hungry by closing. *It would be best to wait.*

"Becky Jean, how's it going? First day on the job?" said Mack as he waved his hat at me when he came through the door.

"Second day," I said. "I worked yesterday too. I washed enough dishes to fill a castle."

I doubt he heard me as he ordered, "Coffee, scrambled eggs, and two orders of rye toast." Then he added, "I'll sit right here at the counter."

I turned in his order to Ron and poured his coffee. "Back so soon?"

"I unloaded in International Falls and drove back to Virginia. Slept at a rest stop there. Now I'm headed to Duluth to get another load." He took a sip of his coffee. "Oh, that's good." He grabbed my hand. "You look sharp in that uniform, hair looks nice. You must have had a shower since I dropped off your pathetic self yesterday."

"Thanks for the compliment, Mack. I feel a lot better, too." I leaned over and whispered in his ear, "Drained the hot water tank dry."

He roared with laughter. "Wish I could have been there." He smiled.

"You got a wife and kids to take care of, remember?" I said as I winked at his lurid grin.

He seemed to compose himself. "Yep, and I called my wife last night from Virginia. She even answered the phone, so I said what you told me. I think we're making progress. At least she'll talk to me now. She said maybe she would let me back in the house soon."

Mr. Lloyd interrupted our conversation, "Becky Jean, the dishes are piling up."

"See yah." I said as I waved to Mack and disappeared into the loud solitude of the dish washing room. My isolation was only interrupted by the banging of more dishes pushed through the wall opening. Connie was sure efficient. I worked fast to catch up with the constant flow of egg-encrusted dishes, dirty oatmeal bowls, and piles of utensils. Sweat rolled down my back, between my breasts, and across my belly. I feared I would need to change uniforms before I covered Connie's break.

The solitude gave me time to think. *I have a job and feel content, first time in a long time. Cotton, Minnesota is my new home.* "M-DOT," I said out loud, recalling the conical building across the highway. I liked the sound. I thought about the fish swimming between the rocks under the bridge as I sprayed the dishes and then scooted them into the dishwasher, closed the hood, and started the wash cycle. I pulled up the next trolley and readied the next load. I returned to thinking about the fish under the bridge. *I'm going to eat some of you little swimmers someday.* I was hungry already, yet it wasn't even mid-morning. I reminded myself that my meal break was hours away. I pushed my empty stomach up hard against the stainless steel counter to stop it from growling. The next load was ready to wash. I switched the machine to the rinse cycle and took a deep breath as I watched the temperature rise to the required 180 degrees. Now if I could just keep my secret.

Chapter 3
Job Satisfaction

"Would you like a refill on your coffee, Mr. Johannsen?" *He must be a school teacher*, I surmised as he scribbled red ink across papers he was correcting in a pile next to his plate. "Grading papers?"

"Yes, teaching summer school to students who are behind in their reading skills. Thanks for the coffee. I need it."

I was covering for Connie's morning break, rushing back and forth to each customer. Every seat at the counter was full as were most of the tables and booths. I flicked a glance at the coffee pot. It was almost full. Good thing that Connie had started a new pot before she took her break. But I would need another full pot for this crowd. They were drinking the coffee as fast as the pot could brew it.

I was adapting well to the job. In the last month, I had enjoyed meeting and serving the customers during Connie's breaks and when it was busy. Most of the customers introduced themselves to "the new girl," so during the course of the month, I'd made a point of remembering their names. After the first few weeks on the job just covering Connie's breaks, I knew the regulars by first and last name. They were all friendly, but I still cherished the privacy and solitude in the back surrounded by the din of the dishwasher.

"Miss, could I have some catsup for my eggs?" a hungry voice spoke behind me.

"Coming right up, Mr. Rollifsen," I said as I grabbed the full coffee pot, pushed the button to start a new brew, and grabbed the catsup.

He shifted his MDOT-labeled hat over his balding head. "Call me Rolly. You've served me enough times, and besides, everyone does." He opened the cap on the bottle and dumped catsup across his eggs. "Where are you from, Becky Jean?" he asked. "I know every family around here, so I know you're not from here."

"As far as I know, I am living in Cotton, Minnesota, Rolly. You should know that." I smiled. "Besides, I've been filling your coffee cup for weeks now."

Mr. Johannsen grabbed my arm, his bill in hand heading for the cash register. "I'm sorry to interrupt, but if I come back for lunch, what kind of pie will there be?"

"Beatrice is bringing in fresh blueberry pie today. She delivers about ten o'clock."

"All right, I'll be back. Blueberry is my favorite." He slipped a dollar on the counter for a tip as he gathered up the student papers he had been grading.

"I'll make sure Connie sets a piece aside for you."

He pulled out another dollar. "That one on the counter is for you, this one is for Connie," he said as he slipped the cash into Connie's tip jar near the cash register. "I'll make sure she knows how well you tipped, Mr. Johannsen. Mr. Lloyd will ring you up."

"Thanks," he said, shuffling his papers and dropping his red marking pen on the floor. I rushed around the counter to help him, but he held up a hand. "Got it."

"Order 12," Ron said from the kitchen, re-focusing my attention on my other customers.

"Excuse me, Rolly. My order is up." I grabbed the plate from under the hot light and brought it to Mr. Pykkinen. He was an elderly man, thin as a wire, but he ate with an unquenchable appetite. I wondered if he had some disease that allowed him to eat so much.

"Here's your cheese omelet and hash browns with two sausages," I said as I turned the plate so that the omelet smiled at him.

"Just the way I like it, Becky Jean. Now, remember to tell Mrs. Pykkinen that I had oatmeal if she asks. It means a good tip for you to keep my secret."

"Yes, sir, your secret is safe with me. Waitress-customer confidentiality, you know."

Mr. Rollifsen was waving at me. "Yes, Rolly, more coffee?"

"No. I'm fine, but you didn't answer me. Where were you from before you came to live here?"

His enunciated question required a less flippant response, so I settled with a slightly more honest answer. "South of Minneapolis."

"Ah, so you're a city girl. What possessed you to come to Cotton, population zero?"

"I needed a break from the chaos of the city. How's that?" *I also needed to change the subject.* "Do Wickstrom's live above their store?"

He laughed. "They used to, but now they built a house south of town."

"So why is this place called Cotton; how did it get its name?"

He put cream in his coffee and stirred before he answered. "This area used to be called 'Whiteface' after the river north of town. That's what the Chippewa called it. Then a lawyer, wouldn't you know it, Joseph Bell Cotton, wrote up the township papers and got his name stuck on our dear town. The people who lived around here had proposed the name 'Moberg.' Esquire Joseph Bell Cotton didn't charge the community to draft the legal documents, so they named it 'Cotton' to thank him for his generosity. I doubt if it was that much work."

I laughed, "Would Moberg have been better?"

He drank a big gulp of coffee and laughed. "I guess not."

"But I like Whiteface the best." I filled his cup and waved, "Ah, the ladies are here."

Out of the corner of my eye, I noticed a troop of elderly women coming through the door, the ladies' Bible study group. Leading the way was an imposing woman, Mrs. Lawrence. She was hefty and buxom, but it didn't slow down her authoritative gait. Her demeanor made crowds part. Her bulk emanated an aura of confidence. Today she was wearing a black dress with large red flowers in the print. It made her look even bigger than she was. The ladies parading in her wake appeared fragile in comparison. Most were half her size and twenty years older. They followed her like ducklings into the private back room where they held their study session.

They were a problem for Connie because they seldom ordered more than tea, spread themselves out through most of the back room, and stayed well over an hour. On special occasions some of the ladies would add toast to their orders. But they insisted on separate checks and seldom left more than a dime tip, apparently unaware that the depression years were over. But I overheard Bert reprimand Connie one morning: "The ladies' husbands order more when they eat here, and they tip well, so just serve them. Just be nice to them."

"Excuse me, Rolly. I have to take care of the Bible study ladies. Thanks for the history lesson. Joseph Bell Cotton, right?"

"Right." He smoothed the catsup around his eggs with his fork and took a bite, winking at me as I left to attend the ladies.

I ran into the back room with a stack of slips for each lady and my pen poised, "Welcome ladies. Who's having coffee and who's having tea this morning?"

Mrs. Lawrence said, "Now you know, Becky Jean, that I'm the only one who drinks coffee. The other ladies all drink tea." They seated themselves in the prescribed order where they always sat and opened their Bibles.

"Beatrice has brought in the caramel rolls. Can I interest any of you in having one? They're especially good today."

"They're always especially good," said Mrs. Lawrence, "but I will forgo the pleasure today." She put her hands on her ample hips. In fact, she had always forgone the pleasure. She had never ordered anything but black coffee in the month I had served them. She clearly maintained her bulk at other meals. Several of the ladies ordered dry toast with their tea. I had no trouble remembering which ones because it was always the same. I stuck my pen back behind my ear. I already had their receipts made out. "Your orders are coming right up, ladies."

"Thank you, Becky Jean," sang the soprano chorus.

I put four pieces of bread in the toaster and smiled at Connie as she came back from break. I poured the one cup of coffee and set up the pots of tea on the serving tray. "Thanks, Becky Jean," she said. "I get so frustrated waiting on those ladies, and in three years I doubt if their tips have added up to five dollars."

"It's all right, Connie. I don't have two children and a husband to support." I hustled the tray to the back room as Connie said, "Thanks, again," over my shoulder.

They were already deep into the Word, so I served in silence and left to attend my swarm of dirty dishes in the dishwashing room. As I returned to my solitude, spraying down the breakfast dishes and putting the next load into the dishwasher, I thought about the rhythm of the day. Ron, the fry cook, took his smoking break after the initial breakfast crowd left. He always went out and sat on the steps of Mr. Lloyd's coop, now my house, while he smoked two cigarettes. It took him exactly fifteen minutes. While he took his break, Mr. Lloyd cleaned the grill. There was a brief lull in the commotion between the early and late breakfast crowd, then another pause before the lunch group came.

The traces of fried eggs and sausages on the grill had to make way for noon hamburgers. When Ron finished smoking, the grill was clean and the lunch crowd started coming. Connie asked me to help keep the wolves at bay until the hamburger orders started flying off the grill and the dishes started piling up again.

Connie always took her lunch break at two o'clock. Sometimes she drove home if she had a sick child or just drove down the road somewhere to get away from the restaurant. It was the most difficult time of the day for me. I had no backup and had had nothing to eat yet. I was hungry and had been running since before 6:00 A.M., smelling and gazing at delicious food that I was not allowed to eat. Every day I was tempted to eat the scraps off the dishes, but I disciplined myself, despite the gnawing lust in my belly, to feed it all down the garbage disposal.

Today was no exception. Before I came to Cotton, I was under the false impression that people finished their dinner by one o'clock, but not this crowd. The truck drivers hauling loads to International Falls, people from the saw mill, and pulp wood lumberjacks got as much done as possible in the morning before they came for lunch, so every table was still full at two o'clock when Connie left.

I filled orders and had little time to chat with the customers. I was frantic when Ron yelled that he was out of hamburgers. I ran to the freezer to get more, informed by Mr. Lloyd that running to the freezer for Ron was "part and parcel" of my job. Connie came in through the back door just as I was pulling forty pounds of frozen hamburger patties out of the cooler. "You can go on break now, Becky Jean." It was music to my ears.

Adjusted to the routine, I would put in my order with Ron and tell my stomach to be patient. It informed me that it was adjusting to eating once a day at two-thirty. I could have set my watch by the hunger pangs that tore at my gut about two o'clock. Sometimes my stomach would complain if customers delayed Connie's break, but I had a vested interest in getting her out on time. "I'll take over," I would insist. It wasn't altruistic. I was sure that my stomach would eat me alive if she returned late.

"Order up, Becky Jean." I swallowed the saliva pouring into my mouth as I smelled my lunch frying on Ron's grill.

Just like Pavlov's dogs. That is what I've become, a Pavlovian dog.

Sunday was the problem. The restaurant wasn't open, so I often went without food, sort of a spiritual Sunday fast, I told myself. I signed my checks, and Connie had her husband cash them, so I got my money on Friday after he returned from Duluth. So sometimes I used my cash to buy a candy bar or some crackers from Wickstrom's store. They weren't open before or after work, so I had to gulp down my food and race down there on my Saturday break to get anything to eat on Sunday. But I hated to spend my money, saving every cent to return to the university.

For a distraction on Sundays, I had been hiking through the woods following what I assumed were animal trails. I had gotten pretty good at recognizing deer tracks through the woods, wolf tracks in the deer's wake, and raccoon tracks along the edges of the corn fields and in the mud near the shore of the Whiteface River. The exercise and the new discoveries kept my hunger at bay. But Sunday night when I came back from my hike was the worst. I was so hungry I couldn't sleep, and I discovered that extending my hikes farther into the woods to exhaustion didn't really help. Mondays at 2:30, I was ravenous. One Monday morning I took some left-over omelet off a plate to shove into my mouth, but caught myself just in time as Mr. Lloyd opened the door to check on me.

"Am I keeping up?" I asked. He nodded. I shoveled the delectable-looking omelet into the garbage disposal.

Chapter 4
Vacation Days

The last Friday of August, when Connie returned from her break she grabbed my shoulder as I turned to head to the kitchen for my daily meal. "Mr. Lloyd wants to see you in his office. He said that you could bring your lunch."

Now what? Had I broken some rule? I ordered my food, proceded to his office, and balanced my tray on my lap as I sat down in front of his desk.

"Go ahead, eat." He motioned and went to his closet and pulled out a large box. "I found a hotplate among the stored supplies in the coop this morning."

I had never explored all the stuff stored in the boxes in the coop, respecting his privacy. I did not even recognize the box he was holding. I kept eating.

"I plugged it in and it still works. I haven't used that thing in over a decade. It can be your kitchen. And one of our customers remodeled their kitchen and asked if I needed an extra refrigerator. He's bringing it in his truck and will put it wherever you want it in the coop. Now you will have a refrigerator and can cook your own meals on your vacation days." His smile was so exaggerated I was sure that he was quite proud of himself.

I panicked. "Vacation days?"

"The days off that you've accrued."

"I didn't know I accrued any days off." *I imagined additional days of fasting. Now I have a kitchen, but where can I get food?* "That probably uses a lot of electricity. How about if I pay for it by working my vacation days instead of taking them off?" I said with a smile at my creativity.

"No need for that," he said as he pulled out an old pan from under his desk and gave it to me. "See, it even has a cover. You can take a couple of dishes and silverware from the restaurant until you can buy your own."

I felt both anxious and excited about my new "kitchen." But what would I do with days off? I had no transportation, and Wickstrom's store didn't offer many staples. The expense of buying food would eat into any savings for college. I couldn't afford to buy food and have enough to return to college to complete my degree.

That Saturday, I gobbled my food down and ran to Wickstrom's to buy something. They did have jars of popcorn and oil, so that Sunday evening I broke my fast and used my hotplate and the discarded pan to pop some corn while reading a New York Times best-seller that one of the customers had given me as a tip. I was in heaven. I couldn't believe how happy I was. But I knew this couldn't last.

Many weeks later when Connie came back from her break, she twisted her long straight hair into a ponytail and gave me a crooked grin, staring at me with her black-brown Ojibwa eyes. "Bert needs to see you in his office. Get your lunch and eat there. He's waiting. This is important."

I grabbed my plate as soon as Ron prepared it and dashed to Mr. Lloyd's office. I set my plate on the edge of his desk and stood with my hands at my sides, a soldier at attention. That's when I realized what day it was. Today, my probation period ended. I panicked. *Did I still have a job? Would I be fired? Had I done something wrong? Did I work fast enough?* I knew today was the last day he could fire me without a reason.

"Go ahead, sit down and eat, Becky Jean." I swallowed as the smell of the juicy aroma informed my salivary glands of the coming nourishment. The wooden chair creaked as I sat across from his desk. I balanced my plate in my lap. "You've been working here almost three months now. I need to know your plans. Are you going back to the university this fall? If so, I need to find a replacement."

He didn't mention that my probation period ended. That must be good. My eyes focused on the grease stains on his apron from cleaning the grill. I had learned that despite his rough exterior, he hid a gentle spirit. I licked my lips and picked up my knife and fork to seize a bite of my roast beef sandwich swimming in gravy, slopped over with a quarter of a bottle of ketchup. I hid my mouth behind my hand as I gobbled a mouthful. The ketchup squirted out the side of my mouth. I wiped my mouth with a tissue he gave me off his desk. *Clumsy, you forgot a napkin. Remember to bring a napkin next time.* I chewed with slow deliberation before swallowing, using the time to think through my answer. *I wanted to return to college to finish my degree. With three years behind me, I only needed one more year to graduate with a bachelor's degree in sociology. Think before you speak, Rebecca.*

"You have treated me so well, Mr. Lloyd. I hope that I have proven to be a hard worker and a good employee."

"Yes, you have, but that doesn't answer my question."

I took a deep breath and cut another bite expecting him to continue with some sort of evaluation. I finished chewing while he looked at papers from my folder. *Was that my college transcript?* The silence increased my anxiety.

"Originally I was only going to work through the summer and go back to UMD, the University of Minnesota, Duluth, to finish my degree this fall. But…"

I had saved every spare cent, fasting on Sundays. Yet I did not have enough money to go back to school. I could resume my studies at the Duluth branch if I bought a junk car and commuted the thirty miles. But I had no place to live in Duluth and to live in the dorm was expensive. Going back to school would mean that I could only work part time, and then I wouldn't have the money to stay in school. I was trapped, but I had good food every day and with no place in Cotton to spend my money except at Wickstrom's. Toothpaste, deodorant, and shampoo hadn't eaten significantly into the money I had saved under my pillow.

Digesting my juicy roast beef calmed my anxiety. "May I keep working here? If I stay the winter and work another year, I could maybe reconsider going back to the UMD next year, when I have saved a bit more money." *I'd call it a working sabbatical. I liked the sound of that word. It meant I wasn't giving up. I promised myself that I would go back to finish my degree.* He gave no verbal or facial response. *Maybe if I sweetened the pie.* "You haven't charged me rent to stay in the chicken coop. If I stay the winter, I think that I should start paying rent."

He twisted his pencil between his fingers. Silence. *Was I about to be fired? Did he have someone else he had promised my job to?*

I took the opportunity to take another bite of roast beef, scooting some of the gravy with the sandwich bread, and gobbled down a few French fries. *Was this my last meal before I was out on the street again?* I had slimmed down working on my feet all day and eating only what Ron gave me each day at

2:30. I drank lots of water to quench my stomach rumbling in the evening, but I was so exhausted that I seldom had trouble falling asleep—well, except Sunday night.

I set my knife and fork down on my plate after each bite, but before he spoke again, I had finished my sandwich. I ate half my French fries, checking him for a response after each one.

"I've hired a young woman, Leah Thomas, to do the dishes. She just graduated from high school last spring, took the summer off, and now needs a job. I've known her parents for years. She should be a good worker."

My chest tightened. *I am going to be fired. Where will I go? How will I get there? I have no vehicle. Should I hitchhike farther north or west or…? The money I have saved won't even pay for a month's rent in a cheap hotel in Duluth.* My stomach churned as it tried to digest all the greasy meat I had just swallowed. Nausea erupted like a volcano. I swallowed to keep from vomiting.

"If you're going to stay…" Now he was spinning the pencil from his desk between his fingers. That was usually a good sign. I took a deep breath. *What? I could stay?* I blinked my eyes to clear my confusion, swallowed, and concentrated on what he was going to say next.

"After reviewing your college transcript, I noticed that you took several business administration courses."

"That was my minor."

"I've decided to make you the assistant manager."

"But Connie…"

He held up his hand to stop me from objecting. "I already asked Connie. She likes her tips, and she's not interested. I could pay you a little more as a salary, but you would still need to waitress to cover the busy times and Connie's breaks. What I need is for you to do some of the buying and bookkeeping. You would have to go to Duluth for supplies. I assume you do have a driver's license."

"Yes, Iowa."

"You'll have to get a Minnesota license, but that should be just a formality." His eyes seemed to burn into me. *Was he questioning his decision?* "You would need to be bonded to do the cash register and use the café credit card to purchase supplies."

I choked up my last French fry and chewed it better. "What does bonding involve? I assume they would contact the nursing home where I worked and my references at the University of Iowa, but would they have to contact my parents?" Hives swelled across my chest. "I really don't want them to know where I am, and…"

"I can ask the bonding company to be discreet, but if you are buying supplies, I have to trust you with my credit card and money, so you have to be bonded." He stood. "Do you have something to hide? Have you any felony convictions?"

I shook my head, "No, no felonies. It's just that, well, my parents…My father sort of kicked me out of the house, so that's why I don't want them to know where I am."

He stood. "Becky Jean, you have been a hard worker. Any father that kicked a daughter like you out of his house needs to have serious psychological treatment."

I stood, grabbing my plate at the last second off my lap so it didn't fall on the floor. The rule was we had to pay for broken dishes. My knees were shaking. I locked my elbows into my sides. "Thank you, Mr. Lloyd. You have been kinder than a father to me."

"As assistant manager, I insist that you call me Bert."

"Yes, Mr. Lloyd, I will practice that tonight and start calling you 'Bert' tomorrow."

His belly jiggled with laughter.

I headed for the door and then turned. "What about the rent?"

"For that little place? Consider it part of your new salaried position," he pointed to the closet in the corner, "Oh, there are your new uniforms. They should fit you much better."

I stood stunned and stammered, "How did you know I would accept? How did you know my size?" I picked up one of the uniforms and read my name with *Assistant Manager* embroidered underneath. They were sharp-looking with wide lapels and a cute pocket with the *Bert's Café* logo.

"Call it a hopeful, educated guess."

I hung my head, "You've been so kind. I hate to ask for anything more, but…"

"Yes?" his bushy eyebrows rose over his glasses.

"May I use the restaurant van to do a little shopping when I go to Duluth? I will pay you for the extra gas and keep track of personal time. You can dock me for that."

"Any time," he said as his concerned visage changed to laughter. "I won't dock you a cent. Now, get back to work. I hear customers out there. Leah will be here at four o'clock to find out what is required of her new job. I expect you to give her a good orientation, Assistant Manager."

"Yes, sir, Mr. Lloyd…Bert."

Connie met me at the door as I left Mr. Lloyd's office. I hung my head. "Did you really turn down the assistant manager job? You deserve it, not me. You have been faithful to Mr. Lloyd for years. Will you resent me?"

"Why would I want to go traipsing around the county buying supplies? I want to be able to go home on breaks, and I certainly don't want to lose my tips to you." Her harsh gaze turned to a smile. "Besides, even when I have been nasty to you, you have always been nice to me. I've watched you like a hawk, ready to tear you apart at the first chance, but I've grown to like you." She gave me a hug.

"We can be friends then?"

"More than that, Assistant Manager, you are family now, you scrawny kid."

Chapter 5
Winter's Approach

Things slowed as the land prepared for winter's snow-covered rest. There are not many oak or maple trees scattered among the pine trees in this part of Minnesota, but the few that there are turned brilliant red among the bright yellow of the poplars interspersed among the blue-green jack pine and spruce. When fishing season closed, we lost the customers with their big boats and trailers from Minneapolis and St. Paul. They were a comical lot as they bragged about the fish they caught and described our restaurant as a "wilderness outpost." They would return opening day of fishing season the middle of next May. We still had a few tourists, families looking for fall hayrides advertised by local farmers. They came with a bevy of children, all wanting hot chocolate and cookies. But now most of our clientele were local farmers, pulpwood lumberjacks, and truckers.

It was a lovely October afternoon. All day I had been looking out the window, past the parking lot at the beautiful kaleidoscope of color in the trees among the pines across the highway. But I knew it would be dark soon, so I took advantage of the pause in coffee refills and hoped the leaves wouldn't blow off the trees before my Sunday hike. I was planning my route when I was interrupted.

"Is your real name Rebecca, Becky Jean?"

"Yes, Charlie, my name is really Rebecca. Do you need more coffee?" I said, jarred out of my daydream. Charlie Butler was a regular customer. He annoyed Connie with his constant questions, but he gave good tips, so she tolerated him, but she warned me not to engage him in much conversation, especially about religion. "Just be civil, that's all," she told me.

He ordered the special of the day, a hot roast beef sandwich. He was cleaning his plate, wiping the gravy with a last piece of bread. He was a rough-looking man who seldom shaved, but at his age, I assumed well over seventy, he didn't need to shave often. His smile was enough to scare a person, with only one upper tooth and two lower teeth that didn't quite meet. He dressed like a lumberjack, with a black and red flannel shirt, scuffed blue jeans with prominent patches, and boots that tied to mid-calf. His hands were gnarled from arthritis, but his forearms displayed well-developed muscles. On warm summer days, he smelled like pine sap. When it got cold, he smelled of smoke. So I suppose he heated wherever he lived with wood. I asked several other customers, but no one was quite sure where he lived. He always arrived in his beat-up pickup truck which was at least a couple decades old.

"Well that is a beautiful Bible name. Rebecca was…"

I finished his sentence, trying to abort conversation. "Isaac's favorite wife. I know. That's for whom I was named."

I felt his eyes travel over my physique. "Well, Rebecca, it suits you just fine. You are as lovely as your namesake," he said as he grinned and displayed his mostly edentulous gums.

"How do you know what Rebecca in the Bible looked like?" The question just came out. I knew I shouldn't have asked.

"It says in Genesis that she was a beautiful woman, and so are you."

"Thanks, Charlie." I filled his coffee cup even though he hadn't asked. "I'll take that as a compliment."

He picked up his coffee cup and nodded thanks. "Now here's the important question: do you know Jesus Christ as your savior so you can see your namesake in heaven?"

"Yes, Charlie," I leaned over and whispered in his ear, "I'm a Christian." I turned to escape further interrogation and put the coffee pot back on the heater. Charlie raised his hand like a school boy. "Is there something else you would like?"

"I would love to have a piece of that coconut cream pie. Is there any left? Coconut cream is my favorite. My mother could never make it, try as she might."

I glanced over to where we kept the pies. "One piece left. It's yours." I placed it on a plate and served it with a fresh napkin and dessert fork. He put his gnarled hand on my arm. His skin was coarse as sandpaper, so I pulled away.

"These coarse hands have operated many a piece of heavy equipment, Rebecca." He shoved a piece of the pie into his mouth, gumming it well before he swallowed. "I worked on those highways up in Canada and North Dakota, you know."

He had told me several stories of those times when I had waited on him before. My favorite was his story about going cross-country in a blizzard because he lost track of the road. He ended up in some farmer's back yard. "Scared that poor fellow and his wife, but he invited me in for coffee." Retired, he still did welding at a shop somewhere near his home upon special request. "No weld of Charlie Butler ever broke," he always said.

"But do you believe in the full gospel?" his long, wispy eyebrows twitched. He leaned over the counter and whispered, "Can you speak in tongues?"

"Unser Vater in dem Himmel! Dein Name werde geheiligt. Dein Reich komme. Dein Wille geschehe auf Erden wie im Himmel. Unser täglich Brot gib uns heute. Und vergib uns unsere Schuld, wie wir unseren Schuldigern vergeben. Und führe uns nicht in Versuchung, sondern erlöse uns von dem Übel. Denn dein ist das Reich und die Kraft und die Herrlichkeit in Ewigkeit. Amen." I smiled. "Does that count?"

A Cheshire grin spread across his face, and then he started laughing and slapping the counter. "Rebecca, you are special. Now, do you know why my name is Butler?"

"No, why?"

"Because my relatives were butlers for the king of England. But my father left all that and came here. Now I serve the King of Kings."

I whispered in his ear, "So do I." He reached over the counter and gave me a hug that about smothered me. I gasped for breath when he let go.

"I am so glad that you are full-gospel, full of God's spirit, and beautiful as your name."

"Excuse me, Charlie, I have other customers."

"You just go serve them in the power of the Holy Spirit, Rebecca Jean." He slapped the counter again with a tumultuous laugh.

"Charlie is usually so aggravating. What was that all about?" asked Connie who turned at the commotion. "I've never seen him act like that. I thought I was going to have to rescue you." She tied on her apron, back from her break. My stomach was grumbling right on schedule. "Do you really speak in tongues?" she asked, her forehead wrinkled in consternation.

"That was the Lord's prayer in German, so I suppose I do. My parents made me memorize it. Don't you know the Lord's Prayer in Anishinaabe? It might get you a better tip next time."

"I never thought of that," she said with a laugh. "Yah, we used to go to an Anishinaabe church on the reservation. I'll have to practice."

After that day Charlie always called me Rebecca Jean and gave me five dollar tips even when he only ordered a cup of coffee. Connie was jealous of my tips, but she said that he really wasn't worth the aggravation. But I did catch her whispering the Lord's Prayer in Anishinaabe for practice.

Since Halloween was coming soon, I picked up some decorations on my weekly trip to Duluth. The stores were full of masks, pumpkins with faces, and ghosts with happy faces. Bert said that he usually ignored the holiday and planned to close early to avoid any teenage mischief, but he didn't object to the pumpkin pictures, New Orleans-type masks or happy ghosts that I hung from the walls, attached to the windows and hung from strings in the ceiling tiles. But he insisted there was to be nothing scary, no witches or goblins, skeletons or zombies.

As part of the festivities, Bernice made pumpkin pies as our special for the whole month of October. Bert explained to the customers that Bernice's pumpkin pies would return before Thanksgiving as well. I caught myself drooling at the sight and smell of them, but I remembered the rule: No desserts.

During the week prior to Halloween, I talked Bert into offering free hot chocolate to any children dressed in costume. Lots of children came, and the parents loved it, usually adding a piece of pie to the order. But we almost ran out of whipped cream, and that would have been my responsibility. I added the last we had to a piece of pumpkin pie and hoped no one would order more. I made a mental note, *More whipped cream for Thanksgiving*.

At 5:30 on Halloween, just as we were about to close, eight motorcycles parked in front of the window. A rough-looking bunch of men in leathers appeared with their three buxom girlfriends. Connie was in the back getting ready to go home, so I met them alone at the counter.

Grizzled with a full beard, a tall, muscular man who seemed to be the leader walked in, and the others, all in black leather with some kind of skull insignia which I assumed to be the gang logo, followed. "What do we have here?" he said as he grabbed my arm and pulled me from behind the counter. "A frail little butterfly."

"Can I serve you, sir? We are about to close."

He pushed me to one of his partners. I almost lost my footing. "Your frail little ass wouldn't service me, butterfly." His partner pushed me to another member of the gang. He jerked me around and tossed me back to the leader. This time I grabbed his leather jacket as tight as I could, looked into his face and said, "Since you are all in costume, I could give you free hot chocolate." He pushed me away.

Then they all started laughing, formed a circle, and tossed me back and forth. Each time I was tossed back to the leader, I held on as hard as I could. The three buxom women joined the circle, laughing at their boyfriends' antics, grabbing at my breasts and yelling, "No boobs on that one."

Ron appeared from the kitchen. His serious visage stopped the hilarity. He never said a word. He just stood silent and ominous.

The leader held up his hand motioning to the gang to stop. "Just having some fun with the little butterfly here," he said. "I think we'll forgo the hot chocolate, little bitty lady. We were looking for something a little stronger." The whole gang started to back out towards the door, but the leader held me until everyone was outside. As Ron approached him, he stuffed something down the front of my uniform. "See you all." He pushed me toward Ron and squirmed out the door.

I pulled a twenty-dollar bill out of my bra. The gang leader winked and yelled, "Just a little tip for the butterfly." They revved their motorcycles and left in a cloud of noise and exhaust.

I had tears in my eyes as Ron's hug filled me with comfort and security. I choked out a, "Thanks." It was all I could say.

Chapter 6
Mall Shopping

Deer hunters started arriving for breakfast before going out to their deer stands during the first weeks of November when the season opened. First the bow hunters came at the opening of their season and then the rifle hunters when gun season opened. I had seen deer on my Sunday walks almost every time, both in the fields and along the Whiteface River. But when deer-hunting season opened, it seemed like they disappeared. I never saw another deer on my walks until the Sunday after hunting season was over. Charlie Butler had given me a red coat to wear, "So you won't get shot when you go out for your Sunday strolls, Rebecca Jean." The coat smelled of pine sap and smoke and was way too big for me, but I wore it faithfully during hunting season. Yet I never understood how he knew about my Sunday excursions.

I enjoyed meeting the hunters, who were the new guests to the restaurant, because I could never guess what they would order. I was terrible at predicting. On the other hand, the local people were my family. Most of the time, I knew what they would order before they sat down. They were so predictable it made me giggle when I called in their orders to Ron. Often he anticipated my requests and had the meals ready. The regulars were always amazed at the quick service.

I enjoyed my assistant manager job. It got me out of town, or out of the woods, depending on perspective. I usually went to Duluth, but sometimes there were sales at the wholesale warehouses in Superior, Wisconsin. Bert had never investigated them for supplies, so he was pleased with my extra efforts to save the restaurant money. I usually went on Tuesday afternoons because the restaurant was less busy and Leah didn't mind bussing the dishes and helping Connie waitress while I was gone. She made a few tips, and it gave her a break from the steam and noise of the washing machine room.

I felt like an escapee from prison when I entered the mall for the first time. I kept track of my personal time and turned it into Bert, but he just laughed at me. I always returned the van in good shape with a full tank of gas well before closing, but he never seemed to care. He even gave me a set of keys for the front and back doors in case the restaurant was closed when I returned to unload the supplies, but I never needed them.

I seldom bought anything at the mall, but I did open a savings-checking account at the bank outlet with the money I had accumulated under my pillow. It was fun seeing the balance increase every two weeks but it was still almost nothing compared to what I needed for tuition if I were to return to university life at UMD the following year. It was nice to not have to sign my checks and wait for Connie to bring back my money, which I no longer needed to hoard in a sock under my pillow. I could just deposit my checks in my account. There was no longer a lumpy sock disturbing my sleep. After a few deposits, the teller, who now recognized me when I came in, told me that I qualified for free checking. Maybe she thought I was a student, but I didn't object. I seldom wrote any checks, so I expected my initial free packet would last a long time. But I felt sophisticated having them tucked away in my purse.

By the middle of November, it was getting cold in the mornings, so I needed to buy some winter hiking gear for my Sunday strolls through the woods. Charlie's red jacket was warm, but it was not warm enough for the sub-zero temperatures I anticipated in December. Connie and other customers had warned me that it wasn't unusual for the temperature in Cotton to drop to forty below zero by January. I felt jubilant walking into the sports store to check out warm clothes and accessories. I planned to buy a sweater, a parka, and boots and promised myself that I would be tempted by nothing else no matter what caught my attention.

Amazed at the choices, I found a warm parka that wasn't too expensive, and a handsome salesman fit me for hiking boots. The sweaters were on sale, stacked on a table near the cash register. A teal pullover caught my eye. I mentally added the price tags then shook my head. They added up to a whole week of work. But I convinced myself that I needed them, so I pulled out my checkbook.

"Cash or credit?" the clerk asked. She tossed her blond curls behind her ears as she looked at the check I was writing. "Ah, we don't take checks."

"I'm local," I pleaded.

"Sorry, no checks." She turned and called over the manager. "I told her no checks." He scrutinized my check.

I protested, "I bank right here at the mall. You can walk over and see if I have enough funds." I paused, waiting for a response. Frustrated, I added, "I can go down the hall to the bank and get the cash. No problem. I really need these things so I don't freeze to death." I thought that added a nice emotional touch.

The manager scanned my new Minnesota driver's license I had provided. I felt like a criminal in a line-up. "I'm a waitress at Bert's Restaurant in Cotton," I added.

He looked up at me. "Ah, I remember you. I stopped there on the way to Lake Vermillion to go fishing. Good coffee, wonderful hamburgers, and the pie was outstanding, but I was pretty tight with the tip." He grimaced, which I construed as an apology, and he turned to the cashier, "We'll accept her check. I owe her." He returned to his other customer. The clerk stuffed the check in the cash register with what seemed like a forced smile that accentuated her purple lip gloss and turned away. I thanked her, but she ignored me.

I returned to the nice bank teller to ask if I could order a debit card on my account. She helped me make out the application and said that my debit card would be in the mail within a week. I used the Café's address for my "Home." I would have to tell Bert to watch for it.

As I walked out with my precious purchases, I passed the garden store. The displays for spring planting were gorgeous. I'd always wanted a garden, but our yard had been too small to have one and my mother had no interest even when I suggested it. As a little girl, I had dreamed about the plants and flowers growing in the garden that I would have some day. I loved flowers. I stood at the window fantasizing about a garden of my own. *Maybe when spring returns, I'll plant something around my coop. I'm sure Bert won't mind.*

The last store before the exit was a toy store. The twinkling of the lights in the window display caught my eyes. Fascinated by the creative items on display, I thought back to my childhood. I never had many toys. I just stood there mute, focusing on the miniature railroad, then the dolls in the corner with porcelain smiles, and finally the whimsical Santa Claus hugging a red-nosed reindeer. How much fun it would have been to play with such toys when I was growing up? But Father thought these things were frivolous. The manager waved through the window as he completed the Christmas display. I waved back and left. *It seems odd to have a Christmas display when Thanksgiving is still a week away. Silly,* I chided myself, *why are you looking at toys? What would you ever do with toys?*

As I put my purchases into the van, I recalled Connie telling me that I needed to replace my t-shirts. They had become see-through from washing them by hand in the sink with industrial detergent. I really didn't need them for modesty with my new uniforms, but they were nice for hiking. My bra didn't fit right anymore either, so, back to the mall.

The clerk at the clothing store was much nicer than the clerk at the sports store and took my check for my new bra and t-shirts without question. She was an elderly woman who said that she had a daughter my age. We talked for a while, but when she mentioned grandchildren, it was time for me to go.

Several days later, Bert called me into his office. There was the letter with my new debit card on his desk. "I used the restaurant for my home address. I hope that was all right."

"Not a problem," he grunted, still focused on his paperwork. "That coop doesn't have its own address."

The following Tuesday, my debit card bought drapes for my "chicken coop" and Chantilly paint for the walls. I just couldn't stand urine-colored walls any longer, and Bert said that he didn't care how I decorated the place. I was surprised how much brushes and supplies cost, but it was worth every cent when the next Sunday night I sat on my bed, eating popped corn and rejoicing at the fresh, frilly drapes and lovely shade of paint on the walls. My joy was only quelled by the acrid smell of the latex in the air that took several days to clear. It was just too cold to leave the windows open to air it out. I sniffed and sneezed, but it was still worth it.

That Sunday afternoon before Thanksgiving, I hiked along a trail that I assumed was a deer trail. I lost track of time in the bright sunshine despite the brisk cold. Just before sunset, I came upon what I thought was a small pond because it was glassy smooth with no apparent current. But on closer inspection, it was just a wide place in the Whiteface River. If the river changed course in the spring, it would become a lacunar pond.

As I contemplated its reflective surface, I heard a soft noise like the crinkle of snow. With stealth, I approached, hiding behind a tree. A doe and her well-developed fawn held up their heads. I didn't move. They went back to drinking as I knelt to watch. It was magical. As darkness enveloped us, I backed away. It was a challenge to find my way back along the trail in the dark, but the image of the doe and her fawn overwhelmed me with peace.

Back at my coop, all painted, cleaned and hung with new curtains, I stripped and crawled into bed. Hungry again, but too tired to make more popcorn, I rubbed my belly. Contentment filled me as I recalled what I had seen at the pond. I fell into a deep sleep.

Winter descended that night. In the morning, it was very cold, and several inches of snow had fallen covering the trees out my back window. Bert had supplied me with an electric space heater that turned on when the temperature dropped. I had set the threshold at 65 degrees so as not to use unnecessary electricity. It was the sound of the snowplow Bert had hired to clear the parking lot that awakened me. I smiled with pride as I looked at my new parka hung in the corner and my boots stacked below. My new shades and pretty walls told me I was home. *All I need is a fireplace and a couch in which to snuggle.*

Chapter 7
Thanksgiving

"Mrs. Lawrence, what is the theme for the Bible study today?" I asked as I seated the ladies.

"Thanksgiving, of course. Philippians Chapter 4 is our text since tomorrow is Thanksgiving, you know," she seemed indignant.

"I am thankful to be serving you ladies."

"There is never a reason not to be thankful, Becky Jean."

"Oh, every day I've been here is Thanksgiving day for me, Mrs. Lawrence."

She smiled at my response and patted me on the shoulder. "That's good to hear, dear." She turned to the group, "Isn't it ladies?" They all cheered, sitting in their usual places. Mrs. Lawrence asked, "Mr. Lloyd will be serving turkey and dressing, I presume?"

I looked over the group. "Regular orders, ladies?"

"Yes, thank you, Becky Jean," they sang in synchrony.

"I'll check on Thanksgiving dinner, Mrs. Lawrence, just a moment." I wondered whether the restaurant would be closed on the holiday. I hadn't thought to ask. When I returned, I affirmed to Mrs. Lawrence that the restaurant would be open and serving the usual Thanksgiving spread.

"Oh, I won't be here," she said. "I have twenty-some coming for dinner. But some of the other ladies will come. You're coming, aren't you, Agnes?"

The frail lady at the end of the table who always dressed with white lace over her blue dress answered. "Oh, yes, I wouldn't miss it. All my folks are in the grave. I outlived them all, so every year Thanksgiving with Bert is special to me."

"I'll save you a place, Agnes. All right, I'll get your coffee, Mrs. Lawrence, and tea for the rest of you. Right?"

"Of course," they sang.

As I was getting the ladies' orders, I queried Bert on the details, "So you said we are open tomorrow for Thanksgiving?"

"Oh yes, Becky Jean, Thanksgiving is our biggest day of the year. I'm the cook for dinner, but Connie has family to attend to and Ron takes the day off, who knows what happens to him. I always make my world-famous dressing, turkey with all the fixings. We serve buffet off the counter. Are you going somewhere?" He wiped his hands on his apron. "You can have the day off if you want."

"No, I'm not going anywhere. I'd rather work. Especially with all the Thanksgiving decorations I purchased—" I paused to correct my statement, "That you let me buy at the party store yesterday." Then I lowered my eyes to ask, "May I join the festivities tomorrow?" *When Mrs. Lawrence asked, I panicked thinking that it might be another day off. The thought of sitting in my coop with nothing to eat on Thanksgiving made me cringe.*

"I really liked the decorations. Good advertising. So if you don't mind, it would be great to have some help. I'll pay you time and a half." He explained the routine. "It's always festive. No breakfast. I'm too busy preparing the Thanksgiving fixings, so we only serve dinner eleven to six, but we are busy. I'll have the turkeys in the oven by sunrise. I always promise my customers real potatoes on Thanksgiving. Could you possibly come in early and help peel?"

It sounded gruesome. In my mind I saw piles of potatoes to peel. Besides if he made the promise, he should peel the potatoes. What came out of my mouth was, "I'll be here at six o'clock. Will that be early enough? I could go to Duluth today and get some more decorations."

He wrinkled his brow. "No, what you bought yesterday will do just fine," he said. "That's more than I usually do. My dear wife was in charge of decorating, and since she died, I just don't do it. But what you bought and put up yesterday brought back so many pleasant memories."

After hours of peeling potatoes, I went to open the door at eleven o'clock. The parking lot was full of cars and people standing around in small groups. I greeted every customer as they paraded through the door, "Happy Thanksgiving." Sure enough, Agnes was one of the first to arrive. She gave Bert a peck of a kiss on the cheek as she came in the door.

My fingers were like prunes from peeling and slicing and rinsing potatoes, so shaking hands was a welcome change of venue. Every table was filled. Bert had the buffet set with mountains of mashed potatoes, gravy, turkey, cranberries, and his famous dressing. We used ornate serving dishes and crystal glasses that I had never seen used in the restaurant before. I wondered where he stored everything. I poured cranberry juice into crystal glasses as I seated the customers. Then they descended on the buffet. Everyone seemed starved. I hadn't eaten a thing, and I knew my stomach was going to start complaining at 2:30 that afternoon. *Can I wait until closing at six? I doubt that Bert will let me eat with this many clamoring customers. It just isn't going to happen. Sorry, stomach.*

Carl and Edna Pykkinen brought their children, Paul and Christine, with their spouses and children. I lost count as they marched in, but I just held the door open till the stream of children and grandchildren ended.

Carl was dressed in a suit I had never seen before. With a grand smile, he introduced his son. "Paul works in Denver. He's in charge of repairing airplanes at the Mile-High Airport."

Paul, dressed in casual clothes, extended a firm, commanding handshake. Edna presented in a Chantilly lace blue dress with a white, wispy, veiled hat. She looked like an actress in a silent movie. "And my lovely daughter, Christine, works for a publishing company in New York City."

I didn't get to shake her hand as she rushed ahead, wiping little hands and adjusting bibs. Bert had warned me that the Pykkinen family would fill the Bible study room, so I arranged it with additional chairs, high chairs, and booster seats.

"There are just too many grandchildren for me to do the cooking," Edna said. "I would have been exhausted, and that husband of mine couldn't wash a dish to save his life. So here we are, and you get to wash the dishes."

I laughed, "And glad to do it, Mrs. Pykkinen." Their family filled the room as air rushes into a vacuum. Soon children were running around the tables laughing, little ones were crying in excitement, and Edna was beaming with pride.

"And that's my oldest granddaughter, Kathleen, Christine's daughter. She's a New York City girl, very sophisticated," Edna giggled and whispered in my ear, "and she has a boyfriend." Kathleen was a late teen, maybe even college age. She seemed quite skeptical of the whole celebration. She was tall, maybe five foot ten or eleven inches with a gorgeous figure and wore a stylish name-brand dress that seemed inappropriate for the wilderness of Cotton. She turned away when I smiled at her.

Carl stood at the door watching his brood. He grabbed my hand and pulled me close. He was wearing an exotic aftershave lotion which would have been more appropriate on Waikiki beach. "Thanks for keeping my secret," he whispered in my ear, "She doesn't suspect a thing." A hundred-dollar bill was in my hand as he released his grasp. I slipped it into my pocket to examine later. I had never seen one before.

I scurried around keeping the serving counter supplied with mashed potatoes, cranberries, and dressing. Bert stood by the turkeys cutting large slabs of meat for each guest. I replaced dropped silverware and a few dropped plates that surprisingly didn't break and kept coffee cups full.

At three o'clock, I just had to go to the bathroom. I grabbed my belly, and Bert understood. *Was it hunger or bladder spasms? I wasn't sure. I ran to the restroom to find out.* I relaxed in the stall. It was the most peaceful calm moment of the day. I wanted to just stay there for a few minutes and drink in the solitude. *"But duty calls,"* I could hear my father say. As I came out of the stall to wash my hands, I heard a voice behind me. I looked up at the mirror and recognized Edna Pykkinen.

"I know what he orders when he comes for breakfast," she said. "All I ask is that you substitute egg beaters and see if he notices the difference. We've been married a long time, and I'd like to keep him around a while longer. He has so many unhealthy habits, the dear. Besides, Bert couldn't possibly store all the oatmeal he claims he eats here."

I lowered my eyes, but a giggle came out.

She handed me a twenty-dollar bill. "It will be our little secret, all right, my dear?"

I took the twenty feeling like a wolf betraying the shepherd. "All right, Mrs. Pykkinen, I promise."

Back in the restaurant, I was assaulted by children churning around the restaurant. I played with some of them and teased others between coffee deliveries. I had bought little turkey stickers, crayons, and coloring books which

I passed out to each child as they finished eating. They seemed charmed and better behaved with something to do. It quelled some of the chaos.

Mrs. Halstrom held out her plate. "Remember, just white meat, Bert."

"Yes, madam," he said as he carved off a slice from the juiciest breast. "Those twins of yours, Tim and Tom, are getting pretty tall."

"Yes, and so smart, Bert. They're both top of their class. They're going to be engineers someday, I suspect. You should see their grades in science. The teacher said he couldn't give them a grade high enough for their performance."

I looked at the twins. *Tall, handsome boys, juniors or seniors at Cotton High School,* I guessed, but I couldn't tell which one was Tim and which was Tom.

"The coloring books and decorations were a great idea, Bert. How come you haven't done that before?" Mrs. Johannsen added. "This is the best behaved my grandchildren have ever been."

"It was Becky Jean's idea."

She turned to me, "Becky Jean, Assistant Manager," she said, reading my name tag. "You're a little young for that position aren't you?" I didn't respond. "Well, anyway, you did well. Oh, and we need more coffee at our table."

I grabbed the pot and said with a smile, "Coming right up, more coffee for the Johannsen's." Their table was busy. Relatives from Norway had come to see what American Thanksgiving was all about. Bert was proud that his dressing would now be "internationally famous." He spoke a little Norwegian and spent some time at their table showing off his few dozen words.

Charlie was there with his wife, Ruth. She was tall and frail and didn't say too much. "It is great to rejoice in the Lord for all these great blessings, isn't it Rebecca?"

"Yes, sir, Charlie." I poured coffee in their cups. "Pleased to meet you, Mrs. Butler."

"Oh, just a half a cup for me, dear." She looked up at me. "And just call me Ruth." Her wispy white hair must have been long because it made quite a knot on the top of her head. "My stomach is very delicate ever since I had those children."

"How many children do you have?"

"Too many," she said.

"Five daughters. They all live in Wisconsin," said Charlie. "We see them in the summer."

"I don't do any traveling in the winter, dear," she said as she dipped her spoon into the mashed potatoes with no gravy. "And all five are very busy." She wiped her mouth with her napkin before eating her dollop of potato.

At four o'clock, Bert instructed me to set out the pumpkin pies. Bernice had delivered them Wednesday afternoon. I recalled the look in Bert's eyes when they arrived. Knife in hand, he had been ready to slice into one of the pies then. If it hadn't been for Connie putting them away so fast, I'm sure he would have eaten one on the spot. As I announced the pies' arrival, our guests swarmed the counter. I thought we would have a riot as people complained that Bert was serving too slowly. A commercial mixing bowl of whipped cream set off to the side allowed people serve themselves. That quelled the crowd. I was concerned that we wouldn't have enough. Several truckers had told me Bernice's pies were famous throughout St. Louis County.

I brought the turkey carcasses back to the kitchen to avoid more chaos and have a few moments of solitude. I was so hungry that I decided to nibble a piece of turkey, but then I heard, "We need more coffee here, Becky Jean." *So much for quiet time and a snack in the kitchen.*

After he finished serving the pies and every piece was gone, Bert helped keep the drinks flowing. The restaurant was jubilant as laughter permeating the atmosphere. Bert seemed happier than I had ever seen him. It was obvious from his demeanor that this celebration meant a lot to him: his guests having a great Thanksgiving.

At six o'clock, Bert flicked the lights. "Party's over," he said. "Time to head for home."

I heard children complain, "Do we have to?" "I'm not finished with my picture." "Can't I have more pie? I still have whipped cream left."

Adults just seemed to sigh. I searched for lost mittens and hats, helped put on coats, and accepted checks. This was the only day of the year Bert accepted checks, but he knew every family. As people filed out, everyone got a warm handshake or a hug from Bert, even the children. As the last customer left, he flipped over the 'closed' sign, pulled the drapes, and both of us collapsed in a booth.

"Did you get anything to eat?" he asked, lifting his head out of his hands.

"Not yet," I stammered. My belt felt loose. I felt weak from running on adrenaline since 2:30, the break time that didn't happen.

"Me neither. I saved a plate for each of us." He smiled, "And one of Beatrice's pies somehow did not find the counter." He smiled as he got up to get our food. I sprang up to help him. "No, you sit down, Becky Jean. I will serve you."

"What?"

"I will serve you."

As I waited, I looked outside. Night had enclosed us, perfect silence except for the buzz of the mercury light that flooded the now empty parking lot. The smell of Thanksgiving trimmings filled the air, accentuating the hunger gnawing at my insides. Yet, I felt such a sense of peace, but maybe it was exhaustion. *You just celebrated the best Thanksgiving of your life, Rebecca.*

Bert returned and set our booth table with bone china and crystal goblets. I had never seen anything like this. In fact, I had never seen such delicate, intricate china in my life. I wondered where in the restaurant, in which cubbyhole, these were hidden. "When my wife was still alive," he said as he served me, "we would eat off this china every night after the customers left." He laughed. "I only have service for two."

Twelve hours of preparing and serving food sure makes a girl hungry. I was ravenous. I just wanted to gobble everything down like a famished dog, but the elegance of the serving set improved my etiquette. Every morsel was ecstasy. I rolled the spicy dressing around my mouth. It was good, the flavors unique. I held a bite on my fork and commented, "So this dressing is now world famous?"

Bert laughed at me, "At least it will be famous in Norway. The Johannsen relatives were quite impressed."

"This turkey is still juicy. I expected leftovers from those carcasses I hauled back to the kitchen."

He smiled as he rolled a piece of dark meat around his plate, soaking up the gravy, "Those will be for *soup de jour* and creamed turkey on toast next week. But I put a small bird in the oven about three o'clock just for us."

"I saw the oven was on. I almost turned it off thinking you had left it on by mistake. But I got distracted by someone calling out for more coffee. Good thing, eh?"

"You're starting to sound Minnesotan." He became silent, nibbling his food. I saw a tear in his eye. He looked up at me, "Helen, my wife was the best

51

woman in the world for me. She wanted this restaurant. I would never have started it without her." We ate the rest of our turkey and mashed potatoes in silence, too hungry to talk.

"She was a lot like you," he said as he scooped the last mouthful of mashed potatoes into his mouth. "She greeted people and made them feel at home. Our customers were like guests in our kitchen. I owe the success and reputation of this place to Helen. Twenty-seven years of marriage were sheer bliss." He sighed, "I sure miss her. One morning I woke up, and she had died in her sleep. I guess it was a heart attack from the coroner's report."

"I'm so sorry." I wiped my mouth. "Do you have any children?"

"Two sons. One is in the Air Force. He's a navigator or something, not a pilot. The other lives in Georgia. He does accounting for a toothpaste company."

"Colgate?"

"I think so. I'm not sure." Bert got up, picked up our plates, and returned with two pieces of pumpkin pie with a mountain of whipped cream on top.

"I'm not allowed desserts, restaurant rules," I said, holding my hands up to quell my sarcasm.

"Tonight you are my special guest. None of my past employees have ever offered to help with the Thanksgiving feast."

"I thought all the pies were gone. You saved one?" I tried to quell my craving despite my bulging full stomach. I loosened my belt. It is amazing how your stomach shrinks when you only eat Ron-type portions once a day. I dipped my fork in the whipped cream and added a touch of pumpkin pie. It was sweet and smooth as silk. I decided that I was going to finish it even if it took all night to get it down.

"What about your family, Becky Jean?"

"I have an older sister. She's married and has a daughter. They're missionaries in Guatemala. They left when I was in high school. I haven't seen them since." He looked expectant, so I felt that I needed to continue. "And my parents, well, I'd rather not ruin this lovely dinner talking about them."

As I sat back, holding my distended belly, I licked whip cream off my lip. "I am very thankful for what you have done for me, Bert." I wedged myself out of the booth. "We have to start fresh tomorrow, so we need to wash all the dishes. I'm an experienced dishwasher, so let me do it. My previous job, remember?"

He laughed and picked up his plate. "I'll help," he said, "I'm experienced from my previous job too."

"Leave my pie, Bert. I'm going to finish it, but I need a little exercise first."

Chapter 8
Pregnant

It was storming outside, episodic lightning sparkling across the snow, which was coming down in sheets. I thought lightning only happened with rainstorms, but there was no doubt about this thunder-snow. The lights in the restaurant even dimmed for seconds at a time.

The truckers laughed at me when I jumped to a loud clap. "This is just a typical Minnesota December blizzard," they said.

It started late in the afternoon, so by closing time the accumulation of snow hadn't closed the roads yet. We had been besieged by late customers who ordered hearty meals and explained, "In case we get snowed in tomorrow." As I was putting on my parka, Bert asked me, "Is Leah still washing dishes?"

"I haven't seen her yet."

He twisted his cap on his head and buttoned his coat. "Would you check on her, Becky Jean? I'm not paying her overtime. She should be done by now."

"I'll check on her and get her home. I can lock up."

"Thanks, I got to go home and work on the books, taxes, inventory, and all that." He skipped out the front door and locked it.

I went to check on Leah. The dishes were done, and all the pots and pans had been put away. She was sitting on the stool in the washing room with her back toward the door, her head leaning against the wall, banging her fists on the wall.

"Are you done, Leah? The roads are getting bad, lots of snow. It's time to go home."

She was such a pretty girl. Even with her long blond hair coiled up in the hair net, her features were lovely. Her tall, lanky, well-developed figure must have been the envy of her friends. She quivered on the stool.

"What's wrong?"

"I'm pregnant." She burst into tears and started banging her head against the wall.

"Who's the guy?" I asked, not sure what to say as she seemed so upset.

She covered her face with her hands and folded her head between her knees, "I don't know." Then she jumped up and screamed, "How much does an abortion cost?"

"I don't know." She ran into my arms, shaking uncontrollably. I held her from collapsing on the floor. "We're the only ones here. Tell me about it."

"They all said they loved me," she whimpered. "They said it, and then we had sex, and then they haven't even talked to me since. Every one of those guys has a new girlfriend. They all lie, don't they, Becky Jean?" She spit out the words in a snarl, "All men lie."

"Do you really want an abortion?" I asked.

"What I really want is to find someone to love me and have a couple of children and live in a nice house where it's quiet and peaceful with no yelling and screaming and," she sobbed, "now that's all down the drain."

"Do you want to keep the baby?"

"I'd love to have a baby. I've always wanted to be a mother. But would any guy date me carrying a kid around? Besides, it's cheaper to get an abortion than raise a child. I don't make that much money washing these stupid dishes." Her eyes were furious as she drove her fist into the stainless steel carousel. "You should know that. You're not stupid, are you?" A look of horror creased her face. "Oh, I'm sorry, boss, Miss Assistant Manager. I didn't mean to be disrespectful. Please don't tell Mr. Lloyd. I can't afford to be fired."

I took a deep breath and then sighed. "I think the more important question is whether you want to raise this child who is a part of you?"

"And part of some shit-head guy." She grabbed my uniform put her head on my shoulder and sobbed, "I think that I want this baby. Yes, I do. I do." She let go of my uniform and straightened it and wiped the wetness of her tears from the fabric. "No, maybe not." Her face was swollen and red. "But what am I going to do? Dad will kill me. How will I pay for the baby? How can I raise a child? Do I go on welfare the rest of my life?"

I led her out to the employees table under the security light. We sat down beside each other and held hands. "Let's start over. Tell me how you got pregnant."

She snuffed her nose, and I gave her a napkin from the dispenser. "I was being careful," she said. "When I went out on dates, I only had sex just before my period was coming. You know, when you feel that fullness and you're getting ready?"

"Yes."

"But four of the guys from the football team asked four of us girls from the cheerleading squad to come to Jim Toumala's cabin." She looked up, "He played defense, a real hunk." She sighed, "Oh, what's the use? It was my fault." She pulled away and yanked off her hairnet.

"Continue." I grabbed her hands and held her.

"It was during those last hot days in August. I had my period first of August. Oh, I was so stupid." She slammed her fists on the table upsetting the condiments. "I thought it would be safe going with the other girls. But I lied to my parents. I told them I was going to a cabin but that it was just girls from the squad. So they said I could go. Anyway, we had a good time, swimming, canoeing, and Jim even took us for a ride around the lake in his father's speedboat. It was great. I was really having fun. I had dated all four of the guys before. I liked them." She wiped her eyes. "I thought they liked me. I agreed to have sex with them on dates because I thought they respected me."

"So what happened at the cabin?"

"We had a couple of beers during the afternoon. I didn't get drunk, well at first. I was careful. Then we went into the cabin when it got dark, and Jim lit a fire in the fireplace. It was so romantic. We were all cuddling, and then Jim suggested that we play strip poker. We girls weren't too keen about that, but Jim said that if we didn't want to take off an article of clothing we could do an alternative. So we agreed."

"They cheated, didn't they?"

"I think so. All four of us girls were sitting in our bras and panties, and the boys only had their shirts off. Anyway, the next hand I lost. So I didn't want to take anything more off, so I asked, 'What's the alternative?'

"Jim pulled out a bottle of his father's whiskey, and everyone agreed the alternative was to drink a shot of whiskey. We should have just quit right then and gone home."

"Then what happened?"

"See, I don't know. Sometime later I woke up on top of a mattress totally naked, didn't have a stitch on, not even a sheet covering me. It was still dark. My nipples hurt like they had been chewed; my breasts were sore and bruised. When I sat up and turned on the light to look for my clothes, I noticed that my thighs were chaffed. Stuff squirted out of my vagina. It even hurt to put on my panties. I tiptoed into the living room. The other girls must have gone because I only found the boys sleeping or knocked out, drunk on the floor by the fireplace. I found my car keys, got dressed, and beat it home."

She stared at me. "September, no period, first of October, no period, first of November, no period, now it's December. So, I must be…" She paused to calculate, "I did the little pregnancy test on my urine. Let's see, one and half, two months, no, three months pregnant? Right? Don't I have to get an abortion before three months? Legally?"

I hugged her. "If you really want one."

"I got to go." She grabbed her coat off the hook in the employee's room and dashed out the door. The snow was now almost an inch deep.

"Wait, Leah, you can stay with me. It's not safe!" She didn't respond but jumped in her car, a beat-up Ford, spun in the slippery parking lot, and left.

The next day, Leah came to work carrying a little pink suitcase. She grabbed my arm and pulled me into the dishwashing room. She slammed a load in the washer and waited for the dissonance of the dishwasher to give us privacy. "My parents didn't take it well. Dad said, and I quote, 'If you're going to have sex with every guy in St. Louis County and get yourself pregnant, then you aren't welcome in this house.' He called me a tramp, Becky Jean. My own father called me a tramp." She hunched over the stainless steel drain sobbing. "Mom said, 'If you're going to make adult decisions, then you should live like an adult, on your own.' But where can I go, Becky Jean, where?" She pointed at the pink suitcase. "That's all I had time to pack before they kicked me out. They just kept yelling, saying I was a disgrace. That was last night, in my own bedroom. Mom said I wasn't a little girl anymore and wasn't welcome to sleep there anymore. 'Be gone in the morning,' she said."

"Start washing the dishes, then Bert won't come in here. It will give you some privacy. I'll talk to Connie. We'll think of something." I hugged her and turned to leave. Customers filled the counter to be served their breakfast.

Connie was standing in the doorway outside the dish washing room with her hands on her hips. She pushed her way in. "I heard the whole thing. You're pregnant, aren't you? Got knocked up by one of the football players is my guess. I'm sure my husband and I can take you in, you pathetic mongrel," Connie tousled Leah's hair.

"She's not a stray dog, Connie."

Leah sobbed, "It's all right, Becky Jean, my father called me a bitch." She snuffled. "Same thing, right?"

Connie softened her tone and held Leah in her arms, "Come home with me, Leah. You can live in the basement. I'll charge you twenty percent of whatever Bert pays you. Now quit sniffling and get these dishes washed. We're serving breakfast, and there are a lot more dishes coming. You are not the first nor the last woman on earth to get pregnant. Get to work."

Leah washed dishes in a fury that day. Although I suspect that some of them were rinsed with tears.

Chapter 9
Charity for Leah

"Bert wants to see you in his office, Becky Jean. You're in trouble," Connie warned as she returned from lunch.

"Can I get my lunch first?"

"I don't know. He's pretty angry." She grabbed the coffee pot and started making rounds of the tables.

"I've filled all the orders of the people here," I told her as I left. I went straight to Bert's office. His face was red and his chin was set. He glared at me as I entered and motioned for me to sit in the chair across from his desk.

"You wanted to see me?" I said, timid as a fawn before a wolf.

"What is this, Becky? I didn't authorize any money-making schemes." He shoved one of the customer receipts across his desk, flipping it over to the handwritten note on back.

I sat down. "It's true, Bert. I wasn't being dishonest."

"So all of your tips today are going to Leah?"

"Every cent. Well, except for the ten percent that goes to Ron, right?"

He read my scribbled note, "Leah is having a baby. All my tips today will go for hospital expenses."

"I should have talked to you first. I'm sorry. I figured I could do that with my tips. It doesn't affect anyone else." I sighed. "It's just that she has nothing, Bert. She was going to get an abortion but decided to keep the baby. I thought it would be like a baby shower. Washing dishes is her only income. You said you have known her parents for many years, that they were good people. How could they just kick her out of the house?

Poor kid came to work last week with a little pink suitcase. And Christmas is coming."

He looked up. The anger in his face seemed to diffuse.

"And whoever got her pregnant has refused to help her," I continued, the tears choking in my throat. "Actually she doesn't know who got her pregnant. It sounds like she was gang-raped, but she doesn't know for sure. She was unconscious at the time." I thought that I should probably not share any more of her history. "Anyway, we are her only family," I paused for full effect, "now."

He picked up a pencil and twisted it in his fingers. Silence. Then he tapped the pencil on his desk; the sound amplified in my head. I couldn't tolerate the sound. It was like a brass drum beating in my temples, so I decided to give him more to think about. "When everyone else thought she was a tramp and a female dog, that's what her father called her, 'a tramp and a…'" I took a deep sigh, saying "bitch" under my breath. "You, Mr. Lloyd, hired her. She works hard. We've had no complaints of dirty forks or 'This dish has streaks,' nothing like that." I took another deep breath to adjust my rampage. The pencil tapping stopped. "If she can't look to you, Connie, and me for support, where should she go, to the streets?"

I looked at my feet. My stomach grumbled. I felt faint with hunger. The little clock on his desk showed that it was almost three o'clock and my Pavlovian stomach wasn't tolerating the delay. "I apologize. I was wrong. I should have asked you first." I wrinkled my face anticipating a harsh reprimand. "Did you get a lot of complaints?"

The pencil spun in his fingers. "Mrs. Lawrence…"

I opened my mouth but felt paralyzed to say anything. *Mrs. Lawrence would probably complain because the pregnancy was illegitimate. Anger boiled inside me just to speculate what she had said to Bert. I prepared to attack.*

His response seemed calm and deliberate. "She wanted to know if it was true."

My defensiveness curdled my voice. "True that Leah has no support or true that I was donating all my tips?"

His demeanor was not what I anticipated. He put the pencil in his empty cup, pushing it to the side of the desk, and fumbled with papers in front of him. "She gave me a check for a hundred dollars but wanted me to be sure that it was going to help Leah before you were allowed to cash it." He chuckled, mimicking her alto voice, "No administrative fees."

Exhausted by my misplaced anger, a weary smile crept across my lips. Guilt for my malignant attitude spread hives across my chest. Despite the fact that I hadn't said anything evil, I wanted to apologize to Mrs. Lawrence for my feelings. In a soft exhale I said, "That's more of a tip than all the Bible study ladies have given in three years according to Connie. But she has a fine collection of dimes they've given her." I raised my eyes to watch for his response.

He adjusted his bulk; his chair creaked. "Oh, I have checks from each of the ladies in the Bible study, too. They were studying the rape of Tamar in Second Samuel some chapter and said that the spirit moved them to give." He stood and gave me a manila envelope. "All the checks are made out to you, so I want an accounting of every cent, Becky Jean. I've written down every check. It is not that I don't trust you, but this is a lot of money, and the ladies want an accounting. You know how they are."

Tears welled up in my eyes. He handed me a tissue off his desk. I blurted between sobs, "Yes, Mr. Lloyd. Every cent will be accounted for."

"Please don't do this again without asking. I had in mind to fire you if this wasn't legitimate. Well, until Mrs. Lawrence explained what it meant to all the ladies."

I bowed my head and examined the dry skin on my knuckles. "Yes, Mr. Lloyd. It will never happen again. It was a dumb idea. I'm very sorry."

His face turned stern. "Becky Jean."

I straightened my posture like a soldier. The rungs of the wooden chair poked into my muscles. "Yes, Mr. Lloyd, sir."

"I didn't say it couldn't happen again. It was a very clever idea, and I doubt that you're at all that sorry. I just ask that you keep me in the loop." He came out from behind his desk and put his hand on my shoulder. The gentle touch lifted me to my feet. "And I will fire you if you call me Mr. Lloyd one more time. I've warned you about that, Assistant Manager Gottwald."

I backed up toward the door, "Thank you, Bert. I won't call you Mr. Lloyd ever again. I promise. I don't want to be fired." I rubbed my stomach. "May I have some lunch now? It's three o'clock. My break time is up, and my stomach was expecting to eat at two-thirty."

He looked at his watch. "Your break starts as of now. I'll help Connie. Any tips I get will go to the Leah Hospital Fund as well."

Chapter 10
Christmas

I had decorated for Christmas with Santa, reindeer, and a crèche in the middle window. Holly hung over the door, and several couples took advantage of it. The customers were festive, and everyone seemed to be in an especially good mood. I was apprehensive.

I filled Mr. Johannsen's coffee cup. "Bert made his special mincemeat pie for the Christmas season. Would you like that for dessert, Mr. Johannsen?"

"I would," said Mr. Rollifsen at the end of the counter. "I wait every year for a piece of that pie."

"I'll be right with you, Rolly."

"Me too. Bert's mincemeat pie is better than my mother's. God rest her soul." said Mr. Johannsen. He didn't come that often to the restaurant when school was in session, except to grade test papers, but this was the beginning of Christmas break and the first time I had seen him since Thanksgiving.

"Two mincemeat pies, coming up," I said, returning the coffee pot to brew a fresh pot. My stomach growled. *If it's that good, I wish I could try it, but rules are rules, no desserts.*

As I was cutting the pie, Connie came up behind me. "Cut two for my customers." She pointed to the two in a booth. They waved at me, apparently eager to bite into the pie. "I'm going on break."

"Does Bert have more in the cooler? That's six pies we've gone through so far today."

"He made some for tomorrow. We can use those if we get more orders. He'll just have to make more. He won't mind; his mincemeat is his pride and joy."

65

"Have you ever tasted it, Connie?"

"Never," she said as her expression grew stern. "Remember, no desserts for the help."

I thought back to the Thanksgiving pumpkin pie with the mountain of whipped cream as I served the mincemeat dessert to the customers. *Only dessert I have eaten in six months, how healthy.* I served Connie's two customers, then my own. "Remember, on Christmas Eve we close at two o'clock, Rolly."

"I've got my Christmas shopping done, Becky Jean, so I'll be here for breakfast."

"Who do you shop for, since you're a bachelor?"

"I go over to my sister's house in Eveleth for Christmas Eve. They always have a big party and open their presents around the tree. What fun it is watching her kids rip their packages open and toss the bows in the air. So I buy all kinds of stuff for them and wrap it up with lots of decorations." He drank the last of his coffee and took a bite of his pie. I filled his cup. "Christmas day we're supposed to have a blizzard, so I suppose I'll be busy plowing. Got to keep the roads open so everyone can get to their Christmas parties, you know."

When Connie came back from her break, she told me to go for lunch. I put in my order with Ron and listened for the sizzle of meat hitting the grill. I took my plate when Ron set it up: a spinach salad with hot vegetables, a small sirloin steak, and a mountain of fruit in a bowl on the side. It looked tasty, but I was puzzled. "This is beautiful, Ron, but it's not on the menu. I just asked for a hamburger. I don't want to get in trouble with Bert."

"It's what he ordered for you," his crooked smile rose over the grill as he stood on tip-toes. "Merry Christmas."

When I returned from lunch, I was satiated and happy. I hadn't eaten steak in so long I couldn't remember. Father always said it was too expensive and a waste. Connie came up behind me and gave me a gentle shove. "So what are you doing for Christmas? Are you seeing any family?"

"No," I said taking a sip of water, still relishing the flavor of the steak in my mouth. "I don't really have any family."

"You want to come to our house for the holiday? That is if you don't mind spending it with a bunch of wild Indians."

"Orders up," said Ron.

I took the orders to my customers and returned to Connie. She seemed sincere. "I wouldn't want to infringe on your family time." I hung my head wondering what I was going to do.

She grabbed my chin and lifted my face to hers. "No problem, homeless one. With my husband's parents, my parents, and my brother and sister and their families, what's one more? They won't even know you're there. Besides, I have a little present for you, and then I won't have to bring it here."

"Really?" My voice cracked.

"Just come home with me on Christmas Eve when we close. If you feel guilty about my hospitality, I'll make you help me in the kitchen, washing all the dishes."

"Thanks, Connie."

"And plan to stay overnight," she said hugging my shoulder. "If Rolly is right, we'll be snowed in by morning."

•　　•　　•

I was surprised how many came for breakfast on Christmas Eve. I was expecting it to be slow, but it seemed like the whole community showed up. Mr. Johannsen came with his wife, Doris. "We had to get away from the kids for a while, they're driving us nuts," she said. "They can't wait to open their presents. Besides, it's nice to be served breakfast even if it isn't in bed."

I served the biggest bowl we had filled with oatmeal and a side of raisins and brown sugar to Carl Pykkinen since he came with Edna. I added a pat of butter melting on the top. He called me to his table when his wife went to the restroom. "Maybe I will have oatmeal in the future. This tastes great. But you know," he smiled. "She complained about the butter, 'Too much butter for your heart, sweet,' I was given a lecture about how I'm not supposed to have that, but it sure tasted good."

"I'll sneak the butter under the oatmeal next time. It will be our deep inside secret."

He patted my hand. "Good girl."

The women's Bible study had their Bibles open to Isaiah when I brought their coffee and tea. I was surprised to see them as I expected the Bible study to be suspended for Christmas Eve. "We've all decided to celebrate the Christ child and have a pastry today," Mrs. Lawrence spoke for the group.

"You don't have any day-old ones on special do you?" Nadine whispered in my ear. She was dressed in red with a bright green scarf. She had tiny bells pinned into her hairdo.

"All sold out yesterday. The truck drivers ate them. You'll just have to have fresh. Beatrice brought in fresh caramel rolls this morning," I said as I pulled out the slips and added pastries to each bill. I saw one of the ladies slip a quarter under her tea cup. *And a big tip besides*, I thought. *No dimes today.*

The restaurant cleared out just after noon. Connie and I stood at the counter with no customers. I could hear Leah singing Christmas carols as she rinsed the last of the dishes.

"We're closed," Bert announced at exactly two o'clock. "I'll lock up the front door. Both of my sons and their families are flying into Duluth on the midday flight from Minneapolis. They should be arriving pretty soon. Can you lock up the back?" Without waiting for an answer, he ran out the front door, pausing only to click the lock with his key.

Connie turned toward me. "Are you ready for screaming kids and wild pandemonium?"

"Ready as I'll ever be."

We went to the dishwashing room to check on Leah. "Are you going home to your family?" Connie asked.

"I'm not welcome there." Her four-and-a-half-month pregnancy was now obvious. The top button of her blouse strained from her engorged breasts, and her uniform was tight around her middle. She was sitting on the stool taking gasping breaths with a tray of dishes that still hadn't been washed piled up beside her.

"Well then, join the party. I won't have you moping around by yourself in the basement," said Connie.

"She even invited me, the homeless vagrant," I said, "so don't feel embarrassed." We each put an arm over her shoulder.

"Is this for real?" Leah said. She seemed to be searching Connie's expression.

"For real," said Connie. "Now let's get these dishes washed up. Bert's already left, so he will never know that we helped you."

• • •

Less than an hour later, all the dishes were done and put away. We scrunched together in the front seat of Connie's pickup truck. "The clouds look threatening," I said looking out the windshield and watching the heavy snow start to fall. There was only a pittance of snow on the road as it seemed to be melting as it hit the highway, but I knew that would change as soon as the temperature dropped. Connie turned on the radio just in time to hear the announcer predict, "Hazardous driving in the morning, folks. Get where you're going for Christmas and stay there." Then the Christmas carols blared out. Connie turned down the volume. She needed to turn the windshield wipers on maximum speed by the time we were half way down Highway 53.

"My husband and I grew up on the Fond du Lac Indian Reservation," she explained as she turned off the highway on to a dirt road. "We've know each other since we were toddlers, and then we were high school sweethearts. After we graduated, Hal got a job hauling pulp wood for the paper company, and I started working for Bert. We bought a piece of property and managed to build our house in our spare time. The commute was terrible for a while, but we were young and foolish. When the children were born, we were glad that those days were behind us. Besides, Cotton has a better school than Fond du Lac, so our daughters are getting a good education."

South of Cotton, we turned onto a dirt road. The Jack Pines crowded alongside the narrow roadway. The fallen packed snow froze on the surface making a blanket-smooth ride on the level, and the truck's snow tires had to dig into the grade as we went up a hill. Several miles down the road, Connie turned into her driveway. If it hadn't been beaten down by company traffic, I would never have known that it was a road at all. The woods opened into a Christmas card meadow. The house burst into view in the far corner. Framed by snow-encrusted maple trees, the green siding of the ranch-style home blended into the surrounding pine forest. There were several cars already parked in the drive.

Leah jumped out of the back seat and ran around to the side of the building. I was curious as to where she was going. Connie responded, "She has her own entrance. She wanted privacy, so we gave it to her." I nodded. Connie added, "Hal wanted a walk-out basement when we built this house. It was a good decision, although I was opposed to it at the time."

"Welcome to our humble home," said Connie as she opened the door and we strode inside depositing our coats in the closet.

"Something smells good," I said, catching a whiff of warm kitchen air.

"Mom got dinner started while I was working," Connie explained. We walked toward the living room. A checkers game had the attention of several teenage boys and two girls. "Those are my brother and sister -in-law's sons," said Connie, "but let me first introduce you to my daughters." She whistled like the call of a chickadee.

Two girls jumped up, left the crowd playing on the floor, and presented themselves in response to Connie's whistle. "Shawnee, Sherrie, this is Becky, the assistant manager at the restaurant."

"Pleased to meet you," said Shawnee, the older of the two. She was a shapely, young, high-school-age girl. She had a plastic poinsettia bobby-pinned into her long, flowing black hair. A red sweater that was at least a size too small and tight slacks that didn't quite meet the sweater accented her figure and displayed her muscular midriff, of which she appeared to be quite proud judging by her gait.

"I am glad to meet you too," said Sherrie with a grin that accentuated her dimples. "Mother says nice things about you."

I guessed that she was finishing grade school or in early junior high. Her hair was cut short, and she was dressed all in black but wore a flamboyant beaded necklace. She noticed my attention to it. "Did you make that necklace yourself?"

"Yes, I did. I'm wearing it because it's Christmas. Is it too much?"

"No, it looks just fine, Sherrie," I smiled and asked, "So, what are your favorite subjects in school?"

Sherrie scuffed her patent leather shoes. "English, because I like to write poems. But I write poems in Anishinaabe too." she said and turned away with a blush. She curtsied. "I also play the flute. I could play for you sometime."

"It is my pleasure to meet such a gifted person like you, Sherrie." She almost smiled.

"She's our shy one," said Connie.

"How about you, Shawnee?"

"I like everything science—chemistry, biology, stuff like that," she answered. "I'm really good in mathematics."

"I'm impressed. Not many girls in my high school liked science and math classes."

She whispered in my ear. "That's where all the smart boys are. Besides, I get all A's in science and math classes." She winked. "Mom said that you're staying overnight, so I am sure we will have lots to talk about. If you will excuse me, I have some checkers games to win."

Connie looked stern. I laughed and added, "You're excused. Are you sure you will win?"

As she backed away to join her cousins who were intent on their game, she grinned and said, "No doubt about it!"

"I don't understand where she gets her arrogant attitude," said Connie. "It's not from her Anishinaabe genes. It must have been from my husband's side of the family. Some French voyageur must have married into his family years ago."

I laughed. "She'll do fine in the world."

While Connie checked on dinner, I sat on the couch and listened to the hubbub as strategic checkers were removed from the board. Sherrie got up off the floor and sat next to me. "I always lose first. Checkers is too rough for me."

"What kind of poems do you like?"

"I write nature poems about animals, trees, and sunsets. Would you like to read one of my poems?" I nodded and she ran to her room to get her notebook.

"She's a romantic," said Shawnee, turning her attention from the game she'd just won against her cousin.

Sherrie returned to read several of her poems to me in a soft voice. I had to lean close to hear her. "Can you read them a little louder?" I asked amid the confusion of another game Shawnee clinched.

"Shawnee teases me about my poems," she whispered in my ear.

There were boisterous greetings from the front door. Sherrie left her notebook of poems in my lap and ran to greet more cousins as Connie's sister arrived with her brood. When everyone was distracted by the new arrivals, Shawnee backed away from the crowd heading to the door and sat next to me on the couch and asked, "Did you have a steady boyfriend when you were my age?"

"My father didn't want me to get too serious about boys," I said.

"Dad doesn't want me getting too serious either. What a drag." She stared at me in silence and then whispered, "Did you ever have sex with your boyfriends?"

Connie interrupted and shot her daughter a stern look. "Shawnee, your Aunt, Uncle, and cousins from Wisconsin are here. They want to see you,"

"Talk to you later, Becky. I got to do the relative thing." She ran to greet her cousins.

With everyone present, including Leah who tramped up the stairs at the last moment, we soon sat down at an extended table to enjoy the feast together. Spiced wild rice casserole and bear meat were the main course for what was sure to be my most memorable Christmas dinner. I had never eaten wild rice or bear meat. But by the time I finished tasting everything, I wished I had been raised in a Native American family. Each person treated me so well in spite of my obvious attempts to ward off personal questions about my family. Everyone was involved in all the conversations between bites. There was a massive amount of food consumed, more than I could imagine. It wasn't even three o'clock, and I was already stuffed. My biological rhythms were in a state of confusion over my good fortune. Leah was the only one silent during the meal, but I noticed that she ate well.

"Do you go bear hunting every year?" I asked Hal, Connie's husband, when the subject came up as to the source of the delicious roasted meat.

"Every year my lovely wife lets me," he said. Connie was sitting beside him. He reached over and gave her a hug, adding, "And deer hunting too."

Connie said with a hint of indignation in her voice, "You didn't mention duck hunting, partridge hunting, and oh, you've never missed a pheasant season either."

"Yah, she lets me do all the fun stuff," he laughed, "not to mention sex."

She jabbed him in the ribs with her elbow. "There are children present, Hal." He laughed. Out of the corner of my peripheral vision, I saw Shawnee perk up at the mention of sex. Everyone smiled.

On some cue to which I was oblivious, Hal stood and everyone else around the table did as well. "I guess the women folk have things to do," said Hal. "We men folk certainly do not want to interfere."

As part of the "women folk," as Hal put it, I helped clear the table and worked on washing the dishes. Connie and her sister dried what I washed, and they put things away including the leftovers, which I envied as they were stored away in the refrigerator. Leah sprang to life grabbing the pots and roasting pan to wash. "Let me do those, I'm a professional."

I was delighted to meet Connie's sister from Wisconsin and her sister-in-law from Fondulac. The three of them danced about the kitchen as they worked, moving lithely to unheard rhythm. "You should work at the restaurant with Connie and me. Your dancing would draw in a lot of customers."

Angela, the sister-in-law from Fondulac, laughed. "Keeping three hungry boys fed is enough restaurant work for me."

"I bring in plenty of customers, and I wouldn't want the competition," said Connie. "I'm glad you live in Fondulac."

"Thanks for the compliment, sis."

"I only saw two boys," I said "Do you have another son?"

She laughed, waving her towel, "My husband is my biggest boy."

When the kitchen was spotless, everything was put away, and all the leftovers were properly stored, Connie announced, "Time to read the Bible story." This must have been a custom because everyone seemed to anticipate it. A hush fell on the house as we all gathered in the living room on couches, chairs, and benches arranged about the Christmas tree as Connie and Hal took turns reading the story of the Christ child's birth. Connie read the story from Luke, and Hal read the story from Matthew. Nobody moved. Anishinaabe, the correct name for Ojibwa First Nation people, are disciplined to listen carefully to stories. All stories are considered sacred, whether Biblical or from oral tradition. Connie finished her part of the story, and Hal prayed for all of us by name. It was heartfelt and so different from the family prayers to which I was accustomed. He finished with a resounding "Amen. God bless us everyone."

Shawnee sat next to me and had stared at Leah the whole time we were listening. As Connie and Hal closed their Bibles, clamor and chaos erupted as the presents were passed out. Shawnee whispered in my ear, "Pretty bad deal having a kid with no sex. I feel sorry for the virgin Mary."

"I think you're obsessed with sex, Shawnee," I whispered back.

She giggled, "No, I'm not obsessed. I'm just a teenager. I don't mean anything by it. And don't you tell on me either." Connie's stern look from across the room quelled any further whispering.

"You two sure are thick today," said Connie, sidling over onto the couch next to us.

"You have a delightful daughter, Connie." Shawnee put her finger over her mouth behind Connie's back. I pulled out a small present from my back-pack, "A little gift for you, Connie, for being such a great co-worker."

She opened the box and took out a silver necklace I had bought on one of my excursions to Duluth. "This is beautiful." She gave me a hug and a kiss on both cheeks. "You didn't get this at the food warehouse, did you?"

"No, but I did get permission from Bert to make a little side trip to Bagley's jewelry store."

Leah had been quiet, sitting in a chair in the corner with her chin in her hands, elbows on her knees. Connie surprised her with several presents. "What's this?"

"A few little baby things," Connie said.

"And maternity clothes from me," I added.

Leah blushed. "I guess," she smiled, scanned the room, and announced, "Everybody here already knows I'm pregnant right?" Her voice drifted off.

There was a chorus of, "Congratulations," from Connie's relatives. Angela asked, "When's your due date?"

"April 18th."

"Pray for a cold spring, kid," Angela said. "I had my first one in August. That was miserable. Sweat like a pig, unable to move."

Connie interrupted, "Don't tell her your obstetrical history and scare the poor kid."

"All right, I'll spare you the eighteen-hour labor and episiotomy story. Gosh, that hurt. But two active sons later, I'm still alive. It's worth the an-guish, Leah."

Connie jabbed her sister in the ribs.

"I had no problems at all," Connie's sister Aida added. "My babies just popped right out."

"Some encouragement, that's what I needed," Leah said as tears filled her eyes. Then she smiled. "I am so thankful to all of you for accepting me the way I am." It was the first time I had seen her smile since the day she told me that she was pregnant. I got up and gave her a big hug. Aida and Angela did the same.

Children were playing with toys, and the other adults were focused on their gifts when Connie brought a package to me. "And here is your gift, Becky Jean."

"It is such a huge box," I said, embarrassed that I seemed to have the largest present. I couldn't imagine what she would give me and in such a big box. I anticipated a prank.

After a lot of unwrapping and slitting boxes open with Hal's pocket knife, I finally opened the box to declare, "A toaster oven." I burst into a cheer of joy. "Now I can expand my cooking beyond hot-plate food in my little chicken coop." I felt the sheen of the glass and the smooth stainless steel and burst into tears. "Thanks so much, Connie."

"It's just a toaster oven. Why is she so emotional?" Hal asked his wife. "We got it on sale."

"The poor kid's got almost nothing, Hal. Bert gave her a hot plate and a cast-away pot. Some customer donated a decade-old refrigerator. That's all she has."

I felt like an orphan under his gaze. He got up and gave me a hug, "My wife says that you are the best co-worker she has ever had. You deserve better, but it was marked down, so we got it."

Connie interrupted, "Too much information, Hal."

He smiled and looked around the room at the men, "Ready for some target practice? I got to try out this new rifle my darling wife bought me for Christmas." The men and boys jumped to attention. The menagerie of men and boys put on their boots and parkas and headed for the door.

"You want to try shooting, Becky Jean?" Shawnee asked me.

"I've never shot a gun before."

"Come on; it's easy." The two of us put on our boots and coats and followed in the male wake.

I glanced back at Sherrie sitting in the corner working on a Christmas cross-stitch. "She won't want to come," Shawnee assured me.

Hal had set up three targets on hay bales at the end of the yard. A dense forest of Jack Pine formed the protective backdrop. He was correcting his nephew's aiming technique as we approached. Shawnee and I stood near the others, waiting our turn.

I looked up to see the large snowflakes coming down. Snow on the ground was now a couple inches deep and piling up rapidly. There was still plenty of sunlight, which the men appreciated as they handled the firearms. "Did you get it sighted in already?" I asked. I had a vague memory of my grandfather telling a story about sighting in his new rifle.

Hal laughed. "I sighted it in before Thanksgiving, but Connie made me put it back in the box till Christmas." He turned to the boys. "Let's see if Becky Jean can hit the target."

"I bet she can't," said several of the cousins to their fathers. I overheard them whisper something about me being a girl.

Hal showed me how to hold the rifle and to sight down the barrel. I got the bull's eye in my sight. It was quivering into view as the rifle was heavier than I expected.

"Now squeeze the trigger slowly," Hal said. "Don't jerk it."

I tried to remember to breath and squeeze at the same time. When it fired, I fell over backwards into the snow to the joyous entertainment of the cousins. But when Hal checked the target, the bullet had gone through the outer yellow circle. "Nice shot, Becky Jean," Hal yelled from the other end of the yard with his finger in my bullet hole. "She hit the target, boys. You lost the bet."

Hal's brother-in-law corralled his sons, "You lost the bet fair and square. Extra chores all next week."

There was a terrible groan among them. The older son looked at me, "We could have doubled our allowance. Why did you have to hit the target?"

"I'm sorry. I didn't know how important the bet was to you. Maybe I could have been bribed."

They erupted in a yell, "We should have bribed her."

"Still, it was funny watching you fall over," one of the younger sons said. "I'll just remember that and laugh when I'm doing my extra chores." He covered his face and laughed.

Hal pulled a pistol out of his holster. "Let's see what you can do with this. It won't knock you over, Becky Jean. But be careful, it's loaded."

The pistol felt cold and malicious in my hand. Hal held my hands in his and then showed me how to hold it with both hands and sight the target. I squeezed off three rounds. It was a 22 caliber pistol, so there was little recoil, and I stayed on my feet. When we looked at the center target, all my bullet holes were within three inches of each other but on the lower edge of the target.

"Nice pattern," said Hal's brother-in-law as he put his fingers in the bullet holes. "You just need to pull it up a bit."

As we returned to the shooting line, the cousins congratulated themselves on refusing their father's double-or-nothing bet.

Shawnee joined in. "Good shooting, Becky Jean. May I have a turn, father?"

Hal handed Shawnee the pistol. "Go ahead, shoot a couple rounds."

The fathers both requested bets against Shawnee. "No way," said the cousins as they laughed at their father's request. I was intrigued at their insistence.

We all lined up and covered our ears. Shawnee took the pistol and shot six rapid-fire rounds. We checked the hay bales. There were two bullet holes in the bull's eye of all three targets.

Her steady confidence deserved my response. "Wow, I'm impressed."

She smiled and turned to her cousins, "Yah, nobody better mess with me, right dad?"

She curled her arm around her father and gave him a hug. She took my hand, and the two of us headed off to the house. "Thanks, dad," she said over her shoulder. "Now, Becky Jean, let's talk about boys." She led me into her bedroom, and the two of us plopped on her bed. She seemed giddy and expectant.

"So you want to discuss how Leah got pregnant?" I began.

She stared at me and became silent. She looked away; then in halting sentences, she said, "Leah was the best cheerleader in our school. All of the girls were jealous of her. She was so pretty, and everybody admired her out on the basketball court doing the cheers." She twisted the ties on her quilt and peered into my eyes. I felt her dark brown eyes investigate my integrity and confidentiality.

"So you don't think she's so pretty anymore? Pregnancy does things to your body."

"It's not that," Shawnee said. "She's still pretty, but..." She swished her hair out of her eyes. "Her parents have rejected her and whoever fucked her—" She covered her mouth. "I'm not supposed to say that word. Don't tell on me."

"I believe that's the word Leah used when she first told me she was pregnant."

Shawnee put her hand on my arm. "It's just that, how could someone who was the star senior at our school...Now she doesn't even have a place to live. She has to live with us. And what's going to happen to her? She will never have another boyfriend."

"So what are your dreams, Shawnee? What do you want to do with your life? How you interact with boys has a lot to do with your dreams coming true."

We talked for over an hour. Shawnee shifted her hair behind her ears. "I lose my temper sometimes, and I'm impatient. That is not Anishinaabe. Dad says that I chatter like a white woman…well, sometimes." She ran her fingers down my pale white arm, "Please don't take offense at that, but Anishinaabe are supposed to be patient and not talk too much. I'm a hundred percent, you know."

"You're a wonderful, sincere young woman, Shawnee. You're intelligent and have a great future."

Connie burst through the door. "What have you two been up to? I've been looking all over for you, Shawnee. I need help serving coffee and dessert."

"Just girl talk," I smiled. "And don't ask me, it's confidential."

"I'll give you an extra ten minutes on your lunch break and my tips for the day to tell me."

Shawnee looked back and forth at the two of us.

"Not a chance," I said with a smile to Shawnee.

"I'll just wait until we've had a busy day at the restaurant and you're really tired. I'll get it out of you."

"My lips are sealed till my dying day." Out of the corner of my eye I saw Shawnee sigh.

"All right," she twisted a smile, "join the party. Come on, Shawnee, you promised to help."

I followed in their wake wondering what was going to happen to this lovely young woman who was struggling to be Anishinaabe.

Chapter 11
Birthday Party

After the festivities slowed to everyone's mutual fatigue, I was assigned to sleep with Shawnee. Sherrie begged me to be her guest, but her bed was too small. I did spend some time in her room with her, and she played some simple tunes on her flute. For her age, I thought she was quite talented. I gave her a hug and went to Shawnee's room, passing the cousins who were sprawled out in blankets on the floor in the living room.

Shawnee was delighted to have me as her guest. But after a few moments of girl talk we were both fast asleep.

•　　•　　•

I awoke in a peaceful fog on the window side of her twin-sized bed. I was so thankful to sleep in a comfortable bed quite unlike my sleeping bag on the sagging mattress over rusted springs in my coop. I wiggled in place just for the sheer joy of comfort. The sun filtered through the window shade was bright, but I knew heavy snow had fallen all night.

Shawnee was gone. To my chagrin, she had made her side of the bed leaving my side, with me in it, undisturbed. I realized how hard I must have slept since I never sensed her leaving or straightening up her quilt and pillow.

I climbed out of bed in one of Shawnee's nightgowns and looked out the window. Everything was covered with at least a foot of Christmas snow. Rolly was going to be busy today. I wandered about the room noticing the tanned hides, science fair awards, and honor roll certificates. Off in one corner was a first prize ribbon for a pistol shooting contest. *Now I understand,* I thought of the preceding day's activities. Plunked down on the end of the bed, I scanned the trophies of a most amazing young lady.

Fixing my side of the bed to match Shawnee's and dressing in my clothes hung over the chair, I was ready to discover what the Anishinaabe did for Christmas morning since we had already opened all our presents. If they served breakfast, it would be my first in over six months. I felt my belly, surprised that I wasn't still full from the Christmas Eve feast. Opening the door, I found the hallway dark. It was so quiet. Even my stocking feet shuffling on the floor sounded discordant against the silence.

Wandering toward the dining room, I still heard nothing. *Where was everyone?* A candle was lit on the table. As I approached, the lights went on. I was dazzled blind. A single greeting erupted, "Happy Birthday, Becky Jean."

I grabbed my chest, mute in response. The table was stacked with small packages wrapped with huge ribbons and bows. Glitter scintillated across the gifts. Everyone started singing "Happy Birthday" to me. I burst into tears, gasping for breath. When I got part of my voice back, I squeaked, "How did you know it was my birthday?"

Connie laughed. "It's on your job application, silly."

In the center of the table was a small cake decorated with "Happy Birthday, Becky Jean" written in gobs of frosting. Twenty-three candles were strategically placed among and sometimes in the letters. *A cake was unnecessary with all the Christmas treats available.* I stood and stared at it, speechless. After lighting the candles, the crowd cheered as I blew them out. I stood paralyzed until Connie put her arm around me and said, "Start opening your presents. We all want to see if you like them." Commotion filled the next hour as I ripped open the wrapping on the presents. I was presented with little boxes filled with small items: costume jewelry, candy, and the last, largest one had a small basket made from wooden strips. I held it to the light trying to understand how it was made.

"Don't worry," said Hal. "None of this was expensive."

Connie jabbed him in the ribs as he explained the small basket, "Connie's aunt made the little basket. It's an Anishinaabe thing. It's woven from Black Ash and tied with dyed cedar roots."

After the presents were all opened and I hugged and thanked everyone around the room, we feasted on the chocolate cake. I was told that it was

Shawnee's favorite, made with rich buttercream frosting. People danced with me around the table, and I received more hugs than a person ever deserves. When the hubbub calmed down, I was filled with emotion. I grabbed my parka and ran outside, shouting to the boisterous crowd, "I can't breathe. I need a little air."

Despite the cold and the wind whipping snow in my face, I burst into tears. I couldn't stop crying. Sweating and hyperventilating, I opened my parka to the cold and tried to regain my composure. I closed my eyes focusing on the cold blasts of wind biting my face and freezing the tears to my cheeks. I slipped on gloves from my pockets as my hands were stiffening from the cold.

A gentle hand on my shoulder interrupted my panic. "What's wrong, Becky Jean?" Connie started rubbing my back. "Was something we did upsetting?"

I turned to face her. She wiped my face with a tissue then hugged me. The warmth I felt was more than her body heat. Her face on my cheeks melted the new gush of tears. "Come on, spill it out, kid. Don't hold onto evil stuff. Not allowed in Anishinaabe camps."

"I've never had a birthday party before."

"What? Never? Girl, that needs some explaining."

"This is Christmas day, right?" Connie nodded. "My father always said that it would profane the Christ child to celebrate my birthday. So he refused to let me even tell anyone that it was my birthday. Besides, he said that I got enough presents for Christmas. He even told me that I was lucky to be alive since in the Middle Ages children born on Christmas Day were sometimes abandoned on the steps of the church."

"What a horrible thing to tell a daughter." She gave me another hug and held me by the shoulders. "So this is your first ever birthday party?"

"Yep, first ever." Tears sprang out of my eyes and dribbled down my cheeks. Connie wiped them away with a now soggy tissue. I felt like a two-year-old toddler. "I'm sorry I made such a scene."

"No problem. We Anishinaabe like scenes." She laughed, "We are honored to start the custom of celebrating your birthday. It is not profane in the Native American calendar, so come inside before you turn into a human popsicle and enjoy your first ever special birthday party."

I followed her inside turning back only to see chickadees gathering on the birdfeeder hanging on the porch. "Sorry little birds, I didn't know I was inhibiting your breakfast."

"Don't worry everyone," Connie announced to the hushed crowd as we walked in the door. "She was too happy to breathe. She had to get some iced air in her lungs. Her parents didn't allow her to celebrate her birthday, so this is her first *ever* birthday party. Leave it to Anishinaabe to be the first to celebrate." Everyone cheered as I spilled more tears.

The rest of the day was vibrant. I played checkers with the children. Shawnee beat me soundly, but I held my own with the boys. Sherrie read me more of her poems. Some were in Anishinaabe. I loved the sounds and rhythm of her reading. She translated them each time afterwards, so I relished the rhythm twice.

Hal decided I needed a winter hike, so he took me outside that afternoon, all bundled up with parka, boots, scarves, and gloves. We hiked on snowshoes through fresh-fallen, foot-deep snow behind their property checking out deer trails and listening to the ravens cawing. He explained that ravens were symbols of wisdom to the Anishinaabe because they could survive the harsh winters without migrating. I was amazed as he pointed out the rabbit tracks and the brush piles where they hid out in winter. I was fascinated by how alive the forest was despite the heavy snow and the below-freezing temperatures. I was so distracted by all the discoveries that I didn't pay much attention to my snowshoeing, which was another first for me. I just shuffled along behind him. I'm not sure if "shuffling" is the right term for snowshoeing. But when we returned and I took off the contraptions, my gluteal muscles were so sore I could barely walk.

In the afternoon, despite my sore buttocks, Hal and Shawnee had me practice shooting the pistol some more. This time the cousins refused their father's bets. I improved a lot, not only hitting the target but getting much closer to the bullseye. I declined the offer to practice with the rifle, although if I had been knocked over I would have fallen in soft, fresh snow.

It was not only my first birthday party but the best Christmas celebration ever in my life. I was so happy and emotional that I experienced spasms of joy and tear bursts all day long. Connie explained my responses to her relatives, which meant more unconditional hugs. I felt more loved than ever before in my life.

Chapter 12
New Year

We celebrated the New Year at Connie and Hal's, another first for me as father always said it was a rite of Bacchus and we had no business celebrating it. Since alcoholism is a problem among Anishinaabe, each guest was limited to one drink at the stroke of midnight. It was a fun night of games and dancing.

I didn't expect to be busy at the restaurant afterwards. January had record low temperatures. Some days it never warmed up to above ten below zero. Almost a foot of snow had fallen during the previous night, and yet the temperature plummeted to 35 below zero. How could anyone get to the restaurant when roads were closed and school canceled? Even Bert had trouble getting in, but since I lived in my nice, warm coop on the other side of the parking lot, I had everything opened up and fresh coffee made by the time Bert arrived. Ron was an hour late, but since no one, not even Bert, knew where he lived, it was impossible to help him or contact him if he needed help. He had given Bert a post office box number but no street address. No one knew how he got to work. He just appeared every day, seldom was late, and never missed a day of work. Connie called in and said she would be late but arrived an hour later in Hal's pickup truck with chains on the snow tires.

It was quiet from six o'clock. I asked Bert, "Do you think we will have any customers today?"

"Oh, yes, we will, but they just won't come at the usual time or in the usual way." He returned to his office with a hot mug of coffee.

By eight o'clock, customers started coming in trucks, snowmobiles, or anything else that could navigate the blizzard. Connie pulled me aside just as we got busy. "Tell me now. What were Shawnee and you talking about?"

"I'll never tell, but I would make a humble suggestion."

"What's that?"

"Let Shawnee coach Leah through her Lamaze classes. I think it will resolve what I won't tell you that we talked about. Leah needs a coach and doesn't have a husband to do it, but I think Shawnee would need written permission from you to be in the Lamaze class, because of her age." I smiled and patted her shoulder.

"I don't know."

"Trust me. That is just what she needs."

"You're sure? She is so hung up on sex as it is."

"It will solve the problem you have with her."

She seemed to get defensive. "I don't have any problem with her. She is just a stubborn…"

I smiled. "Give her permission to be Leah's coach." I turned and walked away, not able to argue with Connie's logic.

"Coffee, please," said Rolly as he walked in from the MDOT barn, across the unplowed highway in Mukluks. "I should have worn snowshoes. Boy, that snow is deep." He stomped his feet to get the snow off and plunked down at the counter. He looked forlorn. He pulled off his tassel cap, shook off the snow, and unzipped his parka.

"What's the matter?" I asked as I poured his coffee.

"The snow is so heavy and it is so cold that I broke the blade on the plow. It needs to be welded. Where am I going to find a welder today? I need a big cheese omelet with my coffee today, Becky Jean, to bury my problems. And add an order of cinnamon toast."

"I checked our thermometer. The red stuff is all hidden and huddled in the little bulb at the bottom," I said as I brought him his omelet, "if that is any consolation to you."

"It snowed all night and then about four o'clock in the morning the temperature plummeted. Now plowing is like moving cement. That's why I broke the plow blade."

"So what are you going to do?" I set a spoon beside his coffee and a side of cinnamon toast, placing the omelet Ron had prepared so that it smiled at the customer. "I'm glad that I don't have a car or need to drive to work living in the little coop in the back. It has a nice heater."

Rolly smiled. "I'm sure that is like camping. I've seen Bert's coop."

"It must be well insulated because the electric heater doesn't go on very often." I added ketchup to his place setting and smiled. "I made my trek to Duluth for supplies the day before the blizzard on your recommendation, Rolly. I see now that was a wise decision."

He covered his omelet with ketchup and then tasted his toast, gave me a nod, and sipped his coffee before adding two packets of sugar. Stirring his coffee seemed to calm him. He dipped his toast in the coffee and let out a sigh. "I called for a backup plow from Duluth. It might get here in a couple of hours after the highway to Duluth is passable. But they're not sure when that will happen. The guys in Duluth said that they're not even bothering to plow the secondary streets. It's just too difficult, and with the schools closed, it isn't a priority. So coming to Cotton, Minnesota will not be a priority either." He slurped a forkful of omelet, cheese dripping down his chin, as he continued stirring his coffee.

"Could you send a snowmobile out to Charlie Butler's place? I hear that he's a pretty good welder. The rumor around the restaurant is that Charlie's welds never break." He stopped stirring, wiped his chin, and took a sip of coffee. His disgruntled face seemed to reflect that he was thinking.

"Sounds like a rumor Charlie started."

"So, Rolly, do you know any other welders here in Cotton?"

"Well, no but…"

Just then the Halstrom twins flew through the snow on their new twin snowmobiles they got for Christmas. Rolly gave me a disgruntled look, "They shouldn't have cancelled school for those kids. Just because their grandfather made so much money doesn't mean he should indulge those two the way he does. Look at those snowmobiles. I could never afford something like that."

"Yes, but maybe that is the answer to your welding problem."

"Yah, how is that?" He took another bite of his omelet. "Their father is the science teacher at Cotton High School, right? He couldn't afford such machines, so their grandfather must have bought them." A bite of toast later, "Frank Halstrom married Carol Hendricks from Duluth. Her father started that chain of hardware stores. Now he is worth millions, maybe billions. And those twins…" he pointed his coffee cup at them as they spun around the parking lot, "are his only grandchildren. He spoils them rotten."

In a flurry of snow that hit the front window, the twins stopped right in the handicapped space. Of course, the sign was covered with snow and we seldom had any handicapped customers to park there, certainly not on a day like today. They came in the door and shook the snow off their snowmobile suits, leaving an instant puddle at the door. After stomping the snow off their feet, they plunked down at the counter. "Do you have any hot chocolate?" asked Tom.

"Me too," said Tim.

"Coming right up," I answered. "Anything to go with it, boys?"

"Something hot, Becky Jean, like pancakes," they said in unison. "Yah, pancakes."

Rolly slid what remained of his omelet, toast, and coffee cup one seat over to be next to Tom. "So, Tom, do you know where Charlie Butler lives?"

"Down in the swamp below Marais Road, right?" Tim answered as he took off his stocking cap, bowed and added, "Mr. Rollifsen, sir."

"Yes. And do you think your snowmobiles could fetch him and bring him to the MDOT building? I need some emergency welding or the county roads will never get plowed."

"We won't have to go to school if the roads don't get plowed, will we?" Tom said with a smile.

"Oh I'll find a way to get the roads plowed so you two can go to school. It's a big problem today, but it sure would be nice if you boys could be part of the solution."

"Just teasing, Mr. Rollifsen, sir. Sure, these snowmobiles are the top of the line. They can go anywhere where there is snow. And there is plenty of snow today. We can get you there," said Tim.

"Don't you need him and his equipment?" asked Tom.

"Yes, I suppose so. We don't have welding equipment in the MDOT building."

"Grandpa gave mom a sled that attaches to the snowmobile for her Christmas present," said Tim. "Maybe Mr. Charles Butler's welding craft tools would fit in mom's sled."

I interrupted. "Sounds like you boys have been practicing speaking very formally?"

"Yes, Ms. Becky Jean, mother said we need to be more respectful of our elders," said Tom. Then he whispered with a grin, "Not that we were ever disrespectful, you understand." I laughed.

"You'll make sure he doesn't preach at us, won't you?" asked Tim turning back to Rolly. "I can't take much of that full gospel stuff he puts on everyone."

"In the middle of the blizzard, I don't think he'll expect you to speak in tongues," said Rolly. "He really is a very kind, compassionate—"

"No sermons, please," said Tom as he took a sip of his hot chocolate and plowed into the pancakes I served. He emptied the syrup pitcher over them. I fetched another for Tim.

"And I hear that he is a great welder," Rolly continued. "If you boys could bring it upon yourselves to go out and get Charlie, there might be some caramel rolls in your future."

"Sure, we'll go get him," said Tim.

"I'll get mother's sled and pick up his equipment," said Tom.

"Bring these nice boys a couple of caramel rolls," said Rolly, "when they return. Charges on the MDOT."

"Wow, thanks Mr. Rollifsen, sir," both boys chorused. They turned to me, asking for more hot chocolate. We'll be freezing cold when we get back, Becky Jean."

"What happened to the Ms.?"

Both boys smiled. "Oh, we're done practicing that formal stuff. We got things to do." They scooped up the last of their pancakes, left their money, and scooted out the door with, "Keep the change."

"Did you know he worked on the Alaska-Canadian highway?" Rolly filled in the story of Charlie's adventures during the war as the boys started their snowmobiles.

"Yes, he's told me some of his adventures up north." I smiled to think that a blizzard and a few good stories could weld a rift in generations. "You want a refill of that hot coffee, Mr. Rollifsen, sir?" I said, mimicking the boys.

"Later," he said as he followed the boys out the door. I watched Rolly climb on behind Tim as they spun in the drive. Another flurry of snow hit the front window as they headed out the driveway and then cross-country to Charlie's place in the swamp. Rolly seemed desperate to hold on to his hat.

• • •

A couple hours later with another flash of snow on the front window, Tim and Tom saddled up to the counter. "Ready for our MDOT caramel rolls," said Tom. "And more hot chocolate," said Tim.

"How is Charlie? Was he able to weld the blade?" I asked as I served them.

"That guy is amazing," said Tom. "When he welds, it is like watching an artist."

"And he was willing to teach us too," said Tim, "and there was no sermon. Besides, he really thought our snowmobiles were great. Made us open up the engines, examined how the treads were attached, everything."

"He said he might go home and make his own," added Tom. They both laughed. "Did you hear the story of God making him sick so that he didn't go out plowing one night. Several of his coworkers died in the storm that night."

"No, I hadn't heard that story."

Between bites of caramel rolls and doses of hot chocolate, the twins related several more stories. "Charlie is one amazing guy!"

I laughed again at the bridge a storm had formed between generations.

Chapter 13
Flashbacks

February cold was just as miserable as January. For many days, the high temperature at four o'clock in afternoon didn't reach ten below zero. I learned that when it was 40 below zero, Centigrade and Fahrenheit were the same. I didn't really think I needed to know that.

It was on one of those cold February days that I was helping Connie with hungry customers. Around noon, there was a minor explosion in the kitchen. The customers didn't seem to notice. But everyone heard Ron yelling, "Incoming." Bert ran to the grill. Connie gave me a nod that she would keep the customers happy, and I followed. We found Ron was curled up under the sink, shrunk into a frightened mass.

Bert tried to comfort him. "Ron, it's all right. It was just a delay in lighting the burner under the gas grill. There's no incoming. Trust me."

"Get down," Ron yelled. "The mortars are next. Watch out!" He curled up even tighter, his head between his legs, and shook like he was seizing.

Bert tried to grab his hand, but Ron only crawled farther under the sink. "Ron, you're at the restaurant. You're not in Viet Nam."

"Get down," Ron yelled, "or you'll all be killed. Get down, sergeant."

Connie appeared in the window. "We got orders, Bert. Is the grill working?"

"Yah, there's nothing wrong with it." He grabbed the orders. "Coming right up." Bert turned to me. "Talk to him Becky Jean, would you?"

I curled up next to Ron under the sink as Bert started frying hamburgers. The sound of the meat sizzling on the griddle made Ron cringe more. I put my hand on his shoulder. His eyes were wild. "You'll all be killed. Get down. Get down. Get down."

I rubbed his shoulder. "We're safe now, Ron. We're all safe." His voice softened, and he started to sob, covering his face with his hands. I rubbed his shoulders some more and then massaged his neck muscles until they relaxed. "Let's go outside, Ron. The mortars have stopped. It's all safe." I stroked his hands, and he placed them in mine. He acted like a child yearning for his mother.

He glanced at Bert frying the hamburgers. "Oh, Bert, I'm sorry. I'm sorry. I'm so sorry." He sobbed. "I got to go out. Out. Out."

I helped him put on his parka and hat. He stepped into his boots, and then he ran out the back door.

"Stay with him, Becky Jean," Bert yelled. "He's used to going in the coop to recover. I don't know what he'll do when he finds it locked."

I scrambled to put on my boots, grabbed my parka, took my keys, and ran out the door after him.

Chapter 14
Sordid Story

Despite the snow and the blowing wind, Ron was huddled by my door smoking one cigarette after another. He was bundled in his military parka with a wolf fur-lined hood. I couldn't see his face but only saw the smoke curling out from the wolf fur. He was fumbling with the doorknob, knocking his head against the door.

"I got the key, Ron, just a minute."

"This is your house now, isn't it?" he said as I put the key in the door. "You don't smoke do you, Becky Jean?"

"No, Ron I don't smoke." My blue-cold fingers fumbled with my keys making a desperate attempt to unlock the door. I finally lodged the key in the lock and turned it.

When the door swung open, Ron stamped out his cigarette butt and ran inside. "May I come into your house if I don't smoke?"

"Sure, come on in." I followed him. His eyes sped about the room. He seemed to be surveying everything.

"You don't have much in your house, Becky Jean. You don't have much furniture. Is this really your home, Becky Jean? Where you live?"

"Yes, it's my home, but you're right, I don't have much furniture."

"The curtains are so pretty. Bert never had curtains like that in here before. Oh, I like the walls. Very nice paint color."

"Sit on the bed, Ron, and I'll sit on the chair. We'll talk." We shed our parkas at the foot of the bed.

"You want me to talk to you, Becky Jean?" He sat on the bed, and I pulled the wooden chair to face him. He held his head in his hands as he started crying. I got him several tissues. He blew his nose. "You want to listen to me talk now?"

"Yes, Ron. You can tell me anything you want." I sat down knee-to-knee with him and held his hands in mine. They were sweaty despite coming in from the cold. At first he seemed to resist my touch but then he grabbed my hands and held them tightly together.

"You want me to tell you even bad things?"

"Yes, tell me even very bad things."

He dropped my hands and stood, almost knocking me off my chair. "Private First Class, Delta Company 1st Battalion 5th Marines will honor your request." He saluted, "Hand-to-hand combat specialist, sir." He looked at me, "I'm sorry, Ms. Becky Jean, madam."

"At ease, Private," I said shifting in my chair. The smell of his breath from the freshly smoked cigarettes stifled the air and made me cough.

"You don't smoke, do you, Becky Jean."

"No I don't. Now tell me the story, Private." I tried to sound as commanding as my petite frame could muster.

"All right, Madame Becky Jean, sir." He took a deep breath and sighed. "I was trained to kill a man in less than thirty seconds—garrote, knife or bare hands," He said as I persuaded him to sit back down on the bed.

With both hands on his shoulders, I demanded in the strongest military tone, "Now, your story, Private."

"You want to hear my story? Nobody wants to hear my story. They spit at me when I came back from Nam. Why do you want to hear my story?"

"I want to hear it because it will help both of us heal."

He stared at me, shaking his head. "You need healing too, Becky Jean?"

"Yes, I need healing too. Your story might help heal me."

There was a long silence as his eyes searched mine. I wondered what he was thinking. Then his sudden staccato speech erupted. "It was just supposed to be a reconnaissance mission. We weren't supposed to engage." His eyes welled with tears, so I gave him a tissue from my bedside table to wipe his eyes. Then he continued, "It was a hot, humid morning, but it was always like that in Nam. You sweat when you worked, you sweat when you slept, and the noise of mosquitoes on your bed net became a lullaby that put you to sleep. I was the lowest rank in our squad. We had a good sergeant, Sergeant Thomas. He had two kids back home and the most beautiful wife. He always showed us pictures of her. We would sneak away his letters and read them, especially those of us who had no one back home to send us sweet letters. Carol was her name. Boy, could she write romantic letters. Some of the guys used to fantasize about her. Jock didn't because he had his own girlfriend, but she couldn't write letters like Sergeant's Carol."

I interrupted his rambling, "You were telling me the story about that day you went on the reconnaissance mission."

He scrunched his forehead. "You want to hear that story?"

"Yes, Ron, I want to hear it."

"It's not nice. I shouldn't tell that story to a nice girl like you." He stood up and headed for the door.

I grabbed his arm. "Tell me, please."

"All right." He sat back on the bed and hunched his back. "Jock and Brains got the gear ready. We all had nicknames. I was Cookie because the guys found out I liked to cook. I tried to go to cooking school but ended up in demolition. My CO said it was almost the same." He giggled, and I smiled back at him. "That's funny, isn't it, Becky Jean?"

"Yes, Ron." I laughed to accommodate him. "Now continue the story."

"The Huey dropped us off in this rice paddy. The pilot buzzed the field to get the water buffalo out of the place where we needed to land. Face, he was the handsome one, hardly needed to shave, and Rad, he had the radio. We set off toward the jungle. Jock, Brains, and I advanced down the trail we had seen from the Huey; Rad and Face followed. Sergeant was always careful. We respected him and knew that he wouldn't put us in harm's way. He had that pretty wife and two children to go home to.

"I didn't exactly understand the mission, but that wasn't unusual. I didn't even understand why we were fighting the Cong. But we were supposed to find out where they were keeping their military supplies. They couldn't find the depot from the air, but everyone knew it was around there somewhere.

We followed this trail. Brains was good at tracking. He could look at the mud and tell how many people had walked that trail and when. He was from Tennessee. His grandfather was full-blooded Cherokee and had taught him tracking. We followed tracks all morning but didn't see a single Cong. By lunch time, it looked like our mission was just about over. The guys were talking about heading back for supper. They always had big juicy steaks if you asked the cook for them. But you had to ask very nicely." He nodded his head and smiled, I assume to exaggerate the point.

Nothing bad had happened in his story. I was sure he was holding back. "Continue, please."

"Anyway, we were eating our rations and salivating about our anticipated supper. Sergeant was studying the map. I was munching my ration cookies and playing with my M-16. I loved that rifle. I always kept it shiny and clean. Sometimes I would talk to it like it was my girlfriend.

"Sergeant called us together and showed us on the map where we had been wandering around all morning. 'We need to head over here,' he said as he pointed to the map. 'It's the only area we haven't checked.'

"I wasn't much for maps. I just knew that my feet were soaking wet and cramping and tired. I would probably need to see the Doc about foot rot in the morning. Anyway, off we went to the place on the map we hadn't been. I unbuttoned my shirt. It was so hot, and the sun made the moisture on the ground rise. It was like raining upside down.

"Sergeant hand-motioned us down. We were on the edge of a rice paddy. But this one had no farmers working in it. Face took the binoculars and searched the perimeter. 'I don't see anything, Sarge,' he said. Rad reported our position. Command said that there were no reports from that area. I guessed our objective must be on the other side. The rice paddy was in a river system. It was hard to go around it, so we decided to cross it. I can't blame Sarge for that decision. He was as careful as could be.

"We scattered to cross so we wouldn't be easy targets. We agreed to meet on the other side by a tall tree. It was quiet, too quiet. But nobody saw anything move. There wasn't even any wind, just quiet and still. I remember smelling the buffalo shit. The farmers used it to fertilize the rice paddies. I smelled it, but I didn't dare look down to see it. I remember the sun blazing over the treetops like fire in our eyes, so we must have been heading straight west. We were in the middle of the muck when Sarge yelled, 'Down!' Like good Marines, we hit the deck.

"I remember a piece of buffalo shit floating right by my face. 'What is it?' asked Jock. 'What did you see?' Sarge answered something about movement at the far end of the rice paddy. No one else had seen anything. Face still had the binoculars and said he'd take a look.

"Bang, those binoculars, reflecting in the sunlight were a perfect target. Face was down, and half his skull was blown into the next rice paddy. His body quivered like a seizure, and then it stopped. I knew he was dead, but I couldn't get to him to pull his dog tags."

I gasped, and Ron put his hands on my knees. "He was the lucky one, Becky Jean. He didn't suffer. He never knew what hit him." He twisted on the bed. "I shouldn't be telling this grisly story to a nice, pretty girl like you, should I? I'll stop, Becky Jean. I'm sorry. I won't tell you anymore. Let's go back to work."

I put my hand on his shoulder as he tried to get up. "I need to hear it, Ron. I know it is important." I promised myself not to cringe as he continued even though I felt nauseated and wanted to go to my bathroom and vomit the story away.

"But it gets worse, Becky Jean. I suppose I should get back to flipping burgers." He shifted to get up off the bed.

I pushed him back down again. "No, this is important. I want to hear the whole story."

"All right, if you're sure, Becky Jean, I'll finish the story if you're commanding me to."

"I am commanding you to finish the story, private."

He took a deep sigh, and I heard a wheeze as he exhaled. But he continued. "Jock tried to get Face's dog tags, but the bullets were whistling over his head and he couldn't get over the foot trail. Rice paddies are terraced with trails all through them on the top of the dikes, like a miniature labyrinth, except the foot paths seem gigantic when you're up to your face in muck.

"Rad called in our position. The Huey came and strafed the edge of the paddy but didn't hit a thing, and when he tried to land near us to get us out, he took fire and left. I remember all of us asking, 'What next, Sarge?'

"He motioned for us to crawl a little closer together. 'Maybe we can get a glimpse of those Cong that are shooting at us and take them out,' he said to encourage us. We made some progress, but still none of us could see the enemy who shot out Face. Brains put his helmet on a stick and lifted it up. The helmet took a bullet just like that. 'They know where we are, Sarge,' he yelled.

"It was so quiet and still. I remember rolling on my back and looking up at the sky. It wasn't any different from the sky in Minnesota. 'I got to take a crap,' yelled Jock. 'Go ahead, I give you permission,' Sarge replied. Jock added,

'I'm stuck in this muck, where do I go?' 'In your pants, stupid,' said Brains. 'Yah, just mix yours with the buffalo shit, it's all the same,' I said. 'Shut up, Cookie, that's disgusting.' But he went anyway. We all laughed when he sighed, 'I needed to do that so bad. And I don't want to hear any jokes about pooping my pants, guys. What happens in the paddy stays in the paddy, right? Just wait till your bowels have to move.' We had to chuckle at his joke. I turned to the side and saw Brains lying on his back squirting his urine up into the air. 'Oh, what a relief it is,' he sang the Alka Seltzer jingle a couple of times.

"Sarge interrupted our potty break, 'We got to get closer, men. I still can't spot those Cong.' He had dug a trench so he could see the far end without exposing his precious head. We tried to regroup but only succeeded in getting pinned down closer together. I looked over at Rad and saw smoke. 'What are you doing, Rad?' I asked. 'Just taking a pot break,' he said.

"Sarge exploded, 'Rad, what have I told you about smoking Marijuana on duty??' He responded, 'Oh, are we still on duty? I thought we already returned to base.' Sergeant didn't like that response, but he was too many rice paddies away to do anything about it. Then the radio signaled. Rad explained, 'The Huey flew high and took on some fire. But they were out of range. No damage.' 'This is Rad, out.'

"We all heard the Huey pilot explain, 'There's a machine gun nest on the west side beside that big tree. I'll try to take it out, but it's pretty well covered by trees.' The gunner on the Huey strafed the area. but when Brains lifted his helmet on a stick it took another hit.

"The radio squawked, 'Take it out, guys, and we'll come and bring you home for supper. Over.'

"Brains carried an anti-tank gun. He wedged it in a crevice and aimed. He missed. Then the enemy mortars started coming in. 'They must have finally calculated our position,' cried Jock.

"Brains got hit first. Blew him to pieces; arms and legs flew in all directions. I looked up as soon as he got hit figuring they wouldn't fire again right away. Scanning the area and then getting down I told Sarge, 'There's a truck at the end of the rice paddy. I could hot wire it and drive it right into that machine gun nest.'

"Sergeant didn't respond, so I started crawling. It was getting dark, the sun now just glinting over the trees, but the Cong just kept sending mortars to where they had hit Brains, one right after another. The shadows hid me as I crawled over the paths between the paddies. I'd wait until the light flashed from the mortars, blinding the enemies' vision, then I crawled over to the next paddy. The blasts were so bright that I knew anyone watching would be temporarily blinded. It was my chance to advance.

"It took most of the night, but just before dawn I made it. Nobody was around. I panicked. *What if the truck wouldn't start? Maybe that's why it was abandoned.* I crawled into the cab. Still there was no one around. The ignition wires were hanging down. I'd worked in a garage during high school, so I knew what to do, but my hands were shaking.

"I was so excited, Becky Jean, when it started. I crouched real low and drove that truck at top speed right into the machine gunner. Unfortunately there were mines around the perimeter, so I guess you could say the truck with me in it was blown into the machine gun nest. Anyway, the truck and I landed on top of the machine gun nest, killing all the Cong that had pinned us down. I was stunned but mobile. There was blood dripping from my fatigues. I figured I must have been hit with shrapnel, but everything moved—legs, knees, and toes—so I grabbed my rifle and jumped out of the truck. There was no one to shoot. The truck had killed them all. In my excitement, I didn't even notice the pain in my legs, not until later.

"I ran toward my squad. 'Call the Huey, Rad. We're free.'"

Ron hung his head and rubbed his eyes of tears. "When I got to where my squad was, Rad was dead. Jock and Sergeant were badly wounded. I grabbed the radio. It still worked and called in the Huey. They were there in less than ten minutes and carted us all away." Ron sobbed after finishing the story. His whole body convulsed as if in pain.

"You're a hero, Ron. That was amazing." I got up and rubbed his shoulders and neck.

"Yah, I got a bravery metal and a purple heart for all the shrapnel they dug out of my legs." He looked up at me, "But they all died anyway, Becky Jean. They all died in the hospital, but they all died. I didn't save anyone. It was all worthless. The whole ordeal was worthless. I had seven surgeries at the hospital. I threw blood clots into my lungs from my legs. Each time I hoped that I would die. I should have died with them. I should be dead now."

"It was not worthless, Ron. You're here for me."

"What have I done for you? Nothing, that's what."

"You're my friend, and I am richer because you're my friend. You've made me rich, Ron." He stood and hugged me as he sobbed on my shoulder.

Bert entered without knocking. "Is he all right?"

"Yes, he'll be fine. He just needed to share a story with a friend."

"He usually smokes a whole pack of cigarettes when this happens," said Bert.

Ron looked up. "I only smoked two. I must be getting better, right, Bert? Becky Jean doesn't smoke, so I couldn't contaminate her house. Look at the nice curtains she put up, Bert. Aren't they pretty?" He smiled like a two-year-old who had just succeeded at potty-chair training. "Need some burgers fried, Bert? I'm ready."

"We had a momentary lull, so I came to check on you. But if you're able, I really need you back in the kitchen. Hop to, soldier."

We put on our parkas and trooped back to the restaurant as if we were in a Veteran's Day parade.

Chapter 15
Frozen Waterfalls

I stood enchanted at the window, viewing the snow drifts and icicles from the comfort of my nice warm coop. The sun glinted and twinkled off each snowflake. *What a morning*, I thought. The thermometer outside my window registered way below zero. I couldn't even read the temperature as the red alcohol was frozen in the little bulb at the bottom of the thermometer. I sipped some hot tea, content to watch the diamond spectacle scattered across the new snow.

It was my day off. Bert said that he was obligated by law to give me time off. I resented it since I had no idea what to do with myself, but I had prepared by buying Michelina pasta from the freezer section at the grocery in the mall and expected to heat it up in my new Christmas toaster oven. The Michelina factory is in Duluth, and I'd heard from several customers that the recipes came from the owner's mother, so I concluded that they should be quite tasty. There were lots of choices, too many, in fact, but I chose a cream pasta with broccoli. We didn't serve much broccoli at the restaurant and I thought it would be something special. It was to be my two thirty afternoon stomach quencher. What a treasure Hal and Connie's Christmas gift had been. Because of it, I had been eating better. Oatmeal for breakfast, boiled on my hotplate, and sometimes I splurged and had something hot for supper in my toaster oven, but I still depended on whatever Ron gave me for my main nutrition.

After a hot shower, I heated up some oatmeal for breakfast. I spooned it slowly into my mouth while watching new snowflakes fall. They were so tiny and delicate when it was this cold. But now I felt restless. It had been snowing all week so I was limited on how far I could hike in the woods. I thought back to the snowshoes I had learned how to use at the Christmas party. But I didn't have any. I should have asked Connie if I could have borrowed theirs. Maybe on her break she could get them for me. The snow was so deep it would have gone right over my new boots. I heated up some apple cider and resumed my vigil at the window. I was sipping hot apple cider when I heard the roar of snowmobiles. Out the window, I recognized the twins' snowmobiles as they spun to a stop in front of my door instead of in the restaurant parking lot.

I opened the door to two grinning twins in matching snowmobile suits. The subzero burst of wind shocked my face.

"Becky Jean, you want to go for a ride?" the two asked.

"I don't think I have the proper gear, but I sure do appreciate the invitation. I'm afraid I will have to turn it down. I'd freeze to death with my flimsy parka. And that's all I have."

Undeterred, Tim said, "We heard it was your day off, and dad said you never get to do anything."

"And you always treat us nice, not like crazy kids," said Tom.

"Besides, we brought my mother's snowmobile suit for you to wear," said Tim.

"It should fit," said Tom, "Mom's gigantic compared to you."

"I don't think your mother would appreciate being referred to as gigantic."

Tim smiled. "Right, but you'll never tell. Besides I was only using it in comparison."

"I'm not sure if that's a complement or a put-down, but come on in, boys, and warm up."

Tom grabbed the snowmobile suit out of a compartment on the back of the snowmobile. The two then stomped into my coop. "Is this really where you live?" asked Tim.

"We have bigger closets in our house," said Tom.

"I'm very thankful for my little place. It's easy to keep clean."

Both boys laughed and headed for my bed. "That's because you have nothing to clean up." My bed springs yelped under the strain of two teenage boys jettisoning onto my bed. I was afraid they would break the springs.

"Yikes, you need a new bed." Then they turned to me and said, "Try on the suit. We'll watch to make sure you put it on correctly." Their chins rose like supervisors at a factory.

I had never worn a snowmobile suit and wasn't quite sure how to approach it. After some inspection I unzipped it and angulated into the suit. The boys flopped back on their elbows staring at my movements. "You find this interesting?"

"It's not like you're naked or anything," said Tim.

I stared back at them. "But you wish I was?"

Their faces flushed. Tom said, "Well, right. But we're just pretending."

I twisted my hips to imaginary music for their entertainment and made a show of zipping up the suit. "Show's over. I guess I'm ready to go."

"Not quite," Tom said laughing. Tim handed me goggles and a wool scarf. Since the suit was a couple sizes too big, I felt like a snowwoman waddling out the door. Somehow with a lot of help they managed to mount me on the back of Tom's snowmobile.

Winter is magical tucked inside a snowmobile suit, zipping along between the snow-covered trees at about thirty miles per hour. The wind catches your face despite the scarf and goggles and reddens your cheeks like bad rouge. The smells of pine and cedar hit your nose in rapid sequence as the visual impact of light scintillating off the crystals enchants you.

I held Tom so tight I thought I caused him pain. We followed a trail off the highway that followed the power lines through the woods for a while. Tim took an abrupt turn ahead of us, and Tom and I followed down a steep bank. Light, fluffy snow whisked across my numb face and blurred my vision. I wiped the snow off my goggles with my gloves, daring for a moment to release my grip on Tom, and discovered that now we were speeding across a lake.

Tim was focused on some unknown goal, but Tom and I switched back and forth along Tim's straight bias. I held tight as we swung first one way and then the other. When I looked back, I saw a French lace pattern across the lake. "Was that for my entertainment?" I yelled in Tom's ear over the motor noise.

"Sure."

These two intelligent young men were obvious candidates to become engineers. Maybe they would continue being creative, I thought, and someday they could solve some complex physical problem more complicated than making pretty patterns in the snow.

At the end of the lake, we slowed. The engine noise diminished so they could yell at each other and be heard. "I wanted to follow the river, Tom, but there's open water ahead," said Tim.

"Let's follow the bank. There should be enough snow in the reeds. We'll just have to slow down."

How could there be open water when the alcohol was frozen in my thermometer? No self-respecting water should be flowing. I guess I have a lot to learn about winter.

The engines revved beyond hearing, and we followed the river that flowed into the lake we had traveled across. The ride was bumpy but slower. I was used to the trail along the power lines and the exhilarating smoothness of the lake. Now we were in a river canyon with steep banks on both sides, flying over snow-covered boulders. We kept to the edge as we passed open water that swirled around rapids. *That's what prevents ice from forming despite how cold it has been for the last two months: current.*

A sudden turn left me breathless. We bounded over a snowbank, and they killed the engines in synchrony.

"Wow," blurted out of my mouth as my eyes scanned the frozen waterfall in front of me. Stalactites of ice coursed down the falls. Crystalline ice prisms muffled the roar of the Wagnerian cascade, imprisoned by stalagmites that completed the enclosure of the falls. As my eyes focused I could see, drip by drip, the formation of new icicles where the water snuck through the massive frozen pipe organ. I was standing before a maestro playing the music of creation. I was transfixed, paralyzed by sight and sound.

"Dad said that you would like it," said Tom.

"Was it your father's idea to bring me here?" I was still mystified why two teenage boys would want to take a twenty-something girl out snowmobiling for the day. *These handsome boys must have classmate girlfriends,* I reasoned. *Why me?*

Both blushed in spite of the sub-zero cold. "Dad said that we had bad attitudes towards the girls at school," said Tim.

"Yah, and we needed to spend some time with you so we would have more mature attitudes," said Tom. "We're supposed to learn 'proper respect for women,' quoting dad."

"So I am a sociological experiment?"

"Yah, sort of," said Tom.

"But isn't this a beautiful waterfall?" said Tim.

He seemed desperate to change the subject. "All right, I don't mind being your proper-respect experiment." I laughed. "Yes, Tim, the waterfall is spectacular."

I stood silent in awe. There was no sound except the water coursing over the falls. Wisps of cedar filled the air caused by the turbulence around the falls. Swirls of snow devils caught my eye, and one even dissipated around me, kissing my numb face.

Tom opened the compartment on his snowmobile and pulled out lunch and declared, "Mom packed ham and cheese sandwiches and oranges and a thermos of hot apple cider."

I plunked down on the soft cushion of a snow-covered boulder. The snowmobile suit was well enough insulated so I didn't melt the snow and get wet. Tim to my left and Tom to my right, I contemplated being their sociological science project. They were both tall, almost six foot, so I felt enveloped in their protection.

The sandwiches were good, and I enjoyed hearing about the boy's classes. They were both straight-A students but avoided classes that weren't "scientific." They were excited to explain their plans for going to the University of Minnesota when they graduated in the spring. "Not in Duluth, down in Minneapolis," Tim emphasized.

We shared sips from the common thermos. "We're just guys, so we didn't think to bring cups," Tom explained. "And mom forgot to pack them." He looked at me acknowledging my disapproval. "Well, we forgot to pack them. That's better, isn't it?" I nodded.

They coerced me into sharing some of my college experiences as we peeled oranges. They cackled like crows as I finished telling them my chemistry class *faux pas*. "It was just a minor explosion, and no one was around, so I didn't get into trouble." They laughed so hard they fell off their rocks, rolling in the snow for drama.

As we finished lunch, they packed everything. I took off my gloves and hiked to the edge of the falls. The tremendous power vibrated through the ice stalactites. I reached out to touch one of the forming icicles and put the drop of water in my mouth. It was so pure, cold, and refreshing.

"Time to go, Becky Jean," said Tim. "It's three o'clock, and we don't want to be trying to find our way along this river in the dark."

No wonder I had been so hungry, I thought, it's my break time. I rubbed my tummy, so satisfied with the lunch the boys had brought. I went to climb on behind Tom, but Tim protested, "Tom got to have you on the way here, it's my turn."

"I'm an equal opportunity scientific experiment?"

"Of course," said Tim.

We followed the trail we had made along the river for safety. I was amazed at the things I had missed coming the other direction: snow formations bending pine branches, gnomes of snow-covered rocks climbing out of the river, and the delicate lace of newly formed ice along the open water.

When we came to the lake, the twins accelerated to full speed. Half-way across the lake we heard a gunshot and stopped. "Where did that come from?" I asked.

"Off to the west, I'm pretty sure," said Tom.

"Isn't that by Rolly's place?" said Tim.

With an instantaneous visual consensus, we turned in the middle of the lake, off to the west at full throttle. No longer traveling at recreational speed, we were off on a mission. I hid my face behind Tim's back only aware of the white blur in my peripheral vision. In what felt like moments, we had crossed the lake and were headed up the shore. As we jumped the snow bank at jet speed, it sent a shattering sensation up my spine. The boys both slowed to a more reasonable speed to follow a path up between the pine trees to Mr. Rollifsen's house.

He was standing outside a small building with a shotgun. I noticed blood was scattered across the snow bank as we skidded to a stop.

"What's happening, Mr. Rollifsen, sir?" both boys asked.

"I can't understand it," he said as he squatted beside a carcass in the snow.

"It looks like that is what's left of a pretty scraggly fox," said Tim.

"You're right. But why would a fox attack my hens in the middle of the day?"

"My dad says that foxes are nocturnal hunters," said Tom.

"So, maybe it has rabies," said Tim.

He killed one of my hens before I got him," said Rolly, pointing his gun at an eviscerated, feather-encrusted glob in the snow.

Tim grabbed a stick and prodded it. "Look at this."

I joined the investigation as we all squatted beside the dead hen. "Look at the liver," said Tim. "It's full of yellow spots. That isn't the way it is supposed to look, is it Mr. Rollifsen?"

"When mom makes chicken livers for supper they don't look like that," added Tom.

"That was Aida, one of my older hens," said Rolly. "She sure has been productive. Best egg layer I've ever had. But she hasn't been producing lately. I thought it was just because…they let up in the winter. Maybe she was sick."

"Dad says that all chickens die of lymphoma if they live long enough," said Tom.

"So that's why I eat lots of chicken," said Tim, "It prevents the poor things from dying of cancer." He smiled, "Aren't I compassionate?"

Tom poked him with his stick. Tim protested, "Hey, don't get that cancer blood on me."

"Mr. Rollifsen, are you going to send the fox brain into the state lab to be tested for rabies? It is a reportable disease, you know," said Tim.

"I suppose I should." Rolly still seemed lost in contemplation over his poor hen.

"Where's your ax? I'll help you chop the head off," said Tom.

"I get to. I thought of it first," said Tim.

Rolly went to his woodshed and returned with the ax handing it to the boys.

"You do it, Becky Jean. That will be fair. Then we won't fight over the privilege," the boys said as they used a stick to lay out the remains of the fox on a stump. I questioned whether this gruesome task was a privilege, but I took the ax to prevent sibling rivalry.

"See how nice we're treating our date, Mr. Rollifsen?" they sang together. "Make sure you tell our loving father."

He scrunched his forehead. "This is a date?"

"Yes, sir, we're learning respect for women," they said, stiffening like soldiers.

"I'm supposed to be giving them the experience of dating a mature woman. Sort of a sociological science project," I explained as I grabbed the ax and aimed but closed my eyes as I struck with a whack that separated the head from the rest of the carcass. Mr. Rollifsen grabbed the head by an ear. "I'll call the DNR now and see what I'm supposed to do. Thanks for your help, boys. And you too, Becky Jean." He headed up toward the house, and then turned, "By the way, what kind of a date did you take her on? This is an odd neighborhood for a date."

"We brought Becky Jean up to see the waterfall."

"Some date, eh, Rolly?" I said as I slammed the bloody ax into the stump. I blushed and shook my head. "Actually, it's been my best date ever."

"All right," the boys yelled, pumping their fists in the air. "Dad won't believe it. We respected a woman."

Chapter 16
Rachel's Birthday

By April Fools' Day, Leah was struggling to get her dishes done. Her pregnant belly was really in the way as she tried to load the dishwasher and work the controls. Connie kept the customers happy, and I helped Leah finish her dishes. She sat on the stool in the washing room breathless with exertion.

"You'll be a mother soon, Leah."

"Yah, the ultrasound doesn't show any little thing-a-ma-jig, so I guess it's a girl."

"So what's her name going to be?"

"Rachel Tamara."

"That's a lovely name. Where did you get it?"

"Well, I figured Leah was Jacob's wife who had the kids. In the Bible, you know?"

"I know."

"But Rachel was the favored one."

"As I recall, she died in childbirth. Do you think that's a good name?"

"Maybe she will be a physician or a lawyer and never have kids." Leah got off the stool, stopped me from helping her. "And her middle name will be Tamara because in the Bible she was raped, but I won't explain that to her till she is of age to understand." She took over stacking the dishes in the rack. "I can finish now, but thanks for the rest break. And thank you so much for collecting money from the customers for my delivery." She held up her gloved right hand. "I promise to never forget what you've done for me. I know you got in big trouble with Mr. Lloyd over it. Connie told me."

"Oh, yes, a lot of trouble, I think I almost got fired." I slumped on the stool to rest my hurting feet. "But in the end, he even contributed to the fund, but I'm not supposed to tell you that. So keep it a secret or I will get fired."

"My mouth is zipped." She turned as Connie entered.

"Are you two almost done in here?" Connie said. "It's time to go home, crew."

"Almost if my big belly wasn't in the way, I would be," said Leah. "By the way, Connie, I just wanted to tell you that Shawnee has been the best Lamaze coach ever. She has really helped me calm down and not be afraid. Thanks for loaning me your daughter."

"No problem. It gave her something more important to think about than how to impress boys." We all laughed.

Bert came in and discovered Connie and me helping Leah. "Maybe you better stay home tomorrow, Leah. I hired another high school kid, Rick Johnson, Fred Johnson's son, for your maternity leave. He's a senior, so his classes are done at 12:30." He turned to Connie and me, "Can you two manage until he gets here?"

We both gawked at the masculine pronoun, "He?"

"Yes, he," Bert emphasized as he returned our startled looks, "starts tomorrow, but he's working for his father this summer, so he can only work a couple months. His father owns a construction company out of Duluth. Is that enough time for your maternity leave?"

"That is very generous, Mr. Lloyd."

Bert winked at me, "See, I am an equal opportunity employer, Becky Jean. I even hired someone like you."

"And I will always be grateful."

•　　•　　•

Wednesday, the following week, Rolly came in late just before closing and ordered a hamburger with everything. There was no one else in the restaurant. We were cleaning up, getting ready to close. "Those twins were right," Rolly said as he swallowed his last bite.

"Right about what?"

"That fox had rabies. I just got the report back from the state lab. But I haven't had any more chicken deaths, so I think poor Aida gave up her life to protect the flock. I brought that liver to the science class and they looked at it under the microscope. Mr. Holmgren said he is no pathologist but it looked to him like the liver was full of cancer, a lymphoma of some kind. Those twins are pretty smart, aren't they?"

"I think they come by their intelligence honestly. I hear their mother is pretty smart as well."

"Yah, she is the lawyer for her father's company, you know."

"No wonder. A science teacher father and a lawyer for a mother, those boys are destined for great things."

"Yah, I guess I needed to improve my attitude towards them," Rolly said. "They sure were there for me to get that broken blade on the plow fixed and now this." He drank his last sip of coffee. "I see you're closing up. Thanks for the supper." He headed out the door.

As Bert locked the front door, the telephone rang. He looked at his watch. "Whoever it is, they should know that we're closed now," he complained.

"I'll answer it," Connie said. Her face brightened as she hung up. "It's Shawnee. She coached Leah through the delivery. Leah just had her baby— six pounds, one ounce. Mom and Rachel Tamara are doing fine." Connie and I grabbed hands and danced around the restaurant.

Even Bert showed a crack of emotion, "I suppose I'll be required to hire this Rachel Tamara when she gets to high school." He dangled his keys. "It's time to leave, ladies. You can dance in the parking lot."

"Let's go to the hospital, Becky Jean."

I looped my arm in hers. "I'm ready."

"Babies and hospitals both scare me," said Bert, "so give Leah my best wishes but tell her not to expect me to visit. I'll send flowers."

I climbed into Connie's pick-up truck, and we headed south. Bert was laughing at us as we left the parking lot. Connie even squealed her tires. "Oops, don't let Hal know I did that," she said to me. "He'll make me buy new tires with my tip money."

I had to caution her to follow the speed limit as we got to Hermantown, north of Duluth. She thanked me because the police were parked in the Hermantown bakery parking lot watching traffic. Connie's face flushed. "There's a speeding ticket I didn't get. Thanks, Becky Jean. There's another lecture from Hal prevented."

I laughed, "You two are so good for each other."

As we walked into the hospital lobby and headed up the elevator to the obstetrics ward, Connie said, "I'm glad you talked me into letting Shawnee coach Leah through the delivery." Connie fingered the buttons without pushing them. "I thought you were crazy when you suggested it, but without any fighting or squabbling she's gotten a good dose of reality. She was so boy-crazy. Now she's almost a normal person. We haven't even had an argument about dating or sex in months." Connie took a deep breath. "And then with the Lamaze classes in the evening, she has actually been doing her homework so that she is finished before she goes to the classes. Not once have we had to ask her to do her homework."

I laughed as Connie finally pushed the button for obstetrics ward, "Maybe she just needed to see the consequences of teenage libido to think it all out. Besides, she learned a little anatomy and physiology as well as some quality sex education at the Lamaze classes." The elevator jerked to a stop. I added, "I heard from Leah that the two of them had some pretty important conversations."

"I can just about imagine what they talked about. Things I should have discussed with her, but I think she listened better to Leah than she would have listened to me. I'm glad the hospital let her coach. They had some questions about her age, but both Hal and I agreed and signed permission, and the hospital obliged." She paused and then said, "Yah, Hal and I were a little weak on the birds and bees lecture. Now Sherrie has gotten the benefit as well. Those two had quite the conversations behind locked bedroom doors the other night."

As we stepped onto the obstetrics ward, I felt giddy, "I wonder what the baby looks like."

"Especially since we don't know who the father is," said Connie. She gave me a serious look.

When we walked toward the room, the nurse stopped us. "Leah is breast feeding."

She heard us out in the hall. "Let them come in, nurse, they're my partners."

"Well, all right, but we usually limit visits to family."

"But I don't have any family or husband. I told you I was raped."

"Well, all right, if you are fine with that. I guess it's all right." The nurse stepped aside to let us in.

"Partners?" Connie asked. "What's that all about?"

Leah laughed, "Did you want me to say that I'm your dish-washing slave? 'Partners' sounds more elegant," she laughed. "And 'slave' could be misconstrued."

"Thanks," we said together.

We looked at the baby. "She looks just like you," I said.

"Yah, now I'll never know who the father is. I was hoping to be able to tell by looking at the little bugger," Leah blurted out. "Then suing the guy for child support. I still think it was probably Jim Toumala who…"

"Let it drop," said Connie.

Leah blushed, "I guess whichever guy got me pregnant has totally recessive genes. I agree, I think Rachel looks just like me. Isn't it exciting?" We both gave her a hug.

Connie patted Leah's belly as she tried to suck it in. "Looks like you're getting your girlish figure back."

"Not exactly, look at all these ugly stretch marks," Leah pulled aside her gown and jiggled her flaccid belly, "and it's all flabby. I guess I'm destined to be a single mom forever. Who's going to date me? I can never wear a bikini again with a belly like this." Rachel quit sucking Leah's breast and fell asleep. "But I sure like breastfeeding," she said. "It's a lot more fun than being fondled by some guy trying to get into my pants."

"Some day you might find a guy who doesn't care about bikinis who really loves you despite your stretch marks, and then you might enjoy the attention again."

"I doubt it," Leah said, "but I suppose I should keep my options open and not get all fat and ugly."

"Have you told your parents?" asked Connie.

"No, and I don't intend to. I told the nurse not to announce the birth in the newspaper either. Let them find out on their own. They're the ones who kicked me out of the house. Why should they know that they have a lovely, beautiful granddaughter?" She tickled Rachel under the chin. She awoke and cooed. "Who's so cute."

"Don't let your bitterness eat you up, Leah," Connie said. She turned towards me, "Becky Jean would love to have her parents care about her. I'm sure that your parents care, too."

"I doubt it."

We sat on Leah's bed as the new mother twirled Rachel's hair between our fingers.

"Isn't she precious?" Leah grabbed my arm and squeezed so hard it hurt.

"What?"

"Thank you for talking me into keeping her, Becky Jean. It would have been such a mistake to abort her. I will never forget that talk we had."

"She is precious," I said and blushed.

"I want you to be her godmother. In a sense, you gave her life too."

I choked, "That is too great an honor…" I choked on my words, but Leah's eyes were pleading. "All right, I accept, but I don't know what I have to offer her."

The nurse interrupted with a vase of flowers. "These just came." She placed the flowers on the window sill and pulled a card out of the middle of the display and smiled as she handed it to Leah. "You must have some male admirer."

Leah opened the card and laughed. "It's from Bert Lloyd."

"Is he a special friend?" asked the nurse.

"No," all three of us said in unison.

"He's my boss," said Leah.

"Wow," said the nurse as she turned to leave. "Not many bosses send flowers."

• • •

Back at work the next day, in my role as assistant manager, I checked on Rick Johnson, the new dishwasher. He arrived promptly at 12:30. I oriented him to the dishwashing machine and the process required by the Minnesota Health Department. He didn't say much but seemed to be listening. My speech reminded me of the one Bert had given me that day I dropped into Cotton. I finished the instructions with, "Any questions?"

"How's Leah doing?"

"Baby and mother are both healthy. Why do you ask?"

"I was only a sophomore when she graduated, but…I don't know, I guess she was the best cheerleader Cotton High School ever had. I felt bad when those guys took advantage of her. We all heard about it at school."

"Do you know who got her pregnant?"

"Nobody seems to know, but rumors around the school are that Jim Toumala knocked her up. By the way, did you see in the paper that he got picked up for drunk driving? The judge sent him to spin dry."

"Spin dry?"

"Yah, he had to go for a month at the alcohol treatment center. What a loser!" Rick started stacking the voluminous numbers of plates into the rack. I stood there watching him, making sure that he was doing it correctly. "Another DUI and he has to go to jail for three months. That's what the newspaper said."

"Oh." I watched him put a cycle through. He seemed to know what he was doing. He held the rinse until it reached 180 degrees, just as I had instructed him, so I backed out the door. "Come and get me if you have any questions."

"I will."

After that, I started perusing the *Duluth News Tribune* that came to the restaurant every day to see if Jim Toumala's name appeared in the back pages where the court reports were hidden. A couple months later, there was his name: another DUI. The Saint Louis County jail had a new occupant.

Chapter 17
Jailbird

A telephone call revealed that the Saint Louis county jail is only open for visitors on weekends and Tuesdays, so after picking up the supplies for the restaurant I checked the time. There was still an hour left of visitation, so I headed for the jail.

"I would like to see Jim Toumala."

After viewing my photo identification, I was instructed by the jailer, if that was his proper title, "You are not allowed to use tobacco or eat or drink during the visit. You don't chew gum, do you?"

"No, never have."

"Good. If you don't follow the rules, you will be asked to leave and will have no further visitation privileges." He showed me a locker where I could deposit my purse and then directed me to go through the metal detector.

"You have twenty minutes."

I was led to the room, and Jim entered. He had a quizzical look as he saw who wanted to visit him. His address was formal. "Ms. Rebecca Gottwald, the jailer told me that you wanted to visit me. I had no idea who you were, so I agreed." A look of recognition came over his face. "Oh, I know who you are now. You're the waitress at the Lloyd's Restaurant, aren't you? Me and my friends were there last summer. That's where I've seen you before."

"Yes, I am a waitress at Lloyd's Restaurant. Well, actually, assistant manager now."

"You must have just started when we went there last summer. I emptied a whole bottle of ketchup on my fries." He laughed at his antics.

I hated when the teens did that, but I ignored the comment. "Yes, Jim, you may call me 'Becky Jean' and forget the Ms. Gottwald formality."

He had blond hair and fine facial features. A tattoo on his right arm of a naked woman contrasted with his pale Finnish complexion. The guard who accompanied him set him down in the chair and stepped back toward the wall.

"Who are you, some do-gooder?" I thought he was going to spit at me the way the words seethed through his teeth. "You must be Leah's friend here to torment me."

"Neither."

"So why are you here to see me, Becky Jean?" he snarled my name. "Did I forget to tip you?"

I ignored his sarcasm. "I read in the newspaper that you were here and I just came to see how are you getting along."

He laughed, "Longest I've been sober in a long time. Since junior high school, I think."

"You went to an alcohol rehabilitation program. You weren't sober there?"

"Sort of. I got kicked out because one of the guys I met there snuck in some vodka. We didn't think we'd get caught. But of course…"

"So then what happened?"

"The judge thought that this would be a better place for me to sober up. It was quite a scene at the center. Two armed policemen suddenly appeared one morning and took me away.

"I guess I just love to make stupid decisions, Becky Jean." He coughed into his hand then combed it through his blond hair. "I'm amazed you, of all people, came to see me. No one else has, not even my parents or my alleged girlfriend." He hung his head. "She sent a letter telling me that she is done with me and going with someone else now." A tear formed in his eye, he wiped it quickly away and snuffled his nose. "I suppose you know that I'm the one who *fucked*—" The guard approached. He whispered, "Screwed Leah. Did you come here to lecture me about that?"

"Yes, I know what happened. Leah told me from her perspective. And no, I am not here to lay a guilt trip on you."

He laughed. "I got her good and drunk and then…" He turned to look at the guard. "Screwed her as many times as I wanted that night. She didn't even know it. But I didn't mean to get her pregnant. I just was having fun." He cupped his hands. "She has great—" He must have seen my disapproval and broke off his sentence. "I suppose that is inappropriate. Sorry, I'm used to just talking to guys here in the jail." He sighed, "Afterwards, I thought she would just get an abortion and everything would be fine. I hear she decided to keep the baby." He rubbed his hands together before he looked up at me. He was staring right into my eyes. "There is no way I want to be a father. Why didn't she just get an abortion?" He was about to slam his fist on the table but stopped mid-air after another look to the guard. His open palm drifted onto the table. "The only time I am free from guilt for the choices I've made in my life is when I'm drunk and having sex, Becky Jean. I can't help it. I feel normal when I'm drunk and screwing. Can't wait to get out of here and have a nice comforting fifth of whiskey and fuck some cute cunt. Oops, that's jail talk, sorry." He saw the guard take a step toward him.

I shared with him how beautiful his daughter was, how happy Leah was with her child, and how she had decided to resolve her anger toward him. As he listened, the obnoxious disrespect in his demeanor seemed to melt away.

"But I'll never be able to see my daughter, will I?"

"Probably not." I took a deep breath, not sure what to say. "That's Leah's decision, not mine to make. Consequences are harsh, Jim. Leah doesn't ever want to see you again, but there is forgiveness if you search in the right places. Alcohol and meaningless sex are not those places."

I asked about his family, but he was unwilling to share since none of his family had come to visit him. I gave him another opportunity to think of what he was going to do upon release. His coarse manner seemed to have softened. He talked, I listened. Then the officer in the corner signaled that time was up. "I'll tell you what, Jim, any time you stop by at Bert's, if I'm waitressing, I'll give you a free cup of coffee." I stood at the officer's motion. "I've got to go now. Remember to look in the right places for forgiveness."

"Thanks for being my one and only visitor, Becky Jean. I will never forget this time with you. You're the only one who apparently cares about me. I'm sorry I was crude." He stood and the guard led him away.

I went back through the security system, obtained my purse from the locker, and felt the freedom of leaving the jail behind me. Climbing into the van outside in the parking lot, I wondered if I had made Jim's problems better or worse with my visit. Maybe I would never know.

Chapter 18
Fishing Opener

A dense cloud cover and a cold wind blowing from the north reminded the Cotton crowd of February even though it was the middle of May. At least there was no snow. It was going to be a blustery opening for fishing season. Despite the weather, the restaurant was full. Connie and I were both dashing around taking orders, and Bert was helping Ron at the grill. We opened at five o'clock in the morning on opening day so the fishermen could get a hearty breakfast and still be out on the lake before the sunrise awakened the fish to the fishermen's tricks. They ate hearty and tipped well.

I laughed at the comical hats the fishermen were wearing and the lures they had stuck in their brims. "Nice lures," I commented to a group all wearing such paraphernalia as I set down the coffee cups, filled them, and prepared to take their orders.

The nearest customer took off his hat and held the brim so I could appreciate the lure. "My lucky lure," he said. "I caught a fifteen-pound Northern Pike with this one and retired it." The other fishermen smiled and ordered hash browns, cheese omelets, and rye toast.

"Do you need catsup with that?"

"Steak sauce if you have it," they chorused.

"Heinz 57 coming right up."

Connie and I rushed around serving and taking orders, filling the coffee pot innumerable times. I could tell by the way she was scurrying around that she was delighted with the business, but we didn't have time to talk. But by nine o'clock, the restaurant had cleared. "I'm exhausted," Connie said, "I feel like I've done a full day's work already."

"You have. Just look at your tip jar. It's overflowing."

She smiled. "Do you mind if I take a break now? Then you can take an early break too."

"Sure, there's only the couple in the booth, and you already served them. I'm sure all the serious fishermen are out on the water already." Connie laughed and went to the break room. I started brewing another pot of coffee in anticipation of our regular non-fishing customers.

A large SUV with a glitzy boat on a four-wheel trailer drove right up to the window in the disability space. A red Hummer parked beside it in the other disability space. By the way the four men were dressed, I guessed that they were from Minneapolis. Their clothes seemed too fancy for fishing. The three from the SUV walked in and asked for a booth.

"Take any one you like," I answered. Their shirts were pressed; they were smooth-shaven and wearing what looked like brand new hats. I looked at their boots and smiled as the shine of new polish reflected the ceiling lights. My eye caught the back of the fourth man as he inspected his vehicle before coming into the restaurant.

"Four coffees and separate checks," the youngest said.

The oldest, with gray hair and wire-rimmed glasses waved at me, "No, madam, just one check." He turned to the other two seated in the booth. "I'll pay for this round, guys. You've worked hard for me this year. You've all made the firm a lot of money. Just don't order the most expensive thing on the menu." The other two laughed as I distributed four menus.

The fourth man entered and went straight to the restroom. I turned, "I'll take your orders when you've all had a chance to look over the menu."

"I'll have the special," the older man said.

"We will too," said the other two. "Whatever the boss wants is good enough for the rest of us."

"And Max will probably have the special as well," said the youngest, "as soon as he gets done primping." The boss ignored the comment, but the other two giggled.

I left to put in the orders with Ron and then brought more coffee for the elderly couple in the back booth. Standing behind the counter, I watched the north wind whipping the trees outside. I pictured white-capped waves thrashing the fishermen. The walleyes would be hungry but all on the south end of the lakes. Lazy as they were, they would be enjoying the food blown to them, hungry from the long winter and laying their eggs on the rocky reefs. I had read about fishing, I just had never done it.

"Orders ready," Ron yelled out.

I gathered the four specials, amazed how I had learned to balance so may plates in the year I had worked, and headed for the city fishermen's table. As I put down the plates, the Hummer man laid down his Wall Street Journal. "Max," I gasped and caught his plate just before it dropped.

His smile snarled. "Becky Jean, how good to see you."

"Anyone want more coffee?" I interrupted and went to get the pot.

As I walked away I heard everything they were saying. "You know her?" the boss asked.

"From the university, down in Iowa," Max said, "I just didn't expect to ever see her again."

"Old girlfriend?" the others teased.

"Hardly," Max said, "but it's a long, sordid story. She's my best friend's ex-wife." He resumed reading the paper, and I was thankful.

My face flushed, and I went in the back to see if Connie could relieve me. "Connie, can you take over, I feel nauseated."

"My break isn't up. Are you sick?"

"I'll be all right. There are four Minneapolis types that came in. They all ordered the special and I served them, but they might need more coffee. The older couple is just about ready to leave."

"Becky Jean, what's wrong? You look ashen."

"I'll be all right. Just give me a minute. I think I am going to faint." I sat down and put my head down between my knees and told myself to breathe slowly and not to start retching. All the lewd jokes Max had told me in the days leading up to my wedding slammed into my brain. *What was I going to do? Should I leave? Go to Canada?* When my heart rate slowed and I no longer felt faint, I went in the back and slammed some dishes through the washing cycle. Morning dishes were done when Rick appeared for his shift.

"Hey, thanks Becky Jean, but if you keep doing that, Bert will think I'm not needed. I'm enjoying the extra cash."

I slumped on the stool, "Sorry, Rick. I was having an anxiety attack and needed to take it out on the dishes."

Connie appeared. "Lots of customers, Becky Jean. I need your help."

I looked up at her and wiped my eyes. "Are they gone?"

"You look like a basset hound that just had its bone taken away. The stock brokers playing fishermen are gone. They left a tip for you, ten percent to the penny. The one guy, Max, asked where you lived. I didn't tell him. Who is that guy anyway? He's obnoxious."

I opened my mouth. Nothing came out. I couldn't even breathe. I hyperventilated and had to put my head down between my knees again. I focused to slow my breathing and the sensation resolved. I stood and grabbed the table for support.

"Tell me about this later. Back to work. We got customers, Assistant Manager."

It was a comfort to serve the regular customers. A few fishermen came back for lunch but hadn't caught much. "Three foot white-caps," an older fisherman in a faded baseball hat complained. "We saw some guys in a bigger boat hauling in a few fish, but we weren't stable enough. The white-caps came right over the gunnels, so we came in. Almost didn't make it back to the landing. Hope the wind settles down this afternoon or we're done." He smiled through his weathered wrinkles. "But it sure works up an appetite," he said as he put in his order.

I jumped every time the door opened the rest of the day, expecting to see Max again, but by closing time he hadn't appeared. I grabbed my chest, still in a panic. For the first time since I started working at the restaurant, I was glad the shift was over. I headed for the back door.

Chapter 19
Haunted by the Past

"All right my friend with the secret past, spill it," Connie grabbed my elbow and jerked me back as I tried to leave.

"You're hurting me," I complained, hoping it would distract her.

She loosened her grip but still held me. "Who is this Max fellow?" Connie's dark eyes captured me. "Tell me now. You know I will get it out of you eventually."

"I don't want to talk about it. It's none of your business."

She grabbed my face with her other hand. "I don't recall asking you whether you wanted to talk about it. This Max guy disrupted my break. That makes it my business. You owe me big time, Becky Jean."

"All right, if you promise not to tell Bert," I pleaded as tears dripped down my cheeks and on to her hand. "Do I have to?"

"You have to. I'm going home to two teenagers, and you made me miss my downtime."

I sat down at the break table, and Connie sat on a stool across from me. Her brown eyes seemed to burn in my face.

"Max was the best man at my wedding."

"You're married?"

"I don't think so, but I'm not sure. I thought I was, but maybe I'm not anymore. Max called me 'his best friend's ex,' so I guess I'm not married anymore. Maybe my husband divorced me uncontested, something like that."

Rick Johnson finished the last load of dishes and waved goodbye, "See you ladies. Don't fight."

"We're not fighting, for your information, Rick." Connie said as she waved him off. She turned and seemed more intense. "This I got to hear," she said. "Go ahead. Bert went home out the front door and now Rich has left so, the guys are gone. It's just us girls."

I quivered as if a blast of ice had hit me in the chest. I wavered because I didn't want to tell her. I didn't even want to hear my explanation. Connie's wood-splitting grip on my arm increased, so I started my story. Connie relaxed her grip. "Maxwell Holter was the best man at my wedding. He was a business administration major at the University of Dubuque. I didn't like him from the moment we met. He introduced himself to me in one of my classes, freshman English, I think. He sat behind me calling me the 'cute cunt' during lectures. The guy I married, Keith Slagg, was one of the students at the Wartburg Theological Seminary where my father is a professor in Dubuque. How those two became friends, I'll never know."

Connie's eyebrows rose, but she didn't interrupt. "My father, the Reverend," the sound of the word made me want to spit, "chose Keith to be my husband because he was so 'spiritual.' He got straight A's in all his seminary classes. My father was impressed. He seemed all right at first, very polite. My parents kept inviting him over for dinner. I didn't have any objections. He was always appropriate in his conversation and seemed nice in our house. In my German family, you do what father says. Besides, I was focused on getting through classes at the university. So when my parents insisted that I marry him, I agreed."

My eye spurted tears, and I wiped them with the soiled sleeve of my uniform. "When I found out that Max was his best friend and that he was going to be best man, I considered it a warning. I objected, asked my parents to check Keith out more carefully, telling them that I didn't like his friend, but my parents said that I had made a commitment and besides I was marrying Keith not his friend. I complained, 'We're not married yet. I haven't made any commitment. Are we even engaged?' It made no difference to them. I was concerned. How could Max be Keith's best friend and Keith be so 'spiritual?' They seemed so different, opposites."

I started to stammer. "But now I understand. They aren't different at all."

"You're mumbling. Speak up. So what happened?"

"All during the reception, he wanted to dance with me and kept saying…" My eyes pleaded with Connie not to go on.

"Spit it out, girl. You can't keep this poison inside."

I sighed, "Obscene stuff like...I don't want to say it, but he wanted to have sex with me. Imagine, on my wedding night." The memories felt like a knife in my chest. I couldn't say more. I sobbed. Connie held me, and I soaked the shoulder of her uniform with my tears.

She braced me up against the wall, "So, I still don't understand why you don't know if you're married."

"It was pretty awful that night after we got to the hotel. It was a nice place. The wedding suite was decorated in red and white. There was a nice living room, a breakfast nook, and a view over St. Louis where we had our honeymoon. I had read some articles in Cosmo to prepare for the night. You know, about how I was supposed to get him excited about me. So I started to undress." I burst into tears again.

"What happened?"

"He said, and I quote, 'Your breasts are all droopy, and your scar is disgusting. You're damaged goods. I didn't agree to marry a monstrosity like you.' Then he went in the bathroom and masturbated and locked me out of the bedroom."

"What? That's disgusting. You're a little skinny, but you are certainly not a monster. Why would he say that?"

I unbuttoned my uniform and showed her my scar. "I had kidney cancer when I was ten years old. The surgery saved my life but left me with this scar from back to front."

"He doesn't deserve you. What's wrong with that guy?"

"He said that since I was damaged, my father should have told him. He would never have married me if he had known."

"You want to see the stretch marks my two daughters and a stillbirth gave me," Connie asked. She didn't wait for an answer, but opened her uniform and slid down her underwear to show me. "And my breasts are pretty droopy too after breastfeeding those two hungry girls. Now that's disgusting, but that doesn't stop Hal when I'm trying to get to sleep after a hard day at work. He's all over me three to five times a week," she smiled, "although I do enjoy it."

I held up my hands to have her stop. She hugged me, "I'm sorry. That was inappropriate."

"It's all right. That's what I longed for that night. I'm afraid Keith wanted a perfect porcelain doll to play with, not a companion wife. I was just a broken doll to be discarded."

"You still haven't explained how come you don't know if you're married or not," Connie said as she buttoned up her uniform.

"I left him. I have no idea what happened after that, but Max called me his friend's ex-wife, so I guess we're divorced or something. We never had sex."

"Oh, you poor thing," Connie hugged me again, and it felt so comforting, something I had needed for a long time. She massaged my back with hands that had become strong from serving thousands of customers.

"Thanks for listening to me. I didn't mean to bother you with my problems. I'm sorry I short-changed your break, Connie. I'll make it up to you."

"You don't have to make it up to me. You're a precious person. I just can't understand why anyone would treat you like that. Do you want to come to our house tonight?"

"Thanks but no, I need to be alone and just sift through some of my thoughts and feelings. Telling someone has been such a release, but it brought back a lot of horrible memories."

We walked out the back door and I locked it. Connie climbed in her pickup. I scanned the parking lot as she left. The sun floated behind the trees producing an earie light. I saw no one and headed for my coop. A long hot shower, peace and quiet was all I needed.

Chapter 20
Assault and Arson

Max sprang from around the corner of the coop as I tried to unlock my door. He grabbed my uniform, tearing the top button. He grabbed my hair and gave me a swift whack across the face with the back of his hand. I was no match for his six foot, muscular frame. He pushed me off the steps onto the gravel. I fell backwards and then tried to get up and run as he backed me towards the restaurant. Then I noticed a pile of trash spilled out of the garbage cans. Rick would never do that. He was careful when he emptied the garbage.

Max grabbed my arms and spun me around, smacking me up against the building, twisting my arms behind my back, and grinding my face into the brickwork. With a massive shove, he body-slammed me into the wall of the restaurant. "We have some things to talk about, girl."

"Max, let go of me or I'll scream." I tried to wriggle out of his grasp, but he was too strong.

He laughed, yanking my hair, "And who will hear you? Nobody lives in this god-forsaken wilderness. Do they actually call this a town? Unincorporated I would guess. Population: one scrawny cunt. There aren't even any fish in the lakes around here."

He jerked my arms tighter, straining the muscles in my shoulders as he slammed me a couple more times against the brick wall of the restaurant. "Now just listen for a moment." I felt the blood dribbling down my cheek. "I should fuck you. That's what you deserve." He lifted up my skirt, tore my underwear down my legs, grabbed my buttocks and tore at my skin with his fingernails.

I screamed.

He laughed, grabbed a rag from his pocket, and stuffed it in my mouth. It smelled and tasted of gasoline. He hit me in the back with his knee. "Just listen. I'm not going to rape you; you're not worth it. Besides, Keith said that you're pretty ugly without clothes. You don't even have decent breasts to fondle." He laughed at his joke.

I stopped struggling. It was no use. The horror of my time with Keith swam through my brain. Besides, as I resisted, he only scratched more of my face onto the brickwork. He was strong, twice my weight, and there was no one to help even if I screamed.

"I'm listening," I squeaked out from around the rag. The fumes were making me light-headed.

"Good. Keith wants his rings back."

He couldn't understand my response and took the rag out of my mouth and twisted my face toward him with the grip of my hair, crushing me against the wall with his body weight. "Where are the rings?" He put a factory-shiny hunting knife to my neck just nicking my skin. I went limp. "Where are the rings?"

My nostrils flared as I stared into his eyes. I felt new strength at the horror I had endured on my wedding night. "Max, the rings are mine. It is the only thing I have from my miserable marriage to Keith, and I'm keeping them. He burned all my clothes and anything else I owned. I should get some kind of compensation."

"You're not married, you never were. Keith petitioned to have your marriage annulled. He said you wouldn't even suck his cock." His grimace felt poisonous. "Well, that isn't exactly how he explained it to the judge. The respondent, you, never showed up to object, hah, hah." He wrenched my arm. "Keith told the judge you refused to have sex with him, so the marriage was never consummated. The judge saw no reason to object, so you were annulled." He spit the last word in my face.

"I didn't refuse to have sex with him. He locked me out of the bedroom." I was furious now and tried to kick him with my heel.

He wrenched me to the ground. "Keith wants the rings back, you stupid bitch. That's all."

"I don't have them here." He let up some on his grip. "You think I'm stupid?"

"Then where are they?" He picked me off the ground, spun me around, backed me into the wall, and scraped the blood off my cheek with his hunting knife. He cut off the next two buttons of my uniform, smearing blood across my chest. My knees were shaking. I felt faint. He took a paper out of his pocket and stuffed it into my bra, fondling my breast in the process. "Your boobs are wimpy but nice enough. Keith should have fucked you at least once."

He pinched my nipple, twisting it until it bled. I winced in pain and fell to my knees. "Now send the rings to that address within thirty days and you will never see me again. Or if you don't, you are in big trouble, girl. I'll be back with Keith next time."

He kicked me in the belly, and I crumpled on the ground. He lit a cigarette and lit the oily rag that had been in my mouth and threw it into the garbage he had piled against the restaurant. It blazed. "It's amazing what a little gasoline can do to get rid of garbage. You're the next garbage I'll get rid of if those rings aren't in the mail soon," he said as he ran through the pine tree wind break in back of the coop and took off through the brush in his red Hummer.

In spite of the pain in my belly, I stood up. The threat of the garbage burning minimized my pain. The northwest wind had bellowed it into a blazing fire. I ran and unlocked the restaurant and pulled the fire alarm. I grabbed the fire extinguisher from the kitchen wall and ran back out. The fire was crawling up the brick wall where Max had thrown more gasoline. I sprayed the base first and then up the wall. *If it gets behind the brickwork, the whole restaurant will go,* I thought as I sprayed the foam. I inhaled the acrid smoke and coughed. My eyes blurred. I couldn't breathe. The smoke became so intense that I couldn't see the fire, but I kept spraying, using the whole canister. I heard a car behind me and screamed, "Leave me alone, Max." Then everything went black.

• • •

I regained consciousness in Officer Davis's arms on the porch of my coop. The volunteer fire department was all over the parking lot. I craned my neck to look at the restaurant. The fire was out.

"Who did this?" Officer Davis asked.

"Max Holter. He's driving a red Hummer, probably heading south to Minneapolis."

"Stay with her, Rolly. I'll call this in."

Rolly cradled me in his lap. "You're breathing better, Becky Jean. You saved the restaurant with your quick work. Boy, we haven't had an arsonist in these parts for years. What got into that guy?"

"He was threatening me."

"Trying to rape you or something?"

"No," I said but felt my underwear at my knees. I thought through what Max had done. "He said that I wasn't worth raping."

"A pretty girl like you?" He brushed the ashes out of my hair. "I'm sorry. I didn't mean the way that sounded."

"That's all right, Rolly. Can I sit up now?"

He helped me sit up. I stood and turning for modesty, pulled up my underwear. Then I scanned the damage. The wall was black where the fire had started, but it didn't look like it had done much damage. Officer Davis returned.

"Is the restaurant all right?" I craned my neck to ask.

"It doesn't even smell of smoke inside. Your quick work saved the day. I have an APB out for a red Hummer driven by a Max Holter. You don't know the license number, I don't suppose, but we can get it if it is registered in his name."

"It was a Minnesota license," I said with a cough. "I think he works as a stock broker in Minneapolis. The number was…I can't remember, but it had a 6 and a 9 in it. I saw it this morning when he was parked outside the restaurant, in the handicapped space."

"That helps," he said and slid into the open door of his squad car.

"The next thing is to get you to the hospital," Rolly said. His gentle words calmed me. "You were overwhelmed from smoke inhalation."

"I'm fine." I coughed a few more times, spitting out black mucous. "No need to go to the hospital. I faint easily. I'm fine."

"You're sure?"

I got my bearings and jumped around in front of the coop. "See? No permanent damage."

I stumbled. Rolly caught me and sat me back down on the step as Bert drove up. He ran over to me. "What happened?"

Officer Davis became official and explained the situation.

"Arson, huh, never had that problem before." He ran to inspect the damage.

Officer Davis put a hand on his shoulder. "Don't go in there yet, Bert. Let the firemen do their job. Just wait. There first report is that there is no damage inside the restaurant."

Bert sat down on the step beside me. I could feel him breathing in short, agitated gasps. As we sat in silence watching the volunteer fireman follow their protocol, I wondered what he was thinking. *Was I a liability to his business? Was he going to fire me? Would I have to leave town? I supposed that I would have to send back the rings.* The crinkled paper in my bra itched.

The fire chief walked over. "Fire's out, Bert. I'll leave one man here to watch, but I don't see any possibility of a start-up. Good thing Becky Jean responded as quickly as she did. She saved your restaurant."

I tried to look up, but I couldn't. *Save it? Why, I almost destroyed it.*

Most of the volunteers climbed on Cotton's one fire truck and drove off. I had no idea they even had a fire truck. It must be parked in someone's garage was all I could figure out. Officer Davis followed in their wake. Rolly stood, "I guess you two have some things to talk about. I got to go, but if you need anything, let me know, Becky Jean."

"Thanks, Rolly, for being here for me."

"The guy wanted to rape her, Bert," Rolly said as turned to get into his truck. "Look at the missing buttons on her uniform."

Bert shifted his weight on the step. He folded my uniform over my exposed bra. "I don't mean to pry into your affairs, Becky Jean."

Here it comes, I'm fired. Was there any way I could make it up to him? He had been so kind. I determined right then to send the rings back to Kevin. Now that I was discovered, I felt doomed. My parents would know where I was and…I had no other choice.

"You know that I have respected your privacy, even when you didn't know if you were married or divorced." Bert said. He paused. The silence was painful. "Even when you were bonded, I didn't pry into your affairs. But I have to ask, not knowing your history, could this happen again? This restaurant is my whole life."

I sighed and looked up as two mallards flew overhead across the evening sky. I smeared the soot off my face as I wiped my eyes on my sleeve. My uniform was a mess. *Did Bert see my blood stains? Could he tell that Max had wiped his knife across my chest?* As my tears dripped down my soiled uniform, I noticed that even they were black. "The arsonist," I paused; the word sounded so evil, "was the best man at my wedding." It seemed like that explained everything, but Bert's eyes showed no understanding so I continued, "He had no idea where I lived but came north to go fishing with his stock broker partners. I served them while Connie was on break. They each had the special." I sobbed, realizing that fact was irrelevant, but as a waitress, I couldn't help it.

He put his arm over my shoulder, and I took a deep breath. Our eyes were fixed on the black smear across the brickwork. "He came back after fishing today and was waiting for me behind the coop. Connie and I locked up, and after she drove out of the parking lot, he sprang out from behind the pine trees behind the coop. He drove that red Hummer. Maybe you saw it today?" I pointed to where the vehicle had been hidden. "He said that my ex-husband…"

He turned and stared at me. His lips tightened as he listened. I was thankful that he wasn't interrupting. "This part is confusing. He said our marriage was annulled. So I guess I was never married, therefore I'm not divorced." I winced, "So that part of my application is in error."

"Forget your application. You're so honest." He shook his head. "My question is: why did he do this, Becky Jean?"

"My annulled husband," I didn't know what else to call him, "wants my engagement and wedding ring back."

I coughed and broke into uncontrollable sobbing. Bert gave me his handkerchief. I coughed up black stuff, turned red in the face, and started coughing again. "Keep the handkerchief," he said. I thanked him with a nod.

"I put the rings in a safety deposit box at the bank." The tears dripped down my cheeks. "It is the only thing I have of any value in my whole life. I should be able to keep it for all the grief he put me through. We hadn't been married even a week, and he burned all my possessions, everything I owned other than what was in my backpack. He must have missed that in his fury. You remember my backpack when I came into your office the day you hired me."

"Yes, I remember the backpack." He rubbed my back like no father had ever done. I could feel the tenderness as his gentle fingers massaged my tight muscles. I had never felt such compassion.

I stiffened up and he turned away as I pulled the address out of my bra. I glanced at it. I didn't recognize the address. "Some place in Ames, Iowa, that's where I am supposed to send the rings." I turned to Bert and used his hand-kerchief to smear the grime around my cheeks. "I don't want you to lose the restaurant on my account. Do you want me to leave? I'm sure I can find a job somewhere else if you write me a letter of recommendation." I wasn't sure that I could find another job, but it was what I needed to say.

"Let's see if they catch him first," said Bert. "Then you can decide what to do with the rings. No, I do not want you to leave. You are a good employee, Becky Jean." He scuffed his heel in the dirt and whispered, "You remind me of my wife."

"You aren't going to fire me then?" He shook his head no. "Oh, thank you, Bert. I'm sorry I got my uniform all dirty. I'm not sure it will come clean." I held the top of my uniform together approximating the missing buttons. "Max cut the buttons off. I don't know where they landed."

He stood and helped me up. "Uniforms are replaceable. You aren't." He left me standing, holding onto the step rail, and walked over to discuss the fire with the remaining fireman.

"Am I excused?" I asked.

He didn't answer. I turned to go into my coop. When my hand touched the doorknob, I cringed. The key was still in the lock. As I turned the lock, I expecting someone to jump out at me again. I closed my eyes and steadied my shaking legs. I'm desperate for a shower, I told myself. I suddenly wished the hot water heater was bigger.

I closed the door behind me and stripped off my clothes, bundling them up I threw them in the garbage. There was no use wasting detergent trying to clean them. They reeked. The Ames, Iowa address fluttered to the floor. I picked it up and put it under my pillow.

The shower felt good, but as I washed my breasts, I again felt the pain of Max's hand fondling me. There was a large bruise and crusted blood where he had squeezed and twisted my nipple. Why hadn't he raped me? Was I really that ugly? I used lots of soap to wash out the fingernail scratches he left across my bottom. I probably had bruises there as well, but I couldn't contort in a way to see them.

I thought about the effect on the restaurant. I was a threat to Bert's business. Would Max be caught? No matter, I felt trapped. My coop, which had been my cozy sanctuary, was no longer safe.

Chapter 21
Fishing

When Rick left to join his father's construction crew, Leah was ready to come back to work. Shawnee was done with school, so she volunteered to babysit during the summer. She passed her driver's license test after hours of practice under Hal's instruction. Well, Hal called it instruction. Shawnee had another word for it. But with her license in hand, she offered to bring little Rachel to the restaurant during Leah's breaks so Leah could continue breastfeeding. Ron and Bert were informed that when the door was closed to the dishwashing room, they were excluded because Leah was breastfeeding and needed the privacy. But sometimes she sat in the back booth where no one could see her just to get away from the isolation of the washing machine room. I warned her that her behavior was inappropriate, but most of the time I understood her need to get away from work and be a mother. Besides, no one could tell that she was breastfeeding in that booth. I still didn't approve, but compassion dissuaded me from making her stop. Besides, she flipped a diaper over her exposed breast for modesty.

One beautiful summer day, several weeks later, the sun streaming through the windows was so bright that it made me sneeze. I hadn't heard anything from Max and was grateful for it. I knew that Bert was involved in some legal aspects of the arson but he kept me out of the loop. That morning he called me into his office. "Good news, Becky Jean," Bert said as I started the coffee percolating.

"What's that? I got customers to serve. Connie's not here yet." I turned my washed palms outward with my hands on my hips.

"They caught the arsonist. The state police just called. I don't think he'll be doing that again."

"That's great news," I said, but I was thinking, *Max is caught, but what is Keith going to do? He'll know where I am.*

He lowered his voice, "Keep the rings, Becky Jean. You deserve them."

"Yes, boss." I ran up front to check on the customers. Several orders later, I stopped to take a breath and look over the crowd. Roger Halstrom was sitting at the counter. He picked up his cup to show me that it was empty. He impressed me. Not only was he handsome, but he was sincere and polite. I never heard him tell any coarse jokes or use profanity. He was quiet, so it had taken a long time for me to get to know him.

"More coffee, Roger?"

"Thanks, Becky Jean."

I poured the coffee and checked to see if there was anyone else who needed more. Roger was talking with Frank Johannsen. This coming school year he would be one of Sherrie's teachers. "Don't you have a couple years of college, Becky Jean?" Frank asked.

"Three years. I was majoring in sociology; minor in business administration. Perfect for a waitress job, don't you think? Only one year to go for my degree. When I get enough tips, I'll return to the university. Maybe go to University of Minnesota in Duluth if they accept my Iowa credits. Why, are you feeling generous today?" I gave him a pleading smile.

He handed me a five dollar bill, "Toward your education."

I snatched the bill and tucked it in my pocket. "Thanks. I'll fill your coffee cup any time if it will get me back to the university sooner." A truck driver sat down one stool over. I went to take his order but kept one ear to Frank and Roger's conversation.

"I got a couple days off this week, no cement to haul," said Roger. "I sure would like to go fishing. Now I just happen to know that a school teacher with three months off in the summer knows where every good fishing hole is in this county."

"Why don't you go up to Whiteface Lake? I went there with my kids last week, and we caught our limit of walleyes, plus a few pike."

"Sounds great. You want to go with me?"

"I can't. I'm heading up to Canada. Well, actually to Lac Seul, Ontario, to go fishing. I take the whole family there every summer during this week. We have reservations at the Silver Water Wheel Lodge."

"I sure would like to go fishing with someone. It gets pretty lonely if the fish aren't biting."

"Why don't you take some pretty young lady?"

"Now, Frank, you know that since I had my surgery there hasn't been a lady from Wisconsin to Dakota interested in dating me."

Frank slapped him on the back. "You're a fine young man. There must be some pretty young woman that doesn't care that you're shooting blanks."

"Well, I haven't found her." Roger sipped his coffee.

"I'll go fishing with you," I said. "Mr. Lloyd said that I could have a day off sometime this week. When do you want to go?" I filled his coffee cup as he set it down.

Roger looked at me. "A sweet-faced girl like you would go fishing with the likes of me?"

"I sure would. I've always wanted to go fishing but never got the chance. Will you put the worm on my hook?"

Roger laughed. "Becky Jean, around here we fish for walleyes. We use minnows and leeches, not worms, at least not this time of year, and we use jigs not hooks. Where did you grow up anyway?"

"I've never been fishing, but where I grew up I heard about worms on hooks. I don't think that they were fishing for walleyes, though. I think they were after pan fish like Sunfish and Bluegills. So, do I get to go with you or not?" Bert came around the corner. "Decide quickly. I don't want Bert to fire me for fraternizing with the customers."

Roger stood with a big smile and stuck out his hand. "I'd be honored, fishing partner. How about Thursday?"

"I'll ask Bert for Thursday off," I set down the coffee pot and shook his hand, "Partner."

"Five-thirty in the morning. Should I pick you up?"

"I'll be standing right outside the restaurant."

Roger looked at Bert, "Just thanking her for excellent service this morning, Bert." He smiled and went to the cash register.

● ● ●

Thursday morning was unseasonably warm. By the time I dressed, popped a stale, day-old muffin in my mouth that Bert gave me, and ran to the front of the restaurant to wait for Roger, I was drenched in sweat. My coop did not have air conditioning but was well insulated. It had stayed comfortable until about the end of June. Dressed in a light t-shirt and blue jeans, I stood in proud anticipation watching for Roger's pickup truck. I adjusted my Minnesota Twins' baseball cap I bought at the mall on Tuesday as he drove into the parking lot.

The back of the truck was loaded with equipment, and he was hauling a trailer with a shiny new boat. I noticed that it had two motors. He jumped out of the cab to greet me. "Good morning, Becky Jean. Ready to catch some walleyes?"

"Now you remember that I don't know the first thing about fishing. You'll be patient with me, won't you?"

He took off his hat and slapped me on the back. "I'll teach you everything you need to know, partner. Did you get a fishing license? I don't want my gear confiscated by the Department of Natural Resources. Those DNR guys have no sense of humor."

I coughed from his slap. "I bought my license Tuesday at that bait shop just north of Duluth. So I am all set." He smiled as I presented my license. "Now, Mr. Professor of Fishing, why do you have two motors on your boat?"

"I love the way you college girls talk," he laughed and slapped his hat on his knee. "One motor is to get to where the fish are and the other is a trolling motor for actual fishing." He walked me around the boat to the passenger's door explaining the nuances of his boat and the sophisticated equipment along the way. "Complete with GPS and depth gauge. No matter where the fish are, I will find them."

He opened the passenger door for me, and I climbed in. The pick-up smelled of oil and tools. There were some dirty rags on the floor next to a thermos. I crawled in next to a large cooler and wedged my seatbelt behind it.

As he started the truck, he padded the cooler. "I'm not much of a cook, but I make a monster sandwich and my mother made brownies for dessert."

"Sounds delicious. But what if we catch fish, can we eat some of them?"

"I am prepared for such eventualities." Pride seemed to drip off his chin. "Does that sound like how a college guy should talk?"

"Only a very intelligent one." He smiled at my response and put his hand on my shoulder. I pushed it off. "Keep both hands on the wheel, licensed driver."

We drove north past the Covenant church. "They still haven't found a pastor," Roger chattered. "Too bad, it sure would be nice to go to church once in a while."

We crossed the bridge over the Whiteface River and turned off the highway onto a dirt road. Several farm house driveways branched off, and then the road narrowed to a single lane. "What happens if you meet another vehicle on this road?" The Jack Pine encroached, and Roger slowed as the branches scratched across the top of the pickup.

He shifted to a lower gear. "Someone has to back up or pull off into the woods." Several turns and a few hills later, I was surprised by a graveled area large enough to turn around. A well-paved gravel road led down to Whiteface Lake. Horsetail rushes and grasses enclosed the landing where Roger backed the trailer into the water. I was impressed with his expertise. He stopped as the boat was ready to float off the trailer.

I scanned the horizon. I didn't see any cabins, and the morning sun glinted off the water. No waves. The air smelled of fish. Roger interrupted my contemplation. "You won't mind getting your feet wet, will you?"

"No." I unlaced my shoes, took them off, removed my stockings, and shoved them into my jean's pocket.

"Otherwise, I would let you walk out on the tongue of the trailer so you didn't get those dainty little feet of yours in the water." He stopped and pulled up the emergency brake.

"I'm not that dainty," I said as I rolled up my pant legs.

"What do you weigh? A hundred pounds with a soaking wet towel?"

"Now Roger, you know that you should never ask a woman her weight, but you're pretty close, a little on the light side."

"Sorry, just guessing." He released the boat from the trailer and handed me the rope tied to the bow. "Be right back. There's a parking lot just up the hill. Don't let go of that rope."

I watched as he pulled the pickup and trailer into the gravel area and then followed a narrow road that I assumed led to the parking area I hadn't noticed on the way down to the lake, somewhere hidden in the trees. When he returned, he was carrying the cooler and a coffee thermos.

I was holding the rope to the boat, but the rolled up bottoms of my jeans had gotten wet. He noticed. "You told me to wear jeans. If I had worn shorts like you, this would not be a problem."

"I didn't want you to get a sunburn," he said as he walked to the boat, slung in the cooler and thermos, and then returned to scoop me into his arms and carry me to the boat. "You need to eat more, Becky Jean, you're pretty scrawny."

"Catch me some fish, and it will improve my nutrition."

"That's a deal," he said, climbing in and turning the key. The motor started, and he swung the boat around. "We're heading for the narrows." He opened a box of donuts from on top of the cooler, handed me one, and ate one himself. "Up the channel is Hidden Lake. It drains into Whiteface Lake. He revved up the motor. It was so loud, we couldn't hear each other talk, so I sat in silence, scanned the shore, and nibbled on my doughnut. I hadn't had anything so sweet and fresh in a long time. I savored each bite.

The lake was beautiful. Full of islands and bays forested with Jack Pine, cedar, and groves of birch trees. Large boulders the size of small houses, broken off the Canadian Shield and dropped by the receding glaciers, added to the panorama. I was fascinated by a scraggly pine that found a place to grow in cracks of a rock with no apparent soil. It looked like a Bonsai tree. I assumed that the brutal north winter wind manicured its growth. There was not a single cabin, much less any evidence that human beings had ever been here.

Roger turned off the motor as we came close to a cluster of islands. "The river flows into the lake over there," he pointed. "A strong current runs through these islands. It is spring fed, so the water stays cold. The bottom is gravel and boulders, just right for walleyes." His grin was infectious, and I laughed.

"I think I'm ready to catch some. What do I do?"

He pulled out the fishing gear stowed in compartments in the bow. He handed me a rod and reel and then showed me how to put a minnow on my jig. "You don't need all those fancy lures," he said. "Those catch fisherman but not fish." He showed me how the bail worked on the reel and I dropped my jig overboard. "Let it hit the bottom. That's where the fish are," he said as he scanned his depth finder. "Fish at twenty-five feet. When you feel a nibble, you have to set the hook."

"What does that mean?"

"Give the rod a sudden jerk upward, that sets the hook, otherwise the fish just nibbles the bait and you end up with just the head of a chewed up minnow. Then you have to keep tension on the line."

"Poor eating that would be."

"Right."

He went to the back of the boat and started the trolling motor. It was so quiet I could barely hear it. He checked the fish finder again and cast his baited jig to the opposite side of the boat. I watched with intensity, trying to learn this new skill.

"Got one," he said as he jerked up his rod to set the hook and killed the trolling motor. As he started reeling in the line, he explained what he was doing. "You have to maintain tension in the line to reel in a walleye. Holding the line taut, he grabbed the net bringing in the first catch of the day. It measured 22 inches on the tape measure stuck to the bottom of the boat.

"That is a beautiful fish," I said, admiring the bright yellow scales on its belly glinting in the morning sunlight.

He laughed and released the fish back in the water. "Go back and make more like yourself," he said to the fish with a smile.

"Why didn't you keep it?" I asked, nurturing a hunger that might not be fulfilled.

"Too big. Those are the fish that make lots of baby fish for next time."

I didn't understand, but before I could ask for an explanation. I felt a tug on my line. "Set the hook," he yelled and grabbed the net. I jerked the rod up as I had seen him do and started to reel in the line to maintain the tension. When the fish came to the surface I was ecstatic but Roger yelled, "Don't pull up. Leave him in the water, but maintain the tension."

I pulled the walleye closer to the boat as Roger scooped it up with the net. I felt giddy with excitement. "My first fish ever," I yelled. It measured sixteen inches by the tape measure.

"That's a keeper. We need two like that for lunch. The best ones to eat are twelve to eighteen inches." He threw it in the fish compartment and turned on the water pump to keep the water aerated. I set down my rod and reel as Roger put on another minnow. I went to look at my fish. It was swimming around in the live well. It looked so beautiful and delicious.

Several fish later, I was still euphoric with adrenaline and endorphins coursing through my brain. I made several trips to the fish compartment just to look at my fish and watch them swim. *How beautiful. I was a fisherwoman.* I couldn't wait to brag to the customers at the restaurant.

It wasn't long before I pulled in another. "That's the third fish off the same minnow. Way to go, Becky Jean. You're a veteran now. Wait till I tell the guys at the restaurant."

"I want to tell them first. You can fill in the details when you're there."

Toward mid-morning, the fishing slacked off for a while. "Pull up your line," he said as he looked at his watch. "No fish in twenty minutes. It's time to go to my secret spot." He turned off the trolling motor and started the 80-horse. I felt so sophisticated with my new-found expertise. I even knew the difference between an 80-horse and a trolling motor.

Ten minutes later, we were in the middle of the lake. He was watching the depth finder as he slowed the motor. "Thirty, twenty, fifteen, ah, there's my ridge." He turned off the big motor and started the trolling motor. We threw our jigs in the water. My veteran minnow was quite macerated as it searched for a fourth fish.

"I'm going to troll over the ridge. Keep your jig on the bottom. Let out line if you can't feel bottom. It's all gravel down there, so don't worry about snags."

I had learned the feel of my jig bouncing on the rocks below. "What if I do get a snag?"

"You won't, but not a problem, jigs only cost thirty cents and that minnow of yours has already done a day's work. I should put on a fresh one."

"Let me see if the little veteran can catch one more," I protested.

As we trolled over the ridge, I felt the smoothness that happens when your lure is no longer dragging bottom and let out more line. We were in deep water. "Twenty-eight feet," Roger announced.

I felt the jerk of a fish and set my hook. Roger did the same. We both had a fish. "Daily double," I yelled. I laughed when we landed the fish to see that my walleye was quite a bit bigger than Roger's. "See, you taught me well," I said to watch his crest-fallen face smile. Mine was twenty-seven and a quarter inches, so it had to go back. His was smaller, so we had our limit for our shore lunch.

We both examined my veteran minnow. Now it was so macerated it wouldn't stay on the hook. I went to grab a fresh minnow. I could do this. The minnow bucket in the live well was just beyond my grasp, so I had to get up.

Grabbing the minnow, I put it on the hook just the way I had observed Roger do it a number of times. I dropped my bait over the edge. Roger hadn't started the trolling motor yet, so I turned to see what he was doing.

"Want a sandwich?" He had popped open the cooler and handed me a mountainous sandwich. "Corned beef, just in case you're Jewish, tomatoes, onions, and my special dressing, so it's all kosher."

"Can I wipe off my hands first?" I was hungry after all the excitement of the morning, but I didn't want my corned beef sandwich to taste like slimy fish. I leaned over the boat and washed my hands in the lake. They still smelled fishy.

He smiled and offered me a sanitizing wipe. "Courtesy of my mother."

Now my hands smelled perfumed. I liked his mother's choice. When I finally bit into my sandwich, the flavor was explosive. "I'm only a quarter Jewish—grandmother on my father's side. I'm afraid that wouldn't meet criterion at the synagogue, but this sandwich is great."

"Oh, I didn't think you were Jewish. I was just making a joke."

"No offense." I rolled the fresh bread around in my mouth. "This is great bread."

"My mother makes it from scratch."

We sat in the still water eating our sandwiches. My eyes caught brownies wrapped in wax paper in the bottom of the cooler. I pleaded for him to pass me one. With my mouth full, I added, "So, why did Frank say you were shooting blanks."

"I guess," Roger swallowed the last of his sandwich, "since you're my fishing partner, I could tell you. I don't usually tell a girl on the first date, and Frank shouldn't have said that."

"Oh, is this a date? I thought we were just fishing buddies." I thought about my last date with two teenage boys on snowmobiles racing across a frozen lake to find a rabid fox, but I didn't say anything. It would surely have been misinterpreted.

He took a huge bite of his brownie, sighed, and scrunched up his nose. "Sort of a date, don't you think?" I watched two mallards fly overhead as he chewed. "All right, maybe this is not a date. Anyway, when I was twenty-one, I had all the girlfriends a guy could want. Then I found this lump in my balls." He blushed. "I shouldn't be talking to a girl about my testicles." He turned to scan the horizon.

"Go ahead. I'm not embarrassed. Remember, I'm a college girl, University of Dubuque. You can talk to a college girl about anything, especially one that is a fishing partner college girl."

"I can't believe that I'm telling you this." He turned back to me. "Anyway, it turned out to be testicular cancer."

"Oh, Roger, I'm so sorry."

"I'm learning to live with it. After chemo and everything, I'm still a guy. I got testosterone. At least they didn't make me into a eunuch but..." he held his hands up empty, "No sperm. So no girl around here is interested in dating me. News travels fast in Northern Minnesota."

"Well, I think you're pretty nice guy. You always leave me nice tips."

"You and Connie work so hard. I'm just trying to show proper appreciation."

"And we love it. Connie has teen-age girls to support and a husband with expensive taste in hunting equipment. I'm just trying to get back to college." I popped the last bit of brownie into my mouth. "Tell your mother that she makes great brownies."

"I will." He packed up the cooler and picked up the fishing rods. "Back to work, fishing partner."

I grabbed his shoulder. "Roger, I am honored that you shared that. I know it must have been a difficult time for you. You haven't lost an ounce of my respect for you. In fact, I think you are a greater man for being willing to share." I picked up my rod and reel. "So, Roger, can we catch some more fish? This is great."

We caught another dozen or so walleye during the afternoon. I lost count. We had enough for our limit based on the little book I received with my shiny new license, so we gently threw them all back.

By late afternoon, I was hungry, tired, and covered in sweat. It must have been almost ninety degrees in the shade, and out in a boat there was no shade. "You see that sand beach between the rocks?" Roger asked pointing into a small cove. "You want to go there for a fish fry?"

"Yes. My sandwich is well metabolized. Fishing makes me hungry. Besides, you promised to improve my nutrition. Remember?"

"I sure do. I'm hungry too. One fish fry coming up." He stopped the trolling motor and started the 80-horse. In a flash across the lake, we were in the small cove. He revved the engine, killed it, and pulled it up as the boat launched onto the sandy beach. I felt like we were a couple of Marines on beachhead maneuvers. Once on the shore, Roger sent me to gather some drift-wood while he dug a narrow hole in the sand to start a fire. I kept adding scraps of wood to keep the fire blazing as he filleted the fish. "Just let it burn to coals, Becky Jean."

I quit adding wood and sat on a log to watch the fire burn down. We didn't need the heat of the fire. A thermometer I found stowed away on the boat said ninety-two degrees. Once the fire had burned down to coals, he pulled out a skillet, griddle, and wire grate from the storage compartment in the boat. He set the grate over the coals. He dumped oil into the skillet and added some potatoes and onions when the oil started to boil. In the meantime, the fish siz-zled on the cast iron griddle. He even pulled out a container of spices for the fish and catsup for the potatoes.

"You did come prepared. I'm impressed."

He served on double strength paper plates. I squirted catsup all over my fried potatoes. The potatoes were crispy on the outside and hot and moist on the inside. I added the fried onions onto my fish for added flavor. I forked into my fish. The meat was so tender and tasty. Never had fish tasted so good. "What a fish fry," I said, wiping the grease off my chin. *"C'est magnifique."* He smiled, I assumed at my word choice. "It's a college word," I explained. "I stud-ied French at the university."

After eating, we lay on a blanket beside each other on the warm sand in the shade of a tall tree, watching the wispy clouds pass. We were both too full to move. My bloated belly settled slowly as the sun blazed down on the sand. We were hot but comfortable in the shade.

Even lying still, I was sweating. My clothes felt sticky and irritating. I smelled like a combination of worn-out deodorant and fish guts. "Can we go swimming in this lake?"

He sat up. "Did you bring a suit?"

"No," I said and bit down on my finger, "but you said you've had girl-friends, right?" I searched his face for a reaction. It was blank. "So you've seen girls naked before?" He nodded, and I watched his Adam's apple rise and fall. "And I haven't seen anyone else on this lake, not even a cabin, so, you won't mind if I go," I watched his eyes, "skinny-dipping?"

"I guess not."

"Great." I jumped up and stripped off my t-shirt and pants, folded them and laid them in the boat. His eyes widened with a stare. I slipped out of my bra and panties and laid them on my clothes. I spun free in the languid air. I felt liberated.

Roger was staring at me. "I suppose you haven't seen such a big scar before." I traced my finger over my abdominal scar that went all the way across my back and then made a show of trying to cover it with my hands. "Renal cell carcinoma. See, Roger we have a lot in common. They took the cancer out, but it was a big surgery. I had to have chemo and radiation for lung metastases afterwards…" I paused to try to understand his gaze. "My husband said the scar was disgusting."

Oops, too much information. I jumped in the water and swam. The day's sweat and fish smell dissipated in the crystalline water. I felt so refreshed and liberated. I swam under water until I ran out of breath. Roger was standing on the beach with his thumbs stuck in his underwear when I surfaced and turned around. "Aren't you coming? The water feels cold, but it's great."

He yelled across the water, "You're married?" His forehead scrunched with concern.

"Not any more. Come on in. You'll feel refreshed."

As he slipped off his underwear, I noticed the scar in his left groin. It didn't bother me, but he covered it and his genitals with his hand as he laid his clothes neatly on the bow of the boat. Then he dived in and swam out to me. "Are you divorced then?" We swam together about fifty yards.

I laughed and dived down deep to the rocks. Everything was as clear as I imagined the Caribbean to be. When I surfaced I swam to a bare rock, flat with an upward twist like a lounge chair, just a few yards away. The sun shining all day had warmed the black granite. I lay back on it and felt the heat of the smooth basalt comforting my skin. The afternoon sun warmed my breasts and belly as I stretched out on the stone slab and closed my eyes, peaceful and at rest. My scar felt sensitive to the sun, so I covered it with my hand and arm.

As I felt Roger climb up beside me, I opened one eye like a chameleon. He was sitting with his back to me, his eyes focused on the lake. "You want to hear my marriage story?" I asked.

His voice was soft and shy, "Yes, of course."

"It's sort of a long story, but I'll give you the short version so I don't bore you." I shielded my eyes from the sun and I turned over onto my belly. The sun's rays soothed and massaged my back muscles. "We're just fishing buddies, aren't we?"

Roger glanced at me, "Yah." But he still looked away as I started to talk.

I told him about how my father forced my marriage to Keith Slagg. He asked me to continue. "Anyway, Keith seemed nice, but I wasn't that interested in him or in marriage. My parents had this vision that I should marry a minister to keep the family tradition going. My grandfather and great grandfather were Lutheran ministers." I shrugged my shoulders and relaxed my arms on the warm rock. "I don't have any brothers to carry on the family tradition, so father said that I had to marry him, so I married him."

I sat up, and Roger turned to look me in the face. "It was a disaster, right from the start. We went to a hotel suite after the wedding. He carried me over the threshold, dropped me on the couch, and said, 'Take off your clothes. We're married, and your body belongs to me.' I was naïve and didn't know any better, so I stood there and took off all my clothes. He took one look at me and yelled, 'That scar is disgusting, and your breasts are droopy.' He threw me on the living room couch, went back into the bedroom, and locked the door. I spent the night crying on the couch. I knocked and scratched at the door, but he wouldn't even give me a blanket. I wrapped up in a table cloth and slept under the sofa cushions. I didn't actually sleep much, I spent the night crying."

Roger put his hand on my shoulder. "Becky Jean, I'm so sorry."

"All that first week of our marriage, when we went to live in his apartment, I tried to please him. I made nice meals and had the house decorated with flowers. I cleaned the apartment so that it was spotless when he came home from seminary classes. He said terrible things to me. One night I dressed up in what I thought was alluring. I had candles lit on the table and had baked a cake with a buttercream frosting. I put on music and did a strip tease after dinner. He told me that I was a 'fucking freak' and 'damaged goods.' He punched me in the stomach and then started slapping me. He wouldn't quit hitting me, so I got dressed and ran home. Pathetic story, eh?"

Roger's eyes focused on my bare breasts, and then he pulled back his hand off my shoulder. "Oh, Becky Jean, that's terrible."

"I couldn't take it any longer. I had to leave. Where else could I go but home?"

"Right."

"Well, that didn't work out. Mother said that I was supposed to cling to my husband. That's what the Bible said. Father said I was a disgrace to our family for having left my husband. He told me to leave his house at once and go back to my husband. They refused to even let me stay the night.

"I walked the streets all night. I tried to sleep on one of the park benches, but it was chilly and I couldn't sleep. Besides, I saw the police were patrolling. I thought, 'Next time I'll let them pick me up for vagrancy. At least I'll get a cot in jail.' But they didn't come back.

"In the morning, I went back to the apartment to try to make amends. My dear husband was burning my clothes and everything I owned in the dumpster in back of the apartment, even my wedding dress. He didn't see me, so I ran upstairs and grabbed my backpack out of the closet. I stuffed a few things he missed and left out the front door. He never saw me leave. I just started hitch-hiking when I got to a highway. I didn't care where I was going as long as it was a long ways away. I ended up here in Cotton, Minnesota working for Bert, and you know the rest."

I arched my back, enjoying the sun's caress on my skin. "When that arsonist started the fire at the restaurant last May, I found out that my so-called husband annulled our marriage, told the judge that I refused to have sex with him. That was a big lie. So, I guess theoretically, I was never married."

"Do you mind if I give you a hug?"

"No, I don't mind." I laughed as he hugged me to his side. He traced my scar with his finger. "Your scar is not that disgusting. He should never have treated you that way."

"I guess he was expecting some kind of trophy bride, a china doll to put on his award shelf. He said I had a cute face one night at my parents' house when he came for dinner before we were married, but I guess I was a huge disappointment to him naked." I dove back into the water and Roger followed. As we swam back to the beach he asked, "So when did you get cancer? Tell me that part of the story."

"I had a renal cell carcinoma, kidney cancer, when I was ten years old. I guess I'm cured. Keith said 'that bit of information' should have been disclosed before we were married, a 'prenuptial disclosure' he called it. I answered him, 'Should I have paraded around nude so you could see what kind of toy you

were getting? I don't think my parents would have approved of that, do you?'
He never answered me, just slapped my face for being a 'sassy bitch..'"

"What about the skinny-dipping? You seem so comfortable. None of my
other girlfriends would have been willing to do this."

I wriggled my toes in the sand next to the boat and laughed. "I'm sorry if I
embarrassed you. I started skinny-dipping when I was in junior high school. I'd
sneak out of my bedroom at night and go down to the lake in the park about a
block away from our house. I felt wonderful swimming naked, like I was free
from all the requirements my parents laid on me. I guess it was rebellion. Besides,
when I was ten, I had all those pediatricians, surgeons, and oncologists examining
my anatomy all the time. When most girls start puberty, they become shy about
the changes in their bodies. When I had to go every few months to the doctor
who had two oncology fellows, two residents, and a team of medical students
checking me over during my development, I guess I just never developed a
proper sense of modesty, 'a maturation arrest' according to Psychology 101."

"You university girls. I guess I've been dating the wrong crowd."

"One time when I was in high school, my parents caught me down at the
lake. Boy, did I get a sermon. Father sat me down on a hard stool as he read
the first three chapters of Genesis to me and emphasized that I was a fallen
creature and needed to have my private parts covered. I laughed at him, and
he sent me to my room. I got sent to my room without supper a lot after that.
That's how I learned to get along without supper. Maybe that's why I am so
'scrawny,' as Connie tells me."

Roger pulled out a couple of towels from the boat, and I wrapped up in
one. It smelled of fabric softener. "Your mother must have sent the towels.
They sure smell nice."

He smiled, "Nope. I do my own laundry."

"The way these towels smell, a girl would be crazy not to overlook that
you're shooting blanks."

He laughed, but there seemed to be pain in his laughter.

We dressed and cleaned up our beach mess. We caught a few more fish as
the sun was setting, but they weren't biting as well. Venus was sparkling in the
evening sky when we loaded the boat back onto the trailer.

"Drop me off in front of the restaurant," I said, but he insisted on bringing
me home.

"I live just behind the restaurant, silly."

He seemed shocked when he stopped the truck to see where I lived. "I rent it, or it's part of my salary," I explained. "Bert calls it the 'coop,' like a chicken coop."

"I've seen bigger chicken coops," he said, "I thought Bert just stored supplies here. I didn't realize that anyone actually lived here."

"I think that I am the only inhabitant of Cotton, Minnesota. No one else lives in the city limits, if there are city limits. I've never seen any posted, and I've walked several miles in every direction. Well, maybe when the Wickstroms are in town living above their store. But I hear they've built a house down the county road south of Cotton and live there now."

He giggled at my joke, took me in his arms, and tried to kiss me.

I pushed him away. "I'm sorry, Roger. We're just fishing partners. I'm still hurting too much inside to have a boyfriend. But I'll go fishing with you any time you want to go.'

His eyes brightened. "That's a deal."

"As long as you never tell a soul that I like to go skinny-dipping. No one. Ever. Promise?"

He started to back away. I could tell that he was ambivalent. The poor guy was ready for romance, and he had found a soul mate, at least someone who understood what it meant to have cancer. "Your secret is safe with me," he said. He drew close beside me and whispered in my ear, "There is nothing wrong with your breasts. They're not 'droopy,' whatever he meant by that. And I am not offended by your scar."

"Thanks, Roger."

He turned, apparently disappointed that I hadn't kissed him, and climbed into his truck and left.

I was still laughing at his embarrassment and the wonderful time we had together as I got undressed to take a shower. That's when I felt the lump in my right breast.

Chapter 21
Physician Appointment

The following Tuesday I planned to go to Duluth for supplies. I searched through the paper for specials. Pork chops were on sale, and I knew our customers loved Bert's special barbecue sauce. I also found frozen French fries on sale. Bert was very particular about the brand, but his favorite brand was thirty percent off the regular price at Upper Lakes Foods, a wholesale house in Superior, Wisconsin.

When I finished shopping and putting the frozen things in the freezer chest in the back of the van, instead of going to the mall I planned to go to my physician's appointment. As I crossed the Blatnik Bridge returning to Duluth, Minnesota, I checked my watch. At 3:30, I had an appointment to check the lump in my breast. It was only a short drive, and I had plenty of time. After parking in the clinic parking lot, I checked the frozen food in the cooler. I had added some dry ice to the cooler chest. Everything was still frozen hard.

The Family Practice Center is part of the residency program affiliated with the University of Minnesota, Duluth School of Medicine. I figured that I would get two opinions for the price of one by seeing a family medicine resident and then have my case reviewed by the attending physician.

As I sat in the lobby waiting to see my assigned physician resident, I scanned the waiting room. It was clean and neat, a bustle of activity. The seats in the waiting area were soft and comfortable. Everything smelled crisp, not medicinal like so many clinics I had been to before. I felt good about my decision. I was using my body to train a new physician. My medical history should at least be instructive even if my lump was nothing to be concerned about. It would be worth the money spent. The pictures on the wall were scenes of Duluth painted by a local artist whose description was on a plaque next to his paintings. As I read about the artist, Dr. Chee who was a librarian at UMD, the nurse called my name.

When I signed in with the receptionist, she told me that my resident's name was Dr. Cheryl Sheihe. What a beautiful name, I thought. I said it a couple of times just to hear the sound. The name suggested that she was Native American, and when I met her, she was dark complexioned with flowing black hair. Her greeting was as sweet as her name.

"How can I help you?" she asked, timid as a fawn in a new-mown field. I thought that she must be a new resident. I was attracted to her perfume, probably lavender.

"Dr. Sheihe, I found a lump in my breast when I was taking a shower. I would like you to check it for me. I wanted to come and establish with a physician as well. You know, have a good check-up."

She looked startled. "A lump in someone your age is usually not cancer." She scanned my empty chart. "All right, let's see, this is your first time here, so I need to get to know you better, and then I will check your lump and have my attending physician check you as well."

I smiled, *Two opinions for the price of one, just like I figured.*

"Let's review your past medical history."

"There isn't much to tell," I said. But I knew the protocol, so as I related the history of my kidney cancer, I wasn't surprised when she sat up on the edge of her chair. "I will need to send for your records." She reviewed family history and my habits. I was especially pleased to add, "Never married." She explained that she needed to do a "Review of Systems," which was a long list of personal questions. I was familiar with it all, so I started without her initiation, "No, I don't smoke; no, I don't drink alcohol, well sometimes I have had a glass of white wine with fish. I do no illicit drugs including, marijuana, cocaine, and heroin. No I don't have double vision or pain in my chest or diarrhea or blood in my stools." The list goes through the entire body. I knew all the questions. She just wrote down everything as I said it. I thought it would be quicker that way. I wondered when she was going to ask more about the lump in my breast, but I knew from past experience that we had to go through the whole review first.

"Please put on a gown, and I will examine you next. I see that you have been through this before. Since I'm a first year resident, just started July 1st, I appreciate how you did that." She grinned. "My attending physician will be so impressed that I got all this information. Since you haven't had a pelvic exam in quite a while, I think we should do that as well." She gave me a gown and left the room.

I wasn't too excited about the pelvic exam. I wasn't sure that needed to be done to check the lump in my breast, but whatever it took. I had signed up to teach a resident, so I accepted it in the name of education. Undressed, I put on the paper gown and sat on the exam table.

More waiting. I hated the crinkling sound the paper gown made when I moved. When I had my kidney cancer, I preferred a cloth gown, and my oncologist knew it. He always made sure one was available, even when the clinic changed to paper.

The attending physician, Dr. Tagett, introduced himself when Dr. Sheihe returned. He was a tall, thin man with a serious affect. Dr. Sheihe examined everything from my ear canals to my various orifices as he silently observed. The pelvic exam was saved for last. Despite being quite comfortable naked in front of the many doctors who examined me during my bout with kidney cancer, I found it embarrassing having two doctors looking up my vagina. They didn't do that when I was ten years old.

"Yes, you have exposed the cervix properly, Dr. Sheihe" Dr. Tagett said.

Oh, great, my cervix is properly exposed. I wasn't sure that "properly" and exposure of my cervix should be in the same sentence.

"Now do the Pap smear," he instructed. I didn't feel much except the tightness of the speculum stretching my vagina, but I sighed when I heard, "That is correct procedure, Dr. Sheihe. Well done." I took a deep breath as she removed the speculum.

Dr. Tagett asked, "How many sexual partners have you had, Ms. Gottwald? Dr. Sheihe forgot to ask."

My legs out of the stirrups, I sat up and let my gown flop in my lap. "None, but I am concerned about this lump in my breast." I dropped my gown onto my lap.

The two physicians examined both of my breasts. "I can definitely feel what you are concerned about," Dr. Sheihe said. I wasn't sure that was reassuring, but her voice gave me justification for scheduling the appointment.

Dr. Tagett's brow furrowed as he repeated the exam. His manner was more firm and clinical. He looked straight into my eyes. "I'm afraid that lump needs to be biopsied, Ms. Gottwald. Ordinarily, for a woman in her twenties, such a lump is most likely going to be benign, but with your history of chest radiation for your renal cancer, you are at increased risk of malignancy."

I was hoping for confirmation that it was nothing to be concerned about. But the reason I was here was because it felt abnormal to me. His concern was not good news. My eyes pleaded with Dr. Sheihe as Dr. Tagett excused himself with a friendly greeting, "Nice to meet you, Ms. Gottwald. I will see you with Dr. Sheihe when the results return." He closed the door behind him leaving Dr. Sheihe staring at me.

I felt that she sensed my concern as she spoke in halting phrases, "I need to arrange a mammogram. Then I will make arrangements for a biopsy. Well, if that is what is needed." She added, "As soon as possible. Don't worry yet. Let me worry for you. That's my job."

I was confident by the concern on her face that she would worry for me. "I was ten years old when I first heard the word 'cancer,'" I told her. "I cringed on that day because I thought I would die. Now over a decade later, I'm still alive." *Now my abdominal scar could feel sorry for the scar I would have on my breast.*

"I don't think its cancer," she said. "Dr. Tagett is just being cautious. It is very unusual for women your age to have breast cancer." She held my hand and was sweet and encouraging, but I sensed concern in her voice.

Chapter 22
Leah and Roger

Roger came in and took off his hat. "I'm hauling concrete to the taconite plant today," he said. "Do you have a table for me? It looks pretty busy."

I scanned the restaurant. The tables were full. Even the counter stools were full. "What's all this concrete for?"

"They're building a new processing plant to add the flux to the taconite pellets this summer."

"What will that do?" I was stalling as I searched for someplace to seat Roger.

Half listening, I heard him explain how flux minimized the processing of ore to steel. All the booths were full except for one. Leah was taking a break in the far booth in the corner. Shawnee had brought Rachel so Leah could breastfeed. When we were this busy, she should have been taking her break in the employees' room. I glanced over to her booth. It appeared that she was done feeding the baby. Shawnee was talking to her mother as Connie made more coffee. Shawnee looked ready to leave with the baby, so I escorted Roger back to Leah's booth. "Leah, can Roger sit with you and have his lunch? All the booths are full." I tried to control my authoritarian irritation that she was using a customer booth.

"No problem," she answered, "as long as he doesn't mind a fussy baby." She turned to Roger. "Her name is Rachel." She twisted a lock of Rachel's hair in her fingers. The child now had a luxurious mop of hair

I took Roger's order and turned it into Ron.

"More coffee here, Miss." I heard the request from one of Connie's booths and grabbed the fresh coffee pot to fill the cups of a group of fisherman. Connie was deep in conversation with Shawnee, so I filled their cups.

When Roger's order was ready I brought his hamburger and fries with a refill of his Coke. As I set down his food, I asked, "I brought the catsup, Roger. Do you need mustard?" Rachel was squirming in the car seat and looked frustrated.

"Yes, do you have any of Bert's special beer mustard?"

"I'll get it right away." I returned with the mustard. Now Rachel was screaming.

Leah looked at Roger, "This child is still hungry and I'm breast-feeding. Will that bother you?"

Roger took a bite of his hamburger and gave me a knowing look and then back at Leah. "Go ahead," he said, "it won't disturb my lunch."

Leah pulled up her sweatshirt and released her breast from her nursing bra. Rachel was quiet in an instant. Her suck was ravenous.

I gave Roger another glass of Coke and mouthed at Leah, "I'm sorry. I thought you were done feeding the baby."

"Oh, it's all right," said Leah, squinting her eyes at me. "And you know why. I don't care anymore." Her gaze was piercing.

I sensed that she was flashing back to finding herself naked on the bed, her breasts sore from being pawed the day she was raped. She had ranted in the dish-washing room one day that she didn't care who saw her breasts because she was resolved that her breasts were for feeding Rachel and that was all that mattered anymore.

Fishermen and regular customers kept me busy. I kept looking at the back booth to see how Roger and Leah were getting along. All I could see was the tops of their heads. He hadn't gotten up to leave yet. That was a good sign. I saw that she had switched breasts as I bussed Roger's dishes. The growing little girl emptied her mother's left breast and started on the right. Leah and Roger were still talking.

"Dessert?" I asked as I slipped past their booth.

"Any strawberry pie left?" Roger asked.

"Coming right up."

"Bring two forks. Leah can split it with me."

"We aren't allowed to have desserts," Leah explained. "'It eats into the profits,' Bert always says. I can't afford to be fired. I follow the rules."

Not exactly, I thought, *or you would be back in the employees break room.*

"But if Roger is buying, I'm sure Bert won't care." I smiled, "The assistant manager doesn't care." She gave me a toothy grin.

I got the pie and set it facing Roger and put both forks to his side. I looked at Leah and saw the concern on her face, "It's all right. I told Bert. He said, 'As long as Roger's buying, there is no problem.'"

"Okay." She hooked her nursing bra, pulled down her sweatshirt, and shifted the now-sleeping child to her left arm as she picked up the extra fork. One bite and she smiled, "This tastes great. Thanks, Roger."

When Roger stood and put on his hat, Shawnee left Connie's side to resume her child-care duties so Leah could return to dishwashing. I noticed the warm touch as Roger helped her out of the booth. I thought he kissed her, but that may have been my fantasy.

"I suppose the dishes are stacking up," Leah said as she grabbed her pie plate, hiding it under Roger's dessert plate, and made a fast exit to the dishwashing room. Shawnee took content, sleeping Rachel out to her car cradled in the car seat.

Roger stood watching as I wiped down the table. "Did you do that on purpose?" he asked.

"What? It was the only place left to sit," I stammered and sounded as stern as possible. "You saw the restaurant. Besides, she is not supposed to take her break out here. We have an employee lunch room. Should I reprimand her?"

"I still think you did that on purpose. She is a really fine young lady. I admire her decision to keep the baby after what happened. It's just that we know too much about each other." He touched my arm.

I turned to look him in the face. "I'll never tell. Will you?"

He put on his cap. "I got to go. Cement calls me."

Chapter 22
Marriage Proposal

Several weeks later, I discovered Leah singing a Madonna song as she opened the dishwasher. I waved as I bussed dishes to her. She was smiling and dancing as she did her work.

"What are you so happy about? Rachel must have slept all night for a change."

"Well, that too." She filled the empty tray with dishes, pushed it into the dishwasher, and started the cycle.

"And what else?"

She ran to me and did a spin. She tried to hug me, but I backed away not wanting her wet apron imprinting my uniform. "Roger asked me out on a date. And," she caught her breath, "he likes Rachel. Shawnee is going to babysit, and I get to dress up. We're going to Blackwood's Cafe in Duluth for dinner. You know, that fancy place that overlooks Lake Superior? Then he's taking me to the Arena Auditorium for a University of Minnesota, Duluth hockey game." She had a smug grin on her face. "And there's more."

"What?" I asked.

"He promised to kiss me every time UMD scores a goal. And," she took a deep breath, "I have to kiss him every time the opposing team makes a goal. Isn't that just exciting?"

I knew that UMD had an excellent hockey team. What I didn't realize was the romantic implications of the scoring. "I hope they score lots of goals for you." She again tried to hug me. "Save my hugs for after work."

"I'll give you a thousand hugs after work," she said.

"I didn't do anything."

"You did too, you sneaky little devil."

"If you had been in the employees' dining room, nothing would have happened." With that I left to talk to Connie. "No problem with clean dishes today."

Connie laughed. "You've been back to see the enchanted dishwasher I take it?"

"Yes."

"Well you should have seen her this morning. She cleaned the kitchen and made breakfast before I got up. It was spotless. The kid is ecstatic over this date with Roger. How did you arrange that?"

"I didn't have anything to do with it."

"I almost believe you."

Mr. Halverson was raising his cup for more coffee.

It was busy all day. Connie went home on her lunch break, and when I took mine, I was too exhausted to do much but sit at the employees table and scoop my tuna noodle casserole into my baby bird mouth. I wondered whether Leah's renewed enthusiasm would last.

Chapter 23
Leah's Anger

A few months later, Leah was agitated. She was banging the dishes around, making a dreadful noise. She even dropped a plate and broke it. Bert hollered at her and told her to be more careful. He usually docked broken dishes from our pay to encourage us to be more careful, but I talked him out of this one. "She's upset about something," I told him. "Take it out of my paycheck if you have to. I'll find out what the problem is."

"You haven't broken a dish since you started."

"So being docked one dish won't hurt me too much."

He returned to his office, too tired to argue.

Even during my lunch break, I had no time to talk to Leah. I volunteered to close up so I could be alone with her to find out what was troubling her. I assumed she and Roger had had a fight. I locked the front door and turned off the lights. Now it was only the two of us. She glared at me as I returned to the dishwashing room to check on her. She slammed the last load into the dishwasher and started the cycle.

Her voice was harsh, "You know I've been dating Roger. He has taken me out on at least a dozen dates."

"Yes, how could I not know?"

She grabbed the stainless steel with her yellow gloved hands. "I like Roger. He's a real nice, gentle, respectful man."

"Yes." I quenched my desire to say more.

"He's treated me the way I always wanted to be treated. You know, before Rachel was conceived." Now she started yelling, "Before I got fucked up."

I noticed tears in her eyes. She snuffled and wiped her eyes with her forearm and gripped the counter again. I waited. *Patience, Rebecca, patience. Don't speak until you know the problem.*

"He hasn't once tried to make a pass at me or…you know, try to get into my pants."

"Yes, I agree, Roger is special."

"We've been trying to be honest with each other. I told him about all the guys I had sex with." She sighed and looked up at the ceiling. Then she glared at me and slapped me across the face, "And he told me that you two got naked when you went fishing."

Stunned, I closed my eyes and took a deep breath. *So that's what the storm in the dishwasher room was all about. How was I going to explain this? I felt guilty. I hated the thought that my selfish decision that day would hurt my friend's relationship with her boyfriend, the first real boyfriend she had ever had.* My words came out slowly, "Yes, Leah, we were naked."

She whipped me across the face with her gloves. "You deserve that and more."

"I'm the one who wanted to go skinny-dipping. It wasn't Roger's idea. It was a hot day, and I was all sweaty and smelled like all the fish we caught. I hadn't brought a swimsuit. In fact, I don't have one." I shifted my stance. The back of my legs cramped as I stood at attention.

"I know all that," she shouted and punched me in the belly. I fell against the wall. My scar seared with pain. "What I want to know is if you two…" her face was crimson, "fucked after that. And tell me the truth." She glared at me with both fists clenched ready to punch me again.

"No," I shook my head as I regained my balance against the wall. Then I enunciated each word, "We were not intimate in any way. We did not even kiss." I stood still waiting for my execution. The silence seemed eternal. I felt like a criminal standing before a judge. I stared at her, afraid that if I blinked, she might not believe me. I tightened my stomach, prepared for another punch.

Like the evolution of a new creation, her face changed and her clenched hands relaxed. She picked up her yellow gloves, folded them, and hung them on the stainless steel rack. She took my hands in hers. "I'm sorry I hit you. I have been so mad at you all day. Did I hurt your surgery scar? I'm sorry. Anyway, that's what Roger said too. I so wanted to believe him. I had to hear it from you to make sure he was telling me the truth." She sat on the stool and started to cry.

I hugged her.

"Would it be too much to ask," her gaze shifted to the ceiling and then to me, "that you two not go skinny-dipping together anymore, just for me? I think I want to marry him, and the thought of you two naked together. I just can't handle it."

"Never again. No more skinny-dipping with Roger. I promise."

She slumped onto the stool like melting wax. "I hurt you, didn't I?"

I unbuttoned my uniform. There was a fist-shaped red welt where she had hit me over my scar. I touched it, causing an involuntary wince. The area was sensitive to the touch.

She got up off the stool and ran her finger over the welt. "Oh, I'm sorry. I'm so sorry. I was angry…and afraid."

"I'll heal. Don't be angry at Roger. I can tell that he really loves you. You need to see him and make up. It was my fault."

She grabbed me and hugged me. "You are so honest, Becky Jean. It makes me crazy. I thought for sure you would deny it. That would have made me suspicious. I assumed that you would lie to me to cover for Roger and then… My knight in shining armor wouldn't be so shiny, would he?" She paused, her face contorted. When it softened, she said, "Becky Jean, thanks for being my friend."

"Always," I said.

• • •

Roger came to the restaurant the day before Thanksgiving waving a piece of paper in the air. "Our marriage license," he announced and sat down at the counter. I ran in the back to get Leah. She returned giddy, dancing around behind the counter, joining Roger in an embarrassing embrace. Bert appeared to see what all the commotion was about. Connie set down the coffee pot. The ladies' Bible study group came out of the back room.

"We're going to be married," she announced. Everyone in the restaurant cheered. Each of the ladies from the Bible study gave them both a hug and a kiss.

After the eruption of emotion calmed, I told them they had some explaining to do. Leah whispered in my ear. "Well, to start with, we went to talk to my social worker, the one for unwed-mothers," she cringed as she said the words and then continued with a smile, "and it turns out that he just happens to be an ordained minister. He's such a nice guy, always treated me with respect." She twisted a smile and announced to the whole restaurant, "Guess what? The minister will marry us at the Cotton Covenant Church." A pandemonium of cheers filled the restaurant.

Bert seemed excited, "When is this wedding? What time?"

Leah thought a minute, pointed out the date to Bert on the calendar. "How about two o'clock? That's a slow time, so could I get a couple hours off work, Mr. Lloyd?" She glanced at her boss; then added, "It would be the first Saturday in December."

He wrapped his arms around the couple. "Great. Slow time. I'll tell you what, I'll close the restaurant for an hour and, then you can have the reception in the Bible study room. No charge, my present to the newlyweds."

"Really? Free? Does that include food?" Leah's eyes seemed to be sprouting out of her head.

"Free, with food, and I'll ask Beatrice to make a special wedding cake."

"Oh my God, I feel faint." Roger grabbed her to keep her from collapsing.

"God will bless your marriage, but don't use his name in vain, Leah." Mrs. Lawrence said as the ladies from Bible study crowded around her.

Leah started crying. "I wasn't. Mrs. Lawrence. I was praying for strength."

Mrs. Lawrence smiled as big as the floral design on her dress. "Well, in that case, Leah, may the Lord Jesus bless your marriage and give you and Roger the strength of His Spirit."

One of our regular customers, an elderly widow pulled out a delicate lace handkerchief from her purse and handed it to Leah. "I make these for people, so this can be your first wedding present."

Leah sobbed. Connie hugged away her tears and said, "Aren't you glad you came to work for Mr. Lloyd? Otherwise you would never have met Becky Jean and me."

"You two have been my best family. Connie, you gave me a place to live when I was homeless and treated me with love and respect, despite not being Ojibway. Becky Jean, you helped me through the most difficult decisions of my life." She pulled closer to my ear and whispered, "Sorry I slugged and slapped you. Thanks for keeping your promise."

Roger gave the two of us a hug. "You two are her best friends. Will you be the maid and matron of honor?"

"If we get to be the witnesses for that legal certificate," Connie said. "Agreed."

"Who will the guys be?" I asked.

"Hal can be best man for sure," said Roger, "and a truck driving friend of mine can accompany Becky Jean."

After that, the whole restaurant started chatting. The couple went to each table to be congratulated. Some even slipped them some money.

•   •   •

The Wednesday before the wedding, Leah brought a formal blue dress into work to show all of us. "I'm hardly a virgin, as all of you know, so I picked blue. Actually, it was my prom dress that I never got to wear. Boobs are a little tight, but Roger says I look great in it. I just hope Rachel doesn't start screaming during the ceremony and I start squirting milk all over. I'm putting pads in my bra."

Bert covered his ears, "Too much information." He made a quick exit to his office.

Connie and I laughed. "It's a lovely dress. After work you will have to try it on for us." Connie looked around, "Men excluded."

Bert reappeared having gained his composure. "We have customers, ladies. Let's get back to work."

Shawnee came in the back door carrying Rachel. "She's hungry."

As I returned to my customers, I took a glance back at Leah. Her uniform was instantly spotted as her nipples lactated. "See? That's what I'm afraid of," she mouthed as she pointed at her breasts. She took Rachel in her arms and closed the door to the dishwashing room.

Shawnee turned to me, "Mom gave me errands to do. I'll be back later. I have responsibilities now that I have a driver's license. Father says, 'privilege always has responsibility' and I always listen to my father."

"But not always to your mother," Connie added. Shawnee smiled at her and rushed out the door.

"She seems pretty excited about her new responsibilities," I emphasized the last word as I whispered in Connie's ear.

"That girl," said Connie but added no more as a number of men at the counter raised their coffee cups for refills.

We were so busy that day pouring coffee. Many customers ordered dessert with their lunch who had never ordered dessert before. That meant re-writing several checks. Connie and I raced from table to table as more people came. There was standing room only waiting for a table by noon. Many were customers we had never served before. Bert helped Ron keep up with the orders, and Connie and I scurried back and forth from serving to the cash register.

As busy as we were, I could hear the faint cry of a baby coming from the dishwasher room. When I was caught up serving all the customers at my assigned tables and all the coffee cups were full, I ventured back to see what the commotion in the dishwashing room was all about.

Sweat dripped off Leah's face, her uniform was soaked, and Rachel was sitting in her car carrier screaming. I went in and closed the door. "I don't know what's wrong with her. I fed her and changed her diaper and she just screams."

"I don't think Shawnee is back yet. Connie sent her on some errands. But I'll check."

"Thanks, Becky Jean."

I closed the door. "Thank God for soundproof dishwashing rooms," I said to myself. I found Connie pouring coffee. "Is Shawnee back, yet?"

"No." She looked at the clock. She shouldn't be back for at least a half hour. Why?"

"Oh, Rachel is fussy."

The man at one of my tables was flashing his credit card. I ran over to fetch it. I looked at the name and paused. "Just looking at the name, are you related to Leah Thomas?"

The husband hung his head. The wife looked up at me. "We're her parents. Do you know her?"

Without answering her question, I told them, "I'll be back in a minute." I ran back to the dishwashing room and picked up Rachel. She was instantly quiet. Leah was pounding the dishes into the racks. "She'll need the car seat," she said without stopping.

"Not yet," I said as I left. I picked up the coffee pot and headed back to my customers. I plopped Rachel in her grandmother's lap. "The meal is on the house, free, but it comes with a baby." I returned the credit card to Mr. Thomas.

"What's this?" Mrs. Thomas said, looking indignant.

"'Who' is proper when referring to a person," I said, "and this little baby is your granddaughter, Rachel Tamara Thomas. Isn't she cute?" Rachel cooed and smiled, breast milk dribbling out her mouth.

"This is my granddaughter?" Mrs. Thomas choked, patting her chest. "Leah's baby? I thought she was..." She gasped.

"Getting an abortion," said Mr. Thomas, finishing his wife's sentence.

"Nope, no abortion ever looked this cute." I tickled Rachel's chin and she smiled. "This is your very alive granddaughter." On cue, Rachel started to laugh. Well, it looked like a laugh to me. Mr. Thomas slid beside his wife. "She is adorable, so peaceful and content."

Not a moment ago, I thought. I filled their coffee cups and ran to another customer that was waving dollar bills at the counter. There was a line at the cash register, and when Connie saw me start ringing up the receipts she checked on my tables. Before I finished, Leah came out in her soaked uniform. Her hair that had streaked out of her hairnet was matted against her sweating face.

"Where's Rachel?"

I pointed, "Entertaining those two customers."

"What the hell?" Leah screamed. She looked at Mr. Lloyd and covered her mouth. "I'm sorry about my potty-mouth, Mr. Lloyd. I'll be more careful."

"Please do, Leah. I've told you before."

"Yes, Mr. Lloyd." She hung her head, but as soon as he returned to the cash register, she walked over to pick up Rachel. She stopped in front of her parents' table. Her father was bouncing Rachel on his knee, and her mother was tickling the child.

I went up behind her with a full coffee pot. "Go ahead, Leah," I said in a quiet voice, "take a break."

She glanced back at me with what appeared to be an expression of anger mixed with confusion but pulled up a chair to her parents' table. I checked out a few more customers at the cash register, so I couldn't pay much attention to what was going on. But by the time Shawnee walked in the door to retrieve her charge, parents and daughter were hugging each other. I even noticed tears streaming down Mrs. Thomas's face.

"The car seat and the diaper bag are still back in the dishwasher room," I told Shawnee. "Rachel is meeting her grandparents right now. Get the stuff and sit here at the counter and I'll make you a strawberry shake."

"You know my mother doesn't approve of me eating here at the restaurant, Becky Jean." She looked at the shake dispenser with pleading eyes and added, "Who's paying for it?"

"I am." I hit the buttons on the cash register and took the money out of my tips to pay for the shake and gave Shawnee the receipt. I caught Connie glancing at her daughter. I pointed at the money as Shawnee held up the receipt. "One strawberry shake coming up."

I set it on the counter when it was finished and gave her a straw and soda spoon. She giggled and whispered, "You sure know how to get under my mother's skin."

"I do?" Then added in a whisper, "But isn't it fun?"

"Yep." She slurped the shake and whispered, "She's never let me have anything here before."

By the time Mr. and Mrs. Thomas were ready to leave, Leah was smiling. Shawnee slurped down the last of her shake as Leah introduced her as Rachel's babysitter. Leah gave her parents a hug and returned to her dishwashing responsibilities. Mr. Thomas gave me his credit card. "Charge it up. It's unfair for you to pay for our meals. We learned a valuable lesson today."

"If you insist."

"I do certainly insist," he said. I ran the card and then gave him the receipt to sign. He added a huge tip.

"Wow, thank you, Mr. and Mrs. Thomas."

"No, we should thank you. That tip is only a token of what we owe you today."

Shawnee put Rachel in the car seat, grabbed the diaper bag, and ran out the door. Rachel's grandparents waved goodbye through the picture window.

At closing time, I went back to see if Leah was done with the dishes. Bert said it was a record day as he added up the receipts, so I thought Leah might be behind.

The room was spotless. "I was really, really mad at you for what you did," she said as I entered. "I would have murdered you if I'd had this knife handy."

She held a butcher knife from the dishwashing carrousel and waved it at me. "But I probably would have tortured you first." Then she put it back in the carrousel and shoved the last load into the dishwasher. She sighed, dropped her hands to her side, and burst into tears. She grabbed me and hugged me so hard I couldn't breathe. I pushed her away, gasping for oxygen.

She held my shoulders. "But thanks. You sure live on the edge, Becky Jean. You took an awful risk, you know. That could have backfired so bad, real ugly bad." She hugged me again more gently and added a smile that I had never seen cross her face. "They're even coming to the wedding. Wait till I tell Roger. He wanted me to invite them, but of course, I adamantly refused. I got so angry when he brought it up. I pounded him with my fists. We had an all-out fight about it. He'll be so proud of me now for doing it his way."

I was excited that night as I lay in bed trying to visualize how this wedding would turn out. It gave me sweet dreams. I knew it was dangerous to introduce Rachel to Leah's parents, but fate intervened. For sure the grandparents were not regular customers. In fact I had never seen them in the restaurant before. I wondered if Rachel somehow sensed her grandparents' presence and that was why she had been so cranky.

Chapter 24
Wedding

December was on the mild side. Everyone around Cotton was talking about Leah and Roger's wedding. It was anticipated to be a special community event. There were only a few things that drew the community together, for example the Cotton Cardinals basketball games. They won about half the time, so they were exciting to watch. The football team had an equal record but boasted the *best* hotdogs and hot chocolate in the St. Louis County. They were sold just under the bleachers during home games. Shawnee brought me with her a couple of times when I wasn't totally exhausted. Bert said that it was good advertising for me to wear my uniform to the game. The hotdogs and hot chocolate were good, especially when it was freezing cold during the game, but I suspect the concession stand roved around the county at all the local games. Tim and Tom invited me to one of the games as a *date*, so I got a free hotdog and drink for participating in their experiment entitled "Showing Proper Respect to a Woman."

But this event was not a game, this was a community celebration. Roger set up an invitation on a large poster by the picture window so that all the truck drivers who ate at the restaurant knew that they were invited. Leah notified all her friends from the former Cotton Cardinals High School Cheerleading squad to attend. Unfortunately most were in college around the country. The few at UMD were preparing for exams but promised to attend.

The day of the wedding was spectacular, warm and sunny, unusual for a December day in northern Minnesota, but sometimes chinooks happen. These warm days didn't qualify as chinooks by the strict meteorological definition, but that's what the local people called them. The social worker/ordained minister Richard Campbell, who hated being called reverend, was a roly-poly, jolly man. Given a beard, he would have made a perfect Santa Claus. He seemed as excited as the young couple about the wedding.

Connie and I received fancy dresses, in a blue that matched Leah's wedding dress, from a very generous Roger so that Connie could be the matron of honor and I could be the bride's maid. We were embarrassed because the dresses looked so expensive, but he assured us that his mother had made both dresses and he only paid for the material. He explained to me in private that his mother was overjoyed that her 'eunuch' son was finally getting married.

I recalled the day Connie and I were invited to his mother's house for the dress fittings. Roger's mother, Audrey, had come to the restaurant to take our measurements. Then a couple of days later, we were invited to her house. This spry, thin, widow woman bustled with energy. As we entered her simple, orderly home, we smelled yeast and cinnamon. The oven was on and the kitchen must have been at least 80 degrees. Audrey invited us to the cooler living room to try on our dresses. They fit to perfection. We stood on wooden chairs so she could arrange the hems. Then we celebrated with fresh coffee and cinnamon rolls just as they popped out of the oven.

Bert proposed to host the rehearsal dinner in the back room after hours. He did all the cooking and serving. Hal was dressed in his best suit and made a spectacular groomsman. I was paired with Peter, a truck driver friend of Roger's. I didn't know him very well, but I had served him many times. He always paid in cash and left a nice tip. He was not much of a conversationalist, but we had a nice dinner together. Bert had served his favorite meatloaf at Leah's and Roger's request and, yes, we had dessert. Bert had saved one of Beatrice's fruit pies. From the first bite I understood why the customers raved about them.

The whole Cotton community came together for the wedding. Someone, even Roger wasn't sure who, had the keys to the church and had swept and cleaned it out. Someone else, also anonymous, donated flowers and bows for each of the pews. The ceremony was joyous. The only solemn part was when Mrs. Lawrence read several scriptures.

To the music of a portable organ, played by one of Leah's cheerleading friends, Hal and Connie walked down the aisle followed by Peter and me. Pastor Campbell's sermonette was funny and yet thought-provoking. He challenged the couple to overlook the problems they had struggled with in the past and rejoice in their newfound relationship, emphasizing that they were "new creatures" in Christ, who was sanctifying their marriage. Connie and I signed the marriage certificate as witnesses. Never had two witnesses been more excited.

Rachel was very well behaved. Now nine months old and walking, she toddled along between the pews throwing rose petals. During the ceremony, she sat in her grandmother's lap. Leah had bottled some pumped breastmilk just in case, but the child wanted to watch everything going on and even clapped when the minister introduced the new married couple.

As the ceremony concluded, I looked back to the door. I thought I saw Jim Toumala standing just inside the door, but then he disappeared, and I wasn't sure.

The reception, held in the back room of the restaurant, was great. Bernice had made the cake topped with HO train figures of a man and a waitress with a little baby girl crawling in the frosting. Beside the couple was a Peterbilt tractor and trailer. It said "Congratulations Family" across the top.

A few out-of-town customers arrived who didn't realize that the restaurant was closed. Connie and I took turns serving them, and Ron volunteered to short-order their requests. The customers wondered at our formal dresses. We explained that the restaurant was hosting a wedding reception and our outfits made the reception more festive. After eating their meals, these stray customers joined the reception. When introduced to the bride and groom, they donated cash to the young couple.

After the reception, Leah and Roger jumped into his pickup with boat and trailer and headed off to Canada for their honeymoon. I think they were heading for Niagara Falls and stopping to go fishing along the way. Shawnee and the grandparents volunteered to care for Rachel, who waved and yelled, "Goodbye, mommy, be back soon," as they left. Bert found yet another teenage boy to wash the dishes for the two weeks while Leah was gone.

Everything had fallen into place. The whole community was involved. I rejoiced that the two had found each other. But as I lay in bed in my coop that night I was jealous of how meaningful this simple wedding was in comparison to my expensive, meaningless, annulled wedding.

• • •

On Christmas Eve, I was again invited to Hal and Connie's place. Leah was living with Roger, but Connie felt that since she had lived with them for over a year, they belonged with the group, so they were invited as well. We had an exchange of small gifts, and everyone was in a festive mood.

My second-in-my-life birthday party the next morning was not a surprise this time, but I loved it just as much. I held back my tears this time even though it was still emotionally overwhelming. Again I slept with Shawnee, and we had "girl talk until early into the morning, but her questions and perspectives were far more mature.

One thing bothered me. I'd had my breast lump biopsied a few days before Christmas without anyone at the restaurant knowing. Because of the holiday season, there was a delay in getting the results from the pathologist. Dr. Sheihe still encouraged me that it was most likely benign, but the expression on the surgeon's face as I recovered from the anesthesia troubled me.

Chapter 25
Breast Cancer

The last of the customers had left when I told Connie the news. "You've got what?" she said and dropped the bussing container she held. She stooped to pick up several broken dishes. "You never told me about any surgery."

"I had a biopsy of a lump in my breast the Tuesday before Christmas. The pathology showed cancer."

"You're just twenty-five years old, Becky Jean. We just celebrated your birthday. How could you have breast cancer? It's got to be a mistake."

"Some young women get breast cancer, Connie. My mother's sister and my grandmother had breast cancer, although they were older when they discovered it."

Connie hugged me with tears dripping down her face. "Becky Jean, I just can't believe it."

"I got to tell Bert when my surgery is scheduled. I'll need to be off for a couple of days, although I don't suppose I'll have to be gone long just to have a bilateral mastectomy."

"What? You're going to have both your boobs whacked off?"

I tried to make light of her colloquial response. "It's better for balance."

Connie did not appreciate my humor. She seemed horrified, so I became serious. "They biopsied a suspicious lump on my other breast too. They couldn't tell on the frozen section whether it was cancer or not. I'll get the report when I go for surgery, but if it is cancer, then, to use your words, I'll have both my boobs whacked off." I hugged her, "I'm not using them anyway, although I suppose my uniform will fit funny."

She still couldn't respond to my humor. She just clung to me. I said to appeaser her, "I'll get foam jobbies if it makes you feel better."

"Oh, Becky Jean, you are the most amazing woman I have ever met. I'd be devastated. I'd hide in a closet and never come out. You are one courageous woman. No wonder Shawnee likes to talk to you so much."

"How did she do on her SAT test?"

"Quite well. I think she's willing to go to college after the talk you gave her. Maybe she will even get a scholarship. The reservation has scholarships for Anishinaabe who want to further their education. No one in our family has ever gone to college, but she is my sharp one. Sometimes she is too sharp with that mouth of hers, but I suppose that's part of being intelligent. She thinks she already knows more than her high-school-educated parents and most of the time she thinks she knows more than her teachers. She mouths off, and that's why she is in detention all the time."

"You have two very intelligent daughters. Sherrie is just more artistic and compliant as well as less science oriented than Shawnee. They both need every chance to go as far as possible in their education. Who knows? Maybe one of them will become a doctor and cure breast cancer."

"What's going on, ladies?" said Bert. "Cut the chit-chat. Who broke the dishes?"

"I did Bert, it was an accident," said Connie.

"Always is," he said.

"Yes," Connie said and turned away to wipe her tears with her apron. "I need a moment, Bert. Becky Jean needs to talk to you." She turned and glared at him. "And it was not chit-chat. It was serious."

Bert directed me to his office. I sat down opposite him at his desk. As I sighed deeply, his demeanor changed. "You aren't quitting, are you?"

I smiled, "No, nothing like that. I got the report back on my breast biopsy. It's cancer, so I need just a couple of days off to have a bilateral mastectomy."

He pushed his chair back and banged into the wall behind him. "What? Breast cancer? How can that be? You're so young."

"It appears that I have a family history. Listen, Bert, I'll have the surgery and be back to work before you know it. I don't have big breasts, so it should be a pretty simple surgery."

"Oh, Becky Jean." He paused and opened his mouth to say something, but nothing came out.

"I still have vacation coming, I'll just use that."

"Well, oh, just take whatever you need. Get well soon. Oh, man, I'm at a loss for words."

"At least this is the slow time of the year. Things won't speed up until fishing season, will they?"

"Don't worry about that. Just take the time you need to get your strength back." He stood, and a slight smile came across his face. "Don't worry. I won't charge Connie for the broken dishes. I'm just glad I didn't have my hands full of dishes when you told me. I would have broken anything I was carrying too."

Chapter26
Healing

A week later, I was in post-anesthesia recovery. As I struggled to think and clear the anesthesia from my brain, I sighed and grabbed my chest. There were thick bandages wrapped around me. As I moved in bed, a nurse ran to my side and checked my blood pressure, timed my respirations, and said, "Waking up, sleepy one?"

As the fog cleared, I forced myself awake and searched my room. There were several other patients recovering from surgery, each attended by a nurse. I shook my head. She encouraged me, "Don't worry, you are doing fine. Your surgery went well." Then she went to the nurse's desk that I could just see beyond my feet.

I tried to reason, *What was I doing here? What happened?* But I couldn't quite put my thoughts together.

I shook my head again, and the nurse returned. "Your vitals are all stable, so we are transferring you back to your room. You're recovering nicely."

Ah, I had surgery. What kind of surgery? Yes, I had breast cancer. Surgery was to get rid of the cancer. Now I remember. That's what these bandages on my chest are all about. What did the doctor call it? Yes, I had a mastectomy, bilateral mastectomy.

Transport through the hall was an interesting experience. The very handsome attendant—at least in my haze of medication he seemed handsome—escorted me on the gurney into the elevator and down the hall to my room. Looking up at all the ceiling tiles was an interesting view, noting all the holes in each tile. I had no idea where I was going or where I had been. I thought that if I memorized the ceiling tiles I could retrace my passage. *But why?*

My chest complained as he pulled me into my bed, but he was quick about it. "Wish you the best," he said as he left me in the charge of the floor nurse. The anesthesia lingering in my brain was too powerful to fight. I fell back asleep.

Light was flickering through the blinds when I awoke. *What time is it?* Looking around the room, I couldn't find a clock. I tried to reason that as the light was coming through the blinds at an angle it must be late afternoon.

There was a painting on the wall at the end of the bed, but my vision was too blurry to see it. The pastel blue walls were at least not the urine yellow of my hospital room when I'd had my kidney cancer surgery as a child. I hated that color. *I always thought it diabolical that the nephrology ward had yellow walls.*

I fixated on the painting, trying to focus. I had to see it. I swung my legs to get out of bed but when I tried to use my arms to sit up, a searing pain shot across my chest. I pulled open the neck of my hospital gown and saw the tight elastic wrap around my chest with bandages sticking out in all directions. A whiff of body odor mixed with iodine made me sneeze. Excruciating pain shot across both sides of my chest as I again tried to use my arms. Digging my elbows into the mattress, I grabbed a pillow and held it to my chest. Tears shot out of my eyes. I hugged the pillow, and the sharpness dissipated. *I guess they took both breasts just like I asked.*

I edged my feet onto the floor and this time I was careful how I used my elbows to push myself up. Instant nausea and dizziness blocked my attempt. I steadied myself with my hands and felt the tightness of the incisions. With slow, deliberate determination I put my arms through a gentle range of motion. *They still work. I just got to get used to this pain. I have to get back to work.*

As I steadied myself on the edge of the bed, I remembered the nice social worker lady who had come to see me before surgery. *She said that my income was 'inadequate.' Wait till I tell Bert.* I laughed out loud. Oh, that hurt. *No more laughing. With no insurance, I qualified for…* I couldn't remember the rest. My brain wasn't working.

"Do it," I said and jumped up. My gown had been washed so many times that it was like gossamer. I could see my abdominal scar and the dressings on my chest right through the fabric. My arms flexed to my chest involuntarily. "At least I can walk," I said using sarcasm to force myself into moving. I paraded around my bed, holding the bedrail, unsure if I would fall or faint. I planned to fall back in bed if I did. *All right, now go see the picture.* I expected some pastoral of a farmhouse in a meadow with snow-tipped mountains in the background. What a surprise.

Opening the blinds for better light, I was startled. It was an original oil painting. I looked at the copper plate below. "Capri," it was titled. "In memory of my daughter, Lily."

"There must be a story behind this painting," I said as I held my finger just above the oil texture, afraid to touch the rugged, Italian coast painted with a pallet knife. Angry waves hurtled themselves on the rocky cliffs, but on top of the cliff stood a young woman. She was painted in sharp detail with delicate brush strokes in contrast to the rest of the scene. She looked calm and tenacious.

"Ooh! What are you doing up?" exclaimed a shrill voice from behind me. I swung around to see Sherrie and Connie. "I can see your bare butt," said Sherrie as she covered her eyes.

I laughed and pulled my gown together in the back, "These hospital gowns don't cover much."

"That's not much better," she said. "I can see right through your gown." She covered her eyes again.

"Sherrie, she's a girl just like you, calm down." Connie shifted her purse to her other hand. "How are you doing? Did the surgery go all right?" Without waiting for an answer, she added, "Can I use your bathroom, Becky Jean?"

"Sure." Connie went to the bathroom, and I put on a robe that was hanging on the wardrobe door in the corner of the room. "Sherrie, could you help me? It's too painful to swing my arms into the sleeves."

She helped me adjusted the robe to my arms, peeking through her hand. I turned to face her. "Is that better?"

She slipped her hand off her face. "Yes. I'm sorry. I was startled. I brought you a card. I made it myself." She lowered her eyes, "I'm sorry. I have never been in a hospital before. Well, I must have been when I was born, but I don't remember. Maybe mom had me at home, I've never asked her."

She grabbed her bag off the bed where she had thrown it and produced a card. It was simple with a leaf design drawn on the front and "Heal fast" scrawled below. I opened it and something fell out. I tried to bend down to pick it up, but Sherrie scurried over to pick it up for me and handed it to me. She held out a square piece of birch bark as gently as if holding a baby bird.

"Hold it up to the light."

The most amazing design, diamond shaped and symmetrical, shone through the thin bark. "It's an Anishinaabe thing. We do it by biting the folded bark. I did that one especially for you. It is a healing design."

"Amazing. You did it with your teeth?"

"Yes, I did it with my own teeth." She looked up at me. "Do you like it?" She shifted on her feet. "And I wrote a poem for you inside. Read the poem. I'll play my flute as you read it out loud." She extracted a flute from her bag and started playing a simplified version of what I recognized as the melody from Mozart's "Magic Flute." She was quite accomplished.

> *A birch tree stands alone*
> *A lonely birch amidst the pine trees*
> *All alone in the meadow*
> *Until the birds nest in its branches*
> *Then it's not alone.*

"Do you like my poem?"

I put my arm over her shoulder, ignoring the strain on my incisions. "I will treasure it always. No one has ever given me a finer gift."

"Don't show it to Shawnee. She thinks it's stupid."

I kissed her forehead. "I promise."

Connie came out of the bathroom. "Sorry, I picked up Sherrie at school and came right down to the hospital. Your bathroom was sort of an emergency. Busy day at work. Can't wait to have you back."

"She likes the birch bark, mom, and she likes my poem, too." Connie quelled her with a nod. Sherrie's smile faded as she sat in the corner chair folding her hands across her bag held in her lap.

"That's quite a bandage I saw when I came in," said Connie. "What's the verdict?"

"The doctor hasn't come in yet. I just climbed out of anesthesia fog, but they took both breasts. The biopsy last week showed cancer in both biopsies." Connie's face looked concerned.

"So I'll be balanced, at least, just like I told you."

"Becky Jean, your attitude. I don't see how you can make a joke of this."

"I went through a lot when I had kidney cancer when I was ten."

"You had cancer when you were ten?" Sherrie blurted, then looked at her mother and covered her mouth.

"It's nothing to be ashamed of." I sat on the bed, opened the card, and reread the poem out loud. "Yes, I had cancer at ten. I thought I was going to die then. Now that was a painful incision." I opened my robe and lifted my gown so Sherrie could see the scar from my kidney surgery. She gasped. I turned to Connie, "So, I guess I've worked through a lot of those ugly feelings."

"I just don't think I could be so calm about the whole thing," said Connie.

"What I'm focused on," my eyes drifted to the picture on the wall, "is getting through this storm and back to work." I motioned toward the picture. Connie scanned the picture. Sherrie stood to look at it and seemed to focus on every detail. "Our customers are my family." I looked at the silent teen gazing at the painting. "Just like your poem, Sherrie, the customers at the restaurant are the birds in my branches." Sherrie turned to me with a loving smile and then returned her focus to the painting.

Connie broke the silence, "So, what happens next, brave heart?"

"I met my oncologist, she's very nice. She told me that they would analyze the cancer for receptors and that would help her decide what chemotherapy I should have." I held the birch bark up to the light coming in the window. I could see the imprint of Sherrie's molars and incisors and sharp dots that I assumed were her canines. "What an intimate gift," I said.

"Those birch barks were considered sacred in the old days," said Connie.

"This will be sacred to me, forever."

There was a knock on the door and the surgeon entered and introduced himself to my guests. "I'm Dr. Philips, the surgeon who did Ms. Gottwald's surgery this morning. Would you excuse us please?"

"Oh they're family; they can stay," I said. He scratched his head looking at my visitors then back at me, apparently puzzled at the lack of familial resemblance between my Germanic blond, pale visage and my friends' dark complexion and long black hair.

"Well, all right, then." He shifted his weight and opened my chart to review my report. "There were several abnormal lymph nodes on both sides.

The frozen sections the pathologist did at surgery showed the cancer we expected." He nodded at me, I assume to get my acknowledgement. "So we had to remove both breasts."

"As I requested."

"Yes, right." He cleared his throat. "The pathologist's final report regarding estrogen and progesterone receptors will take a couple days. You should review those findings with your oncologist." He looked at Connie and Sherrie. He hesitated before pulling down my gown and inspecting my incisions.

"Don't worry, they're my adopted family," I thought that would go over better. Connie rolled her eyes; Sherrie covered her eyes with her hands.

He set aside my chart and his pen, washed his hands and put on gloves from a box on the wall. He released the chest binders and with meticulous care removed the gauze bandages that covered the incisions. "Good. No bleeding. I'll still have to come back tomorrow morning and check once more for any signs of infection just before you go home." He dropped the bandages in a haphazard manner over the incisions and removed his gloves, putting them in a special receptacle by the door. "The nurse will come and put fresh bandages on your incisions." He picked up my chart from the bedside table and put his pen in the pocket of his scrubs. "Are you feeling all right? You did well all through surgery. Any questions?" He paused, waiting for my response.

"I feel fine, Dr. Phillips. Glad to have all that cancer out of me."

"All right, then, I hope I got it all."

"I know the positive lymph nodes mean you didn't."

"Well, yes, I suppose. Maybe the chemo will take care of that. See you tomorrow morning." He headed toward the door. "I'll need to see you in my office in a week to ten days post-op to take out the staples. My nurse will schedule the appointment." He flashed into the hall, slamming the door behind him.

"Well, wasn't that warm and compassionate," said Connie.

"Don't be sarcastic, Connie. He's a surgeon. His job was to remove the cancer. He did his job. He told me that I was the youngest patient on whom he has ever performed a double mastectomy. He was quite uncomfortable with my case." I attempted to reapply my binder. "Now I have two fine incisions to demonstrate his handiwork. Did you know they now use staples, not sutures, to close the incisions?"

"Oh, yuck, doesn't that hurt? Being stapled?" Sherrie cringed in her chair then looked at her mother and covered her mouth.

"I was asleep, Sherrie. It didn't hurt a bit."

Connie looked at her daughter and shook her head. "Go ahead, you can ask her."

"Are those staples still in you?" She grimaced.

I slipped my gown down and peeled back the gauze till some of the shiny staples were evident, "See."

"Oh, yuck." She covered her eyes, trying to rub out the sight.

Connie turned to me, "I think that is as much reality as a junior high school girl can handle."

The nurse appeared at the door with her dressing cart. She looked at my guests. "It's all right," I said.

She gloved up and proceeded to tuck fresh bandages in place and cinched up my chest binder, helped me put on a fresh gown, even assisting me to re-dress with the terrycloth robe. "Would you mind if I took a walk? My friends here can assist me. I still feel a little dizzy and would appreciate someone holding on to me."

"That's a great idea," said the nurse. "Stay active. You heal faster. You are doing very well, Ms. Gottwald. You should be able to go home tomorrow."

With Connie on my right and Sherrie on my left, we walked into the hall. "When did he say that you would get that pathology report?" Sherrie asked, tripping over the word.

"Soon, Sherrie, when I see the cancer doctor, my oncologist." I turned to Connie, "When do you think Bert will let me come back to work?"

"Becky Jean, don't even ask such things."

I was lost in my thoughts as the three of us ambled down the hall. *And when will I be able to get back to the university and finish my degree?* I wondered. *I have to finish my degree. I'm not going to let a wretched husband stop me, and I can't let this cancer stop me either.*

Chapter 27
Homebound

"Are you awake, Becky Jean?" Shawnee asked.

"I think so." I searched under my cloth hospital gown and felt for the bandages over my chest. I looked up at her. "What are you doing here?"

"I'm your designated driver. When one has a driver's license, the privilege comes with certain responsibilities. You've heard my dad tell me that a hundred times."

"Oh, so you're bringing me home?" I looked at Shawnee. Her tight-fitting sweater accentuated her remarkable female form. "I just have to wait till the surgeon checks my staples. Then I am all yours, my dear chauffeur."

"Sherrie was really grossed out about your bandages and staples." She giggled.

Shawnee had left my door open, and as I sat up I could see all the nurses scurrying about. Shawnee had a name tag stuck to her sweater that said, "Visitor" in black block letters. "All right, I'm up. Let's get that surgeon."

The nurse came to check my temperature and blood pressure. "I'm fully alert now if I might speak with the surgeon. He wants to check my staples for signs of infection before I go home."

An infinite hour later, Dr. Phillips, dressed in green scrubs, twiddling a pen over my chart, stood beside me. "Ms. Gottwald, let me just check your incision, and then you may go home." He looked back at Shawnee. "More family?"

"Yep, she's fine," I said. He turned, washed his hands, and gloved up to remove the bandages. I could see that Shawnee was edging around to get a view. When he had all the bandages off, he poked at the incision to see if there was any drainage. Shawnee grabbed her mouth and collapsed in the corner chair.

"It was a big surgery," he said. "Do you want to stay another day?"

"I have no money and no insurance, doctor. I feel fine and would rather go home." I motioned over to Shawnee, "I have plenty of people to care for me there."

"I've never sent anyone home this quickly. But there is no abnormal bleeding and no sign of infection."

I glanced at Shawnee. The blood had drained from her face so that she appeared almost Caucasian. "Don't worry, I'll be fine. I have plenty of help," I reiterated to Dr. Philips.

He turned to Shawnee, who with a sudden jerk sat up straight to give him her attention. As he applied new bandages and rewrapped the ace binder around my chest, he asked, "Can you help her reapply this binder when it comes loose? She'll need help. It must be rewrapped several times a day so the tissues don't swell. It also helps with her pain."

"Yes, I can, sir. I will be faithful and do it as many times as you say."

I chuckled at her sudden formality.

"Great." He turned to me. "Then I'll let you go home, Ms. Gottwald. Staples need to come out at my office in ten days. I've made an appointment for you. I'll give you my card. It has your appointment time on it." He discarded the old dressings, ungloved, pulled a card out of the pocket of his scrubs, dropped it onto my bedside table, and walked out of the room, closing the door behind him.

"I guess that means I can get dressed." I motioned toward the closet. Shawnee took the jeans and sweatshirt out of the bedside closet. She showed a disgruntled facial expression.

"That's what I was wearing on admission, silly."

"You'll never get this sweat shirt on; it will hurt too much," she said. She slipped off her sweater and took off the button down blouse she was wearing underneath. "Here, wear my blouse, and I'll wear that sweatshirt."

"Cute bra, Shawnee, all lacey and frilly," I said. "Does your father know you bought that?" I giggled.

She gave me a furious glare. "No, and you'd better not tell him."

I was dressed in Shawnee's blouse and button-down sweater. It was much looser on me than it was on her. Shawnee sat on the bed next to me and gave me a hug.

The discharge planner knocked and came in focused on my chart. She looked up at me. "Your income is such that you may qualify for help with your medical bills, Ms. Gottwald." She went down a checklist of questions on her clipboard ending with, "Do you smoke?"

"No."

"Do you own a television?"

"No."

"What kind of a car do you own?"

"She doesn't own anything," Shawnee jumped up, apparently frustrated with all the questions. "She has nothing and owns nothing," she screamed. "All her miserable clothes fit into a backpack. Can't you tell? She's even wearing my blouse." Tears dripped down her cheeks. "And now she doesn't even have boobs."

The discharge planner seemed irritated by this upstart teen. I hugged Shawnee, letting her wipe her tears on my discarded hospital gown.

"Is this your daughter, or...?" the discharge planner looked confused trying to judge our ages and complexions.

"No. She is my best friend's daughter." I smoothed down Shawnee's jet black hair. "I'm sorry about her outburst, but she cares about me as if she were my daughter. I'm sort of an adopted aunt."

I handed the discharge planner the form I had completed from the drawer of my bedside table. She added it to my chart. "Thank you for the information, Ms. Gottwald. I will make an application for you, and you should receive a letter from the Ordean Foundation when the board meets to review your request." She skirted out the door.

"I'm sorry, Becky Jean. That wasn't very Anishinaabe. If my parents saw me behave like that, I'd probably be grounded for the rest of my life. You won't tell on me, will you? But all those questions made me so furious." It was the first time I had seen her look shy.

"Can you help me with these flowers Bert sent me? The orderly with the wheel chair will be here soon." Her face was distressed, so I added, "No, I will not tell your parents what happened. Now, can you please help me?"

"Why are they bringing a wheel chair? Can't you walk?"

"I can walk just fine. It is hospital policy, so don't have another outburst." She put her hands behind her back and hung her head. "Now I have two secrets to hold against you, lacey bra and a nasty outburst."

"Blackmailer," she said as she twisted my old sweatshirt around the curve of her hips.

"Oh, come on, I'm just teasing you. You know everything that happens between us is confidential. Have I ever told your mother what we've talked about or squealed on you?"

"No, never. I trust you, Becky Jean, more than any other adult." She gave me a sigh of gratitude.

I looked at her. Even on Shawnee's youthful figure my old sweatshirt looked disgusting. I decided to throw it away when I got home.

•　　•　　•

At Connie's suggestion, I stayed in Shawnee's room for a couple days. Her twin-size bed accommodated both of us, and she was comfortable sharing. I was embarrassed that I needed help getting dressed, but she gave me some of her clothes that she commented, "I wouldn't be caught dead wearing," but they were perfect for someone healing from bilateral mastectomies. By the end of the week, I was helping Connie in the kitchen and sent a message to Bert that I was ready to come back to work.

Shawnee accompanied me to the surgeon's office. By then she had seen my staples on my bare chest enough times that watching the surgeon's nurse remove them no longer disgusted her. The whole process seemed to be more of an intriguing scientific procedure to her. She kept asking the nurse questions about the staples and the staple remover, and in the end the nurse allowed Shawnee to take out the last few staples. I wasn't sure which was better, having a compassionate teenage friend or being her science project.

Bert said that I had to keep an appointment with my oncologist, Dr. Esther Liebowitz before he would let me come back to work. He even had the audacity to require a "return to work" slip from her. After our brief meeting in the hospital, she had scheduled a follow-up appointment to review my pathologic receptors from the biopsies, the significance of the lymph nodes removed, and my prognosis. Shawnee drove me, but I asked her to stay in the waiting room. She protested but agreed. I wanted to sift through the information regarding chemotherapy and radiation before sharing the details with my friends.

Chapter 28
Oncology Visit

I was sitting on the exam table when Dr. Liebowitz entered. She looked up from some laboratory results in her hand. "Because you're so young and because both breasts were involved, I tested you for the breast cancer genes BRCA1 and 2," Dr. Liebowitz said. "Don't worry about the cost. I paid for it through our research grant."

"If it is to my benefit, shouldn't I pay?"

She was gentle in her manner but all business, "It is over three thousand dollars. Are you sure...?"

"I guess I will be thankful for your research grant. I don't have three..." I mumbled.

She waved off my response. She seemed like someone I would enjoy as a friend in different circumstances. Her dark brown eyes were intent but loving.

"Yes, I remember we talked about that before my mastectomy. You wanted to see if I had a genetic predisposition for breast cancer."

"That's correct. Now listen carefully. It's positive, Rebecca." I liked being called by my proper name, at least in this circumstance. It was so good for my self esteem and made me feel like she took me seriously. It brought back pleasant memories from before my parents decided that I was a renegade.

"So I need more family history," she continued. "When I first saw you, you said that your mother was healthy and that you had a sister. Can you tell me more, especially about their health?"

"My grandparents left Germany in 1939. My grandfather was a Lutheran minister and things were getting awful. Grandmother was Jewish. I think he married her to protect her. Anyway, they left Germany and came to Minnesota. Grandmother's brothers and sisters all died in the holocaust. I remember Grandpa telling about searching for them after the war. He lived into his late eighties, never giving up, hoping to find something about them.

I saw Dr. Leibowitz's downcast gaze. "I lost a lot of my relatives in the holocaust too. My Aunt took my mother to England just before the war."

"I'm so sorry Dr. Liebowitz."

She took a deep sigh, "Please continue."

"Grandmother died of pneumonia in her late sixties, but she was diagnosed with breast cancer a few years before. On my mother's side of the family, she had five brothers and one sister. She was the youngest. I recall mother saying that her sister had breast cancer, but I never met her.

"My parents married at the German Lutheran church. The services were still in German back then. My sister and I were raised pretty strict. No talking at meal-time unless we were asked to respond to a question. Dad set the rules, and we obeyed. Mother is pretty healthy as far as I know. My sister is six years older than me. I haven't seen her in years, but I think she's healthy."

"It doesn't sound like you see any of your family very often." Dr. Liebowitz put down her pen. "Have they been supportive since your breast cancer was diagnosed?"

"My sister and her husband live in Guatemala. They're missionaries, work with the poor people up in the mountains." Tears formed in my eyes despite my attempt to maintain my composure. "I'm sort of the black sheep of the family, Dr. Liebowitz. I married the man my father chose for me, and it didn't work out. My father blames me. Well, my mother does, too. We haven't spoken since I left my husband."

"You're divorced or…"

"I heard by rumor that our marriage was annulled after I abandoned him."

She gave me a tissue to wipe my eyes and waited for me to quit crying.

"The only reason that I bring this up, Rebecca, is because of this gene, your mother and sister are at risk for early breast cancer too. Knowing this risk could save their lives."

"I tried to call my mother to tell her that I had breast cancer, but she hung up on me before I could explain. I could give you the address and you could maybe write them a letter. Could you hand me my purse?" She did, and I pulled a card out. She handed me her pen, and I wrote the address on the notepad she gave me. "But please, please don't tell them where I live."

Dr. Liebowitz put her arm over my shoulder. It felt warm, melting the chill in my chest. "I will be discreet. I'm sorry that this is so painful for you. I've been an oncologist for many years, and it is so important for a cancer patient to have a supportive family."

"I try not to think about my own family too much. I've been sort of adopted by an Anishinaabe family, and I have lots of friends now who are very supportive. I'm very happy. You know the restaurant keeps me busy. I work with great employees and have a great boss who respects me. The community in Cotton has really made me feel at home. We're the only restaurant along Highway 53 from Duluth to Virginia. So, we're pretty busy. The restaurant is like a chapel. People care about one another. The ladies' Bible study meets every Wednesday. It's my church." I laughed, "But the Bible study ladies don't tip well." I paused to see her response, "I'm sorry. I'm rambling."

Dr. Liebowitz interrupted, "Have you reconsidered having chemotherapy?"

"I've thought about it. What were the receptor studies on my cancer cells?"

"Negative, I'm sorry to tell you."

"Well, then I really don't want chemo. I've read about Tamoxifen. Is that chemo? You gave me that prescription when I left the hospital, but it's pretty expensive, $69.99 at Walgreens for thirty pills. I bought it and am taking it, but waitresses don't have health insurance, you know. I'm not having any side-effects from the Tamoxifen," I curled me eyes, "when I take it. Sometimes I skip. I've been trying to stretch the prescription out." She shook her head at me. "I'm sorry to be a non-compliant patient, but I'm just a waitress.

"I'll see if I can get the Tamoxifen for you out of my research grant. We are studying patients that have BRCA 1 and 2 genes."

Dr. Liebowitz thumbed through my chart. "Chemo would lower your risk of metastases, but not cure you. You had two positive lymph nodes. Sorry to be blunt, but I expect my patients to be honest, so I have to be honest with them. I'm not trying to ruin your hope, but with those positive nodes and positive BRCA 1 and 2 with negative estrogen and progesterone receptors, the chemo is not that effective."

"If I get...we called them 'mets' when I worked at the nursing home, I suppose I'll die. My family won't care. My friends will be sad, but they'll get over it. I know the risk, but I can't take time from the restaurant being sick, so no chemo. I can't afford to be sick or nauseated when I work around food."

"All right then. You are always welcome to come back if you change your mind. This is not a closed door." She shut my chart. "Let me take a look at those scars."

She grabbed a gown from a receptacle under the exam table and gave it to me. She turned to give me privacy, but I just unbuttoned my blouse and took it off. "I don't need that gown. I've got nothing to cover up." I laughed. She frowned.

She laid me down on the exam table to feel the incision lines. My ribs felt bare and cold. The blood vessels I could see through the thin skin on my chest fascinated me. The arteries and veins searched to nourish the breasts that no longer existed. She examined my arm pits. I hadn't shaved since my surgery and the fine hair tickled as she checked for abnormalities.

"Everything's fine. I do not feel anything abnormal. I'm surprised that you aren't wearing a mastectomy bra."

"I do at the restaurant. It fills out my uniform. The other waitress bought it for me so I wouldn't need new uniforms." I smiled at her. Thin lines cut her face around her mouth as she attempted a smile. I felt sorry for her as she seemed so serious. "But there's no reason to wear it to come to see you, is there?"

"I guess not." She picked up my chart and stood at the door. "Have you joined a support group?"

I buttoned my blouse. "The restaurant is my support group. I told you, it's like a chapel."

"Have you considered reconstructive surgery?"

"Since my scars are pretty well healed, I've been thinking about 'fake boobs,' as my coworkers say." I looked up at her. "I'm sorry for being crude. That's the way people talk at the restaurant. I should have just said, 'Yes, I've considered reconstructive breast surgery.' I need more time to think about it."

She opened the door and paused. "All right, Rebecca, you're doing pretty well. I'll send a letter to your mother and one for her to forward to your sister. They need to know their increased risk."

"Thanks, Dr. Liebowitz. Remember, don't forget my 'back to work' slip, or my boss won't let me return to the restaurant. Oh, and remember, don't tell my parents or sister where I live, please."

• • •

By the next Tuesday, I was back to work. I wasn't as fast as before, but I was getting things done. I went back to work on Tuesday because I expected to be less stressed buying supplies for the restaurant. Each of the wholesale houses I went to kindly loaded my purchases for me. Dr. Liebowitz had arranged a late appointment with a plastic surgeon since I would be in town and have my shopping done by mid-afternoon.

His office was bright with modern aluminum furniture and pictures of attractive people across the walls. A sign said "Free consultation for cosmetic surgery." I wasn't sure my surgery would be cosmetic. Maybe there were different rules if one had cancer. He seemed nice when he came into the exam room, but the surgery he described sounded painful. Even with assistance provided by my caring medical social worker, it would be expensive, even though it wasn't considered "cosmetic" surgery by insurance or public assistance standards.

When I asked him where he was going to get the fat to reconstruct my breasts, he just scratched his head and forced a laugh, "We don't transplant fat. But your skin is pretty thin on your chest. I would have to stretch it to put in the implants. I think it would be good if you gained a little weight."

Now I had something else to think about. I wasn't sure how I would gain weight on my one allowed meal per day and the popcorn and crackers I ate in my coop. I didn't want to buy a lot of extra food. I was saving everything extra to finish college, if I would survive that long. I thanked him for being gracious and left thinking the foam jobs in my bra would be just fine.

But I had one more mission that day. Just down from the hospital clinic on Superior Street, the main street in Duluth, was Bagley's Jewelry store, a family owned business with a great reputation, I read on the door "since 1885." It was quiet as I entered. The store was dimly lit, accentuating the gems in the lighted cabinets. The jeweler was waiting on a young couple. Eavesdropping, I overheard that they were picking out an engagement ring together. They seemed enchanted with the possibilities the jeweler offered.

"I'll be right with you, madam," the dark curly haired jeweler said.

"Take your time. I'm in no hurry. They look like they need you more than I do." The young couple turned and smiled, hugging each other around the waist.

Watching them made me recall our prenuptials. *Keith and I never went to a jewelry store to pick out a ring. He made all the choices and all the arrangements. The wedding was his, not ours.* I remember when he gave a bill to my father after the reception and told him, "That's your part to pay."

Mother had whispered in my ear, "You better make this work; it's costing us a lot of money."

I remember my sense of panic. I hardly knew Keith Slagg. This was all arranged, allegedly for me, yet I was responsible to make it work. It didn't seem fair.

"May I help you now? Thank you for being so patient. I'm Charles, Charles Bagley." He had a course face and a prominent nose almost like a cartoon, but his manner was controlled strength.

"Yes, thank you. So this is a family owned store?"

He smiled, "I'm the great grandson of the original owner."

"That gives me confidence in the store's integrity. Nice to meet you, Charles Bagley." I pulled my engagement ring and wedding ring out of my purse, still in the envelope that I had retrieved from my bank safety deposit box that morning. "I would like to have these assessed and would consider selling them."

"That's a very valuable-looking gem, and a fine setting." He took out his magnifying lens and peered at the diamond. "We can do that, but why do you want to sell them?"

"These are my wedding rings. I'm *divorced* now, so they don't mean much to me anymore." The word stung in my mouth since I was really annulled. "And, well, I have some medical expenses." I pulled the neck of my blouse over so he could see the beginning of my scar.

"I see," he said, but looked away. He photographed the rings and gave me the Polaroids. I filled out a form with my name and social security number. I showed him my marriage license I had purloined when I left to prove that the rings belonged to me. As I put down the restaurant's address and telephone number, he made a copy of my marriage license.

He scanned the form. "Ms. Gottwald, we have to take the gems out of the setting to properly identify and value them. Then we put them back. I will have to charge you for that. Of course, if you choose to sell them we will just deduct that cost from what we give you. Is that understood?"

"Just call me Rebecca. And yes, I understand that you need to take them apart to do it right. How much will that be? I'm just a waitress. I don't make much money."

He took another look at the rings. "I will try to keep the cost down." He turned the rings over in his hand. It seemed to me that he was already assessing their value. "I can have that assessment completed by next week, Rebecca. I love that name. My daughter's name is Rebecca."

I slipped the photos of the rings into my purse. "Thanks, I like it, too, but everyone calls me Becky Jean. Do you know Dr. Liebowitz? She's my oncologist."

He smiled. "She's my wife's sister."

"Well, then, if you have any questions, ask her. I give you my permission." I walked toward the door and opened it for another smiling couple. "See you next week."

Chapter 29
Jewelry Store

"The rings are worth that much?" I was astounded at the figure on the certificate and receipt he gave me. It was enough to buy a small house. My finger counted the zeros from the decimal point.

Charles explained, "Rebecca, the setting is antique, it must have been made in the late eighteen hundreds, way before you were born. The gems are quite rare and flawless. You're quite young. Didn't you say they were your engagement and wedding rings?"

"Yes, but I didn't get to pick them out or anything. My ex-husband just gave me the ring when we were engaged and then the wedding band when we were married."

"Yes, I did verify your marriage license, but I understand that it was annulled in Iowa. I had to do that to insure that you actually owned the rings. I've never had quite this situation, but our lawyer claims that since the rings are in your possession, you have the right to sell them. They were given to you at the time of your engagement and wedding ceremony, so legally, you own them, despite the annulment."

Wow, he has done his homework. I was surprised that all these details of my life were public knowledge and so discoverable.

He held the engagement ring up to a jeweler's scope and offered to let me examine the diamond. I had no idea what I was looking at in terms of quality, but it was interesting to see the facets close up. They twinkled like sparks of firelight.

Mr. Bagley continued as I gazed at the diamond. "They really are priceless, but that figure is the most I can offer. Take them to New York City and you could probably get ten or twenty percent more for them. We were so awed, we won't even charge for the assessment. We don't see anything of this quality here in Duluth very often." He set them in a cushioned box and pushed them toward me. Next to the box he slid a company check. "Your choice," he said. "You may want to keep the rings since they are so valuable, or you can take the check. My sister-in-law said that you had some pretty expensive medical costs related to your surgery. This will more than pay for those."

Another customer entered. "Rebecca, let me serve this customer while you think it over."

"No problem. I need time to think." *Should I take the money or the rings?* Suddenly I understood why Keith wanted these rings back. But the stench of all my possessions burning in the trash barrel and the sting of Keith Stagg slapping me and calling me damaged goods reminded me that the rings were mine. Hadn't the jewelry store lawyer said so? They were the only compensation from all the anguish he had put me through. Did I need the breast implant surgery? Maybe not. It wasn't like I was going to spend it on some luxury or gamble it away. Mr. Bagley claimed that the diamond mount was fashioned in the late nineteenth century. That caused me to wonder from where Keith got them. Were they his grandmother's rings? Did they have great sentimental value to him? Knowing Keith, he probably just wanted them for some other trophy bride or maybe just for the money. Then a realization hit me like a bullet: the rings hadn't cost him anything. He hadn't spent a single cent asking me to marry him.

"I'll tell you what," said Charles Bagley when he returned, interrupting my thoughts. "I spoke to my sister-in-law and know that you are in the process of making some difficult decisions. I'll keep the rings in the safe. They are yours if you want them back. You take the check, and if you cash it that will tell me you don't want them. The rings will be here, locked up, if you change your mind. Just return the check, and the rings will be returned to you."

"Thank you, Charles. You have been so kind and considerate. I don't know what to do, so I'll take the check and think some more."

I made a quick trip to the bank. I thought about cashing it right then but instead put it in the safety deposit box where I had kept the rings.

Chapter 30
Week of Vacation

"Why don't you take a week off?" Bert said. "With pay." He smiled at me as if he knew something he wasn't supposed to know. "You haven't taken more than three days off in a row since I hired you. Well, except for your surgery, but that doesn't count. That was medical leave. So take next week off. We'll see you the following Monday morning."

"Is that all right with Connie?"

"She's getting the girls ready for the next school year. Shawnee is a senior this year, you know. She needs a little extra money for clothes for the girls, so she said she wouldn't mind. Besides, she always takes her vacation in September for wild rice harvest, and then you have to work without her. Leah can help. I've got a temp coming to wash dishes. Now that Leah's married, she wants more time off." He smiled. "Imagine, she told me that they don't need the money as Roger is doing so well. Anyway, I'm checking out this new dishwasher."

"Thanks, Bert. I would really enjoy some time off." My mind raced. Not exactly. What would I do? It was still warm out. Maybe I could go fishing again. My hikes had allowed me to discover a remote spot in the whiteface river to go skinny-dipping. There was a big boulder in the river, perfect for lying out to dry in the sun. I had gone there on several Sundays already this summer and loved the experience. It was so sensuous. I had to apply gobs of sunscreen to my chest because of the delicate skin left from my surgery, but it was worth it. Now that Roger was married, I doubted that my fishing buddy was available. Besides, I had promised Leah no skinny-dipping with Roger. I presumed that meant no fishing trips alone with him either.

I left Bert's office to check on the customers. "Fresh coffee?" I asked the fellows at the counter.

When Connie whisked by, I asked her, "Is this all right for me to have a week off? With pay? That's the part I can't believe. I didn't think waitresses had that benefit."

"First of all, you deserve some time off. Second, since you are assistant manager, you get that as a benefit and Bert counts it as a tax deduction from his business expenses. Third, I took your suggestion, Becky Jean. I'm actually looking forward to going shopping with the girls, and I want a little extra spending money to do it. With all the tips, I should have what the girls need for school expenses. Shawnee is babysitting for little Rachel. Leah keeps track of the hours and pays her minimum wage. She's made quite a bundle of money to spend on new clothes. She has saved every penny. I am so surprised that working to make the money has totally changed that girl's spending habits. She used to always ask Hal for money to spend on such trivial things, but not anymore. It's been great. And there has been no more whining about 'you spent more on Sherrie than you did on me' or 'why can't I buy what I want?' or 'I want to wear what the cool kids wear.' She earned the money, and Hal and I decided we would let her buy what she wants." Connie laughed and added, "Hal did put some modesty restrictions on what she buys."

I thought about the frilly bra she wore to the hospital, but my mouth was sealed.

She wiped the counter and added sugar to the dispenser. "Sherrie, on the other hand, still has a more humble mindset."

"Anishinaabe mindset?"

"I suppose, but she enjoys having me pick out her clothes. Don't lecture me. I know this won't last forever, but I'm enjoying being her mother. I have never had the chance to feel that way during the entire time that Shawnee has been a teenager. She is so independent and way too strong-minded."

"I'm sure they both will make wise choices."

"We'll see." She rushed off to bring the breakfast orders to the road crew.

Roger stopped in for lunch, so I asked about fishing. "We could go together, you, Leah, and I. Shawnee could babysit."

"Sorry, partner," he said, "but there is a run on cement. They're putting in a new facility at Potlatch, and I'm working overtime all weekend. But as

soon as I have a day off, we'll schedule another fishing trip for all *three* of us."
He leaned over the counter and whispered in my ear, "Leah's not really into
skinny-dipping though. She's still pretty sensitive about 'stretch marks.'"

"I understand."

"I asked other customers about their plans for the week. Everyone was
busy. By the end of the day, all my proposed plans had fizzled. I still planned
to go for a swim in my secret water hole in the Whiteface River, but that
wouldn't fill a whole week.

After closing, I went to my coop, slipped off my shoes, and lay in bed looking at the stains on the ceiling tiles. *What should I do with my week off?* I had no
vehicle. Maybe one day Bert would let me borrow the restaurant van, but certainly not all week. I could paint the ceiling. I still had paint left over from the
walls, but it should be white, and I didn't have any white paint. I got up and
showered until I drained the hot water heater, dried off, and flopped back on
the bed.

I awoke, chilled; goose bumps covered my naked body. It was so dark that
I couldn't tell if my eyes were open or not. I crawled under the blankets and
tried to come up with some sort of plan. *I'll have to buy some food. I sure don't
want to go hungry for a week.* Plans spun around in my head. I should have gotten some cash when I went to Duluth for supplies on Tuesday. I could hitchhike to Duluth. Maybe one of my trucker friends would give me a ride. But
then I would have to hitchhike to a grocery store and then how would I get
stuff home? This isn't working out well. Poor planning might kill me. I envi-
sioned Bert finding me dead a week from Monday complaining about a lack
of two weeks' notice. I had no money, no vehicle, and not much food stashed
away. Even thinking about food made me hungry. *Too bad, stomach, there's only
a few crackers and some popcorn in the cupboard and nothing substantial in my miniature refrigerator.* I laughed, because I didn't really have a cupboard. It was just
a cardboard box. *You'll have to wait till a week from Monday at 2:30. God, help
me.* Somehow in the warmth of covering up in my sleeping bag, I fell asleep.

Sunday I followed my usual schedule. It was warm, so I took a long hike in
the woods. It was beautiful as the leaves were just starting to turn. Sprawled
out on a warm rock after my swim, I looked up into the sky and wondered,
What was I going to do tomorrow? Back at the coop, it was getting dark, so I took
a shower, made some popcorn, and finished a novel a customer had given me.

Monday morning I awoke at five o'clock just like usual. I didn't think I needed another shower, so I just got dressed. I checked the cardboard box where I stored food items, the miniature freezer, and the refrigerator. There was nothing much there. My wallet had two dollars and twenty nine cents, counting all the pennies. What could I buy for $2.29? *Connie better come back from her break on time next Monday afternoon or I might do something I would regret. On the other hand, couldn't a person live a month without food as long as they had water?* I laughed at my ridiculous thinking. I sat on my bed to sip a glass of water. How long could I sip water? I looked at my small stack of paperbacks various customers had given me for tips. I had read them all. I guessed that popcorn and crackers would again be supper tonight.

I had dressed out of habit, not sure why I should bother. I could have spent the day nude. Who would know? I even put on the bra with the inserts Connie had bought me. "All dressed with no place to go," I said out loud. Would more thinking help? But I had nothing to think about, at least nothing I wanted to make decisions about.

An hour later, flashing lights and a knock on the door startled me. It was Officer Davis. He looked very official in his pressed uniform. He was always casual in the restaurant, even joking at times, but now his voice was serious. "Becky Jean, Bert said you were free today, and I hope I didn't ruin your plans, but Mr. Pykkinen needs your help. His wife died during the night, and his children can't get flights until later, probably tomorrow. The poor guy is griev-ing and helpless. Can you help him?"

"Mrs. Pykkinen is dead?" I gasped at the news, shook my head, and re-sponded, "Sure, no problem." I grabbed my keys, locked the door, and ran to the other side of the patrol car.

Officer Davis left the lights flash as we sped toward the Pykkinens' place. He turned them off when he came to the county road. "They have a big house on Strand Lake. They own the whole bay, and most of the land he doesn't own is state forest," he said as he slowed for the gravel road. "Mr. Pykkinen started a construction company. He built it up from nothing and sold out for millions when he retired. He trained his crews working on his own house. Mrs. Pykki-nen got every new device, landscaping and construction innovation before any-one else in three counties."

He downshifted. "But she got real aggravated when he would bring people over to show off the house. I remember hearing her complain, 'I got to keep this place clean all the time. I never know what cat he'll drag home. It's worse than living in a museum.' It's a huge house, Becky Jean." His tone seemed to be a warning.

He turned off the county road onto a paved, private road. "When his children were young, it was great, but now they're grown. One lives in Denver and the other in New York."

"Yes, I met them at Bert's Thanksgiving feast the last two years, plus all the grandchildren."

"With just Mr. and Mrs. jostling around in that huge place, it's been pretty big and empty. That's why you see him at the restaurant all the time. He's a people person but devoted to his wife." He maneuvered the angular driveway. "Now that Edna's died, I'm worried. The guy is not domestic. 'I don't know what he'd do without me,'" he mimicked Edna's voice.

I smiled at his falsetto. "Yes, I've even heard her say that. When they came to the restaurant together, she always explained how helpless he was. So how did she die?"

"He woke up this morning and found her dead. Poor guy, he called me because he didn't know what else to do." He turned and saw my ashen face. "The EMT's have already removed the body. I guess it will be a medical examiner's case. I don't think either one of them have seen a doctor in years."

"I wasn't worried about the body, but thanks for the reassurance." I swallowed the saliva that had been collecting in my mouth and took a deep breath. "But why did you come after me?"

"Carl's request. He said his son and daughter liked you. When he called them, they agreed. As you said, they come every Thanksgiving and met you at the restaurant. Anyway, they fly into Duluth tomorrow, I think, or the next day. Duluth is not exactly a high priority international airport." He smiled at the phrase. "They have flights to Canada, that's why it's *international*. Anyway, Carl asked if I would check to see if you would help him, and Bert said he had given you the week off. Does this ruin your plans?"

"No, it doesn't ruin anything." *It helps a lot of things*, I thought.

He turned into a stone gate and down a double-wide drive through landscaped maple and birch trees. Neglected gardens were evident along the way.

"It was as beautiful as any European chateau when they still had a gardener. I guess Edna just couldn't keep it up this summer. But she told Albert Johnson's kid that she didn't need him this year. I'm not sure why."

Around a corner, the mansion blasted into view. It reminded me of an architectural version of a cross-stitch sampler. Stone work to aluminum siding, alcoves, dormers, and ginger bread moldings gave the house an eclectic appearance. We rang the doorbell beside the gigantic oak door. Stained glass windows graced both sides. We heard a faint, squeaking voice, "It's open." Officer Davis opened the door and we walked in.

I was mesmerized by the architecture. An Italian fountain with a large overhead skylight greeted us in the atrium. But there was no water in the fountain, and neglect had left dried green scum clinging to the marble basin. A weak voice said, "I'm in here."

We found Carl sitting on the massive sofa holding his head. He turned, "Oh, you found her. I am blessed." He turned to me, "Thanks for coming, Becky Jean. I feel so hopeless and helpless. I was hoping you would come. My precious bride died. She's dead. I was supposed to die first." He burst into tears.

"Becky Jean knows what happened," Officer Davis intervened. "She has no plans this week, so she can help you, Carl. Bert gave her the week off."

I sat next to him, put my arm around his shoulders, and rubbed his neck.

"She could have gotten along without me. She planned to live with the children when I died. I'm the one who eats unhealthy food at the restaurant and sneaks cigars in the back yard. She was the healthy one. What happened, Becky Jean? What happened? She's not supposed to die. We had a wonderful time last night, even played a game of chess and she beat me. What happened? Is she really dead? Are you sure?"

"I'm sure, Carl," said the officer.

I said nothing. I had no idea what to say. I just kept rubbing his back and neck.

Officer Davis backed toward the atrium. "Now if you need anything else just call, Carl. I'll come. I put my number by the telephone. If I don't answer, just call 911 and the dispatcher will send me the message. I got to go. Crime continues, you know." He looked at me, "Will you be all right, Becky Jean?"

"I'll be fine."

He turned and left. After the sound of the door closing, there was complete silence.

We sat quiet and still for a long time. I massaged his neck and rubbed his back until he said, "I'm hungry. Can you fix me an omelet like Ron makes with lots of butter and ham?"

"That I can do. Do you want me to bring it to you here in the living room?"

"No, I don't want to be alone. I was so anxious till you got here. I'm so glad you came." He tottered to his feet. I thought he would fall, so I held him for support. We moved like two wounded soldiers into the kitchen. He sat at the solid oak kitchen table and pointed to the stove. The kitchen range was a Viking, top of the line. He snorted as I played with the dials. "I never learned to use the crazy thing. Can you figure it out?

"The eggs are in the refrigerator, don't use the eggbeaters. I hate those things. Dump them out. I told Edna that I could tell the difference. Oh, my precious Edna." He sniffled and blew his nose in a tissue. "Cheese is in the circular drawer, and sliced peppers and mushrooms should be there as well. In the crisper there is some ham I hid." He pointed, "Salt and pepper are on that shelf. The omelet pan is in that top drawer."

For someone who didn't know how to cook, he sure knew where everything was. I found the pan and the ingredients he wanted and broke the eggs into a dish. Margarine was sitting on the counter. I stuck the knife in it to add to the hot pan.

"Don't use that wretched stuff. I'll toss it out to the squirrels. Use real butter."

When my mother had gone to work to supplement the family income, I had learned to cook for myself. Of course I was criticized for my choices but figured that, if mother wasn't home to make it for me, I would ignore her yelling when she came home.

Carl got out of his chair to stand beside me as I put the whipped eggs into the omelet pan, adding the other ingredients as he directed. "Oh, it smells so good." I flipped it over and grated cheese over it before I folded it to a smile. He was right at my side watching. "I might as well learn. I can't expect my kids to take care of me the rest of my life." He looked at me, "Cheese omelets have always been my favorite food. Have you had breakfast?"

"No."

"Well then make yourself one." He sat down at the kitchen table and dug into his food. He looked up at me, "Sorry to be rude, I couldn't wait. This tastes so good."

He pulled a serving plate out of the cupboard. "I sure could eat another one of those. Make two more, one for you, and bring them into the dining room." He tottered off to the other room.

When the second omelet was done I flipped it onto the serving plate and started making one for myself. My stomach growled in anticipation. How long had it been since I had eaten breakfast?

Chapter 31
Carl's Housekeeper

Two omelets served in the dining room. The room caused me to pause. A crystal chandelier hung over the solid cherry dining table. Large floor-to-ceiling windows looked out over the lake. The credenza was a museum piece with an Italian china soup taurine displayed on top. Carl had set the table with imported china and cut-glass crystal. "Got these glasses while on a vacation in Ireland." He had filled them with orange juice, which glistened as the morning light broke through the window and caught the facets of the crystal Lismore goblets. "Got these lace napkins on a trip to France." He had folded the napkins so that they stood like alabaster towers at each place. "Waitress at our hotel taught me how to fold them." He smiled at his creation. I noticed the silver service had Rococo designs accenting its heft.

I served the omelets onto the china plates and sat down. Never had I eaten in such style. He started talking, and I listened. I was so thankful, not that Mrs. Edna Pykkinen had died, that was a terrible thing, but that during the week I expected to go hungry, I was feasting. I felt conflicted as the melted four-year-aged cheddar cheese rolled around in my mouth, tantalizing my taste buds, but I controlled my guilt, reminding myself that I was providing a much needed service to a grieving widower. He seemed sad as he related wonderful stories of their more than fifty years of marriage.

"I loved her so much. I just don't know what I'm going to do. Should I sell this big house and go live with my children? Both of them are flying in tomorrow night. Can you pick them up at the airport? I suppose they should rent a car. Then they can get around as they please. But I already have two cars, and I don't feel like driving anywhere." He burst into tears.

He rambled, thinking out loud as I twisted the toast he'd made for us around my plate, cleaning up the buttery scraps that had escaped my fork. I suddenly realized that this was my first breakfast in over a year except Christmas and New Year's at Hal and Connie's, and that was really a brunch. Feeling full in the morning was a new sensation for my stomach. It liked it.

"She will never find out that I ate two omelets this morning. Never find out," he sobbed.

I didn't know what to say. "I'm here for you, Mr. Pykkinen."

"Call me Carl. You're my friend, Becky Jean."

I stood and rubbed the back of his neck. His muscles were tight and spastic. With deep massage, they relaxed, and he calmed. "What fun is eating an omelet now? There is no risk that she'll find out."

"No, she will never know, but didn't yours taste good? I enjoyed mine, and thank you very much, Carl." I started stuttering with emotion. "I haven't gotten to eat an omelet in over a year. It was tasty, and that aged cheddar cheese exploded with flavor in my mouth."

His glazed eyes focused, and his voice became soft and comforting, "Over a year?"

"Over a year, Carl."

"No wonder you're so skinny." He got out of his chair and marched with renewed vigor into the kitchen. "How long has it been since you had hot chocolate?"

"Almost forever." I smiled, reciprocating his changed mood.

"I always made Edna hot chocolate on Saturday mornings." He went to the cupboard and pulled out the ingredients. "It's the only culinary thing I know how to make." He poured half milk and half cream into a pan and turned on the burner. "It is Saturday, isn't it? I am really confused. No matter, this will be the best hot chocolate you have ever had."

"No, it's Monday, but I still would enjoy hot chocolate."

He did appear to know his way around the kitchen, at least to make hot chocolate. "So you are not completely unfamiliar with the kitchen," I teased.

"I can also make tea if I have to," he responded with a laugh.

He grated some special, imported chocolate into the steaming milk, added a bit of sugar, and stirred the silky mixture. I had never seen hot chocolate made this way, so I commented on how he was making it.

"Oh, I watched them make hot chocolate this way on a rainy day in Chantilly, France." He laughed as he filled our mugs. "Do you know what 'Chantilly' means?" I gave a quick negative nod. "It is vanilla-flavored whip cream." He laughed as he took a container of whipped cream out of the refrigerator and squirted it all over my mug of hot chocolate. He escorted me to the deck outside the kitchen, set the mugs on the teak table, and invited me to sit down. The deck looked out over the lake. The forest encroached on both sides of gardens along a path to the lake, winding its way to a boat house.

The morning sun was warm, but the faintest breeze wafted the smell of fall leaves to remind me that winter was coming. I watched the aspen leaves flutter to the ground when a sudden gust of wind freed them from their branches. I sipped the best hot chocolate I ever tasted in my life. It was pure ecstasy. I even got a whipped cream mustache out of the deal.

I turned my focus to the lake and the miniature waves lapping on the rocks. *This view is so breathtaking. Should I pinch myself? Is this all a dream?* Another sip of hot chocolate forced me back to reality. I suddenly felt sad about the reason I was here. My emotions roller-coastered through my spirit.

Carl stood beside me, "See that little building next to the boat house?" I responded with a nod in the middle of sipping my drink. "That's a sauna. If you want to take a sauna tonight and then jump in the lake, you can. You see, we have no neighbors, so you don't need a swimsuit. I own all the land around this entire bay. The rest of the land around the lake is state forest. I was going to develop it and make lots of money, but Edna and I enjoyed the solitude so I never did." He started to cry. "I miss her so." I put down my mug and hugged him. "She loved this view so much." He whimpered. "We would sit out here for hours. We didn't even need to say anything." I ran in the kitchen and found a box of tissues and brought him one. He snuffled and blew his nose. "Thanks, Becky Jean. That's what Edna would have done." Then he cried some more.

When we finished our hot chocolate, he looked at me. "You're so pale, you need some sunshine, girl. Let's go for a boat ride. I'll get one of my granddaughter's swimsuits. I'm sure it will fit you." He grabbed my empty mug and went inside.

I sat on the deck as if in a trance. *What's happening to me? Here I am in this castle on the lake with this rich old man who just lost his wife, and I'm going for a boat ride on a private bay. Is this really happening? This was not the scenario I imagined to console poor Carl for his loss.*

He returned with a one-piece green swimsuit. "Sorry it is not very fashionable, my granddaughter is quite modest. She is only thirteen. No, that's not right. She must be at least eighteen now. Well, she was modest at thirteen. She just graduated from high school last spring, I think. Maybe she is nineteen, could even be twenty." He handed me the swimsuit, "I doubt this even fits her anymore. Last time she was up here, I pulled it out for her and she said, 'Grandfather, I wear bikinis now.' My goodness, that girl was almost naked." He laughed. "Anyway, change in the bathroom and meet me at the boat house."

I changed, thankful that the one-piece covered my scar and that I could stuff my breast inserts into the suit so I wouldn't have to explain anything. I was pretty sure they were waterproof. I put on my clothes over the swimsuit and followed the path to the boat house. It was lined with roses and perennials on both sides, still in bloom. Edna must have kept up this part of the garden. The lawn path that led to the lake was flanked with groomed birch trees and sporadic gardens of annuals. But beyond the groomed grounds, an impenetrable forest of jack pine, poplar, and spruce encircled the yard and the bay.

Carl was in the boat and had the motor running. He tipped his captain's hat as I approached. "Feeling more relaxed?" he asked as I climbed aboard. I didn't answer. It seemed odd that he wanted me to feel relaxed. I sat opposite his captain's chair and control panel. There were more dials and gadgets than I knew a boat could have. Roger would be jealous.

The boat sprang out of the water and leveled off as he hit the throttle. The polished chrome glistened in the sun as we raced out of the bay and into the larger lake. I expected to see a few cabins scattered around. If there was anything back from the shore, it was obscured by the dense forest. "Over there," Carl shouted above the din of the motor. "Those are shelters placed by the forest service." I would have missed them without Carl pointing them out. I saw no evidence of humans. He killed the motor as we entered a river mouth. The sudden silence aroused me from my daydreaming.

"This was Edna's favorite place. The forest service land ends at that swamp. She made me buy the land around the mouth of the river so no one could develop it. You saw the shelters we passed. She was afraid someone would clean up this area and put some monstrosity of a house here. Want to buy a hundred acres of swamp?"

He pulled out the fishing poles, grabbed some leeches from the live well and put one on my hook. "You got a fishing license?" Before I answered he said, "Roger said you did."

I wondered what else Roger said as he handed me the rod. *Did he know?* I didn't want to think about it. "Got one," I yelled as I set the hook.

He grabbed the net and scooped up my walleye. Within an hour, we had enough fish for lunch and had thrown a dozen back. He laughed with every catch, particularly at my antics trying to land them. As we stored the poles away, he said, "Edna never liked fishing, but she sure knew how to cook them. Can you cook these?" He opened the live box, and we looked at our catch.

"Do you know how to clean them?" I didn't want the job, so I was quick to ask the question.

"Edna always asked me that too." Before we headed back, he took me down the river, which fed into another lake. This one was populated with several cabins in every bay. "See what would have happened if I had sold part of my land?" He pointed at the houses his construction company had built. We cruised by one huge house that was almost as big as his. "The owners live in Minneapolis. They only come up here for two weeks in July. Otherwise, I never see them."

"Pretty big house for a two-week cabin," I said.

"Sad, isn't it? They even refuse to rent it to anyone. I found them some clients, nice people who would take care of the place, offered nice rent, and they turned it down. We live in a grand house, but with the children and Edna, it was a living house, a home. I've tried not to throw my money around. I wasn't trying to impress anyone. But I did put samples of my work into the house. Edna complained when I gave tours."

As we headed back up the river to Carl's private lake he said, "Oh, I haven't let you go swimming yet. I'll take care of that right now." He turned the boat with a sharp twist of his wrist and headed straight into a cove that was filled in with white sand. I hadn't seen much sand around the lake. The shore was mostly rocks jutting out from dense forest, but in this cul-de-sac of an island was a pristine sand beach. He cut the motor just before the shallow water, and we slid onto the sand. "This is my favorite beach." He jumped out and tied the bow of the boat to an encroaching tree. "When we were young, Edna and I used to skinny-dip here," he laughed, "in broad daylight. She was a beauty in her day."

I undressed to my borrowed swimsuit and jumped in the water. The fine sand felt soothing between my toes. I swam out from shore till I was short of breath. He was wading in the shallows. "This is great," I yelled.

"I thought you would enjoy this." He held out a towel for me as I swam back to shore.

It was afternoon before we returned to the house, put the boat away and cleaned the fish. Despite my unexpected breakfast, I was hungry. My stomach was playing tricks on me. At 2:30, just like every day, I felt like I was starving. Now it was 4:30 P.M., and I felt weak.

I changed clothes in my assigned bedroom as Carl cleaned the fish. I met him in the kitchen. The cleaned fillets lay out next to the stove. "Onions, flour, and spices are all here in the pantry," he said, "I assume you know what to do with them."

I had a sudden memory of a recipe I used during the week I was trying to impress my annulled husband. "Do you have any beer?" I asked.

"Sure, in the bottom of the refrigerator behind the...well, you'll find it. Edna didn't really approve of beer."

I pulled out a can and added some spices and flour. "Oh, for the batter," he said. His eyes sparkled with anticipation.

"What did you expect?" I chided. I dredged the fillets in flour, then in a whisked egg mixture, and finally in a spiced beer batter. The fillets sizzled in the melted butter, and the smell was enticing.

"Here," he gave me something from the refrigerator. "We'll fry these in butter too." He pulled out two already-baked potatoes and proceeded to grate them.

Hash browns never tasted so good, fried in the butter I had used to fry the beer-battered fish. We sat down to a feast.

He had set the table with fine china again and poured glasses of dry white wine for us. "I got this wine in Germany when Edna and I sailed down the Rhine." He even lit candles, although the afternoon sun glinting through the picture window upstaged the effect.

"This wine is exceptional," I commented as I sipped it between mouthfuls of fish. "Although I am not sure wine should be served with beer-battered fish."

"Life is short," he said and then started to cry. Tears dripped onto his plate. I set down my fork and folded my hands in my lap.

"Can I get you something?" I said as I got up and offered him a tissue from the cabinet. I stood behind him and rubbed his neck.

"I'm sorry," he said as he turned to me. His smile seemed sardonic but authentic, "Eat up. This is great. Edna never made beer batter." He picked up the tail meat with his fingers and stuffed it in his mouth, snapping his fingers with delight. I sat down and started eating again, but he recognized my hesitancy. "Don't worry, Becky Jean. I'm going to have these emotional outbursts from time to time. We were married for over fifty years, wonderful years. It hurts. It hurts terribly to know she's gone. But you're helping me to realize that life continues." He picked up another bite with his fingers and stuffed the fish in his mouth. "Boy, this tastes good. Eat up. Edna never let me eat with my fingers." His silverware glistened untouched beside his plate until he forked down his hash browns.

That evening, we hiked through the gardens and down back trails Carl had made through the woods. Between occasional tears, screams, and outbursts of uncomfortable silence, he seemed cheerful as we hiked along together. It was painful for me to watch him grieve. I didn't say much. I was there to listen. Somehow, the trail we followed circled around, and we ended our walk back at the sauna and boat landing just as the sun was setting. The loons started their chorus, and the water became calm as glass reflecting the sunset's palate of colors.

He led me into the sauna and seemed to relish demonstrating the technical aspects of regulating the heat, showing me how the shower worked and how to pour water on the rocks. He turned on the heat, and then we marched down the boardwalk out onto the dock. The glass-smooth lake sparkled as now the stars began to show their brilliance. "It will take thirty to forty minutes to heat up, but after a good sauna you can just jump in the lake to cool off and repeat the process as many times as you want."

He turned and headed up the path to the house. "I'm going to bed now. I'll have towels and linens all set for you in your room when you're done. You go right ahead and enjoy, now."

I guessed I was staying the night, not returning to my coop. "I'll come up with you and get your granddaughter's swimsuit. Maybe it is dry by now."

He took out his dentures and put them in his shirt pocket. "Roger said that you wouldn't need one. Besides, it didn't fit you very well."

"You noticed?"

He laughed. "As one who enjoys skinny-dipping to another, enjoy."

I stood on the path stunned. Despite the bright display of stars, the darkness was intense. Only a crescent moon was visible. But as my eyes accommodated, I could see well enough. I turned and sat on the dock, waiting for the sauna to heat up.

When I checked out the sauna, the temperature was about 165 degrees and rising. I shed my clothes, hanging them on birch pegs in the ante-room. Peeking out the door, I saw no one. Carl's room faced the road, and there was very little light on the lake side of the house.

I wandered down to the lake in the nude enjoying the refreshing night air swirling around my body. My chest incisions were well healed, but the thin skin overlying my ribs was still sensitive. I covered them with my hands in a reflex despite having nothing to cover. Without too much thinking, I dove off the dock. It was instant ecstasy. Every care in my world seemed to wash away. I swam out a ways and circled back, treading water near the dock just to prolong the experience. When I chilled, I made a quick climb up the dock ladder and sprinted to the sauna on the boardwalk.

The temperature was now almost 180 degrees. I grabbed a towel and entered, sitting on the top bench. There was an intricate pulley system so that even from the top bench, I could spill water on the rocks. The smell of fresh cedar was intoxicating. Cozy and warm, I pulled the rope, and the water poured over the rocks. Steam like a cloud filled the sauna. Blood rushed to my head. It was exhilarating. Before I thought I would pass out, I raced out, down the boardwalk, and jumped in the lake. It was almost enough joy to stop my heart. Endorphins surged through my brain.

I repeated the process a couple more times. The last time, I floated on my back scanning the sky. Several shooting stars flew across as the loons broke into a sustained chorus. The moon was high in the sky when I finally decided to go to bed. *What a vacation.* Wrapped in towels, carrying my clothes, I ventured into the house. Silent and dark, I managed to find my room. I didn't even bother to switch on the light. I just fell in bed, covered up, and was instantly asleep.

Chapter 31
Preparing for the Funeral

The next morning, I dressed in the clothes I had arrived in and wandered down the stairs. Carl took one look at me and shook his head. "Let's find you something nice to wear," he suggested as we returned to my room and rummaged through the closet. "These clothes were left here by my oldest granddaughter. She told her mother she refused to wear them. They just sort of didn't get packed in her suitcase." He laughed. "She thinks herself pretty sophisticated. Anyway, wear anything you like. I'll see you in the kitchen for breakfast."

I tried them on. They were my size but were all more expensive than anything I had ever owned. Stacked on a small side shelf were lacy bras and undergarments. Stuffing my foam breasts in place, I even felt fashionable. I laughed at my image in the mirror. I twisted and turned in my reflected image and fantasized parading down the Paris runway.

During my second breakfast of the year, we had a morning chat. He was still overwhelmed with the reality of his wife's death but excited about seeing his children. After breakfast, we headed for the garage. "You drive," he said. "You know where the airport is, don't you?

"Yes, I pass the airport sign directing me down Arrowhead Road every time Bert sends me to Duluth for supplies, but I have never actually been there."

"Good. All my life, I've wanted to have a chauffeur. Just like General Eisenhower. Did you know he never had a driver's license? I shook hands with him once. I was in Patton's army."

At the airport I stood in the background and let the emotional pandemonium play out. "Sorry, dad, I couldn't get here any faster," Paul said as he hugged his father.

"Oh, dad, I'm so sorry. I miss mom so bad." There were many tears as Christine gave her father a hug. "Paul and I met at the Minneapolis airport. My flight came in from New York just two hours before his." She gave her father another kiss and hug. "There are six flights a day from Minneapolis, so it was no problem."

They both looked at me, standing in the background at the same time. "Becky Jean," Christine said, "You're the waitress at the restaurant where we had Thanksgiving dinner, aren't you? We're so thankful that you're helping dad."

Carl put his arm over my shoulder. "I hired her as my housekeeper." He turned to his daughter. "You know I can't cook, and your mother always said that I was lost in the kitchen. Did you want me to starve to death till you got here?"

Son and daughter grabbed my hands. "Thanks." They turned back to Carl. "So, when is mom's funeral?"

I became the source of community information as I was directed to organize the funeral. Carl wanted it held in our little Cotton church, but it was too small. All of Carl's former employees and subcontractors intended to come. So I called the funeral director, and he arranged for the funeral at the Methodist church on top of the hill in Duluth. The reception, Carl insisted, was to be at the Cotton School 100 gymnasium. I hadn't realized it, but Edna had taught there for many years in the elementary grades. Many of the older teachers, of whom most were retired, planned to attend.

Bert agreed to cater the affair, and I was assigned to serve. By Thursday night, everything was planned. I felt like a member of the family. I enjoyed talking to Christine about New York City—what it was like, where she worked, what the restaurants were like, where she sent the children to school, and what their apartment was like. I had lots of questions. I had dreamed of seeing New York ever since I was a little girl.

She suggested we take a sauna together where she would answer my questions. "People everywhere, lots of ethnic restaurants, and I love the museums," Christine told me. We undressed in the ante-room. She had a nice figure despite the mild stretch marks from her pregnancies.

I was jealous, not of her figure, as I had long ago adjusted to my scrawny body, but to know that I would never have the changes that attended pregnancy and now I didn't even have the breasts to feed…

She asked about my scars and I gave her the abbreviated version.

"I'm so sorry, Rebecca, you poor thing. You're too young for all this."

I covered up with my towel and changed the subject. "Thanks for your concern, but tell me more about New York City. How do you get around such a crowded city?"

"I take the subway everywhere. I don't even own a car."

"But what about grocery shopping and going to the mall?"

Christine laughed, "It's all right there in our neighborhood. And if we really want to get away, we rent a car for the weekend."

"Wasn't that hard to move to New York City?"

"No, I guess I was a city girl at heart. Have you done a lot of traveling?"

I turned to look at her. She was about forty, judging by having a late-teenage daughter, but she looked like she was just barely out of her twenties. "I used to live in Iowa. I went to the University of Dubuque for three years working on my degree in sociology and management." She seemed to be waiting for the answer to her question. "And then I came here. So no, I haven't traveled much."

"So you haven't been to many big cities?"

"I've been to Minneapolis, St. Paul. That's it. But I think I prefer wilderness." It wasn't quite true about the twin cities. I had only hitchhiked though on the freeway with compassionate truck drivers, but Christine didn't need to know that.

She poured a ladle of water on the rocks. We adjusted to the steam before I continued. "You grew up here on this bay where you can't even see your neighbors. Don't you miss the solitude?"

"Not very often. Dad invites us here for vacations in the summer. I see he donated my daughter's clothes to you. That's great. That rascal said she packed them. We get home and her suitcase is empty. We had to buy all new outfits for her. That kid is so spoiled. She'll never wear them again, so I'm glad they fit you. Now back to your question. Staying here for a couple weeks each year is enough *wilderness* for me." She put more water on the rocks. The steam filled the small room, and we both leaned back to enjoy the sensation as it enveloped us.

Unwrapping her towel to wipe her face, she said, "What Paul and I are concerned about is that there is no one around here. Neither of us can leave our jobs right now to take care of dad." She started crying into her towel. She blew her nose into the terrycloth and looked at me. "Are you willing to be his housekeeper on a semi-permanent basis, until we get things sorted out? At least we want someone checking on him. He trusts you and says that you're a great cook."

"Bert is depending on me at the restaurant, and I don't have a car. I've been living in back of the restaurant."

"In that storage shed? That's terrible."

I blushed in spite of the steam. "Yah, that's my home. Short commute to work."

She laughed but soon became serious again. "Let me talk to Paul, maybe some arrangements can be made. The point is we don't want dad to be alone out here. Before we move him to live with one of us, there is a lot to be done."

At the end of the week, I was anxious to get home. It had been great a vacation. I didn't feel that I was needed while Paul and Christine were there. But I sure enjoyed their company. We had such great conversations. At night in my queen-sized bed, I dreamed of walking the streets of New York City or climbing the mountains Paul described outside of Denver. It was bedlam when spouses and children arrived, but I enjoyed them too, and they treated me like family. Only his oldest granddaughter, Aria, still seemed aloof, the one whose swimsuit and clothes I had borrowed. She was a young woman now, and true to Carl's description she wore a fashionable, if somewhat skimpy, bikini when swimming. She never even mentioned that the suit I wore was hers. I wondered if she wasn't in love with some young man back in New York City.

Sunday night after I had just finished supper dishes, I folded my apron and joined the family in the living room. The children were sprawled out on the floor, except Aria who was sitting by the picture window looking out over the lake. The parents were crowded on the sofa talking to Carl. I hated to interrupt. "I think I'd better head home. Can someone give me a ride? I have to be to work at 5:30 tomorrow morning. My vacation is over."

Paul looked at Christine, and they both stood. "Why don't you take one of dad's cars?" said Paul as he went to the kitchen and took the keys out of the drawer by the pantry. I stood paralyzed. "Go ahead, take the Mazda." Paul smiled, scanning my startled face. "Don't look so shocked. It's dad's idea. You have a driver's license, I assume, since you drove him to the airport."

"Yes, of course." The keys felt heavy in my hand as he handed them to me. I felt like I had just won the grand prize in a game show. "Seriously?"

"Yes, Becky Jean, we've talked it over as a family. We really would prefer that you stay here, but you may use the car as long as you check on dad every day after we leave. Dad will pay you to do his laundry and dust and clean. He'll even give you a gas allowance. Christine leaves for New York City tomorrow, and I head out to Denver the day after. There are plenty of bedrooms in this house. Come back if you want. You don't need to stay in Bert's shack. Let me tell you, that place was a shambles when I was a kid." He handed me a check, "This is what dad said that you earned for this week. I hope it's enough."

I stared at the zeros on the check. "Way too much."

"That is what we've agreed to pay you every week," Christine added, ignoring my response.

I headed home as the sun painted bright crimson across the western sky. I was too excited to think. I had a red Mazda RX8 to drive any time I wanted as long as I checked on Carl. But he was my friend. I would have done it for room and board. I played in my mind whether I should stay at his house. What an invitation. But I had my coop, and it was convenient to walk across the parking lot every morning to go to work. When I came to the highway I turned toward Cotton and drove into the restaurant parking lot. As I turned off the vehicle I noticed that my door was ajar.

Chapter 32
End of Coop Life

"Is someone here?" I asked at the door and then yelled the question. There was no answer. My heart raced. I returned to the car opened the trunk with the button below the steering wheel and crept back to the house with the tire iron out of the trunk. Purple had replaced crimson on the horizon as the mercury parking lot light came on. It was getting dark fast. I felt braver with the tire iron in my grasp.

Again I yelled, "Anyone here?" I pushed the door open with the tire iron. The place was trashed. The few clothes I had left were ripped and strewn about. My backpack lay dumped on the floor, shredded with a knife. The few things I had on my table were scattered about the room. My paperbacks were ripped apart. The refrigerator door stood open. My little toaster oven was smashed. With few places to hide, it took only minutes to search every corner. No one was there.

I opened the restaurant, put in the security code, and called Officer Davis on the restaurant telephone. I was sitting on the porch sobbing when he arrived. "Why would anyone do this to me? I have nothing anyone would want to steal."

He investigated the coop through the open door behind me. "I haven't touched or moved anything," I cried, "except to see if there was anyone inside."

"What's this?" he asked, pulling a paper clipped to the shower curtain. He handed it to me.

It was written in red ink, "I want my rings." I looked up at Officer Davis and swallowed. "My ex-husband, well not really, he had our marriage annulled."

"Is this an engagement ring he wants back?"

"Yes, remember the guy that set the fire, the arsonist who got off because '*I didn't know the garbage would light up*'?" I put as much sarcasm in my voice as possible. "He was the best man at my farce of a wedding. He threatened me for the rings then."

"He was let off for a misdemeanor. They couldn't prove intent to commit arson in court," Officer Davis added the official court result. "He said he panicked and left. The judge believed him. Bert did his best testifying, but it was Bert's word against a wealthy stockbroker, 'outstanding member of the community' were his lawyer's words."

I hung my head.

"So where is this troublesome ring?"

"Two rings," I said, "an engagement ring and a wedding ring. They're both at the jewelry store."

"Oh, you sold them?"

"Not yet. I'm thinking about it."

Officer Davis stammered as he shut my door and put yellow tape over it, "This may be a stupid question, but do you have somewhere else to stay?" He pointed at the car. "I see Carl let you use his Mazda."

"I suppose I could go back to Pykkinen's. They offered to let me stay until he moves in with one of his children or other arrangements are made. They even offered me a job as a housekeeper, but I told them I was obligated to Bert."

"It won't help Bert if you get his property destroyed. I hate to be harsh, but I think you should move to Pykkinen's. He's got quite a security system, and besides, you don't need to tell anyone where you live. I'll tell Carl and Bert to be discreet."

"Can I take my stuff?"

He started to laugh and then stopped. "Your clothes are shredded, and your backpack is all ripped. What could you possibly want? Leave it. Don't touch anything, and we'll try to get prints. I'll tell Bert. If it was your ex-husband, I doubt that he'll be back. He's torn everything apart here. He must know that the rings are somewhere else, and it's not likely they would be in the restaurant."

Officer Davis put his gloved hand on my shoulder. "Now get out of here so I don't have to worry about you."

I headed toward the Mazda. "Becky Jean," he called.

"Yes?"

"See how much those rings are worth. If they aren't worth much, send them back."

"Yes, Officer." I wondered if I should tell him that I had already had the rings assessed. I decided that would only make him worry. My chest itched as I remembered the paper Max had stuck in my bra. It was somewhere in that rubble that used to be my home. I thought I should just end this whole affair, get the rings back, and send them to Kevin. The problem was that I still needed to pay for my hospital expenses and the chemotherapy and radiation treatments, and should I get reconstructive surgery so I could get rid of these foam things stuck in my bra? The rings were mine. Or since the marriage was annulled, were they his rings? He gave them to me of his own free will, asking me to marry him. I kept my part of the bargain. I married Keith Stagg. If he had our marriage annulled, that was his problem. Besides, Bagley's lawyer had said they were my possessions.

I drove back to Pykkinen's home. The sky was still cloudy. Only a few stars shone through the cloud cover, and they were probably planets. I opened the garage with the automatic opener in the glove box and drove in. Paul appeared at the doorway to the garage as I climbed out of the car. "You're back?"

"Am I still welcome?"

"Certainly."

"Thanks," I said as I sat in the Mazda and burst into tears. "My place has been trashed."

Paul led me out of the car as I sobbed. I sat at the kitchen table and spilled out the story. Carl hugged me like a father, and his children comforted me like a family I'd never had.

Chapter 33
Physician Followup

After Carl's children returned to their homes, Paul to Colorado and Christine to New York, I lived like royalty. Being Carl's housekeeper was the easiest job a woman ever had. He wasn't very messy and always had a good story to tell. He had no television as he said that there was 'poor reception' and he didn't want a dish. We spent hours in the evenings, when I came home from the restaurant, sitting by the fireplace as he related adventures of his children. Despite years of being a contractor, he had spent time taking his children to most of the state parks in Minnesota and all the major national parks.

We spent weekends hiking the trails around the bay, canoeing or boating, and there was always an opportunity for me to take a sauna and go skinny-dipping after he retired to bed. I was encouraged to wear any of the clothes Aria had left in her closet, but I stayed in the guest room. With a thick carpet that allowed me to wiggle my toes every morning in its thick plush as I got out of my canopied queen-sized bed, I was in a fairy tale. It even had its own bathroom and a bookcase filled with books with intriguing titles. Several nights I stayed up too late reading and almost arrived late to work the following mornings. It was glorious.

With two full-time jobs, I was incredibly happy. After I came home from the restaurant, I did laundry and fixed supper for Carl and me. I set things out in the refrigerator for him to microwave for lunch unless he came to the restaurant. He ate cereal for breakfast except on weekends when he wanted cheddar cheese omelets. I even asked Bert for the rest of my paid time off and got to enjoy the lake and hiking trails before winter hit.

Carl ordered the greatest cheese. It was imported through the Old World butcher in Duluth. Every week, he went to get his favorite cuts of meat, sausages, and of course his special cheeses. I was embarrassed eating so much, but I was surprised that I didn't gain any weight. Yet, I certainly felt healthier.

I managed to rearrange my morning in order to have things set up for Carl and still be at the restaurant on time. Connie was happy for me that I was staying at the Pykkinen's after she heard about the break-in and the destruction of my "property," as she put it. But I made her promise not to tell anyone where I lived. I added, "It needs to be the best-kept secret in Cotton."

"Now that you've joined the rich and famous, are you still going to talk to us common people?" she teased. "And girl, the way you drive around in that sports car, squealing the tires when you leave the parking lot, that's just not the Becky Jean I thought I knew."

I blushed. "You tease," I said, "the only reason I squealed the tires was because I'm not used to the acceleration. That car has power. I'm getting it under control. Besides, it's not my car, and you know I would never be reckless with someone else's property."

Bert called me into his office to discuss the break-in at the coop. The police found no fingerprints, and so there was nothing to pin my ex-husband, or annulled husband, except the printed note, which Officer Davis kept as evidence. He kept close watch on the restaurant and the coop after the incident but did not expect anyone to return and assured Bert that his property was safe.

I knew it was Keith because of the way he ruined my things, tearing up my pack and smashing my toaster oven. Max would have been sneakier so no one would know he had been there, or he would have burned the place down, but I couldn't prove anything. I bought a mailer box for the rings after Officer Davis found the crumpled paper with the address. I planned to stop by the jeweler, turn in the check, and put the rings in the mail. The post office was just up the hill from the jeweler.

But first I had an appointment at the Family Practice Center. Dr. Cheryl Sheihe seemed upset to see me. "You've been through quite a lot since I saw you last."

She was still wearing that lovely lavender perfume. "Dr. Sheihe, I am so thankful that you took my problem seriously."

She looked at the floor. "From my perspective, I'm embarrassed that I really didn't take your case more seriously. I didn't expect that you had cancer. I probably should not have been so flippant that day. I'm so sorry. Twenty-something-year-old women shouldn't get breast cancer. You're almost the same age as..." She paused, and I saw a tear swell to her eye which she quickly wiped away. "I'm sorry to be so emotional. How can I help you today?"

"I had the surgery," I said as she twisted a tissue in her hand. "Anyway, I have a surgeon and an oncologist but no one to really take care of me. So check me over. I think I will opt out of the pelvic exam today, if you don't mind. I still have had no sexual partners. I am a bit concerned that I am always hungry and eating three times as much as before and still not gaining weight."

"I pulled up your hospital records on the computer to review them." She sat down with my records on her laptop computer, and we scanned them together. We discussed the surgery and the oncology appointment, the BRCA positive result, and the meaning of the positive lymph nodes.

"Please put on a gown, and I will examine you next."

"Oh, that isn't necessary," I said as I unbuttoned my blouse, pulled up my bra, and took out my foam fillers. "I got nothing left to cover."

"Yes, it is necessary. Or I'll get in trouble." She gave me a gown and left the room.

I finished stripping, put on the gown, and spent the time folding my clothes into neat piles and placing them on the bench from where she had taken the gowns. This was a cloth gown, and I liked it a lot better than the paper one I had been given on the last visit. It must have been new, because it wasn't see-through like the one at the hospital.

Where was she? This was taking too long. I thumbed through the magazine from the rack on the door, but it was about taking care of your diabetes, which I didn't have. I sat in the chair for a few minutes and then paced but ended up sitting on the exam table.

Dr. Sheihe came through the door. "I'm sorry it took so long, but I was talking to your oncologist, Dr. Liebowitz."

"Yes, she's nice. I really like her."

"Dr. Liebowitz said that you refused chemotherapy."

"I'm taking Tamoxifen, that's chemotherapy at $69.99 a month."

She paused, looked at me sitting on the exam table, and then at the chart.

Her lip was trembling. "She did some blood tests in her office and asked me to give you the results. Your alkaline phosphatase is elevated."

"So, what does that mean?"

"It means that the cancer may have gone to your bones. I should order a bone scan so we can get you started on the appropriate chemotherapy."

I rolled my gown up under my chin and scanned my scrawny self. She turned her eyes. "There are my bones. I'm thin enough for you to check them all. They don't hurt anywhere. Do you really think they need to be scanned?"

She set down my chart and I dropped my gown. She draped it back over my shoulders. "Propriety, Rebecca," she said. "Now let me check you over properly, maintaining some semblance of modesty." I felt chastised, so I complied. She was meticulous about my review of systems, asking me questions as she completed my physical exam, keeping me properly covered as she checked each part. *She's in training*, I thought. *We have to do this right.*

When Dr. Tagett, her supervising physician came in, Dr. Sheihe reviewed my history and physical exam. I could tell that she was upset that I had refused chemotherapy. He was pleasant.

"Ms. Gottwald, I am not sure that the Tamoxifen is sufficient in your situation."

"I'm satisfied with it. Besides, it's all I can afford. Can I get dressed now? I'm getting chilled." I reached to untie my gown.

He stopped me. "I just want to confirm that this is your choice. This is outside usual and customary care." He was so serious.

I enunciated my answer. "Dr. Sheihe explained things well and did a careful exam. I'm very satisfied, and as long as she is willing to be my physician and check me over if I have a non-cancer problem, that's enough, and I am pleased with her care and concern for me. I do not want any other chemotherapy."

"Noted," Dr. Tagett said as he picked his pen out of his white coat pocket and wrote a note on my chart.

He walked out the door, leaving me and Dr. Sheihe alone. "But you're so young. Don't you want to fight this cancer?" she asked.

I untied my gown and flipped it on the exam table. She seemed paralyzed as I dressed. I put my arm on her shoulder. "I've done all the fighting I can do. Do you still want to be my doctor?"

"Yes." I saw a tear drop down on her cheek. I gave her a tissue. Her eyes were red.

"Thanks," she said and wiped her eyes. "I'm just struggling with this role reversal."

"When I was ten years old, I fought hard to stay alive, and I made it. If God gives me strength, I'm going to finish college and be a social worker. If not, then I have just lived the best years of my life with my new family in Cotton, Minnesota."

Chapter 34
Luxury Living

I loved my royal routine. Living in a beautiful mansion on a lake, I had breakfast every morning with Carl, went to work where I enjoyed the routine of waitressing, including a trip to Duluth on Tuesdays to buy supplies, and finished each day providing Carl and me with a fabulous supper served on fine china and drinking imported wine from crystal goblets. *Three meals a day, how amazing.* Each morning, I was excited to wake up. I looked forward to my time off instead of dreading it, and I celebrated Sundays. Carl let me use the boat to go fishing or just exploring around the lake. And there was plenty of opportunity for skinny-dipping. As fall came and the evenings grew colder, I enjoyed the sauna to warm up after a cold dip in the lake. I was happy, happier than I had ever been, and besides I had decided what to do with the rings. That gave me an incredible sense of peace.

I noticed the rich palette of colors in the leaves as I drove to the restaurant one fall morning. I decided that the colors were so rich because the late summer leading into fall had been so mild. There was plenty of rain that summer followed by vibrant sunshine that fall. The wind was so mild that the leaves lingered on the trees. I left the windows in my bedroom open just to smell the fall air.

Even the ladies in the Bible study remarked that it was a beautiful fall. "And I'm almost a hundred years old," said Martha, "I will be next June 15th, and this is the most beautiful fall I ever remember."

"But then your memory isn't as good as it used to be," said Doris.

I laughed at the ladies as I served each of them their tea and toast.

"You're starting to talk like a rich person," Connie said to me one crisp autumn morning.

"What do you mean? I don't talk any differently." I had just finished telling her that morning about spending the weekend in the speed boat taking in the view of the fall colors along the shore.

"You think nothing about how us, poor, common people have to go for a walk in the woods to see the leaves."

"I'm sorry, it's just that…"

"Forget it. I'm just teasing you. I'm going on break. I haven't taken the order from that corner table." She turned, "Oh, by the way, thanks for inviting my daughters over for the weekend." Her tone seemed sarcastic, so I turned to ask her if there was a problem, but she was already in the back room. I took the order from the corner table and made fresh coffee. The pot was empty. Connie usually made fresh coffee before she went on her break. *There must be a problem.*

When her break was over, I met her in the back room. "What's the matter, Connie? What did I do to offend you?"

She looked at me and tried to walk past, but I grabbed her arm. "Connie, what's the problem?"

"You should know."

"Sorry," I stammered, "I am not Anishinaabe. I don't know.

"All right, I might as well spit it out." She set her hands on her hips. "Now I admit that Shawnee is a lot calmer after she spends time with you. I have no idea what magic you spin on her, but since last weekend she has been more respectful. We haven't had a single argument all week. Sherrie enjoyed her time with you too."

"Then what's the problem?"

She shook her finger in my face. "Why did you take the girls skinny-dipping? I sent swimsuits for them. Shawnee is sex-crazed enough already."

"We were taking a sauna, and then we jumped in the lake to cool off. I'm sorry if you don't approve. There was no one around. It's a private bay."

"That's all she has been talking about since she got home. And no, I don't approve."

I held up my hands. "All right, never again. I promise."

"Sherrie was amazed at how many poetry books Carl has."

"I enjoy your daughters. They are like sisters to me," I said, but she turned away and was gone to take an order. I made my way over to the corner table where the County Sheriff had just sat down. "What can I get you, Officer Davis?"

"Corned beef on rye with an order of wild rice soup."

"Coming right up." I wrote out the slip to give to Ron. "Is crime a little slow today? You're here early."

"You never know about crime, Becky Jean, it pops up at the weirdest times and in the weirdest places."

That day at work was difficult. Everyone was grouchy. I felt relieved to be away from the restaurant as I drove into Carl's garage. As I entered the mud room I heard the telephone ring. It startled me, but I calmed down as I answered. "Carl, your daughter is on the phone."

Then I heard, "I want to talk to you first, Becky Jean. How is dad doing?" Christine said, "And tell me the truth."

I gave her a rundown of his recent activities. "He seems to be resolving his grief. He is certainly more active, not just sitting in his chair when I come home from the restaurant. Now he is usually up walking in the garden, even found him puttering in his workshop making a new bird feeder." Then I added, "He's even learning to cook. He had supper all made yesterday when I came home from work."

"Unbelievable. I don't think he ever made supper for mom the whole time they were married. He still has no clue how the washing machine works, I'm sure of that," Christine said. "Let me talk to him."

They had a long conversation as I cleaned up the kitchen. Things were strewn all over. It was hard to believe that he was such a finicky contractor and yet so messy in the kitchen. I suspected that he had many skills that he didn't want people to know he had.

When he hung up the telephone, he found me washing dishes from his lunch escapades. "Oh, thanks, Becky Jean, for cleaning up. I meant to do it. I had a good talk with Christine. She and her husband and daughter are coming for Thanksgiving. Isn't that great?"

"You know that I plan on helping Bert again this year for his Thanksgiving feast?"

"I expected as such. I have to talk to Paul yet, but I think the whole Pykkinen clan will be here for you to wait on us." He gave me a Cheshire grin. "I only get Bert's world famous dressing once a year, you know."

"I'll be ready for you and the rest of the Cotton clan." I laughed. I couldn't help myself.

"What are you laughing about?"

"I was thinking that now that I live here, there is nobody who actually lives in Cotton, Minnesota anymore. It was population one, unincorporated when I lived in Bert's coop."

"It is still home for a lot of people."

"And it is my home."

"Let's go for a little walk, Becky Jean. I have something to share with you." We finished in the kitchen together and then dressed for a hike. I came down the stairs in one of Aria's turtleneck shirts and new jeans that I had bought during my Tuesday run through the mall. I had been able to buy some new clothes since working for Carl. He was paying me more than I made at the restaurant, so my income had more than doubled, although I kept that information to myself. I didn't want Bert to find out.

Carl put his black and red wool shirt over my shoulders and handed me his stocking cap. Down in the corner of the yard, he pushed aside a fallen sapling, and we climbed over some brush. A new hiking trail came into view. It traced the lake shore, then diverted down into a swamp. He motioned me to be quiet as we crouched behind the bulrushes and watched the ducks, teals, mallards, and even a wood duck couple. "See how they are getting ready to fly away?" he whispered. "This has been their home all summer, but now winter is coming."

"Yes, it's exciting to see them."

"I'm getting ready to fly away, too." He picked up a stick and started drawing in the mud at my feet. "I've decided to sell the house and move to Colorado. I'm going to Paul's for Christmas, but also to look for a place to live. A retired couple from Minneapolis has already enquired about the house. They're willing to pay what I asked for the place."

I cringed. *I would be homeless again. I knew in my heart that all this luxury living wouldn't last forever but...* I didn't know what to say. I cleared my throat so my voice wouldn't crack. "That's fine, Carl. With all the money you've given me, I thought that I would go back to the university and finish my degree."

"Oh, I'm glad you're taking this so well. I feel like you are my adopted daughter. I owe you a lot for helping me during this difficult time."

"You don't owe me anything. I only want the best for you, Carl." Deep down, I was not taking this very well. I wanted to go back to my room and cry. My room, well, it wasn't really my room; it wasn't my house. He had the right to do what he wanted and if he felt like moving to Colorado with his son that was his choice and probably best for him. But I felt homeless, again. The ducks flew away as we stood to hike back. I felt a sudden pain in my hip as I stood.

"Something wrong with your hip?" Carl asked.

"Yes," I said, "winter is coming."

Chapter 35
Snowed In

December hit with a blast of arctic air as the jet stream dipped into the Deep South. I sat in the car with the heater going full blast. It was still cold in the car. I had just delivered Carl to the airport. I sat in the car as I watched his flight take off from Duluth International Airport to Colorado. Carl would spend Christmas with Paul and his family. Christine and her family were flying from New York City to join them. It was snowing so hard I wasn't sure the flight would leave, so I waited to make sure he didn't get stranded in the Duluth airport. When I saw his plane take off for Minneapolis, I drove out of the parking lot and turned toward Cotton. "Goodbye Carl, have a nice Christmas," I yelled at the airplane.

I turned up the radio and listened to Christmas music as I headed north on Highway 53. "*O come, O come Emmanuel and ransom captive Israel that mourns in lonely exile here… Disperse the gloomy clouds of night and death's dark shadows put to flight…*" The minor key and six-eight-time fit my mood and my Jewish-Lutheran heritage as snow started coming down in heavy sheets. How could it snow when it was so cold?

I slowed as the visibility deteriorated. I was determined to make it back. Pykkinen's was still my home, Carl assured me, until the closing date. That was important because he told me that if he found a place to live in Colorado over the holidays that he might not be coming back. Despite the Minneapolis couple agreeing to Carl's asking price, there were still things to settle for the multi-million dollar purchase, not to mention his personal things that he needed to pack up. Closing wasn't until spring. I hugged the yellow line when I could see it and strained to watch for deer.

Despite my caution, I hit a bank of snow drifting across the highway. I hadn't seen it, and the steering wheel jerked out of my hands. I grabbed it and swerved back onto the road. The back wheels swung to the side. I hit the accelerator trying to avoid the ditch and spun an entire circle. I came to a jarring stop hitting another snow bank. It took a moment to see which way I was heading. I got out of the car to catch my breath and inspect for damage. The snow was so heavy it hit me in the eyes and forced me to blink. There was no traffic, which was good for my safety, but it also meant that I probably shouldn't be on the road either.

The car was sideways on the shoulder, but not in the ditch. One more foot and I would have been down a five foot embankment. No scrapes and no dents. I lifted the hood and inspected the engine, scooping snow away from the fan belt. Back in the car, everything seemed to be working. I shifted to first gear and eased out of the snow bank, thankful for the snow tires Carl had asked the mechanic to mount. I opened the window to make sure there was not another car in sight in either direction, then, with a wide arc, I crawled back into my lane.

As I gripped the steering wheel with clenched knuckles, I said a prayer of thanksgiving and a request for traveling mercy as I peered into the whiteness ahead of me. I was gasping for breath out of sheer exhaustion when through the snow I saw the green and white sign announcing my arrival in *Cotton, unincorporated*. "Almost there," I said as I accelerated in familiar territory. I waved at the restaurant, aglow in its Mercury light and even thought about bunking in the coop for the night. But, by the time I reached the county road north of Cotton to Carl's place, I was committed to a comfortable bed in my palace.

Going less than twenty miles per hour into blinding snow, I edged my way to the house. I flicked to bright headlights, but that made it worse, a total white-out. Dim headlights were better. I crawled along, thankful that I would probably not meet any cars on this road, but I worried that I wouldn't remember all the curves. At times I slowed just to see the trees on each side forming a pathway to the house. It was a relief when I finally saw the yard light with its halo of snow. I thanked the Lord when the garage door opened, and I slipped across the snowdrift on the threshold into the garage. Once inside with the automatic garage door closing, I turned off the motor and collapsed. My hands cramped. Every muscle in my shoulders twitched with relief. I sat and cried, too emotional to get out of the car.

After a good sob, I said out loud, "If this keeps up, I'm not sure I can make it to Connie's for the Christmas Eve party tomorrow." I pictured Rolly out plowing the roads, but I was sure that the snow was filling in the gaps as fast as he plowed. When I finally had the energy to go into the house, the car door stuck from frozen snow. I shoved with all my body weight, and it opened. Thankful for a heated garage, I rubbed my hands together. They were numb not so much from cold as from the death grip I had on the steering wheel. Once in the house, I shivered. Hat and coat put away in the closet, I headed for a hot shower. I thought about a sauna as the hot water warmed my blue skin, but it would have required too much effort.

Warm again, I crawled in bed with an extra quilt. Like a caterpillar in a cocoon, I felt secure. I wiggled and squirmed, hugging my pillows and enjoying the way the queen mattress comforted my form. But I couldn't sleep. My mind raced through all the things I had to do in the morning: snow-blow the drive way, shovel out the end if the plow came, and wrap the presents.

I had anticipated a spectacular Christmas Eve party. With the money Carl gave me for being his housekeeper and making omelets for him every morning, I had presents for everyone. Leah and Roger were going to be there with precious little Rachel. After they married, they had built a house on a piece of land just down the road from Connie and Hal's. They would make the party even if they had to snowshoe to get there. All of Connie's relatives had arrived at the beginning of the week. I was the only one that needed to somehow get there. It was to be a wonderful Christmas Eve celebration and of course I knew that Connie would do something special for my birthday on Christmas Day.

As I pulled the covers over my head, my thoughts turned to being thankful that I was not frozen in a ditch along the highway. I wiggled my toes and legs between the warm sheets. A pain hit me in my hip just like that time Carl had brought me to the swamp to see the ducks, but as I twisted my hip around, the pain resolved. Maybe I just twisted wrong when I hit the snow bank? It's probably just a bruise. If it persists, I will schedule an appointment with Dr. Sheihe. But as I drifted off to sleep, I knew what it was.

Somehow, I must have fallen asleep, but I awoke early the next morning and wrapped the presents. They were so pretty, and I knew that they were just perfect for each person. But I was discouraged when I looked out the window. Snow obliterated the landscape. I put on my long underwear, several shirts, some Aria's and some Carl's, and my wolf-fur hooded parka and ventured into the garage and opened the garage door. A drift almost waist high had blown in front of the door. The snow blower started on the first pull. I had to snow-blow slowly because the snow was so heavy that the blower strained if I tried to take too much at a time. It took several hours. I took several breaks and warmed up with hot coffee, wishing Carl was home to make his special hot chocolate. After snow-blowing and some shoveling where I couldn't snow-blow, I rewarded my efforts with a big bowl of oatmeal and switched on the radio in the kitchen as I scooped brown sugar and a large gob of butter onto my oatmeal. I watched it melt, as my face hovered over the steaming mixture.

The radio announcer on the local station sounded quite vehement. *"Record snowfall last night. Eighteen inches so far and still falling. Stay off the roads and let the plows clear them. Lots of people in the ditch, and if you get stranded emergency crews are going to have trouble getting to you. There is already one death in St. Louis County blamed on the weather. Everyone is advised to stay put. Enjoy Christmas Eve wherever you are. Don't travel. The Governor has declared all the major roads closed."*

Oatmeal stuck in my throat. I turned off the radio. I hovered over my oatmeal as tears dripped down my cheeks and mixed with the brown sugar in my bowl. I looked at the presents I had wrapped and sobbed. This house was so big. I felt lonely and abandoned. My birthday was tomorrow. I had enjoyed celebrating it recently, no longer feeling like I was a mockery to the Christ child. My friends had given me a whole new perspective. But it looked like this birthday was never going to be celebrated, just like the others when I was growing up. Oh, well.

I called Connie. At least the telephone lines weren't cut off. "I'm not sure I can make it. I cleared the driveway, but Rolly hasn't gotten our road plowed yet. There was so much snow the snow blower stalled a couple of times." My tears dripped onto the telephone. I grabbed a tissue to wipe them off and blew my nose.

"You've got to come. Everyone wants to see you. And there are lots of presents under the tree for you." Connie said. "When you see the plow come by, you get in Carl's four-wheel drive Volvo and get here. Besides, it's your birthday tomorrow."

"Yes, Connie, dear, I'll try."

"Don't Connie-dear me. Just get here." She hung up.

I walked out to the end of the driveway. No plow in sight. The drifts across the road were over the tops of my new boots. I suppose I could snowshoe to Connie's. Carl had snowshoes in the garage. I calculated in my head how many miles it must be. I didn't think I'd make it, and I certainly didn't want to be the second fatality related to the weather. Larger flakes started to fall. They were so beautiful, and when one hit my nose, it tickled.

I'd check the road again later. It was time to take a sauna. I had sweat so much from clearing the driveway that I stunk. Trapped by the snow, I couldn't even attempt to go anywhere until it was plowed. I shuffled through the deep snow and turned on the heat in the sauna. While it was getting warm, I shoveled a path back up to the house. There was a huge drift the wind had blown between the sauna and the lake.

I was exhilarated as I stripped and entered the sauna and sat on my towel. The thermometer was bouncing on the red zone. I laughed at being so warm and naked when it was so cold outside. I put on a ladle of water. Steam filled the room. I could hardly breathe. I gasped and ran out the door and rolled in the snow. My skin prickled all over, especially the thin skin on my chest from my bilateral mastectomy. The scars ached. I jumped up, throwing the snow in the air, thrilled to feel it land on my bare back. It was glorious. I was a steaming girl spinning in a magic snow wonderland.

When my feet got cold, I returned to the sauna to warm up. Another ladle of water on the rocks and I was warm and sweaty again. It felt so wonderful that I paused to think. *How privileged I am. I felt like Cinderella. I haven't found a handsome prince, but I am sure living like a queen.* I felt ashamed that I had been so disappointed about the Christmas party. I was safe, had food, lovely house, why was I so upset.

Another ladle on the rocks, and I steamed myself right out of the room. "I need a shower now," I told the walls as I turned everything off. Bundled up in just my parka and boots, carrying my clothes, I streaked to the house. I was glad I had shoveled the walk. After a long, cleansing, soapy shower, I dressed and searched the bookshelf for a good book.

Carl had more books than some libraries. I had read some of the books since my arrival, mostly classics that I had always wanted to read. I fingered through the titles. I was in the "Adventure" section, as Carl called it. I came across a poem book by Robert Service. I heated up some milk and cream just like Carl had shown me and grated the imported chocolate into the steaming mixture.

Out the picture window, facing the lake, it was snowing more heavily than before. Sipping my hot chocolate, I went to the garage and opened the door. My snow-blowing job had been obliterated. I would need to snow-blow again even if the plow came.

Disappointed and discouraged again, I turned on the gas fireplace and curled up in Edna's afghan, sipped my hot chocolate, and read Robert Service. Somewhere in the middle of the *Cremation of Sam McGee*, as I was feeling warm and cozy, I heard the roar of engines. Fear shot through my spine. What if my annulled husband or his lackey, Max had found where I lived? How could anyone come out in this blizzard What about the security system? That should have alerted me. Had I forgotten to turn it on? And how did they get in through the gate? I jumped when I heard a pounding on the front door. I looked through the peephole. Two people with ski masks stood at the door. I grabbed the pistol from Carl's gun cabinet as I went to open the door.

"Becky Jean, are you all right, alone in this great big house?"

I laughed with relief when I saw the Halstrom twins remove their ski masks. "Yes, why do you ask?" I slipped the gun, hopefully unnoticed, into the pocket of my parka hanging beside the door.

They walked in and stomped their feet on the plastic mat, shaking off their mantle of snow. In their snowmobile suits, they looked like a couple of snowmen. "We came to get you for the Christmas party."

"What Christmas party?"

"Shawnee said that you're supposed to come to their house for Christmas," said Tim.

"And your birthday party tomorrow," said Tom.

"I sure wanted to go, but Rolly hasn't plowed our road, and I'd get the car stuck if I tried to drive through that snowdrift at the end of the driveway."

"We came across the lake," said Tim.

"We're here to bring you to the party. We brought my mother's snowmobile suit for you. You'll stay nice and warm," said Tom.

"With our mother's permission," Tim added. "We are learning to treat adults with respect."

"And women," added Tom.

I stood and looked at their rosy cheeks. "And just why are you two so concerned about whether I go to Connie and Hal's Christmas party? I suspect ulterior motives."

"You tell her, Tim."

"No, you tell her."

"Somebody better tell me, or I'm staying right here." I shifted the afghan across my shoulders and set my stance.

They looked back and forth at each other. "All right, but it's supposed to be a secret." They scuffed their feet and looked at the floor. "Shawnee promised to date us if we came and got you." They became animated, and their faces brightened as their eyes pleaded. "She's the hottest girl at school, but she turns everyone down that asks her for a date," said Tim.

"She even turned down the captain of the football team," said Tom.

"So you two will get big status points if you date her, is that it?"

"Big time," said Tim.

"But Tim and I really like her too, and we will treat her with great respect," said Tom, emphasizing the words. "Are you coming? Our social future depends on it. We'll drive slowly."

"And make sure you're comfortable," said Tim. "We're at your service," they took off their knit hats and bowed, "Your highness."

"You're not just trying to take advantage of Shawnee are you?"

They both blushed. "You mean trying to have sex with her?" said Tim.

"Never," said Tom. "She or her father would kill us."

"Have you seen her shoot a pistol?" said Tim. "She is way too dangerous to mess with, Becky Jean. No, it's just that she is pretty and smart. She's a whizz in science class. None of the other girls score in science. She has all A's in chemistry and physics and, well, you know, she's…"

"Hot." said Tom, nodding his head like a woodpecker.

"As long as your intentions are honorable, I'll go with you. You did bring the snowmobile suit…with your mother's permission." I stared them down. "I have every reason to trust you, don't I?"

"Yes, of course."

"All right, I'll come." I put my hands on my hips. "But I want a full account of this date you take Shawnee on, a full account of every minute."

"Agreed."

"Let me lock up and check the security system, and then I'll be ready to go," I said to their cheers. "Do you have room for all my presents?"

"Sure. We brought mom's sled, with her permission, of course." They bowed again, "Your highness."

I laughed at their antics, glad they had come to bring me to the party, but I was concerned that now too many people knew where I lived. "You must never, ever tell anyone where I live. Is that understood?"

"As you wish, your grace. We will make sure this is your best Christmas and birthday ever."

It was.

Chapter 36
March Anxiety

That winter brought days of severe cold and multiple blizzards; the governor closed all Minnesota schools several times when the wind chill dropped to fifty below zero. So it was a surprise when the week of spring break was warm and beautiful, very unseasonable for Minnesota. As the snow melted, flowers covered the forest floor. The ditches along the road, that I had so feared falling into during the winter, blossomed forth with wild flowers. Connie was in a tizzy trying to keep Sherrie and Shawnee occupied. They both had spring fever. and Connie was sure they would get into trouble while she was working. So the Tuesday of spring break, I offered to bring them to Duluth with me to get supplies and a stop at the mall.

"At least that will give me a couple hours that I won't have to worry about them," Connie said.

"And it is too cold to go skinny-dipping in Lake Superior," I added.

"I guess I did overreact to that," said Connie. "I'm sorry I got so mad at you. But pay attention to what they buy at the mall."

"It's all right. You're a good mother. I should have asked first." I changed the subject. "So how are the dates going with Tim and Tom? I understand that they are the only young men worthy of Shawnee."

She laughed, "They're very respectful boys, and Hal approves of them. He even took them out back to do some target practice. Actually I think it is safer for Shawnee to date two at once than be alone with some of those guys that have asked to take her out. They even took Sherrie with them one time. Boy did she think she was hot stuff to go out with senior boys."

"They're good kids. Did you know that I require Tim and Tom to give me a written account of their dates? They have to write an essay about their date each time and turn it into me before they can date Shawnee again."

"They do? That's ridiculous."

I laughed, "Yes, and even more ridiculous, I correct their grammar and send them back. Tim and Tom say that they are both becoming better writers and that writing about their dates is a lot more interesting than their English assignments." I saw Hal's pickup truck out the window. "They're here. We'll see you later."

We returned mid-afternoon. Shawnee ran to talk to her mother. "Mom, you won't believe it." Sherrie ran in the back to help me unload Bert's supplies to the back room and put the frozen food in the freezer. I smiled at Connie as we came out.

Sherrie shivered. "It's cold in there, mother. Do you have to go in there very often?"

"Yes, my little fawn, I do."

Shawnee interrupted, "Becky Jean set up a college account for me and Sherrie. It has gobs of money in it for us to start at the university."

"Becky Jean, what did you do?" Connie glared, shaking her finger at me.

"That was why I wanted to take the girls with me on my weekly trip to Duluth, so that I could set up a little bank account in both girls' names. They have to sign for that, you know. It's just some money for their education."

Shawnee showed the papers to Connie, "Isn't it exciting, mother? Sherrie and I have our own bank accounts."

Connie examined the bank statements. "Rebecca Jean Gottwald, this is inappropriate."

"We can discuss that later. You have very intelligent daughters, and they deserve a college education."

Connie turned to her daughter, "Shawnee, I expect you to study hard to show Becky Jean how much you appreciate this gift. I don't want you out dating all the guys in the dormitory next fall when you start."

"Oh, I'll study hard, mother, I promise. May I date one or two if I get straight A's?"

"Perfect straight A's. One B, and you are grounded for the rest of the semester."

"Deal." She extended her hand to her mother. "I won't even argue. Aren't you impressed?"

Connie was shaking her head, "Unbelievable. You're a magician, Becky Jean. How do you do it?"

"And mother, I'm going to college too when I graduate. I intend to become a famous author, or maybe a musician playing my flute," said Sherrie. "Becky Jean says I have a gift for writing."

Connie turned toward me, shaking the bank statements, "Becky Jean…"

"There is one condition," I said to Connie, "The money should only be used for education. I want you to make sure of that." I took her hand in mine. "We can discuss this later. We have customers."

I turned away and went to the front of the restaurant, picked up the coffee pot, and checked on the customers. "Great weather, right?" I asked as I filled a customer's cup.

Carl was sitting at the counter. He motioned me over. "I waited for you to come back, Becky Jean. Now remember the closing on the house is just after fishing season opens, May 28th. I'm leaving for New York today. Don't worry. I'm staying with a friend in Duluth tonight and have a ride to the airport in the morning. You're in charge of the place, so you can stay till the new owners move in. They bought the furniture and everything." He smiled, "For a little extra profit. Besides, what would I have done with that stuff? My children don't want it."

"And the china and crystal?"

He grabbed my hand. "Now that will go to my granddaughter. I think it is sophisticated enough for her, don't you think? I've already shipped it off this morning. I left the regular stuff for you, though."

"Thanks, otherwise I would have to buy a lot of paper plates." He laughed and let go of my hand. "I'm happy for you, Carl, and yes, I remember the closing date."

"Have you found a place to stay yet?"

"Don't worry. Connie said I could stay at her house until I find another place to live. They set up a nice room in the basement. It's all arranged." It was only a partial lie. The room had been set up for Leah, but since she married Roger, no one was staying there. I was sure that Connie would let me stay.

"I am so excited about moving to Colorado. I have the cutest little place with a great mountain view, and I'm just up the road from Paul's house." He stirred his coffee. "Just think, I'll get to see my son's grandchildren every day, and Christine is planning on spending her vacations in Colorado."

"I'm very excited for you."

"But first I'm flying to New York City. My oldest granddaughter is getting married. Can you believe it? There is an engagement party for her this weekend." He grabbed my hand again. "Becky Jean, I can never repay you for helping me grieve over Edna's death. You were an angel to me.

"Now here is a paper I need to have you sign."

"What's this, Carl?"

"Transfer of ownership." He smiled, "I'm giving you the Mazda RX8. My friend in Duluth wanted the big car."

I signed the paper as I broke into a sweat. "The Mazda is mine? I don't deserve that, Carl."

"Oh yes you do, and more." He pulled out his wallet and pushed a check across the counter. I almost fainted at all the zeros. Breathless, I couldn't speak. He passed his house keys to me. "The house is yours until closing. You drove the Mazda in this morning. It's yours. Here's my ride. I love you like a daughter, Becky Jean." He kissed my hand and walked out the door.

I stood stunned.

When I drove my new Mazda home that night, I realized that I had forgotten to buy any groceries. I checked the refrigerator to see what I would need. It was a good thing I had not bought anything. Carl had stocked the refrigerator and freezer. I had enough eggs and milk, steaks and sausages, and yogurt and cheese to last until the house transferred to the new owners. I shook my head in disbelief. *Oh Carl.*

Chapter 37
Rachel's Birthday

Out of the corner of my eye, I saw Roger and Leah get up from their table. They must be ready to check out, I thought.

"Mommy, mommy, I love you so much."

I squatted down as Rachel ran to me and gave me a hug around my legs. I grabbed a rag off the counter to wipe the grape jelly off my left leg. "Leah is your mommy, honey. But I love you too."

"My mommy says that you're my other mommy 'cause you saved me."

I wiped the jelly off her face hoping that it would be a long time before she understood what that meant. Leah and Roger were beaming. Roger had his arm around Leah's waist as she picked up the diaper bag full of toys, bibs, and a few diapers. "All right, I'll be your other mommy, because I love you *soooo* much." I held apart my hands to show her how much since I was stuck in position with the toddler hugging my leg. I turned to Leah, "She sure is walking well."

"Yes, she is. Now, remember her birthday party is Saturday, Becky Jean," Leah said.

Rachel interrupted, holding up her fingers. She couldn't decide which fingers she wanted to use. "I'm going to be *soooo* many," she said.

"You're invited if you can tolerate seven toddlers and their parents running around," said Roger. "It should be quite a party." He gave me a hug and whispered in my ear, "I never dreamed I would get to be a father."

"I plan to be there. Wouldn't miss it." I gave Leah a hug. "We've never had a better dishwasher than you."

She gave Roger a peck on the cheek. "I've never been so happy washing dishes as washing them for Roger and Rachel. Wages aren't as good, but the benefits are wonderful."

I put an arm around Roger. "Take good care of her, stud."

"I will, Becky. I'm the best." He gave me a breathtaking hug. I felt a twinge of pain in my left chest.

A couple weeks, later a sudden sharp pain in my chest awoke me from a sound sleep. I glanced at the clock: two o'clock. The pain grabbed my breath, and I sat up gasping. It dissipated after a while but wouldn't go away. Every breath was excruciating like a knife stabbing my rib. I took two Tylenol and went downstairs to sit on the sofa. The pain only got worse.

"I guess I know what it is, so time to go," I said.

I drove down to St. Luke's Hospital, Emergency Department. The pain grabbed me as I drove, but by taking small breaths and calming my mind, I made it. Fortunately the roads were well cleaned, not even wet. When I complained of "chest pain," they took me right into the examining room, and the nurse gave me a gown to put on and asked me to remove my top. The physician came in within minutes and took my history and listened to my heart and lungs noting my past surgical history. "You were awfully young to have a bilateral mastectomy."

"I had positive lymph nodes, and they found cancer in both breasts." I said pulling aside my gown, "and I had kidney cancer when I was ten years old followed by radiation and chemo." I smiled, "But I've survived so far. I'm pretty sure this pain is a metastasis."

"Really?" he said.

"It's only logical, right?"

He ordered a chest x-ray, a CT of my chest for pulmonary emboli, and some laboratory tests. Then I waited. *What is happening to me? This pain is not like any pain I've had before. Is the physician going to order some expensive medicine I can't afford?*

The nurse interrupted my thoughts to give me some kind of pain medicine in an injection while I waited for the physician to return. He returned with the results of my tests and showed me on the chest x-ray and then on the CT scans that there were spots on my lungs. "No emboli," he said. He showed me the place on my left fourth rib that looked like a mouse had been chewing on the bone. "That's what caused your chest pain. It's a pathologic fracture."

"Aren't all fractures pathologic?"

He explained, "Yes, I'm sorry. What I meant was that this fracture happened because something ate away at your bone."

"My breast cancer metastasized to my rib, and that's what caused the fracture?"

He hesitated, "Well, yes, probably." He reviewed the blood tests that were all normal except for the elevated alkaline phosphatase and then added, "I called Dr. Liebowitz and told her about your pain. Since your pain when you breathe is related to the lytic lesion in your rib, it is likely that your breast cancer has metastasized to your rib," he seemed to hesitate but continued, "and to lungs and it may be irritating your pleura as well." He put his hand on my shoulder, "I'm afraid that your cancer has spread fairly extensively."

"I'm sorry you woke Dr. Liebowitz in the middle of the night."

"It's all right. She was on call for the oncology group. She said she didn't mind being awakened for you."

I wanted to cry, but the tears wouldn't come. "Oh, well, I expected the pain to be from metastasis. I had positive lymph nodes."

The emergency physician nodded. "Take this pill that Dr. Liebowitz suggested, and I will check on you in thirty to forty minutes. If this medicine doesn't take away the pain, I will have to admit you to the hospital."

"It isn't a narcotic, is it? I can't go to work with narcotics in me."

"I wanted to give you a narcotic, but Dr. Liebowitz suggested this prostaglandin inhibitor."

I was determined that the prostaglandin inhibitor would make the pain tolerable. I was not interested in admission to the hospital. A half hour after taking indomethacin, my pain was gone, completely gone. I got dressed, left my cubicle exam room, and thanked the doctor. He was sitting at the desk working on charts. He looked surprised to see me.

"Pain free," I said. "Thanks."

He stood with a look of unbelief that I wasn't in pain. "Now don't forget to keep your appointment with Dr. Liebowitz. And I'm sending a copy to Dr. Sheihe as well."

"Thank you, doctor. I feel much better." I looked at the clock on the wall; I would be able to make it to the restaurant before Bert got there.

The next Tuesday morning the pain woke me before my alarm went off. I swallowed another indomethacin pill with cold water and sat in the recliner chair in my room. Thirty minutes later, I felt better and headed for the shower. Scrubbing my chest, I felt tightness across my rib cage. If I pressed on the left forth rib, it was tender. "I guess I better keep that appointment with Dr. Liebowitz and have her check out all these tender spots." I turned off the water and toweled dry. "Today," I promised myself.

I laughed as I put on my bra with the foam inserts. It always felt odd across my chest as my surgical scars were still somewhat sensitive, but as Connie said, it filled out my uniform. The left insert seemed to push on my tender spot. I loosened the strap on my bra. For distraction, I pictured Shawnee starting at the University of Minnesota next fall as I got dressed. *She was so excited when she got her acceptance letter. Sherrie will join her in a couple of years. I can keep wearing my foam boobs until the breast cancer kills me. The money is better spent on the girls' educations than some ridiculous chemotherapy that will give me a few more days of suffering.* I was so glad I had put the ring money into the girl's bank accounts. But I had one more thing to do. I had to see a lawyer. "Today, after my oncology appointment."

Dr. Liebowitz was matter of fact with her explanation. She was glad that the indomethacin was controlling the pain. "But let me give you a prescription for narcotics if the pain gets out of control."

"No need," I said. "Thirty to forty minutes after I take indomethacin, the pain is gone. Well not completely, but so I can ignore it. I don't want narcotics. It will interfere with my work and driving. You wouldn't want me to get into an accident because I was impaired from narcs, would you?"

She sighed deeply. "So I suppose chemo is out of the question too, then."

"Dr. Liebowitz, I appreciate everything you have done for me. You are a good listener and have been compassionate with my case. You explain things well. I doubt that I have long to live, but right now I live in a mansion on the lake, I have a great boss and coworkers, and I love my job. What more could I ask out of life? I feel so rich." I took her hand in mine. "Why take chemo that I can't afford to spend my remaining time nauseated and sick for a few more moments of life? You know that won't cure me."

She took her hand away and sighed. "You're right. I just feel that I have failed you."

"No way. You have been great. Thanks." I hugged her and then walked out of the office, waving at the nurse and receptionist. I figured it would be a while before I returned. Maybe when the cancer got a hold of me I would come back. But then again, probably not, this was likely my last visit.

The lawyer was quite surprised that someone my age wanted to write a will. I didn't fill him in on my medical condition, and the will was "simple," in his words, so he didn't charge me much. But he was curious, "So everything goes to these two girls who aren't even your relatives, and their mother is the executor of the will. What about your family, your parents, any relatives?"

"Nothing to any relatives, absolutely nothing," I said with a vehemence that seemed to shock him. He backed down, but then I added, "Is this will likely be contested?"

He laughed, "Not likely, although it is a significant amount of money. I will make sure that if they contest the will, that it will cost your family much more than what they will get out of it. I promise you to make it so. All the tremendous expense will be theirs."

I smiled. "Good." He asked me to list my bank account number, the title to the Mazda, and any other assets, of which I had none. I was out of his office in less than an hour.

Chapter 37
Fishing Season

Fishing season opened with a bang. The weather was mild with a gentle breeze. Fishermen complained at breakfast that by lunchtime they might already have caught their limit. The restaurant was crowded. I was glad because if I kept moving I could ignore my chest pain and the new pain in my hip. I took my indomethacin every morning before I left for work. For over a month, that had been enough to get me through the day. But this morning I felt like I had to take another one when Connie asked to go on her morning break.

As she headed to the back room she said, "That guy back in the corner booth sure is a grouch." She mimicked his words with a snarl, "Just serve me and leave me alone. I'm waiting for someone."

I turned to look, but the grouch had his back to me. The ladies' Bible study trooped in the door, and they seated themselves in the back room. "I'll be right with you, ladies." I swallowed another pill with a glass of water before I went in to take their orders. The restaurant was a buzz of activity. *I hope my medicine kicks in soon. Otherwise it is going to be a hard, painful day.*

When Bert showed up, he pulled me aside. "Those steaks you finagled from the Old World Butcher look great. I'm planning on steak for the lunch special. I made those little signs this morning." He pointed at the sign in the window.

The signs were adorable—A smiling chicken with an apron and a fork with a hunk of meat saying, "Eat more beef."

"I'll put up some more if you have them," I said. "I'm sure the customers will love them, but isn't the price a little high?"

"Only you and I know what you paid for those steaks, Becky Jean. It's a fair price with a nice profit margin. Besides, if our usual customers order steak today, it will pay your salary." He handed me more of the signs.

"And I'll be rich?" I teased.

When Connie came back from break, she looked in the corner. "Is that grouch still here?"

"Yes, still here. He hasn't asked for anything, not even refills on coffee. So I haven't gone back there."

As we started the lunch menu, the steak special went over well. "Even the grouch ordered steak," Connie said as she passed me at the counter.

In the next hour, there were seventeen orders. Ron was humming. It seems he was enjoying flipping steaks instead of hamburgers. I even considered having one myself for my 2:30 meal. Customers were remarking about Bert's special steak sauce, although some wanted creamy horseradish sauce instead. I had anticipated that, so I had bought a large supply. Somehow word had gotten around the community. Not only was the restaurant busy, but the lunch crowd arrived early.

"I can't believe that I can bite into such a great steak for the price," said Rolly as I filled his coffee cup. He held up his steak knife. "Bert must have pulled these out of the back drawer. I've never seen steak knives served with lunch before."

"You're such a tease, Rolly." I brought him a full catsup bottle. "Has the road crew gotten that road to Whiteface Lake all paved?"

"Should be done today."

"Becky Jean," Mr. Johannsen called for refills on coffee. "You know, Sherrie is doing wonderfully in my class. That girl sure knows how to write poetry, and her prose is excellent too. Grammar, spelling—she's a natural. I hear you gave her some scholarship money to attend UMD."

"Yah, something like that. She wrote a poem for me when I was in the hospital. I've read some of her other poems. I think she's pretty talented. I wanted to give her a chance to show it."

"Oh, what kind of pie can I have with my steak?"

"We have strawberry on special, and I think there is one piece of pecan pie left. They're going fast." I set the steak knife beside his other utensils. "Your steak will be ready in a moment."

"I'll have strawberry pie. I had pecan yesterday."

"Do you want it now in case there is a run on strawberry pie?" I laughed at him. Thin as a poplar tree but he ate pie every time he came to the restaurant. He amazed me.

"You just set it aside for me."

Ron called out. "Steak order ready."

"There you go, Mr. Johannsen, and I'll set aside the strawberry pie for you."

I took a glance at Connie. She was flitting between customers like a bumble bee pollinating hungry flowers. She caught my gaze and gave me a thumbs-up. I checked my jar. I had quite a few tips as well. *It's going to be a very productive day for Bert's Café.*

Connie had served the grouchy guy the special, but after his lunch he just sat there in the corner sipping cold coffee. I was busy serving the tables in front of the counter, so I didn't hear or see him get up. I was too distracted with orders and some of my favorite guests. But when I felt the painful grip and a harsh jerk on my arm, I knew who it was. As he jerked me around to confront him, I glanced out the window just in time to see the red Hummer pull into the handicapped space. Keith Stagg crushed my right arm. Intense pain made me drop the coffee pot. The crash drew the attention of everyone in the restaurant. Hot coffee splattered over my legs, and I shrieked.

His boisterous whisper reverberated around the restaurant. "I want them back. Now."

The restaurant hushed. Max entered and stood just inside the door, blocking the exit. "Come on, Keith, let's settle this outside."

I was determined to stay where I had witnesses. I glared at him as his left hand tightened its grip. I felt a snapping in my arm. "I don't have the rings. Besides, where did you get those rings? I know you didn't buy them."

His sardonic smile added pathos to his response. "An old woman had no use for them anymore. She gave them to me."

"Well, that's all I got out of our so-called marriage. But I guess you made arrangements so that it never happened. You had our marriage annulled, didn't you?"

He laughed, "You didn't come to the annulment hearing, so I was awarded the rings."

"Liar, I am sure that never was part of the conversation with the judge."

"Come on, Keith, let's do this outside," Max insisted from the doorway. He motioned to Keith. "I found out where she lives. Couple of teenage boys told me, so we don't need to make a scene here. Besides she must have sold the rings judging by the car she's driving." Max took a couple steps closer. I assumed he was going to grab my other arm.

I stood my ground, forcing him to push me. The restaurant was silent. Bert moved from the cash register closer toward the door. I saw Officer Davis get up from his booth behind Keith and start walking toward us. Keith jerked me toward the door. I almost fell. He yanked me upright and turned to the customers. "Fuck you all. Mind your own business," he yelled. Max moved closer.

I noticed his right hand was inside his coat. How odd to be wearing a coat when it was such a warm spring day. Then it came to me. He must have a gun.

Just then the bell tinkled on the door. Roger and Leah entered. Rachel trotted in through the door. Rachel escaped her mother's grip and screamed as she ran through the door, "Mommy, mommy, I love you." She ran to me, grabbed my leg and clung to me, sending me kisses.

"You fuckin' bitch." Keith said, grabbing Rachel by her hair. He pulled out the gun and pointed it at her head. "Who have you been screwing?"

Around Keith's shoulder, I saw Officer Davis unlatch his holster, pull out his service revolver and say, "Police, drop the gun." Keith grabbed Rachel around the neck, getting a firm grip on the toddler, and then turned toward Officer Davis's drawn gun.

Rachel yelled, "Mommy, he's hurting me. Make him stop."

Keith snarled, "I'm sure you don't want to see this lovely little girl get hurt, Officer. I'm just here to get what's mine and then I'll be gone." He pointed the gun at me. "This woman is a thief. I just want her to return what's mine."

As they glared at each other, I glanced around behind me. Max had stepped closer, but not close enough to grab me. He seemed unaware that Bert was right behind him. I needed to make my move before Max could grab me. I focused on the gun Keith was holding to Rachel's head. My mind raced to the target practice at Hal and Connie's. *Can I grab that gun and turn it on him? Can I get Rachel away from him?* I felt a searing pain in my right upper arm where he had grabbed me. *I might have to use my left hand.*

"You never said anything about guns, Keith," said Max. "I'm out of here. I don't want to have anything more to do with this. I found her for you and set this up, but I'm not going to be part of shooting little girls." He started to back up right up until he bumped into Bert. That threw him off balance.

Keith turned. "You god-damned chicken shit, Max. I need those rings."

While he was distracted, I had my chance. I grabbed the barrel of the gun and yanked it toward me, away from Rachel. With a reflex response, he lost his grip on Rachel. She squirmed away and ran to Leah. I jerked the gun as hard as I my strength allowed. *Could I grab it and turn it on Keith and end this nasty affair?* But as I buried the weapon in my belly, he squeezed the trigger.

The sound of the shot reverberated through the restaurant. I saw Rachel cover her ears as Leah and Roger grabbed her. Customers shrieked. I felt a sudden pain like hot spattered grease burning in my groin. Then another pain seared down my right leg. I extended my right arm to break my fall, and it telescoped into a weird posture. I heard a loud snapping in my left hip as my leg collapsed.

I turned my head to look at my assailant. A silent scream of apparent confusion flashed across his face. Then he just collapsed. What happened? Had Officer Davis shot him? But I hadn't heard another shot being fired. As Keith hit the floor, his face was white as a cadaver. He looked dead.

The pain in my left hip that had been bothering me over the last couple weeks suddenly increased. I attempted to get up, but my right leg was bent in an odd direction. I couldn't turn it. Still holding the barrel of the gun in my left hand, the burning from the hot barrel cramped my attempt to drop it. I pressed it into the intense heat filling my groin. Where was Rachel? Was she all right?

Looking around, I saw Rachel. Focusing on her sweet face, I tried to maintain consciousness. I tried to motion for her, but only my hand seemed to work. "I'm…"

She broke free from her parents and came to me. I managed to move my arm around to hug her to my chest. Feeling light-headed, my head fell backwards. "I love you, precious."

"I love you too, my other mommy. You're tired, aren't you?"

"Yes, very tired, Rachel. I'm going to rest for a while. Is that all right with you?"

"You rest now, mommy. I love you." She gave me a kiss on the cheek.

Loosening my grip on the gun, my hand started to relax. I looked at my palm to examine the burn from the barrel of the gun and shook my head. *It will never heal.* Distracted by the chaos surrounding me, I felt a sense of peace, confident that Keith was no longer a threat. In fact, he hadn't moved and his face was like wax. He hadn't moved. *How did that happen?*

Officer Davis knelt and took the pistol from my hand. "I called the ambulance, Becky Jean. They're on their way."

Looking back through the crowd around me, I saw Bert wrench Max's arm behind his back. "You dirty arsonist," he said. "We got you this time."

Max tried to jerk something out of his jacket pocket.

Officer Davis jumped to Max's side, jabbing his revolver into his chest. "Drop the weapon." Max dropped his gun to the floor. Davis picked it up and cuffed him, forcing him to kneel on the floor, and gave Bert the gun. "Don't let him move, Bert."

I was feeling weak. My burnt hand dropped to the floor. I couldn't hold it up any longer as my strength melted away. *I have to stay conscious,* I told myself and tried to sit up.

The crowd separated back into the restaurant as Officer Davis directed them away from the scene. He knelt beside my collapsed assailant to examine Keith's flaccid form. His impotent hands lay motionless on the floor. He looked more like a porcelain doll that had fallen off a shelf than something human. Officer Davis checked his neck for a pulse. "He's dead."

There was a gasp from the restaurant crowd.

I heard him mutter under his breath, "How did that happen?" He glanced at the assembled customers. "I only heard one shot. Did anyone hear more than that?" The crowd shook their heads. He jumped up and grabbed Max, relieving Bert of his hostage. He jabbed his gun into Max's ribs, "Max Holter, you're under arrest for conspiracy to commit murder. You have the right to remain silent…Anything you say now can be used against you. Do you understand?"

He tugged at his manacled hands. "Yah, I understand, you two-bit—"

Bert jabbed him in mid-sentence, "No fancy attorney will get you out of this, you devil." He spit at him.

"Back off, Bert," said Officer Davis.

"I didn't know he was going to use that gun," Max yelled.

"So you did know he was armed. Thank you for that information. And I see that you were armed as well." He took Max's revolver from Bert and flashed it in his face.

Tunnel vision narrowed my world. Rachel continued to hug me. Leah knelt by my side. "I love you so much, mommy." My arm was too weak to hug her. Roger and Leah pulled her away from the blood that pulsated out of my abdominal wound. Rachel turned to her mother, "She's tired now, isn't she, mommy? She told me she was very tired." She escaped Leah's grasp again and knelt beside me to give me a kiss. "You take a nap now."

"I will, sweetheart."

"Becky Jean, hang in there," Connie yelled as she caressed my aching head. "The ambulance is turning into the parking lot."

I pointed to the jar of tips at the register. "You can have my tips, Connie. There are quite a few. People were very generous today." A gasp of pain escaped from my mouth. "My work is done, Connie, could you please tell Bert I'm giving notice."

"I'm right here, Becky Jean," Bert said kneeling beside me.

"He knows." Connie wept, her tears falling across my face.

"Connie," I managed to say. It was getting hard to breath and my belly was swelling like I was pregnant. "I won't be homeless anymore. But thanks for the offer to stay at your house." I think I smiled before everything went bright.

County Sheriff Ralph Davis's Perspective

Several days later, I was sitting in my office still not sure of what had happened. A full cup of coffee sat cooling on my desk. Looking up at the ceiling tiles, I contemplated the scene. *Why had the assailant suddenly dropped dead? Was there a second shot? But nobody heard two shots.*

I heard the telephone ring in the front office. The dispatcher answered, "County Sheriff's office." There was a pause. "Then would you like to speak to Officer Davis? He has been waiting for your report. Hold a moment please." I turned to look out my office door. The dispatcher was holding the telephone up in the air and shouted, "Sheriff Davis, Dr. Cohen's on line two. He has the autopsy report."

I answered, "Dr. Cohen? You have a report for me?"

"Yes, I have the report on your two homicide victims, Ralph. Don't be so formal. We've known each other for years. You know my name."

"Yes, Dave. Now you said *two* homicide victims? I'm confused. The man shot the woman. I was right there having lunch, Dave. I saw the whole thing. There was only one shot fired. None of the witnesses in the restaurant heard two shots. I pulled my gun and yelled, 'Drop your weapon,' but I never fired. The assailant just collapsed right in front of me. I'm sure no one touched him. But I admit that he was white as a ghost when he dropped. I felt for a pulse when I had the scene stabilized, but he was already dead. I assure you that I never fired my gun."

Dave laughed. "You can keep rambling, Ralph, or you can listen to me. I know you never fired, but you missed something."

"How could I? I was five feet away."

"Let me review the results for you, Officer Davis.

"Yes, Dr. David Cohen, sir."

He laughed again. "The male victim, identified as Keith Arnold Stagg, had several deep knife wounds. Liver and spleen were lacerated, and his right renal artery, vena cava, and aorta were severed. His entire cardiac output poured into his belly in seconds. In fact, at autopsy showed there was no blood in his heart. That correlates with your description that he was, may I quote you, 'White as a ghost.' His death was sudden, probably less than a minute."

"Knife wounds?"

"Yes, I counted three separate entrance wounds in his back."

"I didn't see anyone stab him. But there was a lot of confusion." I thought back to what had happened. "Bert served steak for the lunch special, so almost everyone in the restaurant had a steak knife. There must have been thirty-some people with knives. Could one of those have been the weapon?"

"I just report what I find, but the wounds seem a bit too deep for just a steak knife, but I suppose if they were thrust hard enough. I'll go back and measure their depth and get back to you on that. However, it seems that the murderer must have known exactly how to do the most damage. You have any trained killers there in Cotton?"

"Not that I know of. That is puzzling. What about Becky Jean?"

"Yes, the young woman identified as Rebecca Jean Gottwald had a bullet track in the abdomen, lodged in her pelvis. It perforated her uterus and ripped through the iliac artery. It's a big artery but somewhat retroperitoneal, so the blood extravasation cephalad took a while before she bled to death. She was probably conscious for ten to fifteen minutes before going into cardiovascular collapse, unlike the male victim."

"Well that fits. He shot her. He had the gun aimed at a hostage, a little girl, but Becky Jean, Ms. Rebecca Jean Gottwald, intervened and pulled the gun into her belly to protect the hostage and took the bullet. It's a strange case. I'm not quite sure of everything that happened. It happened so fast." My voice trailed off.

"One more thing," Dave said.

"What's that?"

"She had had bilateral mastectomies. I checked with our hospital records. She had surgery here at St. Luke's hospital over a year ago."

"She did? Oh yes, I remember, Bert said she was out sick for a while, but I didn't know what she had and I didn't know she'd had surgery."

"She had metastatic breast cancer."

"What? She wasn't even thirty years old, twenty-five or twenty-six, how could she have breast cancer?"

"The records from the oncologist show that she had a rare gene combination that predisposed her to breast cancer. Besides, I received records from Dubuque, Iowa. She had renal cell carcinoma at ten years of age and had extensive radiation to her chest wall. That radiation plus the BRCA-1 and 2 genes, she had both, probably predisposed her to have cancer at a young age. That kidney was surgically removed, and I found no sign of additional renal cell cancer. On the other hand, breast cancer invaded her liver, multiple ribs and both lungs and a huge metastasis in her right femur and a pathologic fracture in her right humerus. Her hip was broken. Did she fall?" He didn't wait for an answer. "It's a pathologic fracture there, too, so she wouldn't have had to fall too hard to break her femur. In fact, it might have fractured with simple weight bearing and caused her to fall. I haven't done the brain yet. I'm waiting for it to fix, but I may find cancer there as well. She was dying," said Dave. "I doubt that she would have lived more than a few months with the cancer load she was carrying."

"Do you think she knew that?" My voice was enigmatic.

He responded with what I considered a coroner's chuckle, "Now how could I possibly know that from an autopsy?"

"Right. Bad question. Could you go over those knife wounds again? I'm mystified by that. I was eating steak just like a lot of people in the restaurant, but I would say my knife blade was four, maybe five, inches long at the most. Could that have severed his aorta and what else you said? And he would have been stabbed fairly soon after the shot went off. I'm telling you, when I saw he had a gun, I ran to disarm him. He grabbed this little girl as a hostage. Then Becky Jean grabbed the gun and a shot was fired. He collapsed. By the time I checked him, he was already dead. He had no pulse."

"I appreciate your musings, Ralph, but do you have any more questions about the autopsy? I'll go back and measure the wounds, but just guessing by recall, I would say that it took a longer knife than five inches." He paused. "Ralph? Are you still there?"

"Yes? I was just trying to remember the details of what I saw." The dispatcher passed me a slip of paper from our fax machine. "Oh, Dave?"

"Yes."

"I just received a dispatch. It seems Keith Stagg is wanted in Iowa on suspicion of murder. It appears an elderly woman died under unusual circumstances."

"So Iowa needs a positive identification and notification as well?"

"Yes."

"Consider it done, Ralph."

"Thanks, Dave." He laughed as he hung up.

Funeral: Cotton Covenant Church

Be still, my soul: the Lord is on thy side.
Bear patiently the cross of grief or pain.
Leave to thy God to order and provide,
who through all changes faithful will remain.
Be still, my soul: thy best, thy heavenly Friend
through thorny ways leads to a joyful end.

Kathrina von Schlegel
Translated from German

I walked into the Cotton Covenant Church in my county sheriff's uniform and sat down toward the front. It didn't smell musty as I expected. Someone must have spent hours cleaning it up. Not since the last minister left had it looked so neat.

Not many had arrived yet. Mr. Gleeson, the funeral home director from Duluth, stood by the open casket at the front of the Cotton Covenant Church just below the podium. I waved. He had been the funeral director for my mother's funeral. He was a tall, handsome African American man wearing his dignified black suit. The open casket was simple pine but had a fish engraved on the inside. I left my seat to pay my respects. Becky Jean looked peaceful but was wearing cosmetics that she never wore in the restaurant. I supposed Mr. Gleeson had done that to make her look more natural. I returned to my seat, overwhelmed with memories of all the times Becky Jean had served me.

Becky Jean's father, Reverend Gottwald, I presumed, since I didn't recognize him as a restaurant customer, entered the church with his entourage of a family. Mr. Gleeson greeted them and ushered them to the front right-hand pews just ahead of me. The reverend was dressed in a black suit with a ministerial collar. After greeting Mr. Gleeson he took a glance at the casket and shook his head. He tried to close it, but Mr. Gleeson stopped him. "An open casket was requested, sir."

Reverend Gottwald turned and asked about the funeral arrangements, adding, "So how much will all this cost?"

Mr. Gleeson answered, "Everything is already paid for, Reverend Gottwald." Then he added, "We don't have many funerals here in Cotton. Most people want the service in Duluth at the Catholic Cathedral or at the big Methodist Church on the hill. She requested to have the funeral here, and be buried in the local Cotton cemetery. You're from where, sir?"

"Dubuque Iowa. I teach at the seminary. So let me make sure I understand this. She pre-paid her funeral and plot? Unusual for a twenty-six year old woman, don't you think?" said Becky's father. "So her estate owes you nothing?"

"She was twenty-five, Reverend, sir," Mr. Gleeson corrected.

"Oh, right. I forgot."

"Her estate owes me nothing, sir. It wasn't pre-paid, but I'm not sure where the money came from. Everything was paid anonymously. She paid for her plot in advance. I believe her lawyer helped arrange that."

Reverend Gottwald chuckled. "She had a lawyer? Well, that's good news for you, because I doubt her estate has anything." He gave Mr. Gleeson a thumb's up, "I'm glad for your sake or you'd be out of luck."

The Reverend looked at his watch, "Ten minutes to go." He looked at the fifteen or so people who had filtered into the church. He introduced his wife, their daughter and her husband, and the young girl sitting next to them to Mr. Gleeson. "My daughter came from Guatemala. She and her husband are Lutheran missionaries there. And that is my sweet little granddaughter, Christina. Isn't she cute?"

"Very adorable, Reverend, sir," Mr. Gleeson said. But I noticed no change in expression on his face.

"I suppose we could get started, I doubt that many are coming." He turned to Mr. Gleeson, "The place sure smells stale."

"They haven't had a pastor here for a couple of years. The building belongs to the Swedish Covenant Church. Since the pastor moved on, the church has only been used for local weddings and funerals, and there haven't been many of those. But you best wait until the proper time to begin, Reverend. We expect that more are coming."

Mr. Gleeson walked to where the family was sitting. "Sorry for your loss, Mrs. Gottwald," he said. The funeral home director offered his hand, but she ignored him and grasped her purse with both hands. She was dressed in a gray suit and skirt with a frilly white blouse.

She didn't look up at him and mumbled, "This is my daughter, Heather, and her husband, Philip. She and her husband are missionaries in Guatemala."

"So I've heard. Welcome. I'm sorry for your loss," he said as he moved along the pew to greet them.

Mrs. Gottwald continued, "We're pleased that they could come home from Guatemala. Because of the funeral, they got permission from their mission board to come and visit. We are so happy to see them."

Mr. Gleeson offered his hand. "I'm so sorry." Heather wiped her eyes with a handkerchief and her daughter, Christina, covered her face with her hands. Philip's jaw seemed set as he put his arm over his wife's shoulder. None of them returned his offer.

Reverend Gottwald looked at his watch and climbed to the podium, "Dearly beloved, we are gathered here in the presence of God to…"

I saw Roger stand. He was with Leah and Rachel sitting in the front row on the left. Leah's parents were sitting beside them. Roger interrupted, "I think you better wait, pastor. I know you are the officiating minister, but there are others coming. So please wait." Roger sat down and gave his whimpering wife a hug. He added, "They have to park their trucks."

"I prefer Reverend, sir. I didn't catch your name."

"Roger, Roger Halstrom. This is my wife, Leah and our daughter, Rachel…Reverend." He stood again and extended his hand, but the reverend stayed in the podium and ignored him.

Rachel stood in the pew and yelled. "Wait, wait, Mister."

"Sorry, Reverend." Leah corralled her daughter. "Sit down, honey. That is Becky's father, and he's a minister, not a mister. But we're supposed to call him Reverend Gottwald."

She squirmed in her seat. "I don't care about his name." She screamed as she wiggled out of Leah's grasp, "He has to wait."

"Sorry, Reverend, toddlers think they know everything."

I watched Reverend Gottwald check his watch. He seemed annoyed that the service was not starting on time.

The low throbbing honk of several Peterbilt tractors shattered the silence. Roger stood and ran to the back of the church. "They're here," he said, "they're all here. Just wait a moment until everyone is here and seated, Reverend, sir."

I got up and joined Roger at the back door of the church to see what was happening. The air filled with the smell of diesel as each Peterbilt tractor without a trailer flashed its lights and filled the church parking lot. Each had an orange funeral flag tied to its aerial. A string of other semi-tractors, Whites and Macks, followed with a string of cars lined behind them, each with their orange flags displayed. In the rear, pick-up trucks followed. The parking lot was full, so the pick-ups parked along the highway. The last vehicle was an MDOT tractor.

A van pulled up to the driveway as the parade parked along the highway. I watched Mrs. Lawrence and the ladies from the women's Bible study descend and march toward the church humming "Onward Christian Soldiers." The truckers streamed in, filling the back rows. The Bible study ladies filled the whole second row. Groups of burly truckers came up to view the casket and burst into tears, hardly able to contain their grief, and returned to their seats.

As I returned to my seat, the Reverend attempted to walk to the back of the church to see what all the commotion was about, but the influx of people pouring into the little church forced him to return to the podium. He tucked in his tie, which had managed to flip out of place, back into his vest and buttoned up his suit.

All the pews were soon filled, and still people entered, forced to stand along the walls. Some viewing the casket lost their place and had to stand along the sides of the church. My legal mind thought, *I hope the fire marshal isn't planning on attending.*

"What's going on, Heinrich?" Mrs. Gottwald asked, twisting in her pew, apparently impatient to get on with the funeral. But she didn't turn to look back.

"I don't know. Some kind of a country hick procession, I'd guess," Reverent Gottwald answered.

Roger returned to Leah's side. "Everyone is here now, so you may begin, Reverend, sir." Roger cleared his throat and sat down, folding his arm around Leah.

"Begin, time to begin, mister," shouted Rachel. Leah hushed her. "But mommy, it's time to begin."

"I know, sweetheart." Leah said, trying to settle Rachel in her lap as a crowd filled their pew.

Reverend Gottwald started over, "Dearly beloved, we are gathered here in the presence of God to commit Becky Gottwald to the earth and to remember her short life. Please turn with me to Psalm 103 starting with verse 14. He looked up. No one except the Bible study ladies opened their Bibles, so he read the passage.

"'*For He himself knows our frame. He is mindful that we are but dust. As for man.*'" He paused and looked at the crowd with a sardonic smile. "I'll paraphrase for you. '*As for a woman, her days are like grass; as a flower of the field so she flourishes. When the wind has passed over it, it is no more and its place acknowledges it no longer.*' So ends the scripture reading." He held his hand up and looked at the ceiling, "So, ashes to ashes, dust to dust. Thank you all for coming. I understand the burial is here at the Cotton Cemetery."

"Wait a minute, Reverend," Mrs. Lawrence stood. She was wearing her black dress with a huge, bulky red scarf, "Are you done already?"

"There isn't much to say about Becky." His face turned stern. "She ran off, abandoning…"

"That's where you are so wrong," Mrs. Lawrence said as her face turned as crimson as her scarf. "Maybe you should have known her better, and then you would have had more to say."

The Bible study ladies stood and grouped together around the open casket, sniffling into their lace handkerchiefs. Mrs. Lawrence took the podium. Her bulk forced the Reverend to the side. "We have a song to sing." The Reverend took his seat beside his wife as the ladies sang all the verses of "What a friend we have in Jesus." After each verse, the whole church sang the chorus.

I saw Carl Pykkinen stand. His son, Paul, helped him totter to the front. He grabbed the casket for stability and wept. Clearing his throat and with a bit of a cough he said, "Rebecca Jean Gottwald was my friend. All of you know that when my precious wife died after more than fifty years of marriage, I was devastated. She was the one who knew how to console me. This girl wrapped her arms around me like I was her father."

I thought back to the day that I brought Becky Jean to console him. She had been so tender to him, but I hadn't been able to stay. I'd had to leave to check on a break-in.

Carl turned and stared at the Reverend. "She helped me keep my faith in God and cried with me over the loss of the delight of my life. And she made me some great omelets." A chuckle went through audience. "And oatmeal sometimes." A roar of laughter filled the church. I laughed, too, remembering that he never ordered oatmeal unless his wife accompanied him to the restaurant.

When quiet returned, he continued with tears in his eyes, "I would have died of grief and never seen my first granddaughter marry if it wasn't for Rebecca Jean Gottwald." He turned to Becky's father, "Didn't you even know her proper name?"

Reverend Gottwald mumbled, "Of course I did. I named…" But he didn't get a chance to explain because one of the elderly ladies yelled out, "Great is Thy Faithfulness." The whole church reverberated as everyone sang all the verses of the well-known hymn.

Shawnee escaped from Hal and Connie's grasp and climbed the podium to stand beside Mrs. Lawrence. "I would never have decided to go to the university if it wasn't for Becky Jean." She paused. "Oh, I'm sorry I interrupted you, Mr. Pykkinen."

"I was done, honey," he said as his son helped him back to his pew.

Shawnee continued, "Rebecca Jean inspired me to apply to the University of Minnesota, Duluth. She scanned the audience. "And I was accepted." There was a cheer. "I start this fall. She even set up a fund for my expenses. Now listen, folks, I was boy crazy and might not have even finished high school." She glanced down at her mother. "Sorry, mom and dad, that I caused you so much grief." She refocused on the audience. "When I got my driver's license, I used to drive over just to talk to her. She snuck me a chocolate malted milk once in a while and paid for it so my mother wouldn't know." Connie shook her head. "Becky Jean made me finish high school and encouraged me to go to college. She was more excited than I was when I got my acceptance letter to UMD. And I found out from her lawyer that I inherited her car so I can commute to class." She smiled at Mr. Pykkinen. He returned the smile. "Mr. Pykkinen gave that car to Becky Jean, for free."

Carl struggled to his feet and addressed the crowd. "No, I made her pay a dollar." Everyone laughed.

Connie stood in her place in the pew, still holding Hal's hand, and wiped her eyes, "Shawnee has been a challenge. Hal and I were overwhelmed with her…" She cleared her throat. "With her exuberance. I think Becky Jean taught me that word." Several parents of Shawnee's friends nodded. "Rebecca, I always called her Becky Jean at work, kept telling Hal and me what wonderful daughters we had. We would not have two lovely daughters sitting beside us today if it wasn't for Becky Jean. We would have driven them away."

Sherrie whispered, "She listened to my poems." Hal smiled and squeezed his younger daughter's hand.

Mrs. Lawrence took control of the funeral. "I have a better scripture, Reverend. I don't suppose you took much time finding that dusty reference, but we have spent the last couple years being blessed by the daughter that you threw away."

Reverend Gottwald stood and grabbed his wife's hand, "I didn't come here today to discuss my child rearing with you." He turned to his family. "Let's leave."

"Now you said your piece, Reverend. Sit down." Mrs. Lawrence slammed her fist onto the podium, and the Reverend sat at the force of her tone. Mrs. Gottwald threw her an angry look of protest but refrained from saying anything as Mrs. Lawrence spoke. "Reverend means terrible, as I recall. I won't honor you with the higher title of pastor. Are you going to deny that you abandoned your daughter? Kicked her out of your house after forcing her to marry a murderer?" She spit out the last word. "Oh yes, murderer, Reverend. Didn't know that, did you? He was wanted in two states for murder. One of which was your lovely daughter."

He stood again and grabbed his wife's hand. "Come, dear, I've had enough of this country circus. I will not be insulted here in this joke of a church." Several truck drivers stood in the aisle to block his exit. Mack confronted him, flexing his tattooed muscles and crossed arms. "Please be seated, Reverend, sir, we're not done yet. Your daughter saved my marriage. You need to sit and listen." Forced to return to his pew, he refused to sit down, ready to leave until Mack gave him a thumb's down.

"Don't deny it," Mrs. Lawrence continued. "I've done my homework. Keith Stagg murdered your daughter, but there was a warrant for his arrest in Iowa for murder, too. An elderly woman, I believe. Obviously you did not do your homework before forcing her to marry Keith Stagg, the murderer. So sit and listen. You might learn something. You sure didn't spend much time preparing your little sermonette. What a cliché. You must have grabbed that out of the back of some old, dusty drawer. Now instead of speaking, it is time for you to listen and learn something about your daughter. It is clear that you missed out on the wisdom your daughter taught to those of us who did listen to her." He appeared red-faced and furious.

When the church stilled to silence, Mrs. Lawrence continued to address the congregation. "Turn to Second Corinthians Chapter 5 starting with verse 21 and then on to Chapter 6. The Bible study ladies pulled out their Bibles. Even some of the truckers pulled Gideon Bibles out of their shirt pockets. Mrs. Lawrence waited until the pages stopped turning.

"'*God made him*'—that's Jesus—'*who knew no sin to be sin for us, that we might become the righteousness of God in Him. And working together with him…*' I'll skip down to verse three. '*Giving no offense in anything, in order that the ministry is not discredited, but in everything commending ourselves as servants of God in much endurance, in afflictions, in hardships.*'" She stopped and faced the Reverend and his wife, "A lot of Rebecca Jean's hardships were because of you, yet she never said anything unkind about you. She was a faithful servant of God in this town, working for Jesus with incredible endurance."

The Reverend turned away. His wife took off her glasses and wiped them. Heather covered her face. Philip remained motionless. Christina stood in her pew to see what would happen next.

"I'll continue. '*In distresses, in beatings…*'" She paused. "We heard about the beatings her husband gave her, but I think I'll skip imprisonments, I don't think Becky Jean was ever in prison."

Jim Toumala was standing against the back wall. He waved his hand at Mrs. Lawrence. "Maybe she wasn't in prison, but she visited me when I was in the county jail for my DUI. Does that count?" He looked at Leah. "And I should have been in prison." Rachel stood in the pew, turned back, and threw him a kiss. "I've lived such a God-awful life, always drunk and abusing everyone I met. Rebecca Jean, Becky, came to see me in the county jail, the only visitor I ever had, and helped me turn my life around. It's been hard to ask forgiveness for some of the things I've done." He looked at Leah again and hung his head. "I am sure grateful for forgiveness." He lifted his head, "And I would never have found forgiveness without her." He covered his face and leaned against the back wall.

"Thanks, Jim, for sharing that. We have certainly seen a change in you since you got out of jail. I guess that fits the scripture."

"I've been sober ever since. Not one drop. And I've apologized to most of the people I've offended. She made a difference in my life." Tears flooded his eyes as he slid back to the doorway. He bowed his head and wept. Several of the truckers hugged him.

Mrs. Lawrence looked around the room. "If there are no more prison birds here, I'll continue. *'In tumults, in labors, in sleeplessness, in hunger.'* The poor child only ate one meal a day, and that was thanks to Bert."

Bert stood, swallowed, and cleared his throat. "She and Connie are... were...Ugh. The best waitresses a restaurant owner could ever ask for. They worked hard. I'm embarrassed now to say that on occasion I did give her some of the day-old muffins." He broke into tears, and his belly convulsed as he sat down. "I didn't realize that she had nothing..."

"You did well by her, Mr. Lloyd. All of us here are indebted to you forever for giving her a job." She smoothed out the page of her Bible.

Mack addressed the congregation. "When I dropped her off the day that Bert hired her..." He looked around at the other truck drivers. "Well, she was hitchhiking. I can't say that I picked her up with the most honorable intentions. Anyway, my wife and I were separated at the time." The woman beside him squeezed his hand. "She told me what to do to get our marriage back together." He smiled, "Every time I took a load up to International Falls, she gave me another assignment. My wife and I communicate a lot better now. And I've quit screwing around. Now I treasure my wife." He sat down. She gave him a hug and a kiss on the cheek.

Mrs. Lawrence continued reading the Bible passage, "Now here's more good stuff. *'In purity, in knowledge, in patience, in kindness, in the Holy Spirit, in genuine love, in the word of truth in the power of God.'* Every one of us experienced that from the dear child. Purity, not one word of gossip came from that girl's mouth, ever. There's not a person here today who didn't receive her patience and kindness. She never complained about her tips or how we all wanted our coffee, well, tea for the ladies right here. We were impatient, but she gave genuine love, my friends. That was the power of God in her life."

"And she was filled with the Holy Spirit. Even spoke in tongues," said Charlie Butler. He stood and gave the congregation his two-tooth grin, "I heard her myself. She believed in the full gospel. She was a born-again, four-square gospel Christian. I will personally bear witness to that in heaven."

A loud, "Amen," reverberated from several in the church.

Mrs. Lawrence took a deep breath. "Thank you, Charles. Let me skip to verse eight. *'By glory and dishonor, by evil report and good report; regarded as a deceiver.'* You're responsible for that part, Reverend. You may have regarded her as dishonorable, but she never said a dishonest word to anyone here. She was more honorable than all of us, myself included, I'm sorry to say."

There was another loud, "Amen."

"I'll continue." With a sheepish grin, she held down the page of her Bible and adjusted her glasses. *"'And yet true; as unknown yet well-known, as dying yet behold she lives, as sorrowful yet always rejoicing.'* How many of us knew that she was dying of breast cancer? Her body was riddled with cancer, even broke her leg when she fell. I didn't know that. She never complained."

Connie raised her hand. "I knew it, but she didn't want me to tell anyone. She didn't want to cause Bert any hardship." Connie turned to smile at Mr. Lloyd. "The poor kid had cancer all over. She never complained even when the cancer broke her rib, fractured her leg, as Mrs. Lawrence mentioned. But I know that her liver and lungs were full of cancer, too. I made her tell me when she came back to work from the oncologist's office."

"She had breast cancer?" Heinrich turned to his wife with a look of consternation and disbelief.

"I told you that when I got the letter from the doctor in Duluth. But I didn't know it was that bad."

"Excuse me, Reverend. May I continue reading the Holy Scripture? You can work out your communication problems at home later. *'As poor, yet making many rich.'*" She choked on her own tears, *"'And as having nothing yet possessing all things.'*" She pointed her finger at the Reverend, "I heard you tell Mr. Gleeson she had nothing. You sounded rather prideful about that. Well look around you, Reverend. Every family present in this church today contributed money to pay for her funeral except one: yours, Reverend. We all contributed because she made us all rich."

Mrs. Lawrence pounded her fist on the podium. "All right, I want to hear some more testimonies now." She sat down as others took the podium.

Tim and Tom took the podium first, "She taught us proper respect for girls," said Tim.

"Women," corrected Tom and continued, "She made us write a report every time we took Shawnee out on a date. We had to write down everything we thought or did." Shawnee giggled.

Tim added, "And then she corrected our writing and sent it back to us." Mr. Johannsen laughed; others chuckled at the twins' remarks.

Rolly stood and joined the twins on the podium. "She taught me to respect these twins." He gave each a hug. There was muffled laughter that spread through the congregation. "I thought that these boys were spoiled brats, but Becky Jean taught me a valuable lesson in respect."

The twins hugged him back. "We like you too, Mr. Rollifsen, sir. Becky Jean said you were a real nice man. We didn't believe her at first." The three of them returned to their seats.

"I just feel bad that she didn't get to complete her education," said Frank Johannsen rising to the pulpit. "I gave her extra tips so she could return to the university and finish her degree. I was hoping she would return to UMD this fall, but I understand that she gave her money away to Shawnee and Sherrie so they could get a university education." He started to tear. "At least the money will go for someone's education. I didn't know about the cancer." He sat back down and wiped his eyes.

"Don't worry, Mr. Johannsen, the money will be used wisely. I promise to study hard," said Shawnee, standing. Connie pulled her back into her pew.

For over an hour, person after person came to the podium to tell how Becky Jean had met their needs, counseled them when they were discouraged, stayed after hours to talk to them outside the restaurant. In a continuous flow, people gave testimony to the Reverend's daughter. I sat in awe with tears running down my cheeks.

Forced to hear the testimonies, the blood drained from the Reverend's face. He held his head between his hands as he heard what people said about the daughter that he apparently never knew. His wife cringed beside him.

Heather listened and kept turning to stare at her father. Heather's daughter, Christina, refused to sit in the pew. She kept jumping up to hear and see everything. Philip seemed stunned.

After everyone said their piece, there was a pause. I thought it was all over. Then I saw that Ron was standing in the back blocking the doorway with his muscular mass. He started coughing. Everyone turned toward him. He was fidgeting with an unlit cigarette. "I'm no good at giving speeches." He coughed again. "This is the first time I've been in a church since I got back from Nam. I got a purple heart and a medal for saving my squad. But they all died in the MASH unit later. I tried to save Becky Jean, but I failed again." He dropped his cigarette and cried as he bent to pick it up. Bert got up and rushed to his side to comfort him. "I told her my whole story. She even listened to the bad parts, the parts I have never told anyone else." He yelled, "I've started healing my Viet Nam wounds because Becky Jean listened to me." He rubbed his head and stammered on, "Many times after work she would touch my shoulder and listen to me again and again. No one ever touches me. You all know that. But Becky Jean, she could because she listened to me. She knew all the bad stuff about me." He turned to Bert and sobbed on his shoulder.

I thought about Ron's response. *Viet Nam vet, trained killer, a cook with plenty of access to long knives. He said that he tried to save her. Ah, the murder mystery is solved. He's the one who cut Keith's aorta with a single slash and made sure he died with a slice to liver and spleen.* But as I contemplated Ron's testimony to what Becky Jean had done for him, I decided that the murder of Keith Stagg would remain unsolved. Besides, Ron had only killed a murderer, defending the only person who had ever listened to his story.

Roger stood, "There were five more bullets in that gun after Keith murdered Rebecca Jean. Officer Davis checked and told me. You helped save my daughter's life, Ron. We all know you did. He could have shot Rachel next. He could have shot other people who were in the restaurant that day. You are a hero in my book. You saved us from mass slaughter." Ron dropped his cigarette again. He collapsed in Bert's arms as he tried to pick it up. Bert picked up his cigarette for him and led him outside to smoke.

Leah stood with Rachel in her arms and went to the podium. The crowd hushed. "As most of you know, Rebecca's ex-husband tried to hurt Rachel. I guess he thought she was Becky Jean's daughter since she always called both of us, 'mommy.' Anyway, I meant to abort Rachel." A hush went through the congregation. Leah's parents looked down at their feet. "I didn't even know then who got me pregnant. I was raped. Now I know, but it doesn't matter anymore. He's forgiven." Jim Toumala covered his face with both hands. "And now I am married to a wonderful man who loves us both. Becky introduced us."

"I love you, mommy," Rachel interrupted and kissed her mother.

"Becky Jean talked me out of aborting this precious girl, and I am so glad she did. Then she put herself in harm's way to protect her. She took the bullet that was intended for my daughter." Leah choked, closed her eyes, but I assumed the memory of the blood, the twisted broken leg and Rebecca's gasped words were too dreadful for her to relate. She paused and opened her eyes as tears streamed down her cheeks. She choked again and sputtered, "She saved Rachel's life again."

"My other mommy is sleeping, isn't she?" Rachel said.

"Yes, Rachel, Becky Jean is sleeping with Jesus."

"She was very tired, right, mommy? She told me she was tired."

"She was tired from doing God's work."

"I loved her this much." Rachel spread her arms out wide.

Leah was sobbing as she stepped down. Roger helped her to her seat, comforting Rachel, and then took the podium.

"I was nothing until Rebecca gave me hope. On a little fishing trip she gave me my life back. Told me I was worth something even though cancer took away my dream of having my own children, of being a father. She did some matchmaking between Leah and me. I'm so thankful." He glanced at his wife. "I'm so glad I'm married to you, Leah."

"I love you, Roger," Leah said.

Roger looked heavenward. "Cotton, Minnesota will never be the same because of Rebecca Jean Gottwald."

Everyone in the church whispered, "Amen."

"We all love you, Rebecca. You can rest in peace now. You have changed all of us," said Roger as he stepped down from the podium and closed the casket. He turned to Becky's parents. "You owe your daughter a huge debt that you will never be able to pay. She died for your sins." The other pallbearers joined him: Ron, Mack, Bert, Frank Johannsen, and Rolly. Sherrie stood and played her Anishinaabe flute as the men carried the casket out.

Reverend Gottwald sat silent beside his wife. They both stared at the floor.

Philip whispered to Heather, who was sobbing, "We talked a few Guatemalan Catholics into becoming Lutherans. Your sister saved a whole town."

"I want to be just like Aunt Rebecca when I grow up," Christina said.

I breathed, "So be it Lord." *This is one county sheriff who will never be the same.*

Acknowledgements

This book is fiction. None of the characters are real. However, Cotton, Minnesota is a real place. I lived in Cotton in the late 1950's and have returned many times. The time frame in the book is during the 1980's. I continue to visit Cotton because the friendships that I developed in the 1950's have been long-lasting, even to the present. Nothing too much has changed since I was there last August except for a few new houses along the road.

When I lived on Bug Creek Road several miles outside of Cotton, the Wickstrom's lived above their store, and there was a pastor who lived in the parsonage at the Cotton Covenant Church for a short time. Wickstrom's was a true general store. They sold everything from sausage and groceries to bolts and plumbing supplies. If you were willing to wait, they would order anything you needed. For a while when Wickstrom's sold their store and the pastor left, nobody actually lived in Cotton. The real name of the restaurant in Cotton is the Wilbert. If you ever get to stop, check out the menu selection, though it is 'trucker fare,' the food is great. When we lived there, my mother worked as a short-order cook. It has had many owners who have kept the name. There have been three minor fires to my knowledge, but the restaurant has always been rebuilt and refurbished.

The school bus picked up children from a large surrounding area, so when I attended Cotton School 100, there were always plenty of students. It is still home of the Cotton Cardinals, despite the lack of Cotton's population. The new buildings added to the red brick school are quite modern. They have often had decent basketball and football teams, although they have never won a state championship. Most of the students who graduate from the high school leave town. Many go to college since there is a paucity of employment in Cotton.

They matriculate at the Junior College in Virginia, Minnesota, thirty miles north of Cotton, or at the University of Minnesota in Duluth, thirty miles south of Cotton. I'm not aware of any Nobel Prize winners, but there have been a number of engineers. Today there are people who live in nice houses along the highway, so Cotton now has an actual population depending on where one draws the town border.

I have taken a few liberties with the town for the sake of the plot. The MDOT, Minnesota Department of Transportation, barn never was nor to this day is across from the Wilbert Restaurant. It is down the road, closer to Duluth. But the restaurant, church, school, and Wickstrom's are as described. The restaurant is well known because it has served truckers, teachers, pulp truck drivers, and locals as well as out of town fishermen and hunters for at least sixty years. The food has always been good. Despite the three fires, none were arson as in this novel, but all were kitchen fires. It continues to be the only restaurant between Duluth-Hermantown and Virginia, Minnesota. When I lived there, the postal department rented an end of the restaurant. Now there is no post office in Cotton.

Highway 53 was an old Ojibwa trail known during the time of the French voyageur, Sir D'Luth in the 17th century. The towns along the trail were placed at 30 mile intervals a century ago, as they are today, because that's how far a horse could reasonably travel in a day. Since the highway has always been the main route to International Falls and Canada, snow is plowed early and regularly during winter snowstorms. On a rare occasion, blizzard conditions shut down the highway but usually not more than a day or so. In 1999, the governor shut down all the schools in the state of Minnesota, but that was because the temperature dropped to 53 degrees below zero in Duluth with a wind chill that was difficult to calculate. The highway was open. Cotton does not have official temperatures, but I am sure it was colder there than in Duluth. It usually is in the winter.

The Cotton Covenant Church on the other side of the pine tree windrow that separates it from the school is where my father preached at times in the 1940's and 50's. He was just substitute preaching when the minister was away, sick, or quit, so we never lived in the parsonage. The church and the parsonage have always been painted white, but the paint was peeling last August when I drove by. There were times when the church was well attended, but now that Highway 53 is four lanes, those who go to church, attend churches in Duluth.

The people who live around Cotton are mostly ethnic Finnish, Norwegian, and Swedish. The few First Nation People are Ojibwa or, more correctly, Anishinaabe. As a group, Finnish, Scandinavian, and First Nation people are all very private, but when they do befriend someone, that relationship is forever. The contrary side is that sometimes they hold grudges for a long time as well. They are fiercely independent and are particularly offended by Minneapolis, Saint Paul people who vacation there and think they know everything. Most Cotton people could survive in a woodland wilderness with a knife and a gun; most Minneapolis people, unless they grew up in northern Minnesota, would probably die in three days. This novel is true to the nature of my Cotton friends and the people who still live in the surrounding wilderness.

Since my wife, Priscilla, was a waitress in a small town, she encouraged me to write a story about a waitress who was a strong woman and who could change people's lives. I am deeply indebted to her insight and help making the dialogue realistic. I want to thank Rodney and Becky Lorentszen, whose family housed and fed our family when my father lost his job and we were homeless in the 1950's. They still live in Cotton and were the first ones to critique this book. Becky's response after reading *Rings of Annulment* was heartfelt: "How did you know what's happening in Cotton?" I want to thank Sheri Hughey for editing my manuscript. She found many extraneous errors. And a thank you to Katie Catanzarite from Dorrance Publishing who found the errors Sheri missed.

The book is dedicated to my wife's father, Charles Ebenezer Fillmore. Although sometimes irritating, he was known for his generosity, encouragement, and willingness to help those in need. One neighbor said, "You could always get a ride from Charlie if you needed one, but you usually heard a sermon along the way." Charlie was a resident of Cook, Minnesota, 60 miles north of Cotton. He was a welder by trade and a heavy equipment operator. He invented the machine that made birch dowels for the Cook box factory. His reputation was that a "Charlie Fillmore weld never broke."

He often stopped at the Wilbert from the time my wife was seven years old. He worked on the highway as a gravel crusher operator. Priscilla remembered that he always tipped well. He sometimes left as much in tip as his morning coffee cost. Charlie Butler, in the book, is true to my delightful father-in-law's character, and I hope this fictional setting honors him.

I am deeply indebted to my high school friend Neil Elder, a decorated Viet Nam veteran, for Ron's story. I hope that it honors him and those Viet Nam veterans that we a as a nation shunned when they returned from that horrid conflict. Ron's story is fiction, but it is also a summation of Neil's and many of my patients' experiences in Viet Nam.

If you have a chance to take Highway 53 north of Duluth, stop for a bite to eat at the Wilbert. You won't be disappointed if you like trucker food.